D1235933

"Sex Camp"

By

Brian McNaught

1663 LIBERTY DRIVE, SUITE 200
BLOOMINGTON, INDIANA 47403
(800) 839-8640
WWW.AUTHORHOUSE.COM

First published by AuthorHouse 01/13/05

ISBN: 1-4208-1644-6 (e)
ISBN: 1-4208-1645-4 (sc)
ISBN: 1-4208-1646-2 (dj)

Library of Congress Control Number: 2004099404

Printed in the United States of America
Bloomington, Indiana

This book is printed on acid-free paper.

I LOVE MYSELF THE WAY I AM
Words and Music by Jai Josef
Copyright © 1979, 2001 Jai-Jo Music (BMI)
All rights reserved. Used by permission.

Cover art and design by
Brian "Briz" Ahern
www.brizycomics.com

KEY TO COVER ART
(Left to right, back row:) Charlie, Leona, Carol, Chuck, Dominic, Wendy, Gina, Lisa, Lloyd, Thomas, Dick, Margaret, Joe. (Middle row:) Maggie, George, Betty, Carla/Carl, Dan, Alison, Pam, Gail, Marjorie, Curtis, Bill, Beatrice, Ben. (Front row:) Grace, Judith, Martha, Annette, Beverly, Peter, Kevin, Brian, Joanne, Tonya, Paula.

ALSO BY BRIAN McNAUGHT

A Disturbed Peace
On Being Gay
Gay Issues in the Workplace
Now That I'm Out, What Do I Do?

Acknowledgments

Without the incredible generosity of the staff of the Annual Workshop on Sexuality, this book simply would not have been possible. Dick Cross, Alison Deming, Carol Dopp, Bill Stayton, and Pam Wilson not only allowed me to share the fruit of their life's work, but also surrendered themselves to my loving caricatures of them. They faithfully read and provided valuable feedback on each chapter as it was finished. Any good that might result from this book is theirs to share equally.

We have created an intimate, playful, and supportive family at the Annual Workshop, and our members are many. In addition to the above mentioned, our strong family tree includes Gail Brett, Michael Butera, and Linda Roessler. Sol Gordon, who planted the tree, grafted many cherished limbs, including Steve Allen, Jr., Andrea Parrott Allen, Larry Bass, Gloria and Barry Blum, Peggy Brick, Sandy Caron, Carol Cassell, Sandra Cole, Paul Fleming, Sylvia Hacker, Ruth Kaufman, Bill Kelly, Marty Klein, Lynn Leight, Jan Lundquist, Bianca Cody Murphy, Peter Scales, Peter Sladowski, and Marty Weisberg. These, and many more names, are beloved colleagues whose work in the past made the workshop the highly-regarded success it is known to be.

Besides the staff, I had access for this book to the expertise of Roger Barbee, Jim Braude, Mary Ann Horton, and Joe Kramer in guaranteeing the accuracy of information about disability, gender expression, and physiology. I also had the watchful eye of my spouse, Ray Struble, who swallowed deeply before offering his critique of each page passed to him for comments. Likewise, our friends David McChesney, Tom Roberts, and

Karen Van Arsdale provided helpful encouragement. I was guided along the way too by Barbara Carrellas, Charles Cesaretti, Debra Haffner, Mark Leach, Eric Marcus, Armistead Maupin, and Bob McCamant.

Special thanks go to Brian (Briz) Ahern for his wonderful talent and deep commitment to creating the perfect cover for "Sex Camp," and to Ed Teo and Ron Robin for their dedication to effectively promote this book.

Finally, I acknowledge with enormous gratitude the hundreds of people who have come to our workshop and so courageously and generously shared their stories with us. Fragments of their lives have been lovingly stitched into the quilt represented by the thirty-two participants described herein.

Dedication

For
Mary Lee Tatum,
Susan Vasbinder,
Dick Cross,
and all others who have
dedicated themselves to
our sexual health.

Preface

In the beautiful Finger Lakes region of New York State, on the very private grounds of an Episcopal Church retreat facility, there's been an annual, week-long, intensive workshop in human sexuality that has, over the past 30 years, dramatically impacted the lives of hundreds of everyday people, me included. This fictionalized book seeks to tell the story of that remarkable program.

The Annual Workshop on Sexuality at Thornfield, affectionately referred to as "Sex Camp" by staff and participants, was inspired and initiated by Dr. Sol Gordon, a pioneer in the field of human sexuality. The program has since been lovingly guided and nurtured into maturity by a staff of deeply-committed, highly-regarded sexuality professionals. Their names in this book are accurate, as are the descriptions of the setting and the content of the workshop. The names and personal details of all of the participants, however, are fictional.

Author's Note

   While the intention of this book is to enlighten and to entertain, it should be read with the understanding that neither the author nor the publisher is engaged here in rendering therapeutic advice. If professional help is sought in the areas of sexuality education, therapy, or counseling, or in any area discussed in this book, the reader is urged to contact his or her physician, and/or local mental health facility, or to seek a referral from the American Association of Sex Educators, Counselors, and Therapists (AASECT) by contacting them on the Internet at www.aasect.org., or by writing to them at P.O. Box 5488, Richmond, VA 23220-0488.

Chapter One

SATURDAY

Welcome

The scratched, red plastic bucket overflowed with the bounty of the morning's hunt—-day lilies, black-eyed Susans, Queen Anne's lace, sweet pea, and other roadside wildflowers whose sight prompted happy childhood memories but whose names I still didn't know.

Alison pulled them out a stem at a time, carefully arranging each according to height, color, size, and texture into her favorite green porcelain vase, a prized find from the Cazenovia Craft Fair.

"A masterpiece!" announced a lean, grey-haired man with a broad grin, accentuated by deep-set laugh lines around his eyes.

"Thank you," Alison replied with surprise, her hand outstretched. "I'm Alison Deming. Welcome to Thornfield! And who might you be?"

"I'm Thomas Miller, Alison. It's a real pleasure meeting you."

"Ah, Thomas. How good to have a face to put with the name. You've arrived safely from Santa Fe. Good for you. Have you checked in?"

"Yes, thank you. Gail signed me in and told me how to find my room. Can I help you with anything?"

1

"Why, thank you for asking. Would you be a dear and take these over to Ridings, that handsome building across the lawn, and put them in a prominent place? That's where we'll be gathering for the opening session. Lunch is at noon. We start the program at one. It's all in your packet. Now, please make yourself at home. Take a dip in the lake. The water's marvelous. Or go for a nice walk around the grounds. We've got thirty-seven acres here. Please introduce yourself to whomever you meet, and please be sure to wear your name badge at all times."

"A place of prominence. I'll be sure to find the perfect spot," Thomas said as he headed across the lawn, both hands holding the arrangement.

"Who's he?" I asked as I exited Higley, the staff dorm, and approached the picnic table where a second vase of flowers was being arranged.

"Thomas Miller," Alison said. "He's a hospital chaplain in Santa Fe."

"Gay?" I asked.

"My guess is 'yes.' He let me know in his call to me that he's HIV-positive. That's obviously for staff information *only*," she said looking up briefly and making eye contact to drive home her seriousness.

"You don't have to tell me," I said a bit indignantly.

"I *know* I don't have to tell you," she smiled, "but make sure that the others are clear about it."

"Good morning!" I said to the two women walking toward the table on their way to the lake.

"Good morning," they chimed in unison, now directing their path toward us.

"Welcome to Thornfield. I'm Brian McNaught and this is Alison Deming."

"Good morning and welcome," said Alison.

"Oh Brian. Trish Weaver said to say 'Hi.' I'm Wendy Taylor. Trish and I work at the Cleveland Youth project. She said you'd remember."

"Oh, wow. Sure. Of course. Trish," I lied, already feeling frustrated by the need to remember names and embarrassed by the difficulty I have in doing so. "How's she doing?"

"Great. She insisted that I come. She was here two years ago. Oh, and I'm sorry. This is Barbara."

"No, *Beverly*," smiled the handsome black woman at her side.

"Oh, I'm sorry," said Wendy. "We just met," she explained.

"That's okay. I'm Beverly Johnson," she said.

"From Trinidad!" Alison exclaimed, dropping her scissors and taking Beverly's arms in both of her hands. "How *nice* to meet you. And what a long way you've come. Beverly is a health care worker from Bernadette's agency," Alison explained to me.

"Bernadette was here four years ago," I explained to Wendy.

"No three," Alison corrected. "And Wendy, how nice to have *you* with us. I heard from Trish a year ago that there wasn't any money in the budget to send someone last year, but that she would make sure someone from the agency came this year. We're glad you're here."

"Thanks," said Wendy. "I've heard all about Thornfield. I can't want for it to start."

"It's started!" exclaimed Alison. "You and Beverly have met! And I'll bet you find you have a lot in common. Are you headed to the water?"

"Yea, we just want to get a lay of the land," Wendy said.

"Well, have fun. And remember, both of you, to wear your name badges," Alison said.

"Have you been to your rooms?" I asked.

"We're roommates," Beverly replied with a big smile. "That's where we met."

"Brian, be a dear and take this vase up to the registration desk. And ask Gail if she needs anything. If you see Carol, ask her to put the Kleenex and supplies in each of the meeting sites."

"Carol is picking up people at the airport. Where're our helpers? I'll have them put out the supplies?" I said.

"I have Tonya in town with my car getting food and drink for tonight's party, and Kevin was setting up the resource table the last time I knew, though I think I spotted him heading to the beach."

"I'll put out the Kleenex and supplies," I said. "Where's Pam?"

"She's going through the marked-up newsprint from last year to see if it's all there," Alison said. "Bill's running late. He's got Dick with him in his car."

"Did you remind the chef that lunch is early today?" I asked.

"What do you mean?"

"Every day it's 12:30. Today it's at 12:00 so that we can start the program at one."

"He's been told but maybe you better check," she said as she worked to pick up her clippings.

"Who's that over there?" I asked, nodding at a woman sitting in the lotus position on the hillside, seemingly staring at the lake.

"I don't know. Why don't you go over and introduce yourself?"

"I've got to go put the Kleenex out."

"Go then. We'll find out soon enough."

Up in Peabody, a new arrival glared at an empty mattress.

"Honey, if they think I'm making up my own bed, they're crazy," Leona Mills said with disgust to the empty dorm room. "Will you *look* at these sheets? Which one's supposed to be the bottom? And get a load of that towel. I wouldn't dry my dog off with that towel. I did *not* sign up to go to some kid's summer camp. This is supposed to be a professional development conference. And I'm not sharing no bathroom with three other women either."

"Hi. You must be my roommate," said a tall woman with curly, grey hair as she entered the room, her left hand pulling a rolling suitcase, her right arm outstretched. "I'm Betty Koslowski," she continued, taking Leona's hand. "Just get in?"

"Hi Betty. I'm Leona Mills. I'm with Planned Parenthood in Washington, D.C. Did you know that you have to make your own bed?"

"This is my third time through Thornfield. Making the bed doesn't bother me. I just wish it was a little longer," Betty laughed, taking the other end of Leona's sheet and helping her make up the bed she'd selected by the window. "If you need extra blankets, they're on the top of the closet. Extra hangers can be 'stolen' from the other rooms. Extra towels are put out in the living room every couple of days."

"I'd hope so. Do we actually have to share that bathroom with other women?"

"Probably, if they have a full enrollment. It's not so bad. Actually, it can be kind of fun," she said as she pulled a pillow into its case. "Food's good here, Leona. I put on a couple of pounds every time I come."

"What's this whole week about?" Leona asked. "My director sent me here. She just raved about it, but wouldn't get specific. She said it 'changed' her life, and that I'd have to find out about it for myself."

"It's a really amazing week, but it's really what you make of it."

"So what do *you* do, Betty? What brings you back here three times?"

"I'm getting my masters in counseling. Right now, I make a living doing computer programming."

"Hmm. Well, I work with pregnancy prevention, mostly with inner city schools in the D.C. area."

"Did you come here by yourself?" Betty asked as she started working on making her own bed.

"Yes, but that girl at registration said there were a few others from different Planned Parenthood affiliates here," Leona replied as she began pulling clothes out of her suitcase and hanging them in the closet.

"That's Gail. She's cool. She works with the deaf, and she'll teach you how to sign. She's a great dancer too, and has the cutest butt."

"I didn't notice her butt," said Leona, looking a little nonplused, "but I'm not that kind of girl, if you know what I mean?"

"I do, and I am," said Betty, with a smile but stiffening a bit.

"I do, and I am *what*?" Leona asked, stopping her unpacking.

"I *do* know what you mean about not being that kind of girl who would notice a woman's cute butt," said Betty calmly, "and I *am* that kind of girl who would notice a woman's cute butt."

"Oh," said Leona. "So you're a *lesbian*?"

"Yes, I am," replied Betty. "Is that going to be a problem?"

"Oh, this gets better and better," Leona thought to herself, but said, "I don't have a problem. Are *you* going to have a problem?"

"No problem at this end, Leona. But I can ask Alison to switch our rooms if you want."

"No. I'm fine. But I do think I'll go out and check out the place. If you don't want any help with your bed, I'll see you later."

"This is going to be an interesting week," chuckled Betty to herself.

As she exited Peabody, Leona eyed an encounter taking place across the breezeway.

"Can I give you a hand with that?" the full bodied, round-faced woman asked as she opened the door to Huntington for the good-looking, buffed man in the wheelchair.

"Thanks," he said as he maneuvered himself to the registration desk.

"Do you have luggage somewhere that you need help with?" she continued.

"I got help from the person who dropped me off. Thanks. It's outside the dorm. I'm Ben Ellis," he said, reaching out his right hand.

"Hi Ben, I'm Joanne Douglas. It's really nice to meet you."

"And I'm Gail Brett, the registrar. Welcome to Thornfield both of you," said the petite, curly, black-haired woman from behind the counter. "I have your room assignments, participant packets, and name badges all ready for you. Let me see, Ben Ellis. Yes, here we go. Ben, we have you down in Higley, which is the staff dorm. We thought it would be easier for you to get around down there. But, I need you to first sign in for me here," she said, handing him a clipboard and pen.

"Are there any other participants staying in the staff dorm? I'd really rather stay with the other participants," he said as he started to sign the statement. "And what's this I'm signing?"

"I'm sorry. It's just a registration form required by our host, the Thornfield Retreat Center. And you are, of course, welcome to stay with the other participants in Peabody. We just thought it would be easier for you because the bathrooms down in Higley are wheelchair-accessible. Why not take a look for yourself at Peabody and see how it works for you? If you want to stay there, I'll switch a couple of people who haven't checked in yet, and put them up on the second floor. There's a room on the first floor right near the door that you could have. After I check Joanne in, I'll go over to Peabody with you."

"I'll go with him, Gail. You're busy here. Let me sign in, and Ben and I will check it out."

"Thanks, Joanne. Is that okay with you, Ben?"

"Sounds good to me," he said, rolling his chair back away from the desk, and turning it to face the door. "So when do they start the porn?" he asked with a big grin.

"Oh, so you've heard about the films, have you?" Gail laughed, as she handed Joanne her packet and registration form.

"Why do you think I came?" he flirted.

"It's *not* porn, and the films start tomorrow morning, I think. Anyway, lunch today is at noon. The program begins at one, over in Ridings, which is the building across the lawn. Please bring your packets to every session, and *please* wear your name badges all day, every day," Gail said. "Oops. I forgot to give them to you, didn't I?" she giggled as she perused the counter top filled with circular, laminated tags, each with calligraphy-style first names surrounded by colorful little stars. "Oh, here we go."

"So, we've got our packets, and our name badges, Ben. You ready to go?" Joanne asked, as she moved toward the door.

"Ready when you are," he replied.

"Have you looked around at all?" she asked as she led the way across the breezeway to Peabody. "It's really a beautiful site, and the lake is ..." She stopped herself.

"Yea, it looks inviting, doesn't it?" Ben said as he maneuvered his chair behind her. "I haven't been in the water for a long, long time. I'd kind of thought I'd go swimming this week," he winked.

Twenty-some miles away at the Syracuse airport, Carol collected her crew.

"Okay, we're all in. Everyone's got their luggage?" she asked as she pulled away from the terminal.

"Yep." "I'm here." "All set. Thanks," came the replies from three of the four passengers.

"Why don't you guys tell me something about yourselves? Dominic, you be my navigator, okay?" Carol said, passing a sheet of handwritten instructions to the athletic-looking man riding shotgun. "Where are you all from? What do you do? What brings you to Thornfield? And *please* don't tell Alison that I asked you to do this. You're going to have to do it all over again when we start the program this afternoon. But half the fun for me this week is meeting new people and making new friends. So, I'll start. My name is Carol Dopp. I'm a counselor and a family life educator in a private co-ed school in the Washington, D.C. area. I have a beautiful daughter named Kerrigan, and I've been coming to Thornfield for the past twelve years. I came for my first two years as a participant, and then I joined the staff."

"It looks like you've got a turn coming up," advised Dominic.

"Oh, right. Thanks," Carol said, putting on her turn signal. "Okay, who's next?"

"Well, I'll go," said her navigator. "I'm Dominic Paluzzi, but my friends call me Dom. I'm a football coach at Liberty View High School in Dayton, Ohio, and I've been assigned to teach a family life course to juniors and seniors. I was told by my friend Joyce Evans that she got a lot out of her time at Thornfield, and that I should come to 'Sex Camp'."

"Oh, wow, Joyce!" Carol said with an ear-to-ear grin. "I *loved* Joyce. She was great! We stayed up half the night watching this dumb movie that Brian brought called *Glen or Glenda? I Lived Two Lives*."

"She told me," Dom laughed.

"You're going to *love* this week," Carol said enthusiastically. "I'm *really* glad that you're here. So, who's next?"

"I'll go. I'm Paula Pendergast," came a voice from the back seat. "I'm from Tempe, Arizona, where I'm a sex therapist. I came to Thornfield to work with Bill Stayton and to get the 44 ceus for AASECT certification. I'm a single mom with a handsome son who's gay, and who lives in Atlanta."

"A gay son, huh? You'll have to talk with Brian. How did you hear about Thornfield?" Carol asked.

"From Alison Deming. I met her at the AASECT conference in Miami and she gave me the brochure. And I *do* want to talk with Brian."

"What's AASECT?" Dom asked. "And Carol, it says you stay on this until you get to Route 84."

"Thanks. AASECT is the American Association of Sex Educators, Counselors, and Therapists. They certify people in the field. Bill Stayton was president, a while back. They offer 44 continuing education units, or ceus, for the week. They require a SAR for certification, and our whole program's wrapped around a SAR."

"What's a SAR?" asked Dom.

"Dirty movies," laughed Paula.

"Dirty movies?" came an interested male voice from the back seat.

"They're *not* dirty movies," Carol said. "They're *explicit*. They're not 'dirty.' Years ago, the SAR program was designed in California by the Methodist Church. Explicit sexual films on a variety of topics like masturbation, homosexuality, disability, and aging are used to get people thinking about their feelings and about their values. Bill will be explaining the whole thing when we get together this afternoon.

"There are going to be explicit films on homosexuality?" asked Dom a bit nervously.

"Cool!" exclaimed the same unnamed male voice from the back seat.

"I thought you might like that, Dan," teased Carol. "Why don't you tell us about yourself?"

"I'm Dan Schemp. I'm queer, and I work with high risk kids for AIDS LA."

"What brings you to Thornfield?" Carol asked.

"A couple people from another AIDS agency have been here, and they recommended it to me. I'm actually looking forward to the discussion about queer people and the link between heterosexism, homophobia, and sexism. And thanks for telling us that your son's queer," he said to Paula.

"Gay. My son is *gay*," she replied. "I hate the word 'queer'."

"Whatever," Dan sighed, focusing his eyes on the view out the window.

The car was now silent. It remained so for a couple miles.

"We're about halfway there," announced Carol. "Three down, one to go. What about you, Joe?"

"My name is Joe Cook. My partner and I live in St. Helena, California, and I'm a retired professor of theology from Georgetown. What else? Oh yes, I've come to this program on sexuality because I've done a lot of work with the Center for Sexuality and Religion, and they recommended it. I believe they 'partner' with the training. Is that right, Carol?"

"Right," she said smiling as she made eye contact through the rearview mirror. "We've got a great group of partners now. CSR, GLSEN, Planned Parenthood, and SIECUS."

"Who are all those groups?" Dom asked. "And you know you've got an exit coming up pretty soon?"

"Yea, I know where I am now. Thanks. And I'm sorry about the acronyms," Carol replied. "CSR is the Center for Sexuality and Religion. GLSEN is the Gay, Lesbian, and Straight Education Network. Planned Parenthood … "

"I know Planned Parenthood," Dom jumped in.

"Right. And then, what have I left off? Oh yea, SIECUS is the Sex Information and Education Council of the United States. They're all great groups, and we love having their endorsement," said Carol.

"How long have you and your partner been together?" Dan asked, turning to Joe.

"Thirty-seven years," Joe replied with a smile and a wink.

"Congratulations," said Paula. "I hope my son finds someone he can be with for thirty-seven years."

"Eleanor and I hope our children do too," said Joe, "as long as that would make them happy."

The smile on Paula's face turned to a look of confusion. Dan peered disappointedly out his window.

Chapter Two

Tears at the Table

"They're lovely, aren't they?" Catherine Mitchell whispered as she carefully approached the crouched man who had focused his lens on the mother duck and her eight little ones. "Living signs of God's wonder."

"They're great," he said, maintaining his pose and purpose.

One, two, three quick shots he took as the family of ducks nervously paddled away from the small cove in front of the Thornfield boathouse.

"I shouldn't have interrupted you. I'm sorry," she said.

"No problem. I got a couple of great shots. Hi. I'm Kevin Brooks," he said, now standing and extending his right hand. "You here for the workshop?"

"I am," Catherine said, taking his hand, and noting the strength of his grip. "You too?"

"Yep."

"Are you nervous?" she asked.

"Always a little, but I love this place, and I always have a really good time," he said.

"You've been here before, Kevin?" she asked.

"I'm a little slow, I guess," he said with a laugh. "I have to keep coming back to get it right."

"What do you do?" she asked.

"I'm a graphic artist, and an amateur photographer," he said. "How about you?"

"I'm an Episcopal priest," she replied. "I'm at a church outside of Seattle."

"A woman priest! Far out," Kevin said smiling.

"Episcopal," she clarified. "The Romans don't allow it."

"It's still cool. Oh wow! Look at that," he said as he pulled his digital camera to his face, and focused on the hot air balloon that slowly approached from the far end of the lake. "It's got the rainbow colors!"

"It certainly does," Catherine acknowledged, her mouth turning from a smile to pursed lips. "It's getting about time for lunch," she said, looking at her watch. "I'll see you up there, Kevin. It was nice meeting you."

"Thanks, Catherine," he said as the lean, wiry, salt and pepper-haired woman turned to stride up the hill. "It's nice meeting you too."

"Is that you, Kevin?" came a loud voice from the top of the hill. "Hi, sweetie! How *are* you?"

Pam Wilson headed down the hill with a determined step to embrace her old friend. As she encountered Catherine, she stopped to introduce herself.

"Hi there. I'm Pam Wilson," she said with a big smile. "I'm on the staff of the workshop. Welcome to Thornfield."

"Hi, Pam. I'm Catherine Mitchell. I look forward to working with you," she said.

"What brings you here?" Pam asked.

"I'm an assistant pastor of an Episcopal church outside of Seattle. I'm taking over the youth group, and I was told by a colleague that this week might help me with that."

"Oh, boy, will it ever, Catherine. I'm glad you came. Have you met Bill Stayton yet? Bill's a Baptist minister, an American Baptist, not the Southern kind."

"I've heard of Bill. He's one of the reasons I wanted to come here. I'm counting on getting a handle on these issues from a religious perspective," Catherine replied.

"That's *not* a Seattle accent I hear," Pam said with a grin.

"No, I'm from South Carolina originally."

"I thought I recognized that accent. I've got family there. In fact, I'm missing a big family reunion this week. This is a family reunion here too, but I'll miss seeing my relatives, and I'll miss big time the collards, black-eyed peas, fried catfish, and corn bread I know they'll be having."

"You're making me hungry," Catherine said.

"Mmm. Me too. But before I go to lunch, I want to go down and say 'hi' to my buddy, Kevin. It was a pleasure meeting you, Catherine," Pam said, taking Catherine's right hand in both of hers and squeezing gently. "I'll see you shortly." With that, she was running carefully down the hill with arms outstretched for Kevin.

"Hi, handsome!" she said as she hugged her friend tightly. "You look so good. How have you been doing?"

"Pretty good," he said with a laugh of delight in being so warmly welcomed. "Did you see the balloon with the rainbow colors?"

"Oh my gosh, look at that," Pam said as the balloon and its occupants drifted past. "Isn't that beautiful? So now, Kevin, come clean. Are there any new developments in the romantic arena?"

"No," he said with a shy smile. "Nothing new to report. How about you?"

"Well, now, I do have something to report. His name is Richard. He's wonderful. Brian and Ray met him and they really clicked. He's a great guy, and I'm very much in love."

"That's great," Kevin said enthusiastically. "Here, let me get a picture of you."

"Oh, Kevin, I *hate* my pictures."

"You won't hate this, and if you do, I won't show it to anyone. Promise."

"Okay," she said, taking the place on the log he pointed to as he focused his camera.

"Say 'clitoris'," he said, prompting a smile on his friend he had described to others as Halle Bally's twin sister.

At the top of the hill, in the Huntington dining room, lunch had begun.

"Mind if I join you?" the short, stout man with the jovial smile asked as he set his large plate of American chop suey on the table.

"Please do," replied the young, redheaded, freckle-faced woman with green eyes. "I'm Maggie."

"Hi, Maggie. I'm George," he said, placing down his salad bowl and extending his pudgy hand.

"Hi, George. This is Martha. Right?"

"Right."

"And Beverly," she said.

"Hello," the two black women said in unison.

"Nice to meet you both. Now, can I get anyone something to drink?" George asked as he turned for the table supporting the milk and hot chocolate machines, juice and water dispensers, and coffee urns.

"I'd love a glass of water," Maggie said with a big smile.

"So what brings you to Thornfield?" George asked upon his return with the water, and with a big glass of mixed lemonade and cranberry juice.

"Beverly and I are health care workers in Trinidad," Martha said. "We work with teenagers in pregnancy prevention, HIV, and pre and postnatal care. Colleagues of ours have come here in the past, and returned home with strong recommendations that we come ourselves. We just met Maggie."

"I'm a homemaker from Racine." Maggie said. "I've got two little ones who are going to miss their mommy this week. My husband, Barry, came here last year, and returned home a very different person. Our therapist strongly suggested that I needed to come this time."

"What about you, George?" Martha asked.

"Well, I'm here for the food, as you can tell," he said, raising his eyebrows at the mound of pasta, tomato sauce, and ground beef that filled his plate. "I heard there are no limits on helpings."

"If this lunch is any indication, the food is really good. I'll be a blimp by the end of the week if I'm not careful," Maggie said. "But besides the food, George, what brings you here?"

"A friend of mine came a couple of years ago and raved about it. He made me swear I'd come. I avoided it for a while but he kept hounding me, so I came. I wanted to meet Brian McNaught, and I thought it'd be helpful in my work. I'm a pastor for a small church near Toledo. That's in Ohio," he said to Martha and Beverly.

"I already explained that Racine is in Wisconsin," Maggie said. "What denomination?"

"MCC. That's the Metropolitan Community Church," he replied. "It's a Christian denomination with a principal outreach to gay and transgender people, and their families. I don't think we have a church in Trinidad, but we do have them all over the world."

"Does that mean that you're gay?" Maggie asked.

"Not all of our pastors are gay, but I am," he said. "I was in the seminary to be a Catholic priest, but I got kicked out when they found out I was gay. So I entered the MCC seminary. It changed my life."

"How so?" Martha asked.

"When I was a Catholic seminarian, I was 6'2", blond, and 165 pounds of muscle," he replied with a wink

"George!" Martha protested with a laugh as Beverly giggled, hiding her mouth with her hand, and looking away.

"I found my place in the world," he said with a more serious face. "I found how I could be myself and serve God at the same time. Do you work with any gay youths in Trinidad?"

"Oh, yes, I'm sure we do," Martha said. "But it's very difficult for them to come forward. Pam Wilson came down to work with us a year ago. She raised our awareness of the needs of gay youth. That's what I want to learn more about while I'm here. How can I do a better job reaching out to them?"

"That's not why I came," Maggie said as she pushed her food around with a fork, staring intensely at her efforts.

"Why did *you* come?" Martha asked.

"I came to find out why people *turn* gay," she replied glumly.

"People don't *turn* gay, anymore than people turn colors, although I wouldn't mind being a little browner when I left this place," George said, lifting his arm against Beverly's to contrast his pale, white skin.

"*Yes* they do," Maggie said with a sad sigh. "My husband came here last year as a heterosexual. He came home a homosexual. I came here to find out why," she said, lifting her head to expose her tear-filled eyes.

George reached out and put his arm around her. "I'm sorry," he whispered.

Clang. Clang. Clang. The sound made by Gail swinging the school bell across the lawn at the door to Ridings alerted the dining room participants that the first session of the Annual Workshop on Sexuality at Thornfield was about to begin. Tables quickly emptied as participants cleared their dishes, and grabbed their packets.

Chapter Three

Introduction of Staff

Classical music was playing softly on a boom box as the thirty-two participants filed into Ridings, with its cathedral ceiling and slowly rotating ceiling fans. At the end of the room were numerous full-length windows that provided a panoramic view of Lake Cazenovia, blue in its mid-July splendor through the tops of the hillside oak and pine trees.

Gail was filing through a box of cassettes near the tape player at the front of the room. On the wall above her hung a colorful panel from the AIDS Memorial Names Project Quilt. "In Loving Memory of Michael," the three foot by six foot section closest to her head read. The denim lettering was surrounded by a sewn-on ragged teddy bear, a silver-colored plastic and rhinestone tiara, some sheet music, and a red handkerchief. "1952 - 1984" it read beneath his name, along with "We Miss You!" and a dozen or so handwritten names, including "Mom," "Dad," and "Sis."

Having found the tape she was looking for, and having started its melodic introduction, Gail stood and asked the participants to sing along to "I Love Myself." The words, she said, could be found in their packets.

Several people stood up and started riffling through their powder blue folders.

"I love myself, the way I am, there's nothing I need to change ..." the first verse began, sung loudly and enthusiastically by the staff, scattered around the room, and mumbled by the majority of participants who were torn by their desire to sing but also to watch Gail who was interpreting the song in sign language. A couple of people in the room were noticeably and predictably amused by the words. A couple of others seemed put off by the sentiment. But most of the new faces seemed to show an earnest desire to get right into the intended mood of the moment.

"I love the world, the way it is, 'cause I can clearly see, that all the things I judge are done by people just like me ..." we sang as Gail crossed her arms around herself to indicate "love." The staff, which had seen her sign the song dozens of times did their best to remember the various signs for "world," "judge," and "people," but mostly only remembered the easy signs for "I," "see," and "me."

"Thank you, everyone," said Alison as the song ended, and the staff shot looks at one another of warm satisfaction and affection. "Thank you, Gail," she continued. "That song, by Louise Hay, has become a tradition here. We'll be starting each day with it. We hope you'll join in each time."

"Can I say something about the song, Alison?" I asked.

"Of course you can," she smiled back.

"Jai Josefs wrote that song and Louise Hay introduced it to gay men with AIDS who came to meet with her every week back in the early 80s." I said, standing. "She believed that self-love was an essential aspect of physical healing. We've been singing it here for years because we think that love of self, of others, and of the world are essential aspects of a healthy sexuality too."

"Thank you, Brian. Well, good afternoon and welcome to the Annual Workshop on Sexuality at Thornfield. I'm Alison Deming, and on behalf of the entire staff, I want to say how happy we are to have you here," she said with a room-filling smile, her arms straight at her side, and in a voice that shook slightly with nervousness and emotion. "It's going to be a *wonderful* week of growing, and learning, and stretching," she said extending her arms out to the ceiling and laughing in delight at the image. "We've got a great staff, and a great program that we're very proud of. You'll be working with some of the top people in the field of sexuality education — Bill Stayton, Brian McNaught, Pam Wilson, Carol Dopp and our staff emeritus, Dr. Dick Cross. I'm going to have them all introduce themselves to you shortly, but before I do, I want to tell you a little bit about the program, and get you acquainted with this 'holy' place. Ah, yes, you had a question?" she said, gesturing to George.

"When do we get to see the dirty movies?" he asked with a sheepish grin.

Nervous laughter from some, and applause from a few others, filled the large, open room in which the participants sat in a three-quarter circle.

"You like dirty movies, do you George?" I said to the jolly man I had met on the walk across the lawn from the dining hall.

"I was asking for Maggie, here," he said, putting his arm around the blushing new friend who sat at his side, to the laughing approval of the group.

"Oh no you weren't," she protested. "And you're a man of the *cloth*!"

"Ooooh," responded several in the crowd with mocking indignation, and a few clapped in delight.

"I see no conflict there," Bill Stayton chimed in with a smirk.

"You wouldn't," replied Carol.

"Well, haven't we gotten off to a fun start?" said Alison in a laughing tone that nevertheless regained control of the group. "In good time, George. But they aren't *dirty* movies. They're *explicit*. And they will provide us all with the impetus we need to go to our small group discussions and process our 'feelings.' But I'm getting way ahead of myself. Where was I?" she said, turning to me.

"You're about to tell them about the history of the program," I said.

"Thank you, darling," she said. "Brian's my able helper. He keeps me on track."

"He keeps us *all* on track," Pam piped in.

"Whether we like it or not," Carol added.

"Excuse me," I said in feigned contempt, "you're interrupting Alison. Alison, you were saying?"

"Thank you, Brian. The Annual Workshop on Sexuality started more than thirty years ago at Syracuse University when Dr. Sol Gordon, director of the Institute for Family Research and Education, decided to host an educational program for students in the field of sexuality education. I took on the job of coordinating the week-long summer training. Initially, we met on the Syracuse University campus, but we soon discovered that it was not conducive to the kind of work that we wanted to do, so I moved us out here to this beautiful facility owned and operated by the Episcopal Church. The name 'Thornfield' is that of an Episcopal bishop, as are the names of all of the buildings here — 'Higley,' where the staff stays, 'Huntington,' where you had your lunch, 'Peabody,' where you are all staying, and this

17

building, the newest of them all, 'Ridings,' where we'll be meeting every day.

"Excuse me, Alison, but can I ask a question?" asked Leona from across the circle.

"Certainly."

"These chairs are very uncomfortable. Are we going to be in these chairs *all* week?"

An awkward silence filled the room for only a second.

"They *can* be uncomfortable, can't they?" Alison affirmed. "No, we'll be downstairs for most of the presentations and films, and the chairs downstairs are much more comfortable. But you're always welcome to bring a pillow from your room to sit on, as long as you take it back. Please consider this whole complex yours to enjoy and to explore. There are acres and acres of grounds to walk. The lake is beautiful and a great spot for meditation or a nice swim. But if you do swim, please make sure you swim with a buddy. Don't swim alone. And I don't want to hear about anyone swimming nude," she said, turning to me with an expectant smile.

"You notice," I pointed out on cue, "that she said she didn't want to *hear* about it. Also, please don't pee in the lake. It's been specially treated with a chemical so that if you do pee, a big orange circle forms around you. I was down there earlier and there were some warm spots. Carol was that you?" I asked.

"It was Maggie," George said. "She took a swim before lunch."

"You're *awful*," she said laughing, and swatting his arm with her hand.

"You didn't know about the chemical, Maggie," I said. "But now you're warned."

"Yes, and getting back to our schedule," Alison said. "Oh dear, where was I?"

"The history of Thornfield," I said.

"She did that," Carol said.

"But she didn't talk about who's come here, and how the program has developed," I said.

"Well, the program has developed from a week-long training that incorporated just a three-day SAR to a week-long SAR. Bill's going to tell you about the SAR shortly. We used to have well-known people in the field come to the workshop and gave talks — people such as Mary Calderone, Michael Carrera, and Beverly Whipple — and then they'd leave. We changed that so that the staff is here *all* week. They stay and make themselves available to you all, so please take advantage of that."

"Alison?"

"Pam?"

"Can I take just a minute to echo what you said?" Pam asked. "Don't wait until the last minute to talk to one of us. If you'd like to meet with any of the staff, speak up, and set up a time. We're all happy to do that. Also, can I ask that everyone please wear your name badges all week long, all day long, even at every meal."

"And when you're swimming," I said.

"Very funny," Pam continued. "I don't know about the rest of you, but I'm awful with names, and I want to get to know yours."

"Thank you, Pam. We're getting ahead of ourselves a bit, but I do want to say that this place is a very special place to us, and I think it will be to all of you. We've had in these rooms and in these uncomfortable chairs," she said smiling to Leona, "hundreds of pilgrims like you from all over the world, and from *every* profession you can imagine, sitting, and listening, and sharing, and blooming before our very eyes. You see this wonderful arrangement of wildflowers we've assembled? They come from the fields … "

"And private gardens," I said.

"They do not!" she continued, "from the fields and woods in the surrounding area, and they, in their unique beauty, represent to us the unique beauty of all of you. You are all very different from each other, but each is beautiful in her or his own way. You've come together as strangers this week, and will bloom together in the wonderful arrangement that this time allows. That's why we call this 'holy' ground. It's a special place where many people have connected with themselves, and others, in a very special way. I hope that is true for each and every one of you this week. Now, without further ado, let me introduce to you our wonderful staff, and then we'd like to get to know all of you better.

"I'm going to ask the staff to come up one by one, and introduce themselves to you. And each has a question they'd like you to think about this week."

"Alison," I said, "why don't we begin with you?"

"Right you are," she said appreciatively. "Let's start with me. I'm originally from this area, but I now live in a small community north of Phoenix in Arizona. I'm a semi-retired psychotherapist, and marriage and family counselor. A couple of years ago, I had the adventure of a lifetime when I fulfilled my dream of becoming a Peace Corps volunteer. I'd be happy to talk with any of you about that over lunch. What more to say? Well, that's enough for now. Carol, will you please come up here and continue?"

Carol rose from her chair, and took on a new seriousness as she walked to the head of the circle. She threw her shoulders back, and struck the pose of a teacher meeting her class on the first day.

"Hi. My name is Carol Dopp. It's great to have faces to go with the names. As most of you know from our correspondence over the past year, I'm the coordinator of the workshop. Like you, I was a participant at Thornfield many years ago. Being a slow learner, I came back the following year," she said, throwing her long blond hair to one side, to the appreciative laughter of the group. "Professionally, I'm a counselor and family life educator at a coeducational private school in the Washington, D.C. area. Personally, I'm the proud mother of a beautiful daughter, Kerrigan, and I brought *lots* of pictures to show you. The question that I have for you is about what's keeping you from being the sexual person that you want to be. We're going to have a whole week together to look at the roadblocks to sexual health. In thinking about it right now, what would be the *one* thing you might change about yourself so that you could celebrate your sexuality more fully? Thanks."

"Thank you, Carol," Alison said as Carol relaxed her posture, smiled broadly, and returned to her seat. "Pam, would you go next, please?"

Dressed neatly in stylish black shorts and ironed white blouse, Pam walked to the spot previously held by Carol. "Hi everybody. I'm Pam Wilson, and it's great to be with all of you for what I know you will find to be a truly *amazing* week. I've been coming to Thornfield for 10 years, and it's something I look forward to all year long. I'm a social worker by training. I got my masters in social work from Catholic University of America. Over the past twenty-five years, I've worked mostly as a sexuality educator and diversity trainer. Brian and I work together at different corporations talking about sexual orientation. My biggest chunk of work today is as head of training for an organization working with low income fathers to get them reinvested in their families. I've also been busy writing a sexuality curriculum for the Unitarian Universalist Association and the United Church of Christ. That's about it for me."

"Tell them about your book," I said.

"Oh yea. Thanks," she said. "I have a book out entitled "When Sex is the Subject: Attitudes and Answers for Young Children.""

"It's a great book," I chimed in.

"That's my buddy," Pam said, smiling at me.

"And your question?" I prompted.

"I know. I know," she protested. "And he's also a *nudge*. My question has to do with your feelings about the sexuality education you got as a child. Let me see the hands of those of you who feel you got a 'good' sexuality education at home when you were growing up."

Two hands went up with some hesitation. The other participants laughed together at the dismal but predictable results of the poll.

"Okay, you all didn't see my hand go up either, right? So what do you wish you had been told about sexuality when you were young? I want you to think about what you wished you had learned, and what you think young people today should be hearing. Yes?" she said pointing to a woman in the circle.

"Pam, my mother told me when I had my first period that I was now *cursed*. That's all she'd say," said a heavyset woman in a pink, floral print summer dress. "I cried myself to sleep that night. I couldn't figure out what I had done wrong to be *cursed*."

"Oh, no," Pam said sympathetically. "My mother told me that a married woman who enjoyed sex with her husband was a *whore*."

"Oh, no," another woman said sadly from the crowd.

"Pam, Pam," came a voice from the other end of the circle, pleading with an outstretched arm to be recognized.

"One more, just one more," Pam said, trying to quiet the excitement that she had started. "We'll have plenty of time to tell our horror stories in our small groups. What was it you wanted to share?" she said with a smile to a pretty young woman in shorts and jersey.

"It can wait," she replied.

"No, go ahead, please," Pam invited.

"My father told me that women who love women should be *shot*," she said sadly.

"Ouch!" Pam said with a sympathetic pouting lip.

"Yea," she said. "He later changed his mind, but he said it when I told him that I'm a lesbian."

"Fuck him," said Dan Schemp in a low voice, shaking his head disgustedly as he stared at the floor. The room went silent.

"We're going to be talking about all of this more," Pam said, "and hopefully we won't keep repeating the same horrible mistakes with others that our parents made with some of us. Alison?"

21

"Thank you, Pam," Alison said standing up briefly at her seat. "Bill Stayton. Will you please introduce yourself?"

Bill rose hesitantly from his chair and walked to the front of the room, staring at the floor and smiling impishly.

"Hello there. I'm Bill Stayton. Let me see, what should I say about myself?" he asked, looking quizzically at Carol, Pam, and me. "I'm a Baptist minister. I'm also a sex therapist. How I got on those two tracks dates way back to when I masturbated for the first time. I didn't know anything about masturbation, so when I ejaculated, I really thought I was dying. I knew I needed to go to church, and the closest one to our house was a Baptist church. That's how I became a Baptist. And the more I masturbated, the more I went to church. And the more I went to church, the more I masturbated. They sort of went hand in hand. Actually, they still do," he said with a guilty smirk, swaying his butt back and forth slowly to emphasize the paradox. "I'm also director of the graduate program in human sexuality at Widener University," he continued, switching to a more serious tone. "It's a wonderful program that I'm eager to talk about with you more. But for now, the question that I'd like you to ask yourself this week is, what do you think the Bible *really* says about sexuality, and where did you learn this?"

"Thank you, Bill," said Alison. "And now, Dick Cross. Dick?"

Very tall and gangly, but with perfectly erect posture, Dick stepped to the front of the room with determination amidst some giggling about his faded T-shirt which proclaimed "Jugglers have colorful balls." Striking an imposing stance, he bellowed forth with a strong, deep, but warbling voice, "I'm Dick Cross. I'm 86-years-old, an M.D., and I've been coming to this program for many years. What you might find interesting about me is that I started a sexuality program for medical students at Rutgers University back in the 70s, long before such a thing existed elsewhere. Echoing what everyone else has said, I think you'll find this to be a magical place."

As he headed toward his seat, I asked "Is there any question you'd like folks to think about this week, Dick?"

"What's that?" he said, looking up a bit confused.

"Do you have a *question* for people to think about?" I repeated slowly, and more audibly.

"No questions," he said. "I'll leave that to you." And he sat down.

Alison smiled, and nodded to me as she said, "That leaves you, Brian."

I walked forward to the spot taken by the others. "Welcome," I said. "I'm Brian McNaught. I've spent most of my adult life trying to help others to understand what it's like to grow up as a gay, lesbian, or bisexual person. Most recently, I've added the topic of 'transgender.' I've written some books, and produced some video tapes on gay issues but I make my living primarily working with corporations and colleges as a speaker and diversity trainer on sexual orientation. I've been coming to Thornfield since I was 27 years old, and that was some time ago."

"A looong time ago," Carol chirped in.

"A looong time ago," I agreed. "I think you'll find that you're in for one of the most amazing weeks of your lives. Dick called it 'magical.' It certainly will be that for most of you. But, in truth, you get out of it what you put into it, so I invite you to put *everything* you've got into the week. The question that I'd like you to take a look at is, how does heterosexism, homophobia, or heterophobia impact your life? Do they stop you from living fully? If so, are you comfortable with the limitations they put upon your journey? Thank you."

"Thank you, Brian," said Alison. "And now, we'd like to hear from you," she said, gesturing with her extended right hand in a sweeping motion to the group. "I'd like us to go around the room, and one by one tell who we are, why we're here, and maybe one little thing about ourselves that most people wouldn't know by looking at us."

"Alison?" I said.

"Yes, Brian?"

"Before we do that, I know you wanted to introduce Gail and our staff helpers."

"Right you are," she said with contagious enthusiasm. "You all have met Gail, I assume, our wonderful registrar and song leader. Gail, stand up if you would, and tell everyone a little bit about yourself."

Gail stood, smiled first at Alison and then at me, and then with a sweeping look of warmth to the semicircle of participants. "Hi everyone," she said with a little giggle. "I'm Gail Brett. I live in the Utica area of New York State, and I work with children who are hearing impaired. I came to Thornfield as a participant the same year as Carol. We've been roommates ever since."

"She snores," said Carol.

"Aagh!" Gail yelled in protest. "I do not! *You're* the one who snores." After laughing at her own comment, she said. "I love Thornfield, and I hope you do too."

"Thank you, Gail," Alison said from her seat. "And now, I'd like to point out our two staff helpers, Tonya Lopnow and Kevin Brooks. Tonya and Kevin, would you please stand so that everyone can see you? Thank you. If there is anything you need, please don't hesitate to ask either of them, or any of the staff. Well now, that's a lot of introductions, isn't it? And we still have to meet all of you. But let's first take a little bathroom break. Let's take just ten minutes if you would. There are bathrooms on this floor and on the lower level."

"I *hate* that song," a thirty-something woman whispered to a middle-aged man she had been sitting next to as they headed toward the lower-level restrooms.

Chapter Four

The Participants

"Thomas," Alison said to the person seated at her left, after all of the participants and the staff had returned to their seats, "won't you please begin? Your name, why you're here, and something we wouldn't know about you by looking at you."

"Sure," he said, staring at the floor for a few quiet seconds. "I'm Thomas Miller. I'm an Episcopal priest, and hospital chaplain, in Santa Fe, New Mexico. I came here for both personal and professional reasons. Let's see, what wouldn't you know about me by looking at me? Well, maybe you would. I'm a gay man, but what you wouldn't know is that I have three daughters from a previous marriage."

"Thank you, Thomas. Next? I'm sorry, I'd call you by name but we haven't yet met, and I can't see your name tag," said Alison.

Sitting up straight and turning her body so that Alison could read her name tag, the large woman in the pink, floral summer dress sitting to the left of Thomas said, "Hi, my name is Marjorie Gale. I'm the director of education for Planned Parenthood in Muncie, Indiana. I came here because I've heard so many great things about this program from people at other Planned Parenthood affiliates, and I need some ceus for AASECT re-certification. What you might not guess about me is that I raise cocker spaniels and compete in dog shows."

25

"Hi everybody," said the young woman seated next to Marjorie in response to Alison's encouraging nod, "I'm Wendy Taylor. I'm a HIV-prevention educator in Cleveland. I'm here because almost everyone in my agency has been here, and have *raved* about the week. I kept asking them, 'What makes it so great?' and they all said, 'You have to go find out for yourself.' So, here I am. What you don't know about me is that I'm a lesbian," she said, smiling down the row of chairs at the woman who had spoken of her father's hostile response, "and I like to run."

"We'll form a group," I said.

"Of lesbians?"asked Carol, to the delight of the participants.

"Of runners," I explained with feigned exasperation. Wendy smiled and nodded in agreement.

The process of introductions continued. Catherine Mitchell explained that she was an Episcopal priest also, and had come for help in working with the youth group of her parish. Next to her was Judith Cohen, a college educator in human sexuality in Miami. She shared that she was feeling nervous and already a little overwhelmed. Margaret Johansson was a retired United Church of Christ pastor who was volunteering to be a sexuality educator for the youth of her church. She came to work with Pam. She was feeling a little nervous too.

Curtis Wiley works with people with disabilities in the Chicago area. Sr. Annette Guzzo is with the Sisters of Loretto, and she works with people with AIDS. Maggie Sutherland didn't tell the group that her gay husband had come the year before. She explained that she was a mother of two young children in Racine, Wisconsin, and had come for personal reasons. George Hauser took a moment to explain the Metropolitan Community Church to his fellow participants, and then, by holding up his hand to proximate the state of Michigan, to show where Toledo, Ohio was in relation to Detroit. Leona Mills told of her work at Planned Parenthood, and explained that something people don't know about her is that she doesn't like sharing bathrooms.

Ben Ellis had positioned his wheelchair near the entrance to the room. He said that he was a sexuality counselor and educator for a local agency that worked with people with disabilities. He said he was straight, and that one thing most people wouldn't be able to tell about him by looking at him was that he loved to dance. Betty Koslowski explained that she was pursuing a degree in counseling, and that she wanted to work with the gay, lesbian, bisexual and transgender communities. She said that something most people wouldn't know about her from looking at her, she didn't think, was that she had made a significant change in the course in her life eleven years ago, and, eyeing Leona, that she'd be talking in more detail about that later. Gina DeWitt raised her eyebrows in anticipation of learning about this major change, and smiled as she introduced herself as an AIDS educator from Atlanta, Georgia. "The big change in my life came when I told myself, and then my family, that I was a lesbian. This, was of course," she reminded the others, "in the context of my father saying that women who love women should be shot."

Joe Cook introduced himself as a retired professor of theology. He saw the advertisement for the workshop in the mailing from the Center for Sexuality and Religion and wanted to meet Bill Stayton. Grace Adler, "As in 'Will and Grace'," is a corporate diversity manager from Dayton, and wanted to participate in the "train the trainer" workshop that I was offering at the end of the week.

The only black man in the group was Lloyd Howard, a youth worker and counselor who was led to the workshop by his involvement with GLSEN, the Gay, Lesbian, and Straight Education Network that partners with the workshop. Charlie Tatewell explained that he was a Methodist minister from Oklahoma City, he was married, had two sons, and he came to Thornfield to learn more about gay issues. Dan Schemp said he was 'queer,' and worked with high risk teens on HIV-prevention. What we might not have known about Dan by looking at him was that he had been a member of the LA chapter of Act Up.

Beverly Johnson and Martha Brown told the group that they were health educators working for the government's family planning clinic in Trinidad. Lisa Keene didn't say she had been sent to Thornfield by her therapist. She merely said that she had heard good things about the workshop, and was looking for a nice vacation from her work as a software engineer. One thing the group might not know about her from looking at her was that she liked cats. Tonya Lopnow confided that she liked cats too, and in fact had three. She was a high school teacher in Alberta, Canada, who had been assigned to teach family life. Dominic Paluzzi said that he also had been assigned to teach family life in high school. He's the varsity football coach in his Dayton, Ohio school, and he said that he'd be interested in joining Brian and Wendy's running group.

Joanne Douglas introduced herself as a new staff person at SIECUS, the Sex Information and Education Council of the United States, and said that one thing we might not know about her was that she was at one time a nun. Paula Pendergast said she was a sex therapist from Tempe, Arizona, and the one thing we wouldn't know about her from looking at her was that she had a gay son of whom she was very proud. Beatrice Ramos said she wanted to either teach sexuality education or become a sex counselor. She was a graduate student in the Widener University sexuality program, and came to Thornfield at Bill Stayton's urging.

There were only three participants who had yet to introduce themselves. Carl Gunther was a slight man with fine features. His long black hair was pulled back into a pony tail. "I'm an organist in my church," he said with pride. "I'm married and have two grown children. I came to this program because of my interest in gender issues. What you may not know about me from looking at me is that I'm a cross dresser. I decided to let you get to know me today as Carl. Tomorrow, I'd like to participate as Carla."

"No shit!" drawled the burly, middle-aged man sitting beside him. "Well, I came here to learn, but I didn't expect to learn about 'cross dressing,' at least not on the *first* day. But hey, as I say, I'm here to learn. To each his own," he said smiling a little nervously at Carl. "I'm Chuck Dowd. I'm the junior varsity coach for football and baseball at a small high school in Hattiesburg, Mississippi. I'm also a youth worker in our school, and in my church, which is Baptist. I got the brochure on this program from someone in the school's counseling department. The school paid my way, so I said I'd come."

"I'm glad you came," said Alison. "And, last but not least, Peter, tell us about yourself."

"I'm Peter O'Shea," he said softly.

"A little louder if you would, Peter," Alison said, "so that everyone can hear you."

"Sorry. I'm Peter O'Shea," he said louder. "I found out about this program on the Internet. I was curious about how you approach the issue of sexual orientation. I got my church to send me. I'm a youth worker with the Lutheran Church in the Eugene, Oregon area. What you might not know about me from looking at me is that I'm an ex-gay."

"Fuck!" sighed Dan from the other side of the room.

"We welcome you, Peter" said Alison. "We welcome *all* of you, and invite you to plunge yourselves into this amazing week of personal exploration and growth, and of professional skill-building."

"Alison?"

"Yes, Carol?"

"Did anyone notice that we don't have any two people with the exact same first names? That's a first," she said.

"And won't that make it easier for us to remember who's who?" Alison replied with delight. "Well now, let's take a refreshment break, shall we? There are lots of nice, cool drinks in the cafeteria. But, let's be back here in 15 minutes, please."

"Some interesting dynamics," Carol whispered in my ear as people stood to leave.

"That 'ex-gay' guy is really handsome," I said.

"Dan 'Fuck' Schemp thinks so too," she smiled.

"Am I on next?" Bill asked as he joined Carol and me in front of the Quilt panels.

"No, not yet," I said. "When they come back, we'll go through the schedule, and explain the tracks. Then you do your 'words'."

"Oh, goodie," Bill said with wide eyes, and an ear-to-ear smile. "It's a *great* exercise. They'll love it!"

"What are you three talking about over there?" asked Pam with a suspicious grin as she finished her conversation with Lloyd, and headed our way.

"We're talking about how beautiful you are," I said.

"Right," she responded dismissively. "What do you all think of the group?" she whispered as she got closer. "I just talked with Lloyd. He's a sweetie!"

"So is Peter," I said.

"No, he's a cutie!" Pam corrected. "He's handsome. But 'ex-gay'?"

"Are any of you going over to the cafeteria?" asked Alison as she came up from downstairs.

"Do you want something to drink?" came a voice from the doorway. "I'd be happy to get you something."

"Why yes, thank you, Thomas, but only if you're going. I'd love a cup of coffee, black."

"One black coffee coming up," he said as he joined the end of the procession out of the building.

"I like that man," she said to us as she sat down and looked through her workshop folder.

In small groups during the break, the participants began registering their reactions and starting new friendships.

"Well, so far so good," said Marjorie as she lit up a Kool on the Ridings' wrap-around balcony. "What do you think?" she said, turning to the new smoking buddy she had met outside of the cafeteria at the end of lunch.

Curtis dragged hard on his Merit. "There's a lot more going on than I had expected. Gays and ex-gays, nuns and ex-nuns, he/shes and football coaches. It's not going to be a boring week."

"How far do you go when you run?" Dom asked Wendy who was walking with Gina ahead of him.

She turned back and quickly looked at the round name tag in the upper right-hand corner of the man's Buckeye's T-shirt. "Oh, Dom, hi," she said. "I really run time more than I run distance. I try to run about forty-five minutes every day. You run too, right?"

"Yea," he said. "I run on a treadmill at the gym, and on a track at school. I'm not a fast runner. I do about a nine minute mile, but every other day."

"So, you're going to join our running group?" she said.

"The lesbian group with you and Brian? Yea, sure," he said. "Let's find out where he goes and when."

Carl walked to the center of the vast stretch of sloping lawn overlooking Lake Cazenovia, sat back on his elbows, and tilted his head to feel the warm sun on his thin, angular face.

"So, you're a TV?" said Betty as she sat down beside him. "How long have you been cross dressing? And, does your wife know?"

"Yes, she knows," he said, "but she doesn't much like it. My kids know too, and have asked me not to dress up at home when they're there. You know much about this?"

"I'm an MTF, Carl. I don't know much about the 'queen for a day' thing, no offense, but I know the pain of not being able to express who you are," Betty replied, casually looking over her shoulder to see Dan heading their way.

"Hi doll," Betty said with a sexy wink to the muscular, blond, thirty-six-year-old man who was kneeling down next to her and to Carl. "Was that a 'fuck' I heard out of you a little earlier, cupcake?"

"I'm a little blown away by Mr. Ex-Gay being here," Dan said, shaking his head with disgust, "but I'm sure glad *you* came, Carl. I look forward to getting to know Carla."

"How are you doing so far?" Gail asked Lisa as the two entered Huntington. "Did you get settled in your room, okay?"

"Yea, thanks," Lisa replied with a weak smile. "I'm rooming with Gina, and we're sharing a bathroom with Betty and her roommate, but I can't remember her name. She's the beautiful black woman from Planned Parenthood in the DC area, I think."

"Leona," Gail said with the excited delight of recollection. "Leona Mills. Good. So how's it going?"

"So far, so good," she lied.

"We have an MCC in Oklahoma City," Charlie said as George filled a red plastic glass with ice and handed it to Maggie. "I've met the minister, but I don't remember her name."

"At one time, I used to know everyone's names," George replied. "Try mixing the lemonade with cranberry juice," he said to Maggie. "We've gotten quite big now, but not so long ago all of the ministers knew each other on a first name basis."

"That was a brave thing you did in there," said Catherine to Peter as she caught up to him walking alone across the lawn to the cafeteria.

"What's that? Oh, yea, thanks," he said, looking a bit startled. "I knew when I signed up for this that I'd feel like the Lone Ranger. The words 'ex-gay' can be a lightening rod."

"You're *not* the Lone Ranger," Catherine replied, putting her hand on his shoulder as they continued their slow pace.

"How's that?" he asked with a confused look.

"Oh, I'm just saying that I know other people who have made the same correct choice about their lives," she answered, "and anytime you feel as if you're alone, you come see me."

"What community were you with?" Annette asked Joanne as they made their way along the path with the others toward Huntington.

"I was an IHM, Monroe, Michigan province," Joanne smiled back. "And you're with the Sisters of Loretto? That's a good group of women. I admire the risks you all take."

"Thanks," said Annette. "I'm very proud of the group myself. I always thought IHMs were a good group too. When did you leave?"

"Excuse me, Annette, it looks as if Ben needs a hand with that door," she said scurrying up the path.

"So, you're both from Trinidad, eh?" Leona said to Beverly and Martha as they sat at one of the picnic tables outside of the cafeteria and sipped their waters.

"That's right," Beverly said. "Some of our staff have been here before, and came back with glowing accounts."

"Were there as many lesbians here when *they* came?" Leona asked with a mischievous smile, and a slight turn of her head to check the surrounding area. "Because there sure are a lot this year."

31

"I don't know about that," responded Beverly with a polite smile and gentle eyes, "but I know they said they learned a lot, and that we would too."

"Are you two roommates?" asked Leona, sensing the need to change the subject but still seeking support for her dilemma.

"No, we asked Carol to have us room with people we don't know," said Martha a bit shyly. "We're best friends at home, and we knew that if we roomed together we'd probably isolate."

"Hmm," said Leona. "So, who are you rooming with?"

"I'm with Maggie," said Martha.

"And I'm with Wendy," said Beverly.

"Oh, so you have the same problem I've got," Leona said to Beverly, and ended the conversation as Lloyd and Thomas approached, black coffee in hand.

The sound of a clanging school bell alerted them all to the beginning of the next session. In response, Beatrice and Grace got up from the reclining positions they had taken on adjacent picnic tables in front of Higley, the staff dorm.

"Oh, that sun feels so good, I hate to leave it," said Beatrice.

"And there isn't much time for it this week, is there," said Grace. "Have you looked at the schedule? We go from morning until late at night."

"That's okay," replied Beatrice. "That's why I'm here. I can get a tan at home."

"Me too," said Grace, as they headed across the lawn.

Ben maneuvered his wheelchair through the door leading into Ridings, and noticed the elevator to his left.

"Looks like that's got your name on it," said Curtis. "Alison said we're going to be meeting downstairs for most of the week. I'd be happy to help you, if you'd like, when the time comes."

"Thanks, I think I'll be fine, but I appreciate the offer," Ben said.

As the participants began filing back into the room, they noticed that the staff had changed their seating positions. Most of the people headed back to where they had been sitting before the break, but Kevin made a beeline to the empty seat next to Dan, who was unconsciously staring at Peter, who was staring at the floor.

Chapter Five

The Program Begins

"If you'll please pull out your schedule for the week, I'd like to go over some things with you," I said at Alison's request. The participants began shuffling through the packet of materials that most of them had placed under their chairs.

"It says 'Proposed Agenda' because sometimes we make changes in the time or in the content of the schedule," I continued when it was clear that they had all found the outline. "You'll note that tomorrow morning, after we meet here for announcements and a wake-up exercise, you'll all be getting together briefly with the staff person who is directing your 'Skill-Building' session that takes place at the end of the week. For instance, I'll be meeting with those of you who signed up to enhance your skills as presenters of information on sexual orientation, and gender identity and expression. Bill will be meeting with those of you who want to focus your attention on your spiritual journey. Alison will be meeting with those who want to spend Friday exploring your personal, sexual journey, and Carol and Pam will be meeting with those of you who want to enhance your skills doing sexuality education in schools or in the community. Some of these groups, such as mine, will be meeting periodically throughout this week during lunch or dinner, while others may be only getting together again on Friday. Any questions?"

"Have we all signed up for this?" asked Peter, drawing a small grimace from Dan.

"You were a last-minute registrant, Peter," Carol explained from her chair across the room. "Why don't you and I hook up at the next break and we'll find out which group works best for you?" Peter nodded his approval, and Dan rolled his eyes. "I hope it's not in *my* group," he whispered to Kevin.

"Where do we meet?" asked Grace, pen in hand.

"We'll give those sites tomorrow morning, Grace," I said. "As you may know, throughout the week, you're going to be meeting two or three times a day in a small SAR group. Those SAR groups are different from the one that's meeting briefly tomorrow morning. Tomorrow's meeting is about the 'Skill Building' workshops that take place at the end of the week. The SAR groups, on the other hand, are process groups which you stay in all week, not to talk about what you *do* professionally, but rather what you *feel* personally on the topics that are being presented in the SAR. We'll be talking more about the SAR a little bit later."

"You're getting ahead of yourself," Pam said.

"Shush," I replied with a smile.

"Brian?"

"Yes, George?" I said.

"When do the dirty movies start?"

Before the laughter subsided, I asked, "Are you inquiring for Maggie again, or is it for yourself this time?"

"Neither," he said, "Martha here was asking."

To that, the dark-skinned black woman in the colorful print dress slapped his arm with one hand as she covered her giggle with the other.

"Soon enough, Martha. Soon enough," I said. "But before we get to them, let's go back to our schedule. The SAR officially begins after our morning skill-building meeting. Bill will be setting the stage for the SAR in just a minute. As you can see by looking at the schedule, we go from the general to the specific in our topics. Pam, for instance, starts us off with a presentation on 'What is Sexuality?' Bill then helps us take a look at our 'Sexual Value Systems.' We then explore 'Body Image,' 'Self-Pleasuring,' and then 'Male and Female Cultural and Biological Sex Roles.' From there, Carol moves us to the 'Hurdles to Sexual Health.' Next, we look at the 'Sexual Response Cycle,' and 'Sexual Orientation.' Pam and Bill then help us take a look at 'Heterosexuality,' and Carol and I explore the issues of 'Growing Up Gay'."

"You skipped 'The Touch Factor'," said Leona with a raised eyebrow. "Is that when we all start *touching* each other?"

Nervous laughter came up from a few people. Others clapped.

"I sure hope so," said Margaret, with a smiling, wide-eyed expression.

"Do we have to wait until then?" asked Thomas.

"Touch, touch, touch," laughed Sr. Annette, as she playfully pretended to tickle Tonya, who was sitting to her right. Laughter and pretend tickling erupted in various segments of the three-quarter circle of participants. A few others sat with bemused smiles, and some with folded arms.

"See what you started?" I said to Leona with a grin.

"You *still* haven't answered my question," she said lightly as she tried to escape a feigned attempt at tickling from Charlie.

"My, aren't we a fun group?" Alison said with delight.

"To answer Leona's question," I said in a voice loud enough to be heard over the individual conversations that had started, "I skipped 'The Touch Factor' by mistake. Actually, for me, it's one of the highlights of the week."

"Because he peeks," quipped Carol.

"Don't give it away," Bill admonished.

"Speak to Carol," I said in an aside to Bill, with a disapproving nod at Carol. "Without giving you any details, I promise that you'll *love* the exercise. But personally, I agree with Thomas. I don't want to have to wait until Wednesday night before I get touched. So, if anyone wants to give me a neck massage, know that I'm ready and willing."

"After me," said Pam, circling her shoulders in a gesture to indicate soreness.

"But let's finish the schedule because Bill has a great ice-breaking exercise, not that you all need it. Who spiked the lemonade?" I asked, turning to Carol. "Following Carol's and my presentation on 'The Stages of Coming Out,' Bill takes a look at 'Monogamy and Its Alternatives,' and then Alison and Dick help us explore 'Aging.' Finally, Bill wraps up the week with 'Universe as a Turn On.' Any questions?"

"Brian," Carol said, her hand raised high, "just a quick comment on the word 'Celebration' that you see at the end of the week. Each year we close with a social gathering in which we sing songs, read poetry, act out skits, play a musical instrument, or whatever it is we want to share with the other participants."

"It's lots of fun," said Pam in support.

"So please start thinking about what it is you might like to share with the others on Friday night," continued Carol, sitting back in her chair to indicate that she was finished speaking.

"And just to add to that," I said, "I know that many of you have been looking around the room thinking to yourselves that you'll never remember everyone's name, let alone get close enough to the others that you'll want to stand up on Friday night and be silly performing a skit. But I promise you that by the end of the week, this room full of 'strangers' will become, for most of us, a room full of 'friends,' some of whom we'll feel closer to than we do to many of the people in our families and circle of friends back home. At least, that's been true for me."

"And me," said Pam.

"And me," said Bill.

"And me," said Betty and Kevin in near unison.

"Our return campers," Alison explained with a sweeping smile of delight and pride to the rest of the group. "Thank you, Brian. And now Bill, and an introduction to the SAR."

"The SAR experience, about which I'll be saying more tomorrow morning," explained Bill as he took center stage in his wrinkled khaki shorts, beige socks and sandals, and tucked-in, plaid, short-sleeved shirt, "provides us the opportunity to take a look at those things which stop us from experiencing sexual health. 'SAR' stands for Sexual Attitude Reassessment. Together, we're going to be assessing our attitudes about human sexuality, ours and that of others.

"In sum, we believe that the major impediments to sexual health can be broken down into three categories: Ignorance, Secrecy, and Trauma. This whole week, we're going to be taking a look at how we all have been impacted by sexual ignorance, sexual secrecy, and sexual trauma. We'll be doing so with films," he said with conspiratorial smile and raised eyebrows to George, "with presentations, and with small group discussions. To get us started in this process, I have an exercise that is designed to get us talking with one another about subjects we don't often openly discuss in our lives outside of Thornfield. In a minute, I'm going to ask each of you to break up into groups of two, and please try to pick a person you don't know or work with. Then, I'm going to give you a word, or words, to discuss, and I want you to take turns discussing your *feelings* about the words. I want one person to go first and talk uninterrupted for one minute. I'll tell you when to stop. Then, I want the other person to talk uninterrupted about his or her feelings about the word. Is that clear?"

"What if we don't *want* to talk about our feelings about a particular topic?" asked Leona.

"Good question," responded Bill. "If you don't want to talk, you can pass. You can always pass here. But try *not* to pass. Remember, the more you put into this week, the more you'll get out of it."

"Trust the process," I said in support.

With no further questions from the clearly more anxious participants, Bill said, "Okay, now go find someone to talk with whom you don't know."

Some participants stood up and walked toward the center of the three-quarter circle of chairs, looking quickly around the room for a face that appeared receptive. Other participants stayed seated and merely turned to their right or to their left, looking for eye confirmation that the person sitting next to them was open to being partnered.

"Does everybody have someone to pair with?" Bill asked. Five people seemed to be still milling around in the center of the room. "Lisa, will you go with Lloyd, please? And Tonya, you go with Charlie. Who does that leave? Okay, Gail, you come up with me," he said. "Ready? The first words are 'Masculinity and Femininity.' Begin."

The initial conversation in most couplings involved, "Do you want to go first? Which word are we supposed to do first? Okay. I'll go."

"Oh," Bill interrupted, "if you're a man, talk about your feelings about masculinity. If you're a woman, talk about your feelings about femininity. And," turning to Carl with a big smile of affirmation, "if you're *both*, talk about either or both, but in one minute. So, begin."

"Masculinity," said Carl to his partner Martha. "It's a hard term. What does it mean to be masculine? Does it mean being aggressive? Does it mean having a hairy chest? I've got a hairy chest, which is a nuisance. Does that make me masculine? Is it muscles? Is it making babies? I've made babies. Am I masculine? Or is it how you *see* yourself? I see myself as male. I'm clearly male, and sometimes I feel 'manly,' like when I'm dressed in jeans, and I'm with my wife, and she's in a dress, and the kids are with us. Then, I'm the 'man' of the family. But, let me switch to feminine before my minute runs out." Martha smiled and nodded encouragement. "I know I'm feminine when I relax into a soft and vulnerable mode. Clothes help. That's why I'll be cross-dressing tomorrow. Carla *needs* to be wearing feminine, or 'ladylike,' clothes to feel *permission* to express herself. And when I'm dressed in women's clothes, I feel happy. I mean, *real* joy, as if I've found my safe niche."

"Time's up. Now switch," Bill instructed.

"Feminine," Martha said on cue. "I *love* being a woman. But that doesn't mean that I'm not strong. 'Feminine' to me means my ability to listen, and to feel compassion. It means being free to express my feelings, my sadness with tears, or my joy with laughter. 'Feminine' means my ability to nurture without excuses, to feel soft and vulnerable, as you say. But it doesn't mean to me that I want to be 'taken care' of, or treated like a piece of china that might easily break. It doesn't mean that I feel the need to step back, or be in a role. I like being with my women friends because I generally feel that I can be myself with little judgment or expectation. I like talking with women because I trust that I will be listened to and understood. That's part of being 'feminine,' I think."

"Yes," said Carl excitedly. "When I'm with women, I relax more than I do with men. I don't feel like I have to play any games. I can just be me."

"Okay, time's up," Bill said. "Please thank the person you were with, and quickly move on and find another partner."

Carl hugged Martha as he headed into the maze of moving bodies and found Margaret.

"The next words I want you to discuss are 'Self-Pleasuring'," Bill announced.

"Okay, well that gets right down to it, don't it?" laughed Chuck to his shy-smiling partner, Kevin. "I think I'm glad you and I got teamed up on this one, bud. I don't think I'd want to do this with a nun. You want me to go first? Let's see. 'Self-pleasuring.' Okay. Masturbation. Beating off. I do it," he said leaning forward and whispering as he winked. "I enjoy it, but I don't feel all that comfortable talking about it, I guess. Seems kind of private," he continued as he sat back up straight and raised his voice from a whisper. "But I guess I better get used to talking about it, hadn't I? I know the ball players are doing it. So are the kids at the church, at least the guys. Probably the girls too. Okay, so it feels good, it's natural, and we don't talk about it. Is time up? You want to talk about 'masculinity'?" he laughed. "Okay, let's see. I remember feeling some guilt about masturbating when I was a kid. And I remember feeling some in the first few years of my marriage. It's not something my wife and I talk about, but I don't feel guilty about doing it anymore. Gosh, is the whole week going to be like this?"

"Time's up. Now the other person talks," directed Bill.

"You're up, Kevin," Chuck said with a big grin and raised eyebrows.

"I grew up Catholic," Kevin said, his dark brown eyes bright as he leaned forward in his chair. "Besides hearing that it was a sin, I heard that it would make hair grow on your palms. I kind of liked that idea," he said laughing.

"Well, it seems to have worked pretty well," said Chuck as he casually pointed to Kevin's hairy legs, arms, mustache, and two-day-old beard.

"Yea, well, I was pretty scared to try it when I was young. It was only later that I decided that I was missing something and began experimenting. I'd rub myself on the bed, and then I learned to use a pillow."

"You were a lot more creative than me," Chuck said. "I always just used my hand."

"I started doing that later," Kevin said, still smiling. "My mom caught me one time in the morning when I was still in bed. She told me that she was disappointed in me, and that she wanted me to talk to the priest."

"What did the priest say?" Chuck asked.

"He didn't say anything. I never told him. I didn't think it was any of his business."

"You were a confident little guy," Chuck said.

"I was pretty confused as a child," Kevin replied, "but I had a sense of what to keep to myself."

"Time," Bill announced. "Thank your partner and go find another one."

"Thanks, Kevin," Chuck said. "You're really good at this."

"Thanks," he replied. "I've done it before. It gets easier after the first time through."

"The words are," Bill said as he turned to write them on the flip chart as he had the others, "'Oral Sex'."

A couple gasps of laughter erupted but the mood in the room remained playful, and the participants began again to buzz.

"Do you want to begin, Sister?" Curtis asked with a look of concern, "or do you want me to start?"

"Please call me Annette," she replied, "and I'm glad to go first. Well, of course, the official position of the Catholic Church is that oral sex, in and of itself, is forbidden, as it can't result in pregnancy. I know that for many people, it's a very pleasurable and acceptable way of making love. I tend to focus more on the 'context' of the acts than on the acts themselves. So, I don't have any personal negative feelings about it, and haven't explored the thought about whether it would be 'personally' of interest, if I had the option. I've learned that heading down those paths isn't always helpful to me on my journey. On the other hand, I have given it a lot of thought as a person who works with people with AIDS, and I'm more than a little concerned about the possibility of infection when people have oral sex without a condom. It's always been considered a low risk activity, but there's enough evidence out there to say that we ought to be strongly advising the use of condoms. Of course, the Church's position on condoms is that they cannot be used because they undermine the purpose of sex, which is 'procreation.' This is, of course, a completely irresponsible, dangerous, destructive, and ignorant position."

"You go, Sister," Curtis said.

"Time's up," Bill said.

"Your turn," Annette nodded.

"My focus is different, Annette. I work with people with disabilities, and for many of them and their partners, oral sex is the *primary* means of giving or receiving pleasure. We have to do some really hard work to help some of these folks get past their negative feelings or, better yet, their *guilty* feelings about oral sex. Of course, oral sex isn't just a mouth on a penis or a tongue on a clitoris – am I being too explicit here?" he stopped.

"No, no, please, go on," she said.

"For me, oral sex takes in the use of the tongue in one's anus, one's nipples, one's ears, or anywhere else that provides pleasure to one or both parties. If you have no sensation below the waist, you look elsewhere. And even when you *do* have sensation below the waist, as you say, it's not the 'acts' that are of importance, it's the *context* for the acts."

"Of course, of course," she said.

"Personally, and I get the impression we're supposed to talk 'personally' about this stuff," he said, "I enjoy oral sex. I enjoy the sight, smell, touch, and taste of it. I can't believe I'm saying this to a nun. I know. I know. It's 'Annette.' At any rate, oral sex is a part of my life personally and professionally."

"Time," Bill said. "Please thank your partner and hook up with someone else. This will be the last one."

"Thank God," Maggie said with a sigh of exhaustion from the floor where she was sitting with Lisa. She got up and headed in the direction of Tonya. Dan made a beeline in the direction of Peter, who was parting company with Judith.

"You okay if we partner?" he said with his hand outstretched. "I'm Dan."

"Sure," he said with a look of resignation. "I'm Peter."

The handshake was firm and brief. They sat in chairs that had been turned to face each other.

"The words," said Bill, writing in black marker, "are 'Anal Pleasuring'."

"Of course," said Leona from where she was sitting across from Ben's wheelchair.

"You want to go first?" asked Dan of Peter, working hard to conceal his glee.

"No. You go ahead," Peter replied, slowly tapping his hand on his knee.

"Anal Sex. I *love* it," he said, moving slowly forward, resting both hands on his knees, making intense eye contact with his prey. "I love the feel of a guy's cock up my ass, and I love the feel of my cock up another guy's ass," he whispered softly, and with slowly-increasing excitement. "When some hunky guy has his big, hard cock up my ass, and has his tongue down my throat, and his hairy arms and chest around and on top of me, and I feel like I'm about to explode with excitement, and then he lets loose his man load into me, and I let loose mine all over me and him both, I feel like I'm in fuckin' heaven. And when I'm the one on top, and the guy below me is looking hungry into my eyes, telling me that he wants it bad, and I slip my cock into his warm, wet ass, and start sliding slowly back and forth, back and forth to the rhythm of his moving hips, and I press my body against his, and take his mouth with my tongue, and I see him whimper with pleasure, and feel him squeeze his ass tight, and I let go of the hot juice in me, and feel him spray me with his, I'm in fuckin' heaven again." Feeling his own erection swell, Dan sat back with a satisfied smirk, crossed his legs, and said, "Your turn."

"Time," Bill said.

Peter returned the smile, and moved forward, resting his arms on his knees. He looked for an intense moment into Dan's blue eyes.

"It's clear that you get a lot of pleasure from just the *thought* of anal sex," he said, briefly eyeing Dan's swollen crotch. "I don't. I never have. It doesn't 'disgust' me. It just doesn't 'appeal' to me. When I had sex with other men, it was mostly oral. I liked it. It felt good. Sometimes it even felt *great*. But I was never able to give myself over to it completely because there was always something nagging in the back of my mind that said it wasn't right."

"That's horseshit," Dan said.

"Let me finish," Peter said. "You had your minute. I don't want to argue with you. I just want to use my turn to talk about *my* feelings."

"The topic's *anal sex*," Dan said a bit harshly.

"He said 'anal *pleasuring*,' but for the sake of our discussion, let's stay on anal sex. I've told you that it doesn't appeal to me," Peter responded firmly in a whisper. "I think there are some logical reasons why it doesn't. I don't think it's all that natural. If it was, it wouldn't hurt so much. I just don't think it's what God had in mind when he created the human body. It's just not that sanitary, and as AIDS illustrates, it's not very safe. And last but not least, I'm not so sure that it's in fuckin' *heaven* that you'll find yourself as a result of engaging in it."

"Fuck you," Dan said angrily in a voice loud enough to be heard by a couple of people on either side of him.

"Hey, I'm just giving you *my* perspective on anal sex," he replied in a hushed voice. "I know that it's not your perspective. It's mine."

"And it's God-damn judgmental. Who are you to say that my having anal sex is going to put me in hell?"

"Time," Bill said.

"You're right," Peter whispered. "I allowed myself to get angry, and I apologize. I'm a bit nervous, and I'm feeling a little outnumbered here. What I should have said was that if *I* engaged in anal sex, fuckin' heaven isn't where I imagine *I'd* end up as a result."

"So tell me," Bill said in a voice loud enough to drown out the continuing conversations that were taking place around the room, "what was that like?"

Initially the room was quiet. Bill stood comfortably still, smiling from person to person with eyes wide.

"It was *hard*," said Maggie.

"Why?" asked Bill.

"Because it was so *personal*," she said.

"I don't talk with my friends about that stuff," said Lisa.

"I don't talk with my *wife* about it," said Charlie.

"Would you like to?" asked Bill, with a pregnant pause. "Can you think of any reason why talking about those topics with your friends or partners might be useful?"

"It would sure get things out in the open, wouldn't it?" said Chuck. "Might be fewer guilty feelings."

"Might be," affirmed Bill with a big smile. "What was the most difficult topic to discuss?" he asked, casually checking his watch for the time.

"They were all hard," said Maggie.

"Masculinity," said Carl.

"Femininity," said Marjorie.

"Anal pleasuring," said several people in unison.

"Well, for the rest of the week, we're going to be taking a look at *all* of those topics, and why they're sometimes so difficult for us to talk about," said Bill with a grin.

"Thank you, Bill," said Alison, standing and turning toward him as he walked to an empty seat. "What a *great* way to start the process. Now, it's break time. You've got a nice long stretch before dinner at 6:00. You may want to get settled into your room, or take a quick swim in the lake. Do have fun, and please be sure to be to dinner on time. As a reminder to the staff, we have a meeting in ten minutes."

Chapter Six

Mary Lee's Tree

"Getting ready for the next session?" Lloyd asked as he sat down next to Pam in the rapidly emptying meeting room.

"Well, I'm actually on tomorrow, but you're right. I'm going through my notes," she said, looking away from her papers, and directly at him with her smiling eyes. "So, how are you doing, Lloyd?"

"Pretty good," the handsome young black man said with an eager-to-please smile.

"Was that last session too intense for you?" she asked with a tilt of her head and raised eyebrows.

"Oh, no. It was cool. I like talking about sex. So, I see that you've got the AIDS Quilt here," he said nodding toward the panels.

"Yes, Carol arranged for that. It's great having it here. It brings it right home, doesn't it?" she said, searching his face for a clue as to what was on his mind.

"People forget, don't they. Even people who should know better forget sometimes," he said, peering out the windows that overlooked the lake.

"Forget about AIDS, or forget about safe sex practices?" Pam asked.

"*Safer* sex practices," Lloyd corrected. "Both, I guess, but mostly about the need to play safe."

"That's the work you do, isn't it?" she asked. "Didn't I hear you say you work with HIV issues?"

"Not really. That's a part of what I do, but mostly I work with GLSEN on minority youth issues, among other things."

"That's right," Pam said, gently knocking her head with her fist. "Sorry. You told me that before. It takes me awhile to get names, faces, and jobs straight."

"So to speak," he replied with a grin.

"What? Oh right," she said, rolling her eyes at the unintended humor, and casually looking at her watch. "So now, Lloyd, walk with me, will you? I'm supposed to be meeting with the staff in a few minutes. Tell me specifically about the work you do."

"One of the things that I do is help schools and local groups focus on the unique needs of black and Latino gay youths," he said as they walked toward the door. "We do some work on Asian and Native American gay youths too, but mostly it's with queer blacks and Latinos."

"Talk to me about the unique needs," Pam encouraged as they worked their way across the lawn toward Higley. "I mean, I know that it can be harder to be gay in minority communities, but what specifically do you tell the schools about it?"

"When adults look at young black and Latino faces, they don't usually allow for the fact that the kid might be gay too. Gay minority youths are often invisible. In their own communities, queer boys get a lot of pressure to be 'macho.' They experience homophobia there, and racism in the white gay culture. And, there's a lot of resistance to using condoms. There's also a lot of drug and alcohol use. Then you've got self-esteem issues. People will say 'yes' to unsafe sex because they feel desirable, even people who should know better."

Heading toward them with blankets from their dorm rooms were Maggie and George. After smiling and nodding to Pam and Lloyd, they walked to the center of the hill, spread out their blankets, and sat side by side, gazing through the trees at the late afternoon sun dancing on the lake.

"Please don't be offended by this question," Maggie asked her new friend, gently taking his elbow in her hand, "but Peter said that he's 'ex-gay.' Is that possible?"

"I'm not offended," George said turning toward her with a soft smile. "If I were you, I'd be asking the exact same question. Do I think gay people can become straight? No. Do I think gay men can have sex with

45

women? Yes. Do I think your husband is torn apart by his love for you and by his attraction to men? Definitely yes!"

"Hmm," she sighed. "So, what *does* Peter mean when he says that he's 'ex-gay'?"

"I'm anxious to find out," George replied, "but please don't torture yourself by thinking that your husband 'decided' to be gay, or that he can decide to be straight. It doesn't work like that."

"We were so happy, or at least I thought we were," she said, her eyes tearing slightly as she looked away. "It just felt so out of the blue. He came here last year at the advice of his therapist. He ends up in Brian's group. And he comes home and tells me there's something he needs to say. He says he's 'gay,' and that he's sorry. Sorry? We've been in couple's counseling ever since. Barry, that's my husband, he asked me to come to Thornfield so that I'd understand. Our therapist agreed. I sure hope they put me in Brian's group."

To the left of Maggie and George, on the picnic tables outside of Huntington, Dom and Chuck talked about high school football, and drank coffee from white "Thornfield" mugs.

"Is this what you thought it would be?" Dom asked, changing the subject.

"Well, as I said in the circle, Dom, I came here to *learn*. I didn't think I'd be sittin' next to a cross dresser on my first day, or talkin' about oral sex and anal pleasurin' with a perfect stranger. It's not something we do regularly at my Baptist church in Hattiesburg. And I don't think we'll *start* doin' it either. But I get the feelin' the staff here knows what they're doin', and I'm glad to be here. How about you?"

"I'd have to say it's more than I bargained for," Dom said, turning around to see if he could be overheard. "The woman who suggested that I come here didn't tell me much about it, other than that she was sure I'd come home saying I was glad I came. I didn't know we were going to be watching gay sex films."

"What gay sex films?" Chuck interrupted. "You mean like porn?"

"No, I don't think it's porn. It's just films of guys having sex with each other. I'm not sure I'm ready for that," Dom said, "and I sure as hell wasn't ready to sit near enough to that Dan character to hear him describe in detail to that 'ex-gay' guy why he loves anal sex. Geese Louise."

"I didn't hear any of that. I heard the 'fuck you,' but he's been talking like that since he got here," Chuck said.

"He's an angry guy. I'm steering clear of him," Dom said, finishing off his coffee.

"Are you sorry you came?" Chuck asked.

"No. I can't say that I'm 'sorry.' Not yet, anyway. But I didn't count on it being so intense so fast. Maybe it's not always like this. I gotta believe my friend wouldn't have sent me to this if it was going to be a bad experience."

Squeals of laughter from the beach distracted them both and made them smile in the direction of the lake.

"It's *cold*," screamed Tonya. "Why didn't you tell me that it was so cold?"

"It's not cold. It's great!" Charlie said as he floated on his back further out toward the raft. "It just takes a minute to get used to."

"And it's *mucky*!" Tonya continued in her lament.

"It's not mucky. The bottom's just a little soft," he replied. "But taste the water. It's so *sweet*! What a great lake!" With this, Charlie turned over on his belly and began to swim the breast stroke past the raft and the roped-off swimming area. Turning back, he noticed Tonya wading back to shore, then turned himself around, and swam the crawl back toward the small, sandy beach.

"It's too cold for me," Tonya said to the half a dozen participants who sat fully dressed on a picnic table nearby.

"If it's too cold for you now, doll, what are you going to be saying when we go skinny dipping after dark?" Betty asked with a mischievous grin.

"Skinny dipping?" Marjorie said. "I'm game. But can we do that here? I thought Alison said we couldn't."

"No, what Alison said was that she didn't want to *hear* about it," explained Betty. "It's her little joke. She's one of the most enthusiastic skinny dippers. Her and Dick Cross. The whole staff comes down here at least one of the nights, swims out to the raft, and sits bare assed out there singing, 'You Are My Sunshine' and 'Blue Moon'."

"No kidding?" said Joanne. "That surprises me a bit, but it sounds like fun."

"And we almost always have camp fires down here at night," Betty continued.

"You mean everybody?" Lisa asked.

"No. It's not an organized thing," Betty replied.

"I've never been skinny dipping," said Joanne. "Is that crazy?"

To that, Betty stood up tall, as if at attention.

"Why did you stand up?" asked Marjorie. "Is it time to go?"

"No. I'm playing 'I Never.' If someone says something that *they* have never done, but *you* have done it, you have to stand up. Joanne said that she had never been skinny dipping. Since I have been skinny dipping, I stood up."

"Oh," said Lisa. "Then I need to stand up too."

"Me too," said Charlie from where he stood nearby.

"And I have to sit," said Tonya.

Sr. Annette stayed seated in silence. Grace and Carl stood a little uneasily.

"So, if I say something that I've never done, like maybe have oral sex, then everyone who has had oral sex has to stand up?" asked Joanne with a big grin.

"If they want to play the game," said Betty as she sat back down at the picnic table.

From the top of the hill came the clanging announcement that dinner was served.

"Saved by the bell," smiled Annette, as she and the others got up and headed up the hill toward Huntington.

As the staff entered the dining room, we consciously headed to different tables, and saved places for ourselves with our folders.

"Mind if I join you?" Dick asked Martha, Leona, and Beverly who had already been seated with assorted-size helpings of roast chicken, mashed potatoes, and peas and carrots. This was in addition to their small bowls of tossed salad, and a helping each of strawberry shortcake.

"I'd like that," Beverly said with a beautiful smile as she turned her head up to the top of the six-foot four-inch frame standing beside her.

"I'll be right back," he announced.

When he did return, Dick carried a plate with a small amount of food, but a decent-sized salad. Placing those down, he went to the water cooler and filled a large, ruby-red plastic glass nearly to the top. Upon sitting down, he reintroduced himself, and apologized for not remembering everyone's names.

"It's part of getting older," he explained, "and I don't like it one bit. But there's nothing that I can do about it but acknowledge it."

"How old are you?" Leona asked, after the three women had given Dick their names.

"I'm 86-years-old," Dick said with unabashed pride.

"And what about this T-shirt?" Leona said with a grin, pointing at the statement that "Jugglers have colorful balls."

"Oh, that comes from Steve Allen," he replied. "Not the father, who was a well-known comedian, but the son who is a physician, and used to be a presenter at this workshop. He teaches people to juggle as a way of relaxing. He brought colorful scarves and balls for everyone to practice with. He also brought some T-shirts. I, being one who loves T-shirts with interesting messages, had to have one."

"Were you able to juggle?" asked Beverly.

"Not well," said Dick with a laugh, "but that didn't matter. What mattered was that I tried, and I had fun with it."

"There's not a lot of food on your plate there, Dick. Are you dieting?" teased Leona.

"Regrettably, one of the things you lose when you get to be my age is your sense of smell, and with that you lose your ability to distinguish flavors," he said. "I don't have much of an appetite anymore, but I eat a lot of roughage, and I drink a lot of water."

At a neighboring table, Bill was telling the four others seated with him about how proud he was of his wife Kathy's involvement with Soulforce, the nonviolent, direct-action spiritual group that confronts the hostile responses of organized religions to gay people. "She was arrested in one protest," he said with a big smile. "My wife, the jail bird."

Kevin laughed, as did Joe and Margaret.

"It's a challenging issue," said Catherine with a slight smile but a furrowed brow. "It's not really like some of the other civil rights issues, is it, where the interpretation of the Bible and religious tradition weren't so seemingly clear?"

"There are some good Episcopalians involved in Soulforce, I think," grinned Bill. "Maybe even a bishop or two!"

"I'm sure there are," said Catherine "but that doesn't solve the problem or make it easy. The Episcopal Church is as deeply divided on the issue of homosexuality as are most denominations."

"More so, I'd say, with the consecration of Bishop Gene Robinson," Bill replied.

"A sad day for many in the Episcopal Church," Catherine said. "People still speak of a schism."

"As they did on the issue of women's ordination?" Joe gently interjected.

"As they did on women's ordination," Catherine conceded.

49

"I think it's very clear that the Bible doesn't condemn the loving sexual expression of homosexual people," Bill said more seriously, "but it's even clearer on how we are to behave toward our neighbors."

"No argument on that last part from me," said Catherine.

"Well, it looks as if we have some interesting things to talk about this week," Bill said with a big smile toward Catherine, and then to the others.

"Margaret, tell me about your work," Joe said to change the subject. "I heard you say that you're retired as a pastor – in what denomination?"

"UCC," she said, and then seeing Kevin's look of befuddlement explained, "the United Church of Christ. I retired four years ago but started to get stir crazy. I knew I needed to get back involved in something exciting. When our local congregation's youth worker left to take a job elsewhere, I voiced my interest in being considered. But when they said 'yes,' I started to worry that maybe I wasn't up to date enough on the issues the young people care about to be of much use. So, here I am."

"Here we all are," said Joe.

"The UCC has been in the vanguard on gay issues, hasn't it?" Bill asked with a look of innocence, as if he didn't know the answer.

"Yes, we were among the first, if not the first, to ordain an openly gay man. That was back in the early 70s. His name was Bill Johnson. We ordained him," she said with raised eyebrows, "but he was never called to a church."

"Kevin, you've been here before, and you're a staff assistant this year," said Joe. "What keeps you coming back?"

"I guess I keep learning," Kevin replied as he looked to Bill for support.

"He's one of our best campers," Bill said enthusiastically and with no small amount of pride. "He grows enormously every year, and he's a real gift to all of us."

"I first came here at Bill's suggestion," Kevin explained more confidently. "He was my therapist. Once I came, I decided I really liked it. I came a couple of times, and then Alison asked me to come this year and help out."

As he was speaking, Carol lovingly squeezed his shoulder from behind, and moved on to the table at which I was sitting. Crouching down to speak into my ear, she whispered, "I'm going up to see the tree. Do you want to come?"

"Sure," I answered. "I'll be right with you. If you'll excuse me?" I said to the people at my table as I stood with my stacked dishes and headed toward the dishwasher's opening in the kitchen wall.

Carol and I headed out the door, down the sidewalk, and onto the long curve of the circular driveway on our left. We crossed the stone bridge and a small stretch of grass until we reached a crooked, six foot, blue spruce pine tree that sported an abundance of new growth.

"Hey, Mary Lee," I said.

"Hi, sweetie," Carol replied for the tree.

"She's looking better, don't you think?" I asked Carol.

"Yea, I think she looks great. It must be the trimming we gave her last summer," Carol said.

"And the white wine," I added.

Carol laughed, took my hand in hers and squeezed it. "I love you," she said.

"I love you, too," I answered.

"Oops, time to go," she said looking at her watch. "What's next?"

"You're up, my dear," I said. "It's the ice breaker and mixer."

"Right. Right. Right," she said as if she didn't really need to be reminded.

"Bye, Mary Lee," I said.

"We love you, Mary Lee," Carol said as we headed back up the path toward Ridings. "We love you, too, Susan," I nodded to a nearby tree.

Chapter Seven

Icebreaker

Borrowing a story from *Friedman's Fables,* Carol led us in a "guided imagery" as we gathered as a large group in Ridings after dinner.

"You're crossing a narrow, rickety bridge," she explained to us after we had closed our eyes, "because the life that you have been living on one side of the ravine has been dominated by pain, emotional hunger, fear, and ignorance. You know that if you dare to cross the bridge, you will arrive in a place that is free of those things that have limited your joy. You step forward, but halfway across you encounter a man who frantically ties a piece of rope around himself, hands you the other end of the rope, and proceeds to jump off the bridge.

"You instinctively hold on tight, as the man swings above the abyss. 'You have to hold onto the rope,' the man explains, 'or I will die. Please don't let me die.' You pull as hard as you can, but you can't pull the man to safety. You're only able to keep him from falling. You say to him, 'I can't keep holding this rope. I need to cross the bridge. Everything I want in life is on the other side.' And he replies, 'I'm sorry about that, but if you let go, I'll die. My life is completely in your hands.' So, what do you do?" Carol asked, and paused for a reflective moment. "And what's at the end of the rope that you're holding tonight that might stop you from making the journey across the bridge this week? What is keeping you from being a sexually healthy person?"

Leona rolled her eyes, and looked at the ceiling with a smile. Several people stared at the floor in quiet reflection. Maggie leaned over to George and whispered, "I wonder if Barry had *me* at the end of his rope last year?"

"Think about your own rope," George whispered back, and patted her knee. "This is *your* week."

Carol continued, "I'm going to pass out a small sheet of paper to all of you. I'd like you to sit for a few moments in silence and think about one thing that is tied at the end of your rope that you'd like to let go of. What one thing might keep you from making a journey to sexual health? Then, I'd like you to write the word, or words, down on the paper, fold it up, and we'll place them all in this basket. This is completely anonymous. No one will be looking at what's written on the paper. I promise. And at some point this week, we'll be burning the papers in a bonfire down at the lake."

As she and Pam passed out small sheets of paper, some participants began writing immediately. Others sat quietly, a few with their eyes closed. After a couple of moments, the papers were collected. They contained words such as "My weight," "Guilt," "Fear of the truth about myself," "The size of my penis," "The Church," "Time," "HIV," "Ignorance," "Responsibilities to my family," "Body image," "Anger about sexual abuse," and "This is dumb."

"Okay, good!" Pam said in a spirited voice that quickly changed the tone of the room, "So, let's get to know each other a little better. We gave our names and professions before, and we shared one thing that most people might not know about us, but let's learn some more. I'd like everyone to stand up, as you are able, and form a nice, tight circle. Good. Now, I want all of you who are from big families to move into the center of the circle, please."

Several participants, myself included, moved forward. Our group included Peter, Wendy, Dom, Leona, Kevin, and Ben. We initially just smiled at one another but then, at my prompting, we moved into an even smaller circle and gave an enthusiastic cheer for big families.

"Okay, you members of big families, that's enough," Pam said laughing. "Back into the big circle. Now, people who are the only child in the family, please move into the center of the circle."

Bill stepped forward quickly with a big grin, followed by Joanne, Tonya, Dan, and Grace. Following our lead, they too formed a smaller circle, put their arms around each other's shoulders, and gave a cheer for their being an only child.

The categories that followed included dog owners, cat owners, people who wore contact lenses, people who had previously been through a SAR, people who were feeling a little anxious, and people who had never before been skinny dipping.

"How about people who don't like sharing a bedroom or a bathroom with others?" said Leona, as she stepped forward.

"I thought you said you were from a big family?" I teased.

"Why do you think I don't *like* to share a bedroom or a bathroom?" she shot back with a grin, and stepped back into the circle of participants.

The light chatter and laughter in the room cued Pam to the success of her exercise.

"Well, now, it's party time," she announced. "There's food and drinks and some music. And I, for one, want to see Ben there dance."

Ben smiled at Pam from his wheelchair and said, "Start the music."

Kevin and Tonya pulled back the accordion room divider that separated the main meeting room of Ridings from a smaller, carpeted area. There they revealed a couple of tables that were loaded with bowls of pretzels and nuts, trays of cheese and fruit, plates of chocolate and cookies, bottles of soft drinks and seltzer, a couple of dispenser boxes of inexpensive wine, a couple of ice buckets, and a tray of plastic glasses.

Gail was crouching over the boom box where she selected and started a tape of classic disco songs, and Carol dimmed the lights. Pam then walked over to Ben, stretched out her hand and slowly, walking backwards, led him to the center of the room. Once both hands were freed, Ben moved his arms, shoulders, head, and upper torso in smooth, rhythmic, sensuous waves. His eyes closed, his head tilted back, his arms went up, his fingers snapped, and he commanded the rapt attention of the dancing and non-dancing participants.

"You go, Ben," Leona hollered from the sidelines, where her body was moving in sync to the beat of the Donna Summer song. Pam's agile body elegantly mirrored Ben's movements. Some people started clapping in beat with the song, while others headed to the dance floor. Gail grabbed Kevin's hand and led him to the center of the room. Carol and I danced next to Maggie and George. Peter tapped his foot to the rhythm from his seat at the side, and smiled with delight at the sight of Ben's wheelchair moving back and forth in a nicely choreographed routine. Thomas danced with Lloyd. Betty danced with Wendy, and Dan danced by himself.

"Isn't this fun?" Alison posed to Beverly and Martha, who responded by taking Alison's hands, stepping onto the side of the dance floor, and swaying island-style to the music. Alison proved herself an apt pupil.

At the refreshment table, Dom half-filled a glass with white wine for Joanne.

"Thanks, Dom," she said, swaying gently back and forth, as she nibbled on a pretzel. "This brings back memories, doesn't it?"

"I was never much of a dancer," he explained. "But how did *you* hear this music in a convent? You were a nun, right?"

"You think nuns don't know about disco music?" she asked incredulously. "I taught in an all-girl's high school. I chaperoned a lot of dances. Donna Summer and I go way back. Her, Gloria Gaynor, and The Village People. We're old friends."

No sooner had she finished her sentence when the familiar beat and words of "YMCA" began echoing across the room. Bill immediately excused himself from the conversation he was having with Joe and Margaret, and started bouncing up and down on the dance floor. As The Village People sang out the letters 'Y,' 'M,' 'C,' 'A,' Bill led the dancing crowd in the formation of each letter with his outstretched arms. Sr. Annette squealed and clapped with delight as she watched Bill joyously surrender to the song. In a moment, she was up from her seat and at his side, forming the letters herself.

Two or three songs later, the avid dancers had left the floor for refreshments, and those who had stood near the refreshments had begun to filter out of the room and off to their dorm rooms.

"It looks as if things are starting to slow down," I said to Carol. "I'm heading back to the room. I'll come over tomorrow morning and pick up what Tonya and Kevin miss tonight."

"Okay. I'll be there in a minute," she said.

Thomas saw me leaving, and headed toward the door with me.

"Calling it a night?" he asked.

"Yea, I'm afraid so," I said. "When I first started coming here in my late twenties, I'd be the last one up at night. I'd be down at the lake for a swim after most everyone else was in bed. I'm getting old, I fear. I now find myself going to bed pretty early."

"Me too," he said with a warm smile.

"You're a nice man, Thomas," I said. "I'm glad you're here."

"Thanks," he said. "I'm glad to be here."

"One of the things we didn't mention today, but usually do, is that we encourage groups to have their needs met by organizing their own sessions during the breaks," I said. "For instance, people who are in Twelve Step programs often get together periodically during the week. And for the last several years, the gay, lesbian, bisexual, and transgender folks have been announcing that they would be meeting for lunch or getting together for a discussion during a long break. It's not a suggestion. It's just a possibility I want to raise with you."

"Thanks," he said as we parted company in the direction of our separate dorms. "I'll think about it."

"Oh, and, Thomas," I said after a few steps, "if you *do* start a group, you might want to include 'allies.' It allows those who think that they're 'gay' or 'bisexual' to sit in without having to identify themselves."

"Good thought," he said as he turned and walked toward Peabody. Behind him, Betty walked with a determined gait.

Outside of Peabody, Marjorie and Curtis sat on a bench and shared a smoke.

"Going to bed so early?" Marjorie asked Thomas and Betty as they headed toward the door to the dorm.

"I still haven't made my bed," Thomas explained.

"I want to check in with my roommate," said Betty. "Did you see Leona go in?"

"Yes, she's already in her room," said Marjorie. "I saw her go up about ten minutes ago."

As Thomas and Betty entered Peabody, they walked past a handful of participants sitting together laughing on the front porch. Joanne was pouring wine she had brought from home into small plastic glasses and sharing it with her new friends.

In the living room, Joe and Catherine were talking quietly.

As Thomas entered his room, he found Lloyd lying on his bed reading a book in the dim light provided by the desk lamp.

"Hey, there," Thomas said. "What are you reading?"

"*The Night Listener*," he replied. "It's a book about this kid who says he has AIDS who calls this radio host and develops a friendship. It's by Armistead Maupin."

"I read it," Thomas said. "It's a good book. Freaky though. I saw a piece in *The New Yorker* that said the book is based on a real event, and that the kid with AIDS never existed. He was made up by some sad lady who was desperate for attention. Oops. I think I just ruined the book for you, didn't I? I'm sorry."

"No, you didn't," said Lloyd. "I heard about it too. But I still wanted to read the book."

Taking a breath, Thomas said, "Well, as a guy who is HIV positive, I resent the way that she used AIDS to get attention."

"Me too. So, how long have you been positive?" Lloyd asked, closing his book, and sitting up in bed.

"A little over fourteen years," Thomas replied. "I don't usually bring it up casually, but since 'HIV' was what I had at the end of my rope, I decided to talk more openly about it this week. Besides, I imagined that you were bound to notice the regimen of pills I take. Anyway, I'm not *ashamed* of being HIV positive, but I think it blocks my journey in a lot of subtle ways." He smiled, then turned, and began the process of making up his bed.

"Thanks for telling me," said Lloyd. "I'm HIV negative, I think."

"What do you mean, you *think*? Don't you know?" asked Thomas, turning back with a look of concern.

"I did know, but a couple of weeks ago I did something really, really stupid, and now I don't know. It's making me crazy. I should have known better. I am such a fool."

Down the hall from their second floor bedroom, Betty had finished washing her face and brushing her teeth, and was now sitting on her bed in the room.

"Leona?" she said hesitantly to the woman lying on her back beneath the covers of her bed, staring at the ceiling. "Can we talk for a minute?"

"Sure. Go ahead," said Leona.

"You've made it pretty clear today in the group that you don't like sharing a room with someone else, and I get the feeling that sharing a room with *me* makes it particularly difficult for you."

"Who said that?" snapped Leona.

"I think that my being a lesbian makes you very uncomfortable, and I just want to assure you that you're perfectly safe. I'm not interested in you. I won't be looking at you. If you'd like, I'll stay out of the room while you're getting dressed. We don't even have to talk to each other if you don't want to," Betty said.

"Who said I didn't want to room with you?" Leona persisted, turning to face Betty. "And, why *wouldn't* you be interested in me? What's wrong with *me*?"

Betty laughed. "Nothing's wrong with you. You're a beautiful woman. But, you're straight, and I don't even let straight women on my radar screen. Do you let yourself be attracted to gay men?"

"Honey, once they had a piece of Leona, they wouldn't be gay for very long," she laughed.

"It doesn't work like that and you know it," Betty admonished with a grin.

"I know. I know. What's bent can't be made straight, or so they say," said Leona. "Okay. I admit it. I don't know any lesbians very well. I don't get the whole girl-girl thing. It makes no sense to me. And the thought of rooming with a lesbo, er, a lesbian, just didn't sit right. I don't know how I feel about it. I don't know how I feel about this whole week. I can't believe I had to make my own bed. And what's this 'I love myself' song all about?"

"Leona, do you think maybe you'd prefer to have a single room?"

"I asked about it," she said, "but the additional cost is not in my budget. We'll work it out. I don't want you uncomfortable with me either. Now, what do you say we turn off the light and get some sleep? They start this thing so damn early."

As Leona turned toward the wall, Betty undressed, pulled back the covers, turned off the ceiling light, and climbed into bed.

After a few moments of silence, she said, "Leona, there's one thing more that I want to tell you before you decide to stay roommates."

"You snore?" asked Leona as she turned over on her other side to face the direction of Betty's bed.

"No, I don't snore," she replied in the darkness.

"You sleepwalk in the nude?" she asked.

"No, I don't sleepwalk," she said. "Leona, I'm an MTF. Do you know what that means?"

"I get the 'MF' part," Leona giggled, "but I don't get the 'T'."

"MTF stands for 'male to female'," Betty explained. "I was born 'male.' I've been a biological female for eleven years. I'm what's called a 'transsexual.' But I don't think of myself as such anymore. I just think of myself as a woman. That's the big 'change in my life' that I referred to when we went around the circle in the large group this afternoon. Normally I would have said it then, because it's no big deal for me. But when I saw how you reacted to my being a lesbian, I thought I'd better tell you in private about being a transsexual. I wanted you to hear about it from me first."

Leona's covers were now over her head. The room was silent for several awkward minutes.

"Leona? Do you have anything to say?" asked Betty.

Still, silence.

"Leona?" whispered Betty.

"Go to sleep, Betty," Leona sighed.

The following morning, as the chorus of large black crows announced with loud squawks from the tree tops the dawn of the workshop's first full day, Marjorie made her way through the Peabody living room in her pink floral bathrobe, and an unlit cigarette

between her fingers. As she passed the sofa, she noted that Leona was there, beneath a pile of blankets, snoring softly.

Chapter Eight

SUNDAY

Carla Joins the Group

As Carol and I left Higley, and headed toward Ridings to make sure that the meeting room was clean and reassembled, we encountered an array of early morning activities.

Grace was at a picnic table outside of the staff dorm making notes as she went through the participants' packet of materials. She looked up as we passed and greeted us with a cheery "Good morning."

"Ready to go?" I asked.

"You bet," she said. "I can't wait to get started."

Martha, Beverly, Sr. Annette, and Judith were seated with big cups of coffee at a picnic table outside of Huntington, waiting for the 8:00 a.m. beginning of breakfast. Annette looked up as I looked over and waved "hello."

Curtis and Marjorie sat on the bench outside of their dorm, and smoked their third and fourth cigarettes of the day, respectively.

Out on the lawn that sloped down to the lake, Margaret sat in the lotus position on a blanket, her back perfectly straight, her hands on her knees, and her eyes focused on the ground.

Down at the beach, we spotted three people sitting together, talking at one of the picnic tables. It appeared to be Joe, Thomas, and Charlie. "A ministers' meeting," I said to Carol.

"The God Squad," she shot back.

As we approached the door to Ridings, Leona came upon us quickly on the asphalt path that led from her dorm.

"May I please speak with you?" she said in a strong, declarative manner. It was clearly not a question.

"Good morning," I said as I turned to face her. "Speak to me?"

"No, not to you," she responded without looking at me. "To Carol."

"Sure," said Carol. "Let's walk down to the tables behind Ridings."

"I'll check the meeting room," I said as they walked away down the grassy hill to the flagstone patio behind the building.

"Carol, what's the meaning of putting me into a bedroom with a 'he-she'? It's bad enough that she's a lesbo, but now I find out that it isn't even really a 'her'," Leona said in rapid fire measure as they walked. "How, in your right mind, did you think that would be okay with me? If I stay, and I say 'if,' I want my *own* room, with my *own* bathroom, and I want you to give it to me for *free*. I should sue you. I really should. Maybe I will. This is *not* my idea of a professional development conference. We stand around singing 'I love myself,' you ask us what's at the end of our rope, and then you room us with biological freaks. I'm sorry, but this won't do. This just won't do. You ask us what's at the end of our rope. I'll tell you that *I'm* at the end of my rope. I have half a mind to go home today. I really do."

"Leona, let's sit down here for a minute and talk, shall we?" Carol said as she sat on top of the picnic table and patted the place next to her.

"I'm sorry that you've had such a rough start of it," Carol continued as Leona begrudgingly sat down with a disgruntled look on her face. "I hope that you'll stay. The week offers an amazing opportunity to grow both personally and professionally."

"Rooming with a lesbo 'he-she' was not covered in your brochure, Carol," Leona snapped.

"Leona, I'm a lesbian, so I'd appreciate it if you'd cut the 'lesbo' crap. And Betty is a friend of mine, so I'd also appreciate it if you'd drop the 'he-she' shit," Carol said calmly.

After a few seconds of silence, Leona said more softly, "I apologize. I meant no disrespect. I'm just a little freaked, that's all."

"I understand," Carol said. "Betty is an amazing woman with a heart of gold. I thought you two would be *great* together. If I had known how you'd feel, I *never* would have put you in with her, and I can easily arrange to have you switched into another room right away. I can even find you a single, if you'd prefer, but it will cost you an additional $150. That's what Thornfield charges us."

"I think you should just give me the room for *free*," Leona said with feigned exasperation.

"I can't do that," explained Carol. "There are lots of people here who don't much like the idea of sharing a room, much less a bathroom, and many of them initially don't like their roommates. I don't have singles to give to all of them, even if they wanted to pay, and I certainly can't afford to give any of them free rooms. Besides, by the end of the week, most of them will love their roommates."

"Well, I won't *love* mine, and I sure as hell don't want mine to *love* me," Leona said.

"Okay. As I say, I'm happy to switch you with someone else," Carol said. "That won't be hard to do. But before I do, I'd like you to talk with Betty about your desire to switch. She's a big girl … "

"You can say *that* again," interrupted Leona with a smirk.

"And she won't be shocked by your reaction," Carol continued. "My guess is that she told you that she was transgender so that you could decide for yourself if you wanted to continue rooming with her. Am I right?"

"Yes," she acknowledged. "Although she waited until I was in bed."

"So, tell her that it *does* make a difference, and that you'd like to switch. She'll understand," Carol said. "That's part of her journey, and yours."

"Okay," said Leona, getting up from the table.

"Leona, can you stay just a minute more? You've still got plenty of time for breakfast," Carol said, patting the spot next to her on the top of the table. When Leona sat back down with a big sigh, Carol continued. "What brought you to Thornfield? I mean, what did you want to get out of it?" she asked.

"The truth is, my director sent me. I said 'yes' because I heard from others in Planned Parenthood that it was a worthwhile educational experience," Leona said.

"It is," said Carol, "but you've got to give it a chance. And quite frankly, it feels to me as if you've been fighting it since you got here. I'm not talking about you wanting to change roommates. I'm talking about your complaining about *everything* from the chairs, to the song, to the exercises, to having to make your own bed, to having to share a room and a bathroom with others."

"Are you saying you'd like me to leave?" Leona asked defensively.

"No, I don't want you to leave. I want you to stay. I really do," Carol said firmly and with a smile. "But I want you to give it a chance, and I don't think you're doing that. I think that you're a little like me, that you're a little uncomfortable with new surroundings and new faces. We all cope with change differently. I think you cope by complaining. But I don't think you're as uncomfortable as you make yourself out to be. I think it's just a defense mechanism. Am I right?"

"Maybe," she said, "but the chairs *are* uncomfortable, and the song *is* dumb."

"Well, I agree with you about the chairs," Carol replied, "but I love the song. Anyway, thanks for letting me talk. I hope you'll hang in, and that you'll give the place a chance. Let me know when you've talked with Betty and I'll make the necessary arrangements to switch you to another room. Now, let's get some breakfast. I'm starving. How about you?"

"I could eat," Leona said as they headed up the hill.

The dining room in Huntington was filled with animated chatter as Carol and Leona entered and approached the buffet table. Each moved to a different side of the serving area, took plates, and began scrutinizing the offerings of cereal, fresh fruit, bagels and muffins, scrambled eggs, sausage, and potatoes.

"There's too much food here," Leona said to Carol across the serving station.

Carol looked up quickly with a smirk and raised eyebrows.

"It's *good* food," Leona said a bit sheepishly in response. "There's just a whole lot of it to choose from."

From behind them, Dan distracted everyone's attention with an ear-piercing whistle and a loud series of claps. "Looking good," he announced in a commanding voice to the person who had just entered the dining room in a striking summer dress in playful pastel colors, accented by white sandals, and a white scarf that tied up into a ponytail her long black hair. She blushed in appreciation of the positive attention, smiling broadly with lips of "Passion Pink."

"Good morning," said Carol as she crossed the floor to greet the new arrival. "I'm Carol Dopp, the coordinator of the workshop."

"Good morning, Carol," responded the melodic voice with a laugh. "I'm sorry that I forgot my name tag. I'm Carla."

"Of course you are," Carol replied with a red-faced laugh.

The Ridings meeting room soon filled up quickly in response to Tonya's ringing of the brass school bell, and the majority of the participants were standing with music sheets in hand by the time that the tape of "I Love Myself" had begun to play. Gail stepped forward a few steps from the perimeter, and most eyes were on her as she elegantly interpreted the words with sign language. Some eyes, though, were unconsciously fixed on Carla, who was flanked by Dan and Martha, as she too tried to follow Gail's interpretative gestures.

Leona cautiously shot a quick look across the room at Betty as the tall woman crossed her arms and rapped on her chest to indicate "I love myself the way I am." During the second verse, Leona continued to remain silent, and focused on Gail as the staff and many of the participants sang "I love you just the way you are, there's nothing you need to do."

In the fourth verse of the song, Betty sang loudly, and without the use of the song sheet, as Gail's right hand and arm pushed forth like a blooming plant through the earth. "I love myself, the way I am," we sang, "and still I want to grow. The change outside can only come, when deep inside I know, I'm beautiful and capable of being the best me I can. I love myself, just the way I am."

"Creepy," whispered Lisa to Curtis as the staff and some of the participants smiled appreciatively back and forth.

"Good morning," Alison said in her enthusiastic tone.

"Good morning," responded the staff and half of the participants.

"I hope you all had a restful night," she continued, "and that you're ready for a full day of activity. We'll have announcements in a moment, but let's begin by waking up just a bit with some exercise, shall we? I've asked Dick to lead us this morning in a warm-up exercise. Dick?"

Stepping forward in a T-shirt that illustrated with cartoon-like drawings the proper use of condoms, Dick explained in a strong, animated voice that the weather in Cazenovia, New York can be quite unpredictable. "At any time," he said, "we could get rain, snow, wind, or fog."

Many of the participants smiled with anticipation and amusement as he asked us all to stand and form a tight circle. To that, Ben obligingly maneuvered his wheelchair into formation. Dick then asked for a volunteer, and Tonya quickly walked to the head of the circle and stood beside Dick.

"I'd like you all to turn so that you're directly behind the person in front of you, and then create these changing weather patterns for that person by giving them a gentle massage."

"This is completely voluntary," I quickly interjected. "You don't have to participate."

"Let's begin with rain," Dick said undaunted as he carefully turned Tonya around and began tapping his fingers lightly on her head and then her shoulders. "The rain can get heavier, of course," he advised as he modeled giving gentle chops of the hand to Tonya's shoulders.

"Oh, that feels good," Tonya moaned, as did many of the participants as the person behind them began to tap and massage their heads and necks.

Seeing that Ben was having trouble reaching up to Charlie's neck and shoulders, Gail slipped out of line and stepped carefully in between the two of them. She stooped down a bit for Ben, as did Charlie for her.

"Now it's going to snow," Dick announced. "It can be a gentle snow, or a heavy snow. Ask your partners which weather they prefer."

"Heavy snow," directed Wendy to Gina. "Oh, yes," she said.

More moans of pleasure came from many of the other participants, as well as instructions.

"Don't stop," Maggie said to Lloyd. "It feels so good."

"I think I'd like it to rain hard all day," said Carla with a giggle.

"And now, fog," Dick said as he took his large hands and moved them slowly within an inch of Tonya's head, face, and shoulders.

"Ooooh," said Tonya in delighted response.

After fifteen seconds of fog, Dick said, "Okay, thank your partner." And that was it. When the chatter died down, Alison stepped forward, thanked Dick, and asked everyone to take their seats.

"That was great, Dick," she said, "and now for announcements. Once again, please don't forget to wear your name tags at all times. It's very important that you do so. Also, please make sure that you clean up after yourselves in the dining room. I noticed a few coffee cups left on one of the picnic tables. Otherwise, we're doing a great job. For you nighttime swimmers, be advised that your voices carry up the hill," she said smiling at Gina, Wendy, and Lisa, all of whom blushed in response. "Now, does anyone have anything to ask, or to announce? Yes, Dan?"

"I'd like to welcome Carla to the group," Dan said putting his arm protectively around Carla's bony shoulders. A handful of people clapped, including Peter.

"Yes, indeed," Alison said with a warm smile. "We welcome all of you to the group each day in whatever manner you wish to express yourselves. Thank you, Dan. Anyone else?"

"Alison?"

"Yes, Thomas?" she asked.

"During the break today between 4:30 and 5:30, I'd like to meet with the gay, lesbian, bisexual, and transgender participants, and with anyone else who might want to come as an ally," he said, smiling at me.

"Very good," Alison said. "We encourage you to set up meetings that meet your needs this week. And where would you like people to meet?"

"How about if we start out by meeting at the picnic tables outside of the dining room," he replied. "It's really just a 'get to know you' session."

"Alison, I have an announcement too, though I hate the timing of it," said George.

"What's that?" Alison asked.

"Well, it's Sunday, and I'd like to have a religious service for those who are interested in getting together. It'd be an ecumenical thing. Everyone would be welcome. I thought we'd meet in the little chapel area in the woods, out back of Ridings. But the only time I can think to do it, given the schedule, is at the break at 4:30. I'd really like to go to the gay meeting, and I don't want to take people away from that meeting," George said to Thomas.

"And I'd like to go to the service," Thomas said from across the room. "How about if we have a *dinner* meeting instead for the gay, transgender, and allies group? We'll just take our food out to the picnic tables, maybe out in front of the staff dorm where there's more room. Does that work?"

"It works for me," said George. "Thanks."

"Well, that was handled with a great spirit of cooperation, wasn't it? Well done," said Alison. "If anyone wants more information on the service or the dinner meeting, please see George or Thomas at the next break. Now, we need to move on so that we stay on our schedule. We're now going to meet with the staff person who is directing the skill building workshops on Friday. You all know whom you're meeting with. You just don't know where. Let's see here," she said as she pulled on half glasses to look at her notes. "Brian, you're meeting with those who want to enhance their skills as presenters on sexual orientation down in Higley in the staff living room. I'll be meeting with those that want to explore their personal, sexual journey right here in Ridings in that small room adjacent to this. Bill will meet with his group about sexuality and spirituality in the library on the second floor of Huntington, and Carol and Pam will meet with those of you who are involved in sexuality education in the large room above the dining room in Huntington. Any questions? Okay. We're due back here in forty-five minutes. Thank you all."

Carol pulled my arm as I was heading toward the door.

"I forgot to tell you that Peter is in your group," she said.

"No, he's not," I said.

"Yes, he is. He wants you to help him convince audiences that it's possible to change your sexual orientation," she whispered.

"You liar," I replied.

"I'm serious. Go see for yourself," she said.

Chapter Nine

Skill Building

Carol *was* rattling my cage. I followed Peter across the yard, and slowly released my held breath as I watched him and Catherine walk up the stairs in Huntington toward what I assumed would be Bill's introductory meeting on spirituality. I was relieved. "I owe Carol big time," I thought to myself with a laugh. "She'll pay."

Grace led the small procession in a lively step across the lawn toward Higley. Behind her walked Lloyd, Gina, and Carla. After we all had settled into the orange and brown upholstered sofas and chairs that were arranged in a circle in the staff living room, I asked each of the four to introduce themselves to the group, to talk about their professional aspirations, and about what they hoped to achieve in the "Skill-Building" workshop on Friday.

"I've corresponded with all of you, so I'm aware of your goals, but I want you to think of this group as a 'team'," I explained, "and your team members need to better understand your objectives. Grace, will you start, please?"

"Sure," the handsome woman with short, blond streaked hair said with a confident voice. "I'm Grace Adler. I'm the diversity manager for Salina Systems, Incorporated, in Dayton, Ohio. We manufacture components for high tech companies, and have 3,500 employees scattered around the

U.S. Our headquarters are in Dayton. Brian came and spoke to some of our executives and to our human resource professionals. We do in-house diversity training for our employees, and we need to do a better job on sexual orientation. Since I'm the one who does most of the training, he suggested that I come to Thornfield. So, I'm here to learn how to do it better."

"Thanks, Grace," I said. "I'm really glad that you're with us. As you recall, I requested that all of you read *Gay Issues in the Workplace* prior to your arrival here, and asked you to give particular attention to the model workshop that I outlined in the final chapter. Each of you needs to pick a segment of that workshop that you will present individually on Friday. Grace, have you decided which segment you want to work on?"

"Yes," she said. "I want to practice doing the sex education component. That's where I'm the weakest."

"Good. Okay, Lloyd, how about you going next?" I said.

"Okay. I'm Lloyd Howard. I'm twenty-three, and I live in New York City. I'm on the staff at GLSEN, the Gay, Lesbian, Straight Education Network. I'm gay, and I do minority outreach with young gays, lesbians, bisexuals, and transgender people. I wrote Brian, and told him that I'd like to do more public speaking, and he suggested I get GLSEN to send me here, which they did. I had already read the book, but I read it again, and I think I'd like to spend my time on Friday telling my story."

"That's great, Lloyd," I said. "In this work, the messenger *is* the message, and the most important thing you can do in a program on sexual orientation or gender identity is to tell your story. That's what connects you with your audience. Grace, is it okay if I 'out' you?" I asked turning to her.

"Grace is heterosexual," I said in response to her nod and smile. "I think it's important for heterosexuals to talk about their journeys in becoming allies, but as Grace knows, I think it's *essential* to have a gay or transgender person speak at every workshop on sexual orientation and gender identity to help put a 'face on the issue.' Okay. Let's keep going. How about you, Gina?"

"Hi everyone. I'm Gina DeWitt," said the androgynous and athletic-looking, young woman on my right. "As I said in the big circle yesterday, I'm a lesbian. I live in Atlanta, Georgia, where I do HIV-prevention work through AID Atlanta, which is our local community outreach program. When I signed up for the workshop, Carol asked me which skill-building program I wanted to be in. I wanted to work with Brian, just because I knew of the work you do. I don't know how it's going to fit into what I'm doing. I thought about focusing more on lesbian and gay issues in the future, but I'm not sure how. Anyway, I want to work on my story too. That's what I'd like to do on Friday. And," turning to Lloyd with a smile she added, "I'm twenty-four."

"Well, *I'm* not twenty-four, and I'm *not* gay, and I'm sorry, Brian, but before I got the brochure for this workshop, I'd never heard of you," said Carla with a sweet smile, her hands folded on her lap, and her feet carefully crossed, "but I thought that this particular skill-building workshop was the right place for me. I read your book at your request. I thought it was good, although I think you really do need to add some more information on 'transgender' issues in the workplace. But I'd like to practice telling my story too. Even with all that I may have said privately to some of you yesterday about my wife and my kids not liking it when I cross dress, it's who I am, and I'm *not* ashamed of it. And maybe if I start talking more about it, I can spare others the fear and shame that I've felt for many years, and still do feel, I suppose. And maybe if I'm *good* enough, Grace here, or you, Brian, will have me come in and talk to your audiences. For a fee, of course," she added with a hearty but consciously feminine laugh and wink.

"Well, we'll just have to see what her fee is, won't we Grace?" I said, reaching over and giving Carla's knee a playful squeeze. "We have a lot to do in the brief time we have here, so I'm going to keep talking, but I want you to interrupt me if you have any questions. Agreed?"

Four smiles of affirmation allowed me to continue.

"First, I want you to work this week in teams of two because I feel it's really important that you have the experience of working in collaboration with someone else. Carla and Gina, I'd like you two to be partners, and Grace and Lloyd, I'd like you two to be partners. You're going to be doing your presentation on Friday on your own, but if you have any needs, I want you to let your partner help you out. Understood?

"On Friday, each of you will have a half an hour to make your presentation to me and to the other three. Following each presentation, you will hear a critique of your work from us, so you are also going to be in the role of 'mentor'," I explained.

"I'm sorry," said Lloyd, "but why are we doing partners, and what are we supposed to do?"

"Thanks for stopping me, Lloyd," I replied. "Let me back up for a minute. I'm used to working alone. I give a speech. I conduct a half-day training. It's just me. But when I do an eight-hour workshop, I generally team up with Pam Wilson. When I first brought someone in to work with me, it was *really* hard for me, and for them. Before Pam, it was my best friend, Mary Lee Tatum. She was a wonderful, heterosexual sexuality educator who was so embracing and affirming in her manner that audiences just fell in love with her. I *adored* her. But when we started working together, we both felt a terrible strain on our friendship because neither one of us was used to sharing the stage. We had to work really hard at learning to be honest with each other, at speaking up for ourselves, at listening to what the other was saying, to relaxing, and trusting, and to accepting different standards of success."

"Why did you work so hard at it?" asked Lloyd. "If you were good by yourself, why didn't you just say it wasn't working with Mary Lou?"

"Mary Lee," I said. "Because, for the workshops that we were doing together, the sum of us was better than we were individually. As a team of a gay man and a straight woman, we reached more people more profoundly than I might have as just a gay man. The same is true with Pam. Besides being a superb trainer, she's also a black, heterosexual woman. She brings a credibility to the black, Latino, Asian, and Native American heterosexuals in our workshop that I don't automatically have with them as a gay, white man. In addition, people see a wonderful role modeling in our teamwork that can be applied to their own situations at work."

"Brian, then why don't you *always* insist that companies bring in a team?" asked Carla.

"Money," I said, "and time. Most colleges and corporations can only give you a limited amount of time. Having two people lead a four-hour workshop doesn't make any sense, and it's prohibitively expensive to bring in two trainers for that period of time. Anyway, that's why I want you to team up this week with someone else. I want you to have the experience of being required to take into consideration another person's needs, to listen, to hear a different perspective. You probably won't always be working alone, and I want you to know what it feels like to work with another person."

"I'm sorry," said Carla, "but what happened to your friend, Mary Lee? Why did you and Pam start working together? Did you have a falling out?"

"No, she died," I said with a sad smile. "A few weeks before we were all scheduled to be here for this workshop, she was killed in an automobile accident. It devastated all of us. That was back in 1991. She was a much-loved woman. The staff planted a tree in her memory up near the driveway. It's the crookedest but most wonderful tree in the world. I'll show it to you sometime, if you'd like to see it."

"I would," said Carla.

"Me too," said Grace as Lloyd and Gina nodded their heads and smiled supportively.

"Thanks. Okay. Let's get back to business." Reaching into my folder, I withdrew five copies of a two-page text entitled "Guidelines for Trainers." As I handed one to each of them, I explained, "I put together these guidelines with the purpose of helping others learn from my experiences over the past thirty years. I'm not an expert on all of this, but I have had some successes, and I have had some experiences that weren't as successful as they might have been, and these items represent my thoughts on things to do, and *not* do, to enhance the effectiveness of your presentations. I'd like you to use these guidelines in two ways this week. I'd like you to read them through carefully, and then use them privately to critique my work, and that of the rest of the staff throughout the week. Please make notes. If you see that we did something that you liked, write it down. If we failed to do something that you feel would have made our presentation better, write that down too. Are you clear about what I'm asking?"

"Are we supposed to *tell* the staff person what we felt they did right or wrong?" asked Gina nervously.

"No. No," I said with a smile, "but for your own professional growth as people who want to improve your presentations, listen this week with two sets of ears. Listen as participants who want to grow in your personal and professional understanding of issues of human sexuality, and listen as professionals who want to build your skills as presenters. Just take notes, though, and we'll meet periodically to share our observations. Got it?"

"I think so," said Gina.

"Here, let me give you an example," I said. "Look at the third item. 'Know Your Facts - Admit When You Don't.' Keep your ears open to *that* this week. Ask yourself if the people presenting know their material. If they get asked a question for which they don't have the answer, do they get defensive, do they acknowledge that they don't have the answer, or do they bullshit?"

"Okay, I got it," said Gina.

"Good," I said. "The other thing I'd like you to do with these is let them guide your own presentations on Friday. I'm going to be using these items to critique you, and I'd like you to use them to prepare yourselves, to critique yourselves, and to critique the others in our group. For instance, the fourth item states, 'Know Your Host.' It goes on to say, 'Know the company's history, number of employees, ethnic and religious make-up, competition, history of diversity efforts in training, policies, methods of settling disputes, union policies, history of gay-related problems, and sense of the gay, lesbian, bisexual, and transgender employee group members on the environment.' Prior to Friday, I want you to tell me who it is that you're making your presentation to, and I want you to be able to answer all of these questions about your host before you get up to speak."

"Yikes, this is *hard* work," said Carla.

"You're darn right it's hard work," I said. "I take you all seriously that you want to enhance your skills. I'm going to give you the best I can this week, and on Friday, I want you to do the same with me. Right?"

"Right!" the four of them said with varying degrees of conviction and focus.

"Okay," I said looking at my watch. "We've got just a few more minutes. Let's go over this list together."

"If we promise to go over this list on our own," said Carla who stopped when she saw my response of raised eyebrows, "and promise to do so *today,* can we go see the tree now instead?"

"Sure we can," I said with only a brief hesitation. "That would please Mary Lee, Carla. She'd like the fact that we compromised on our goals to accommodate different views, and she'd get a kick out of the fact that it was you who suggested it."

"Why's that?" she asked.

"Because, among a thousand other things, Mary Lee was the facilitator of a regular meeting of transgender people at her church in Falls Church, Virginia," I explained as I stood to lead the way.

"Oh, I *like* her already," Carla said with delight.

"Everybody did," I replied, putting my arm around her shoulders as we headed up toward the driveway. "Everybody did."

Moments later, as we broke from our circle around Mary Lee's tree, we became aware that other groups had finished their meetings too.

"Hey, George," hollered Charlie as they headed down the stairs in Huntington from their session with Bill on "sexuality and spirituality." "Will you be offended if I *don't* come to your service this afternoon?"

"Heck, no," replied George, turning around to see Charlie coming behind him, separated by Joe and Catherine. "You'll go to hell for not honoring the Sabbath, but *I* won't be offended."

"I thought you left the Catholic Church," said Joe with a grin.

"I did," replied George, "but while you can take the boy out of the Catholic Church, you just can't take the Catholic Church out of the boy. Sorry, Charlie. It's a mortal sin. I hope you have a good excuse."

"I'm going swimming," said Charlie as they stood together in the lobby. "As much as I'd *like* to be with you, I need some time to myself."

"I understand completely," said George. "This is not a command performance. I merely wanted to acknowledge the day and the space, and felt that it was a good way to start my week. We're probably going to have a couple of readings, say a few things about sexuality and spirituality, and ask for blessings on the work we're doing."

"I'll be there," said Joe. "It's at 4:30, right?"

"Right," confirmed George. "We'll meet in that opening in the woods behind Ridings. There's a nice little altar and some benches there. It's going to be very informal."

"Well, maybe I will come," said Charlie.

"No, really," said George. "I think you should swim. Cold, wet skin will make the fires of hell less horrible for at least the first few *seconds* of eternity."

"Oh, you're good," said Catherine.

"Thank you," smiled George appreciatively.

As the four of them headed into the cafeteria for something to drink, members of Carol and Pam's "sexuality education" track started coming down the stairs.

"This is gonna be good," said Chuck to Dom as they hit the landing. "But I felt a little out of my league in there."

"Me too," said Dom, "but that's why we're here. I need to take back some activities for the class that I'll be teaching. They're going to be a lot more useful to me than any discussion on 'anal pleasuring'."

"Still stuck on that one, eh buddy?" asked Chuck in a respectful but playful whisper.

"Yea, I guess I am," Dom replied with a laugh of recognition.

"How was that session for the two of you?" asked Pam as she approached where they stood in the lobby. "Was it clear what we want you to do during the week, and what we'll be doing on Friday?"

"Clear to me," replied Chuck. "We're both lookin' forward to gettin' some ideas about classroom activities. We're both brand new to this."

"Yea, I felt a little awkward when we went around the room and talked about our work," added Dom.

"Hey, that's why we come together here every year," said Pam with a bright face of encouragement. "It's to make sure we're *all* fully equipped to do the work we're doing. You guys will be great! I mean it. The field needs good men like you involved. I envy the kids you'll be working with. They are mighty lucky," she smiled.

"Thanks for saying so," said Dom.

"Yea, comin' from you, that feels pretty good," said Chuck.

"Well, it's the truth," Pam insisted as she reached up to put a hand on each of their shoulders. "Remember this week to do two things: Think about the subjects we're discussing and how you're going to cover them in an age-appropriate way back home. And second, keep your 'teacher' hat off in your small group discussions. While you're in your SAR groups, think about how the subjects impact you personally." Then, looking at her watch, she exclaimed, "Yikes, time to go. Carol," she hollered up the stairs, "are you coming? We're going to be late."

"I'm coming. I'm coming," said Carol as she and Leona picked up their pace, and made the turn down the final set of stairs. "So you're going to talk with her during the next break?" she said in a low tone.

"Yes. Yes," replied Leona with frustration. "I'm going to talk with her, but I'm not sure why *I* should have to. She's the one who's creating the problem." To which Carol sighed audibly.

"Okay. Okay," continued Leona, "I'll talk to her during the break or at lunch. Now get off my back."

"George," Carol said, squeezing Leona's hand "goodbye," and moving quickly out the door to catch up with him and the others.

"What's up, sweet thing?" he asked.

"Oh, I like that," she said.

"Sweet thing?" I exclaimed incredulously as my group and I approached from the driveway. "She's *evil*!"

"Evil?" said George with a look of astonishment. "She's not evil. Charlie here is evil, but not our Carol."

"Thank you," Carol said, ignoring my shaking head of disbelief. "George, how about if we burn the papers from last night's exercise at your service this afternoon? You know, the ones that talk about what's at the end of our rope? We were going to burn them some night on the beach, but it would be cool to do it while all of you are gathered for the religious service today."

"Fine by me," said George as they approached the door to Huntington. "But it may be just a small group at the service. Charlie, for instance, doesn't plan on being there. He's going *swimming.* Is that okay with you that it's just a small crowd?"

"Oh, sure," said Carol. "And Charlie, don't you think twice about not going to the service. Take care of yourself. Of course, you'll burn in hell."

"I told him that," said George.

"I'll ask someone from the kitchen staff to bring a small grill over to the outside chapel after lunch," said Carol. And then, turning to me she whispered with a grin, "So, how did Peter do in your group?"

"Really good," I said. "He told us that seeing you was what made him decide to become 'ex-gay'."

"Because I'm so pretty?" she blushed.

"No, because he found out that *you* were gay," I replied. "Oh, and by the way, when I took my group up to see Mary Lee's tree, she asked 'Where's Carol? Where's Carol?' and I told her that you don't like her anymore, and then she told me that she had *always* liked me the best."

"Come on you two," Gail said as she finished ringing the bell. "You're late."

Chapter Ten

The SAR Begins

With the words "Ignorance," "Secrecy," and "Trauma" written in large letters on the whiteboard behind him, Bill stood up straight in his beige shorts, blue and white striped pullover shirt, powder blue socks, and brown sandals. His highly-animated face was filled with a broad smile of excitement, and his raised eyebrows silently questioned whether we were ready to begin. As he looked around the room, I did so too, in anticipation of the response I trusted he would receive from the participants. I particularly watched the faces and body language of the heterosexual men.

"All of us are sexual creatures," Bill began in a light but professional tone. "We came into the world *sexual*. Male fetuses are known to have erections in the womb. Infant females are known to manually stimulate themselves. So why do we, as adults, feel so much discomfort and anxiety about our sexuality and that of others? Several factors contribute, and I suggest that they can be summarized with these three words: Ignorance, Secrecy, and Trauma.

"Many segments of our society actually *value* sexual ignorance," he continued with a look of concern and genuine sadness. "Society doesn't really value sexual comfort and knowledge. Many people believe that sexual knowledge is 'dangerous,' that it increases promiscuity and irresponsible behavior. The 'Abstinence Only' sexuality education in our schools that has been funded by our government shows how far-reaching this belief is. But research doesn't support this widely-held view. On the contrary, adolescents who have access to comprehensive sexuality education are known to *delay* their first sexual experience. Knowledge is not dangerous. Lack of knowledge is! In my practice as a therapist, I see *sexual inhibition* as one of the most prevalent manifestations of sexual dysfunction, and I find that sexual ignorance is one of the prime causes of that inhibition."

Looking to me a bit like a grown-up Charlie Brown, with his lovable round face, disarming impish smile, and complete lack of self-consciousness about posture, attire, or mannerisms, Bill proceeded to illustrate his point.

"When I was in fifth grade," he said with a look of innocent delight, "my best friend Champ said to me, 'Do you want to know how to turn a girl on?'

"'Sure,' I said," and with a playful look of anticipation for our sake, he added, "But what's a girl?"

"'Well,' Champ said, 'they've got three holes down there. To really turn them on, you find the middle hole, you stick in your finger, and you tickle the thing at the end'."

To illustrate the point, Bill raised his eyebrows with happy expectation, and smiled knowingly as he practiced the tickling technique with his finger. This he accompanied with a little wiggle of his butt, like a puppy wagging its tail in excitement. Many of the women in the room squirmed in recognition of the effect of such 'tickling.' Some laughed or groaned in sympathy of the ignorant fifth grader. A few of the straight men looked at Bill cautiously, questioning perhaps the accompanying wiggle of his butt, and where this story was going. And the majority of the gay men, I suspect, sat wondering, as I did the first time I heard the story, "What three holes?" ("He's counting the urethra as one," Carol whispered to me at the time.)

"Also when I was in the fifth grade," Bill continued with his illustration, "I worked in my father's grocery store. I did inventory. I stacked the shelves. I did everything except touch the Kotex. I was forbidden to touch the Kotex. I was never told what it was. I was simply told not to touch it. In those days, Kotex was wrapped in plain brown paper and tied with string," he explained with great seriousness.

Then, with a Jack Benny ear-to-ear grin, and a silent nod of his head, Bill assured us that the story he had just told was the absolute truth. Many people laughed or giggled as much at his playful facial expressions as at the recollection of their first experience with Kotex.

"Secrecy," he announced to indicate that we had moved on from the topic of "Ignorance."

"Another major source of problems in a sexually repressive culture is the value that is placed on being secretive about our sexuality, about our sexual thoughts, our sexual feelings, our desires, and our sexual behaviors," he said. "When I was growing up, you couldn't talk about your feelings at home, at school, or in the church. You couldn't talk about your day dreams, your night dreams, or your wet dreams, and, for the most part, you still can't. Do you know that it was five years into our marriage before my wife Kathy was able to say to me, 'Don't you *ever* do that to me again'."

Here Bill stopped and peered around the room with a look of total bewilderment and shock. What had he done wrong? Then he wiggled his finger in the tickling motion to indicate what it was he was being ordered to cease and desist.

"She said," he continued, "'I've counted them up, and I figure that in our five years of marriage I've had 1,580 pelvic exams from you. I wish I could put you on your back, put your feet in a stirrup, and stick my finger up your hole, and see how *you* like it'," to which Bill indicated by smirk and repeated raised eyebrows that maybe that wouldn't be such an awful torture. To this, Dom and Chuck shook their heads in disbelief as they grinned in surrender to Bill's mischievousness.

"Trauma," Bill continued when the playful laughter had subsided. "The knowledge and expression of our sexuality have been so repressed in our culture that the majority of people have subsequently been *traumatized*. All of us, at some level, have been traumatized sexually. We have been made to feel shame about our natural sexual curiosity, our fantasies, and our needs. When a culture only values certain sexual activities within the confines of heterosexual, monogamous marriage, thoughts about all other activities and attractions create anxiety, confusion, and trauma. For some of us, the trauma is simple. For others, it is complex, such as that which results from abuse or rape. But the trauma, like the ignorance and secrecy, impacts our ability to enjoy a healthy, happy sexuality. Let me give you an example from my own life.

"A few years ago, I had a urinary track infection," he explained matter-of-factly, "and my doctor gave me a cystoscopy. He told me that there would be a little bleeding afterwards, and that I shouldn't worry about it.

He said that I should just go get some sanitary napkins, wear them for a few days, and that I'd be fine.'"

Bill stopped, and the slowly-emerging look of complete alarm and panic alerted us to his dilemma. He was being asked to purchase something he had been instructed as a boy *never* to touch.

"I went to a grocery store several miles away from the one where I normally shop," he confessed. "I finally found the aisle with the sanitary napkins and I started sweating. I mean, I was *really* sweating. There were so many of them, I didn't know what to do. In a panic, I ran out of the store, and I didn't look back."

Charlie and Curtis began shaking their heads in affirmation and smiling broadly.

"At work on Monday," Bill continued, "I pulled my friend, Carol Meddleton, to the side and said, 'What does "without wings" mean?' She said 'What are you talking about?' and I told her about my predicament. She was great. She said, 'Here's what you do. Go buy Stay Free without wings, non-deodorized, medium days, thin. You'll be fine'."

Bill's face cued us to his excitement. He had the information he needed to accomplish his goal. But he still faced the prospect of buying them.

"When I went back to that store, I found the Stay Free without wings, non-deodorized, medium days, thin sanitary napkins that I wanted. I put them in my basket, and then started buying a bunch of things I didn't need. When I got to the checkout counter, I began to worry that the package I bought wouldn't be marked, and that the checkout person would yell, 'Price check, aisle three, Stay Free, without wings, non-deodorized … But they didn't. I bought the sanitary napkins and everything was just fine. I can't tell you how it changed my life. Now, I feel so comfortable talking about and touching sanitary napkins that I buy them every time I go to the grocery store. I don't need them anymore, and my wife Kathy doesn't need them, but I *love* buying them, and I have them in every bathroom."

Once the laughter and chatter of recognition had subsided, he continued more seriously. "The process that we are about to begin is called a SAR, which stands for Sexual Attitude Reassessment or Restructuring. It is such an important and highly-valued educational process that AASECT, the American Association of Sex Educators, Counselors, and Therapists, requires participation in a SAR of every candidate for certification. The belief is that sexual health professionals need to be aware of the buttons in them that can get pushed by the discussion of the various aspects of sexuality. They need to be aware of their own areas of ignorance, secrecy, and trauma. If a counselor feels anxiety about homosexuality, for instance, he or she is *not* going to be a lot of use to a client who comes in because of problems they're having accepting themselves as gay. All of us, whether we're in the profession or not, need to know about those areas of sexuality that trigger responses of shame, fear, hostility, or anxiety.

"This is a program that began in San Francisco in the1960s in cooperation with the National Sex Forum and Glide Methodist Church," he said. "The SAR has three components: Evaluation of our Sexual Attitudes, Knowledge Building, and Skill Building. To help us evaluate our sexual attitudes, we're going to raise the anxiety we feel about sexuality with the use of explicit films," he said with a smile and nod to George. "We take people at whatever level they're at, and increase their anxiety until it can't go any higher. And then it drops. That's when the person becomes 'educable.' By the end of the week you'll be saying, 'If I *never* see another penis or vagina again, it'll be too soon.'"

"Don't count on it," interjected Dan, receiving some appreciative applause and laughter.

"What we want to accomplish by the end of the week," continued Bill with a wink to Dan, "is that there won't be a topic that creates anxiety for you. Then, you'll be able to take a good look at any sexual subject without fear. You'll be able to ask yourselves, 'How do I *really* feel about non-monogamy, homosexuality, and masturbation?' Along with the anxiety building, we'll also be doing some 'knowledge building.' When we're done with you, you'll have a comfort and knowledge about sexuality that is greater than that of 99 % of the population. Then, you'll be asking yourselves, 'How can I *use* this new information?'

"On Friday," he said, "you'll take all of this new comfort, and this new knowledge, and you'll put them into practice in your 'skill-building' workshops. Does that all make sense to you? Are there any questions?"

"Yes, Bill, I have a question," said George.

"When do the dirty movies start?" replied Bill in anticipation of the question.

"No," George said. "I want to know if we're going to be looking at a lot of naked Methodists in these movies."

"Good question! As a matter of fact, you *are*," Bill said with delight. "A fair number of the early films were made with volunteers from Glide Methodist Church. They really believed that they were making a significant contribution to the field, and I hope they know that they have. In the past 26 years, I have personally led 400 SARs involving over eight thousand people, and I can attest to the powerful impact these films have on people's lives."

"Sex and religion come together," observed George with a smile of delight.

"It's the way it's *supposed* to be," responded Bill with a nod to Alison to indicate that he was finished.

"Okay," Alison said as she sprang to her feet. "Thank you, Bill. That was *very* helpful. We're now going to take a fifteen minute break. Get yourselves something to drink if you'd like, but be right back here in fifteen minutes please, as Pam will be taking a look at the question 'What *is* sexuality?'"

"He's a trip," Dan said to me as we headed out the door toward Huntington. "Is he gay?"

"Bill?" I said with a big grin. "No, he's just free."

"He's cool," Dan replied. "Are you *sure* he's not gay?"

"Yes, I'm sure that he's not gay," I said, still smiling. "Are you disappointed?"

"Disappointed that he's not gay? Hmm. That's a good question," he said thoughtfully. "Maybe I am."

"Why?" I asked.

"Why what?" he said.

"Why are you disappointed that he's not gay?"

"I don't know. Maybe it's because I'd trust him more if he *was* gay," he answered.

"That's honest," I said as I veered us off the path to the cafeteria, and into the center of the lawn where I stood still for a moment. "But is that about him, or is that about you?"

"What do you mean?" Dan asked, standing still with me.

"Do you only trust people who are gay?" I said, sitting down on the grass, pulling my knees to my chest with my arms, and looking up at him.

"This is getting a little heady," he said defensively. "I just asked if he was gay."

"Sit," I said, patting the ground beside me.

"No, I think I'll go get a drink. Do you want anything?"

"No thanks. I'll just sit here and enjoy the sun."

A minute passed, and I was joined by Kevin.

"What were you guys talking about?" he asked as he sat down beside me.

"Not much. He wanted to know if Bill was gay."

Kevin laughed. "What did you say?"

"I said 'no.' So, what do you think of Dan?"

"He's pretty hunky," Kevin grinned. "He's handsome, and he's got a great body. I like the way he's been speaking up for Carla."

"I like that too," I said. "He's got a good heart, I think, though he sure seems angry to me."

"Yea, well, I think that he's pissed that Peter, the 'ex-gay' guy, is here," Kevin said.

"I think it's bigger than that," I replied, lifting my hand to massage Kevin's neck. "I think he's in Stage Five. I think he's a little angry at life right now. But I don't disagree with you about his looks. He's handsome, and he's *butch*. Do you have your eyes set on him? Do you have a plan?"

Blushing just a bit, and laughing with a smile that filled his handsome, thin face, Kevin said, "Not yet." And then with a touch of sadness, he added, "I wish I wasn't so shy."

"I wish you weren't so shy too," I said as I tickled him, "because you're so cute, and so wonderful, and any guy who got you would be so lucky. I wish you could just believe that."

"I know. I know," he said looking at me with his beautiful dark brown eyes. "You going swimming later?"

"I might," I replied. "It depends on whether there's a staff meeting during the break. Maybe I'll go swimming tonight, though, if it's warm enough."

"Do you want something to drink?" Kevin asked as he looked at his watch, got up quickly, and headed toward Huntington.

"No, thanks," I said. "Better hurry, though."

As I lay back on the grass, and let the late morning sun warm my body, I listened to the weekend lake noises that were beginning to make their presence felt. Speed boats pulled skiers, dogs barked with excitement, party barges chugged slowly down the shoreline, and squeals of delight accompanied splashing sounds in the water. Tomorrow the lake would be quiet, as it would for the remainder of the week. Only on the weekends was there any evidence that we weren't alone.

"Lost in thought?" a familiar voice asked, breaking through my drowsiness.

"Lost in pleasure, Thomas," I answered, opening my eyes. "Am I out of time?"

"No, we have a couple of minutes more," he said as he sat next to me.

"So, any new impressions of the week you want to share?" I asked.

"I like my roommate," he said.

"Who's that?"

"Lloyd," he replied. "He's a nice guy."

"He *is* a nice guy. What else?" I asked.

"Bill's session just now was *brilliant*," he said.

"He's a great teacher, isn't he. I hope my 'skill building' group took notes. I've heard him over and over again, and he always has my complete attention."

"He's very *free*, isn't he?" Thomas mused.

"I used the same word myself a moment ago. He *is* free. He completely lacks self-consciousness about his masculinity, his heterosexuality, his authority as a theologian, or as a therapist. He gives great permission to just be yourself, which is what this whole week is about, really."

"We're going to have an interesting discussion in his group on Friday," Thomas said.

"I bet you will, but how so?" I asked.

"We've got quite a mix, from 'being gay is great' George to 'ex-gay' Peter," he explained. "We cover the spectrum from 'liberal' to 'conservative' on interpretations of the Bible. Joe is great. Catherine seems a bit up tight. And Bill is just as easy going about the whole thing as one could imagine. It's going to be fun. Interesting and fun."

"Oh, it sounds like fun," I said. "I wish I could be a fly on the wall, but I've got my own group to work with. Keep me posted, will you?"

"With pleasure," Thomas winked.

"By the way, what instructions for the week does Bill give you in his workshop? I've never asked him."

"Well, we began by each telling the story of our spiritual journey so far," Thomas responded as he leaned back his head to feel the warmth of the sun on his face. "During the week, we're supposed to think about what has happened each day that speaks to our spiritual journey. On Friday, we're going to talk about how we integrate it all."

"That sounds good."

"I think so too," he replied as he looked at his watch. "And now, we *have* run out of time. Just about everyone is back in Ridings. I'm surprised Gail hasn't rung the bell. Will I see you at the gay dinner meeting tonight?"

"You bet," I said, getting up off of the ground. "I wouldn't miss it. For the first several years I came here, it felt as if I was the only openly gay person."

"I bet that was lonely. It's nice to have a family, isn't it?" he asked.

"Yes, it sure is," I said. "In truth, the staff has always been my family, but it's awfully nice to feel the energy of openly gay and transgender folks around."

Chapter Eleven

What is Sexuality?

In the neatly rearranged semicircle of chairs, the majority of participants had settled into comfortable positions, with pen or pencil in hand, and writing paper and packets balanced precariously on their knees. The sexuality educators, particularly, seemed attentive and eager to take notes as Pam began her hour and a half presentation on "What Is Sexuality?"

Combining a delightful blend of professional attention to detail and process, with a warm and playful storytelling manner, Pam drew our attention to the five interlocking circles labeled "Sexual Beingness" on newsprint in the front of the room. Carol, simultaneously, passed out copies of the same diagram to the participants.

"This wonderful conceptual framework was created by Dennis Dailey, a social worker and educator at the University of Kansas," she explained. "It helps remind us that our sexuality is extremely complex. It has far more to do with *who we are* than with *what we do* sexually. In the time we have together this morning, I'm going to talk about the five key components of our sexuality. Each of these major topics will be further explored in greater detail in upcoming sessions."

The five interlocking circles were labeled Sensuality, Intimacy, Sexual Identity, Sexual Health and Reproduction, and Sexualization. On the handouts, Sensuality was defined as "Accepting and enjoying one's own body, and its ability to respond sexually, as well as enjoying the body of a sexual partner." Intimacy was defined as "The basic human need to be emotionally close to another person, and have that closeness returned." The description of Sexual Identity was "An understanding of who one is sexually, including a sense of being male or female." Sexual Health and Reproduction were described as "Attitudes and behaviors that have to do with reproduction and keeping the sexual parts of the body healthy." Finally, Sexualization was defined as "The use of sexuality to influence, control, or manipulate others."

Pam began with the circle representing Sensuality.

"Take a look at the words inside the circle," she instructed us. There we found listed, "body image, skin hunger, sexual behaviors, pleasure and orgasm, and fantasy."

"Body image," she said, "refers to how we feel about our bodies in general, and how we feel about our genitals. How we feel about our bodies is heavily influenced by what?" she asked, extending her arm and upturned palm to encourage participation. "What influences our attitudes toward our bodies?" she repeated.

"The media," Marjorie said strongly from her seat.

"Correct," affirmed Pam with a grateful smile. "The media *really* impacts our standards of what is beautiful. What do commercials, print advertising, movies, and television tell us that we're supposed to have in order to be beautiful?"

"Flat stomachs." "Big muscles." "White teeth." "White skin." "Thin waists." "Money." "Blond hair." "Big penises." "Big breasts." "A hairy chest." "A hairless body." "Legs that work." The responses came quickly from around the semicircle.

"Right," said Pam. "Good. And what else impacts our sense of our bodies? Where else do we look to for direction on what is beautiful?"

"Our community," said George with a sad look of resignation.

"That's right," affirmed Pam. "Our community or our culture tells us what is beautiful, what is *desirable*. For instance, in my culture having a big butt is very desirable. Women are supposed to have a big butt. Now look at this butt," she said turning around and gently sticking out her small bottom to illustrate her point. "This is a *small* butt. This is not what's valued among African American men. Gail, get up here, please."

Gail stood with a giggle, knowing from past workshops that it was her cue to provide an illustration of a "cute" butt.

"Now, look at that butt," Pam said smiling. "That would be a *great* butt in my community, but not this butt," she said again, slapping her own posterior and shaking her head in disappointment and feigned disgust.

"Thanks, Gail," she continued as Gail smiled and hurried to her seat. "So, our community or our culture can impact how we feel about our bodies. And if we don't feel good about our bodies, how comfortable are we having them be seen or touched? Not good. Can you think of any other influences on how we feel about our bodies? Yes, Annette?"

"Religion."

"Right," affirmed Pam enthusiastically. "Religion can play a *major* role in how we feel about the goodness of our bodies. How so?"

"Pam," explained Annette, "there was a time when some women in religious communities were required to bathe under a sheet so that the angels didn't see them naked. Their heads stuck through a hole in the center of the sheets, and they washed themselves beneath it."

"You're kidding," Dan replied with shock.

"It's no longer the practice, but it does illustrate how religion supported negative attitudes toward the body," Annette said.

"More than supported," Bill said loudly from his seat. "Initiated and promulgated."

"There's lots of blame to go around," Pam said diplomatically as she stepped forward, and then shifted subjects. "When you all listed the things that the media promotes as beautiful or as pleasing, no one mentioned odor-free female genitalia. I had an uncle who used to repeatedly tell this awful joke about the blind man who every time he passed the fish market would tip his hat and say, 'Hello, ladies'."

The majority of women in the group groaned in unison.

"Right," said Pam in affirmation. "How are we women supposed to feel good about our bodies, and feel good about offering our bodies to our partners, when we're given so many negative messages about our vulva's and vaginas? We're told that they're 'ugly,' they 'stink,' they're 'nasty.' Don't look. Don't touch!"

"Pam," interrupted Marjorie, who dropped her pen and paper to the floor, and raised her hand with determination.

"Yes," Pam said, nodding to her with raised eyebrows of expectation.

"They cut off the clitoris of young girls in many African countries because they don't want them, as women, to feel any pleasure," she said. "Talk about body image and loving one's genitals."

"It's called circumcision," offered Curtis.

"It's called *genital mutilation*," Marjorie responded firmly.

"It's awful that someone would have their genitals cut," said Maggie with disgust.

"I know someone who did," inaudibly mumbled Leona with a coy look. Kevin, who was sitting beside her, responded with a furrowed brow.

"Imagine how having your clitoris cut off would affect your body image and your ability to respond sexually," Pam said sadly. "It would have a long-term impact, and some of us have heard unimaginable stories from women who have experienced it."

She paused for a moment to allow us to reflect. She then said, "But, let's go on talking about body image. I want to focus on the guys for a minute, specifically on the issue of penises and penis size.

"Once, when I was in Trinidad," she said looking around the room slowly to make eye contact with each participant, and nodding her head in gentle affirmation of the following story's truth, "where I was doing a sexuality education workshop, my host gave a cocktail party for me, and many people who had not attended the workshop came to the party. I met all kinds of friendly people who welcomed me, but some of them were full of nervous energy about the sexuality workshop. Some of the men started telling jokes, and quite a few of the jokes were about penis size. I was a guest, so at first I just listened without comment. Of course, I never laughed at the jokes. I just listened. But by the time the third penis joke was told, I couldn't hold back any longer."

"Surprise. Surprise," I said.

"Right," she said in appreciation of the affirmation. "Anyway, I spoke up and said to the joke teller, 'You keep telling these jokes about penis size. I know that you're just having fun, but I'm sensitive to the fact that some men worry about the size of their penis, and for many partners, penis size is *not* important.' The joke teller just laughed harder. He said, 'Well, in the United States it might be okay to have a small penis, but here in Trinidad, we call that a "ZUT." I tell you, I pity the man walking around with a zut. Even my 10-year-old son has a good size penis that will never be considered a zut.'

"Well, by now I was inspired," Pam continued. "I looked around the room and noted three women that I knew were in relationships with men. I called them over and told them that I wanted to do a quick survey. I asked, 'If you had to choose between a man with a big penis who was just a so-so, not particularly sensitive, lover, and one with a small penis who was attentive and caring, and made it his business to please you, which would you choose?' All three women enthusiastically said they would choose the lover with the small penis.

"The joke teller was not impressed with my survey," she said. "However, there was another man standing around us who was *very* impressed. He spoke up and said, 'Well, I found that very interesting, myself, because if I pulled my pants down right now you would see that I have a zut. And I am so pleased to hear these women say that it wouldn't matter at all to them as long as their lover was caring and attentive.'

"Well, needless to say," Pam concluded, "I was in awe of this man who could stand up and say this at a party. And it proved to me that you never know when you're doing important sexuality education."

After a few seconds of silent reflection, Pam continued with Dailey's category of Sensuality by describing Masters and Johnson's "Sexual Response Cycle," and explaining the stages of Excitement, Plateau, Orgasm, and Resolution. Bill Stayton, she said, would be expanding upon the model at another time. Copious notes were taken by many of the participants as she discussed the vasocongestion and mytonia of arousal.

"Will you please spell those?" asked Grace.

Soon we moved to the next circle in the diagram, labeled 'Intimacy.' The words contained within the circle to describe Intimacy were "caring, sharing, liking/loving, risk-taking, and reciprocity." To help us focus on our own lives, she broke us into groups of two and asked us to take turns talking about the experiences we have had building intimacy with others. Catherine paired herself with Ben.

"You want to go first, or do you want me to?" Ben asked as he maneuvered his wheelchair to face Catherine's seat.

"Whatever you like," Catherine said pleasantly.

"Okay, I'll go," he said. "For me, an intimate relationship has to be reciprocal. I need to feel that the other person is taking as good care of me as I feel I am of him or her. They need to be as honest with me as I am with them, sharing their feelings and trusting me with their scariest secrets. But that's only half of it. I have to feel as much 'like' or 'love' for them as they do for me, and vice versa. Sometimes, people fall in love with you that you're not in love with, and despite how intimate the friendship may feel, it can fall apart when one person has expectations the other can't meet."

"Has that happened with you?" Catherine asked.

"What? Oh yea, I guess," he said. "Sure it has. How about with you?"

"Intimacy," said Catherine, "for me includes respecting people's boundaries. I'm a very private person. I don't feel inclined to tell my 'scariest secrets,' as you say, to others. And I'm not sure I want them telling me theirs, unless, of course, it's in my capacity as a priest. It's just the way I am. It may have something to do with my Southern upbringing or with my family. I do agree with you, though, that intimate relationships need to be reciprocal. They also need, I think, to share values. It would be very difficult for me to have an intimate relationship with someone who didn't share my values."

Clearly sensing Catherine's reserve, Ben pulled back both emotionally and physically, gently maneuvering his chair to give more space between them. For the next few moments they discussed their work.

After calling us back to our places, Pam continued to discuss, and illustrate important points from each component of Sexual Beingness. With Sexual Identity, she used the marked easels at the front of the room to make distinctions between Biological Gender, Gender Identity, Gender Role, and Sexual Orientation. Explaining that I would be covering the topic in more detail later in the week, Pam also briefly focused our attention on Alfred Kinsey's well-known continuum of sexual behavior.

In her discussion on Sexual Health and Reproduction, Pam began with a cautionary note.

"Before I begin to describe this component, let me first say to the educators in the room, that each circle of sexuality identifies important sub topics that should be covered in any good sexuality program. We need to help young people deal with all of these important issues and yet, so often, programs tend to focus only on two of the circles: 'Sexual Health and Reproduction' and 'Sexualization'," she said with a sad and disapproving shake of her head. "We're comfortable teaching youth about puberty, how to avoid pregnancy and STD's, or about the traumas that too many of us have encountered with rape, sexual abuse, etcetera, but we, as a society, are *not* comfortable talking about sensuality and the body's natural ability to respond sexually, or about the importance of emotional and sexual intimacy, and the skills associated with developing and maintaining intimate relationships. Most sexuality education programs do not deal forthrightly with issues of sexual identity and sexual orientation. Yet, a lack of understanding around these issues can lead to personal pain and self-denial, as well as to discrimination against, and intolerance of others.

"Dailey's model of 'Sexual Beingness' makes it clear that the so-called controversial or 'hard-to-teach' topics in sexuality education are key components of our sexual beingness, and should not be ignored," she said.

Having offered that warning, Pam proceeded to provide accurate information on the topics listed under Sexual Health and Reproduction. These included "reproduction, sexual intercourse, anatomy and physiology, contraception, and STD risk-reduction."

Finally, she moved to the last but not least significant component, Sexualization. Reminding us of Bill's earlier comments on the impact of ignorance, secrecy, and trauma on our sexual health, Pam repeated that Sexualization was "the use of sexuality to influence, control or manipulate others." Inside the circle on the diagram were the words "seduction, sexual abuse, rape, advertising, and sexual harassment."

Looking at her watch several minutes later, Pam brought our sober discussion to a close and summarized by reminding us that our task for the week was to explore our sexuality in the framework of it being a complex interaction of components, influenced by a variety of outside sources. As she concluded, and Alison rose to thank her, Thomas led a hearty round of applause. Pam blushed, smiled with gratitude, and sat down.

"Okay," said Alison with an energetic voice. "Well done, Pam. And now it's time for lunch. Following lunch, please be back here right on time for Bill's presentation on our 'Sexual Values'."

"Nice job," I said to Pam as I bent down to give her a kiss on the cheek.

"Thanks," she said, "though it felt a little rushed at the end. Did it seem like that to you?"

"Nope. As always, it was great," I replied.

"Thanks, sweetie," she said.

"Nice job," Betty said as she walked quickly by us. "Hey, Leona, wait up, will you? I need to ask you something."

"Here goes," Carol said from behind me.

Chapter Twelve

Betty and Peter's Explanations

The bright sun created a fortune in diamonds on the lake, and the sound of speed boats filled the air with the roar of activity as we exited Ridings, and scattered in different directions before going to lunch.

"I want to go swimming," whined Maggie.

"So, go, darlin'," said George. "Grab your suit and a sandwich, and have a picnic on the beach. You've got an hour."

"Fifty minutes," corrected Maggie.

"So go," he repeated.

"Will you come?" she asked.

"No, it's too far to walk back for refills on pasta," he said straight faced. "Just kidding. Actually, I thought I'd have some lunch, and then go sit for awhile in the outdoor chapel. I want to collect my thoughts before the service this afternoon. Besides, I look like a beached whale in my bathing suit. I'm afraid that someone would call Greenpeace."

"Uh, uh," Maggie scolded. "Body image."

"Tell me about it," George said with a sad smirk.

As Maggie headed toward Peabody to get her swimming suit, she passed Peter who was already in his.

"That was fast," Maggie said.

"Yea, I'm ready for a swim," he said smiling as he shifted his rolled towel to his left hand so that he could open the dorm door for Ben.

"You guys going swimming?" Ben asked.

"I am," said Peter.

"Me too," said Maggie.

"Well, maybe I'll join you one of these days. I don't have enough time to get this chair down and up that hill in fifty minutes, but I'm determined to get into the water before the week is over."

"If there's anything I can do to help make that happen," Peter said, "know that I'd love to do it."

"Me too," said Maggie.

"Okay. Thanks. You're on," said Ben. "I could use some help. I'll take a look at the schedule and see when there's enough time to manage my 'Operation Flashback'."

"Operation Flashback?" Maggie asked quizzically.

"Yea, I lost the use of my legs in a lake," Ben explained with a sigh and a sad smile.

"Oh gosh, I'm so sorry," said Maggie.

"Don't be, please," Ben said. "It was a long time ago, and it's high time that I got back into the water."

"Well, I'm going to go put on my suit, and then grab a sandwich," said Maggie. "Peter, do you mind if I join you? There's something that I want to talk with you about"

"Not at all," he replied. "I'll meet you down there."

"Thanks," she smiled warmly. "And Ben, can we rename the Operation? How about 'Operation Affirmation?' or 'Operation,' I don't know, 'Recovery'? 'Operation Flashback' sounds a little grim."

"I'll give it some thought," Ben said. "But, you're right. I need a new name. That's an old one, and it doesn't say what I'm about anymore. Thanks."

As Maggie entered her room, she saw Betty close the door to hers.

"Okay, Leona," Betty said, "let's talk. First, thanks for taking the time to do this."

"Carol said I *had* to," Leona said with her arms crossed, peering through the curtains at the stretch of lawn outside of their room.

"Second," continued Betty undaunted, "I want to apologize for the way I sprang it on you last night that I'm a transsexual. I should have sat you down when I arrived, before I unpacked, and told you about myself. I'm so used to being me as a woman that I forget, or at least I *try* to forget, that other people may not be as comfortable with it. Quite honestly, I'm tired of explaining myself to people. Thornfield is one of the few places in the world that I feel safe and fully accepted. I shouldn't have assumed anything about your feelings, though. I'm sorry. And finally," she said, sensing no indication from Leona that she yet wanted to speak, "I'm so sorry that you spent the night on the sofa in the living room. It wasn't a great beginning to your week, was it."

"No, it's not been," said Leona who surprised herself with a sudden choking back of tears. "Hooey," she said, clearing her throat, and stopping herself from crying. "Where did *that* come from?" she asked as she dabbed her eyes with the edge of her pillow case. "Betty, I am *not* a mean person. I do not want to cause you any pain. I consider myself an open-minded person, but I'm having a really hard time getting my arms around the fact that I'm sharing a room with a person who was born male, and who tells me that she's a lesbian. It's just not an experience I was prepared for, and with no disrespect meant for you, I just can't see myself staying in this room. Carol told me that she'd move me, but she wanted me to talk with you about it first."

"I understand," said Betty with a nod and a soft look of acceptance. "I don't want to have a negative impact on the week you'll have here. And *I'll* move. There's no need for you to move."

"No, *I'll* move," said Leona standing. "I'm the one with the problem. I'll go tell Carol that we talked, and ask her to move me into another room tonight."

"Okay," said Betty.

"You're a nice person, Betty. Please don't take offense," Leona said as she walked to the door.

"No offense taken," Betty replied. "I'll see you at lunch in a minute."

Instead of going to lunch as she had indicated, though, Betty headed for the driveway.

"Hey, Betty," I called out from the door leading into Huntington.

"Hey, Brian," she replied.

"Where are you going?" I asked.

"Just for a walk," she said with a weak smile.

"Want some company?" I asked.

"No thanks," she said. "I think I'll just go talk to Susan."

"Okay," I said. "Holler if you want anything."

"Thanks, I will," she said.

"Whom were you talking to?" Alison asked from the registration desk where she was standing with her assistant, Tonya.

"Betty," I said as I walked in. "She's heading up to Susan's tree to think."

"Who's Susan?" asked Tonya.

"Susan Vasbinder was an important member of our Thornfield family," explained Alison. "When she died, we planted a tree in her memory, up near Mary Lee's tree. Mary Lee Tatum was another much-loved member of our family, Tonya. Having those trees on the grounds gives the staff, and those participants who knew them from the past, a place to go and just think. As I recall, Susan and Betty bonded pretty strongly when Betty came to the workshop for the first time. I think Susan had a profound influence on her life."

"I *know* so," I affirmed.

As Alison and Tonya resumed their review of procedures, including what to do if someone wanted to have materials copied, I headed into the dining room where I found Carol sitting at a table in the corner with Lisa.

"So, besides not liking the song 'I Love Myself', how's it going for you so far?" Carol laughed.

"You noticed?" Lisa said a little sheepishly.

"It's no big deal. Every year there's a handful of people who have trouble relating to it. They usually come to love it by the end of the week," Carol said. "But beyond that, how are you doing?"

"Okay, I guess," Lisa replied. "To tell you the truth though, I'm not sure why I'm here. I'm a software engineer. I'm not a sex educator. Why do I need to know about the engorgement of the penis with blood during arousal?"

"Got me," laughed Carol. "You mean that 'vasocongestion' doesn't come up, forgive the pun, in your work?"

"Not usually," Lisa said.

"So, why *are* you here?" Carol asked, knowing full-well the answer.

"Because my therapist thought it would be good for me to come," Lisa replied. "Remember? I told you that when I registered in February."

"I know, but I wanted to help *you* remember it," Carol said. "What is it that you think she or he thought you might get out of the week?"

"She thought it would be helpful to me in sorting out my sexuality?" Lisa reluctantly acknowledged.

"Well, if that's what's at the end of your rope, then you're in the right place. A lot of these people are professional sexuality educators, but most of them know that they're here to sort out their sexuality too. And the ones that don't know that, trust me, *will* by the end of the week. That's the magic that happens here, Lisa. I think that if you hang in and 'trust the process,' as we say, it'll happen for you too."

"Carol, may I please speak with you?" Leona asked as she approached the table.

Down at the lake, Maggie and Peter laid side by side on the green, outdoor carpet-covered raft that was anchored twenty-five yards from the shore. Both were still dripping wet, and breathing a little heavily, not so much from the short swim as from climbing the ladder onto the metal, barrel-supported platform.

"Oh, that felt good," Maggie said, shaking the water from her hair. "I've been dying to get into the lake all morning, but I wouldn't have wanted to miss Bill or Pam."

"Are you liking the workshop?" asked Peter, staring at the cloudless blue sky.

"So far, so good," Maggie answered in a chirpy manner. "How about you? Do you like it so far?"

"Yea, so far it's about what I expected, although Bill's warm-up exercise with the words yesterday felt a little intense," Peter said, his lanky arms folded back, with his hands supporting his head. "I got through it fine, though. Now I'm curious about how he's going to handle 'Sexual Values.' I expect that I'm going to disagree, but so far it feels as if I could get away with disagreeing."

"Why do you think you'll disagree?" Maggie asked, turning on her side and raising her head.

"My sexual values are *biblically* based," Peter answered. "I'm not sure that Bill or any of the rest of the staff look to the Bible for their values."

"Ouch! That's a little harsh," Maggie said with a frown.

"Sorry. You're right. Even when I said it, I knew it wasn't what I meant. What I mean is that I don't believe that any of them take the Bible *literally*. I do, and that's what guides my values," he explained.

"Oh, so is that why you say that you're 'ex-gay'?" Maggie asked innocently. "I mean, does your understanding of the Bible tell you that you *can't* be gay, and that's why you aren't any more?"

"Pretty much," he said with a half smile.

"So how did you *become* ex-gay?" Maggie asked. "When you say that you're ex-gay, do you mean that you're not attracted to men anymore?"

"I mean that I've been 'delivered' from a homosexual lifestyle that I believe is sinful," he replied. "But, how come you're so interested in this? Is that the question you wanted to ask me? I mean, up at the dorm, you said you wanted to talk to me about something. Is this it?"

"Yes," she acknowledged. "It is. I came to Thornfield because my husband, Barry, came here last year. When he came home, he told me that he was gay. So, I guess he's an 'ex-heterosexual,' isn't he? As you can imagine, that blew a great big hole right through the center of my life. Our therapist suggested that I come here to deal with my anger at the place, and to try to understand what happened to Barry."

"And you want to know if Barry can change back into being a heterosexual?" Peter asked.

"Yes, I guess I do. Is there hope for him? Is there hope for us?" Maggie asked.

"I don't know," Peter answered, as he turned to face her. "I'd love to say 'yes,' but quite honestly I can only speak for myself. Is your husband a religious man?"

"Not particularly," she answered.

"Hey, you two, you're going to be late," hollered Charlie from the shore. "You've got ten minutes before we start."

"Thanks, Charlie," Maggie called back as she noticed the flow of participants heading back up the hill. "We'll be right there."

"We can talk more about this later, Maggie, if you want," Peter said with a warm smile.

"Thanks," said Maggie. "I'd like that. I appreciate you being honest with me. Okay. Here goes. One. Two. Three." And with that, she dove into the water.

As Peter and Maggie toweled off, and headed up the hill, she asked him, "Are you going to the religious service this afternoon?"

"Probably not," he said, "but maybe. I need to think about it."

"Why wouldn't you?"

"Mmm, I think I wouldn't be comfortable with prayers that don't represent my understanding of God," he answered. "But, again, I'm not sure. I haven't made up my mind."

"Okay, so this may seem like a really dumb question, but are you going to go to the meeting of gay people and allies during dinner?" she asked.

"Oh, my guess is not," he laughed. "Even if I *wanted* to go to represent my perspective, I don't think I'd be very welcome."

"Well, *I'm* going," she said, "and if you want to come, I'll sit with you."

"You're a sweet woman, Maggie," Peter said. "Your husband is a lucky man."

"*Was* a lucky man," she corrected. "But, thanks. By the way, I know you hear this a lot, but you sure are good looking. Are you a model or something?"

"Thanks," he blushed, and then teased, "Are you flirting with me?"

"Are you *nuts*?" she laughed loudly. "I've already got my hands full of gay men, or ex-gay, or whatever. You know what I mean."

"Yes, I know what you mean," he said with a big smile. "See you back in Ridings."

As Maggie left the dorm, toweling her wet hair she bumped into George who was coming from the direction of the woods.

"Hey, Maggie," he called out.

"Hi, George," she replied, stopping outside of the door into Ridings.

"How was the swim?" he asked.

"It was perfect. Too short, but wonderful," she answered.

"You two have a good talk?" he asked with a gentle smile. "You and Peter?"

"Yes, thank you," she said. "Although, to tell you the truth, I'm still pretty confused. We didn't get very far. He talked about being 'delivered.' But, I'm not sure what that really means. I think it has to do with his faith. Speaking of, did you have a productive time by yourself?"

"I did, thanks," he said. "And don't worry about the whole thing being confusing. It'll sort itself out for you."

"I hope so," Maggie sighed. "By the way, he's a nice guy. He's really cautious, but he's a nice man. I encouraged him to come to the service, *and* to the gay meeting."

"What did he say?" George asked.

"He said he wasn't sure about the service because he wasn't sure he'd be comfortable, and he didn't plan on coming to the meeting because he didn't think he'd be welcome," she said. "I encouraged him to come to both. I told him that *I* was going to the meeting, and that I'd sit next to him if he came."

"You're a gem," he said as he squeezed her to himself with one arm, and gave her a kiss on the forehead. "Time to go in."

Chapter Thirteen

Sexual Values

"Our sexual values are *sacred*," Bill affirmed with a very serious look as he brought our attention to the topic of the session. "This week is not about *changing* your sexual values. It's about helping you identify, clarify, and evaluate them to see if they continue to serve you well. The first task, though, is to *identify* them and, as such, I have an exercise that I'd like to take you through. I'm going to read a few statements one by one, and I'd like you to respond as to whether you 'agree' or 'disagree' with each statement.

"Let's make that end of the room the place where you'll stand if you 'agree' with the statement that I'm making," said Bill, gesturing to the area of the room that was dominated by the mass of windows overlooking the lake, "and this end of the room as the place where you'll stand if you 'disagree' with the statements. Remember, there are no 'right' or 'wrong' answers. Incidentally, I wrote these statements at the Mayflower Hotel in Washington, D.C. the night before a workshop and, as you can see, they're still on the same stationery," he added with a playful little wiggle of his butt. And then, more seriously, "Responding to these statements will help us each clarify our sexual values.

"Okay, are you ready?" Bill asked with a look of excitement and joy.

"Ready!" Thomas answered strongly.

"Good. The first," Bill said, "is this. 'We would probably have fewer sexual hang-ups if we had been allowed to experiment freely as children.' Agree, over here. Disagree, over there. Again, 'We would probably have fewer sexual hang-ups if we had been allowed to experiment as children.' Please move now to the area of the room that best represents your feelings."

Several people hesitated prior to leaving where they were sitting.

"Can we stand in the middle?" Beatrice asked with a slight frown.

"No, you have to go to one end of the room or the other, but you are allowed to change your mind and move," Bill said. "Let's do this quickly," he added. "Go with your first impulse."

Once we had moved to one or the other end of the room, Bill instructed, "Now talk among yourselves as to why you are where you are. In a minute or two, I'm going to ask one or two people from each group to represent the feelings that came up in your discussions."

The buzzing sound of voices filled the room as three or four small groups of participants at each end began talking out loud about why they agreed or disagreed with the statement. After four or five minutes, Bill called our attention back to the center of the room where he was now standing.

"Okay, what did you hear?" he asked. "Why are people standing where they are?"

"If I had felt free to experiment with *my* feelings," Dan announced loudly from the "Agree" side, "I wouldn't have felt so damn guilty about being gay, and I wouldn't have felt so lonely and isolated either."

"Being able to touch oneself without shame would go a long way in eliminating the fear and guilt many people have about masturbation," added Marjorie.

"In societies where there are fewer taboos about sexuality, children grow up with healthier, more mature attitudes toward themselves and others," asserted Judith.

"Good. Anybody else?" Bill asked. "Okay. How about someone from the other end? Tell us why you disagree."

"You don't want kids playing with matches and gasoline," Dom said strongly. "Children need guidance on what will hurt them and what won't."

"By whose standards?" hollered back Dan. "What constitutes sexual matches and gasoline?"

"Let's give this group a chance to tell us what they're thinking," Bill said, turning to Dan with a smile. "Remember, there are no 'right' or 'wrong' answers here. Who else has a perspective to offer?"

After a few seconds of silence, Tonya said softly, "I can't believe that I'm on this end, but I guess it depends on what or who the child is experimenting with."

"Say more," Bill encouraged with a smile.

"About not believing that I'm at this end, or about what the child is experimenting with?" she asked.

"Either," Bill responded playfully.

"If a child is touching itself, it's one thing," Tonya said with a little uncertainty, "but if it's experimenting with something that could hurt it physically, then I don't think it should be completely free to explore."

"Like what?" Dan asked from across the room.

"I don't know 'like what.' I just think there are things like Dom said that children should be kept away from," Tonya answered.

"Like dressing up in your mother's clothes if you're a little boy?" asked Carla meekly from the "Agree" side.

"I don't know," pleaded Tonya with obvious frustration. "Can I move?" she asked Bill.

"You can if you want," Bill grinned.

"What's the purpose of parenting if it's not to offer your children moral guidance on behaviors?" asked Catherine in a strong voice, which stopped Tonya in her tracks.

"This is so confusing," Tonya whined.

"Is it?" Bill asked with apparent delight. "Okay. Let's move on to the second statement. Ready? 'Given adequate safeguards such as safe sex, effective birth control, and freedom from venereal disease, adolescents should feel free, *if they choose*, to experience themselves sexually with another person or persons. Agree or disagree?"

"Will you say that one more time, please?" Marjorie asked.

"Sure," said Bill. "Given adequate safeguards such as safe sex, effective birth control, and freedom from venereal disease, adolescents should feel free, if they choose, to experience themselves sexually with another person or persons."

"Adolescents are what age?" Lisa inquired.

"Teenagers," Marjorie answered. "From puberty to adulthood."

"Thanks," said Lisa.

"Okay, time to move," Bill encouraged. "Agree over here. Disagree over there."

Many people stayed where they were. A handful of others switched places.

"Where are you going?" Charlie asked Martha as she walked toward the "Agree" side.

"He said 'adolescents'," she replied, turning to face him. "The one before was about children."

"Can adolescents choose freely when an adult with power is involved?" asked Dom.

"Let's first take a moment and talk with others in our groups," Bill advised, "and then we'll discuss our differences."

When the conversation began among the "Disagree" side of the room, the issue of pedophile priests and ministers heated the discussion in at least one small group. They were the first to speak when Bill called for reactions to the statement.

"As I said before," Dom explained. "I'm standing here because I don't think an adolescent is capable of freely choosing to have sex with an adult, especially when that adult has power over him or her. The best example we've got is these damn priests who are having sex with innocent children."

"You're talking about two different age groups," insisted Dan from the other side of the room. "If a priest molested a child, it's one thing. If he had sex with a teenager, it's completely different."

"Let's hear from one side at a time," said Bill. "We're starting with the 'Disagree' side this time."

"A teenager doesn't have the ability to give informed consent to a priest," interrupted Dom with a touch of anger.

"*This* teenager did," Dan said with a raised voice, ignoring Bill's instructions. "It was what I wanted. No harm was done. And I'm glad it happened."

"That's you," said Dom dismissively.

"Yea, that's me," answered Dan defiantly.

"Okay," said Bill with an enthusiastic smile. "Clearly we have a difference of opinion, here. Let's go back to the 'Disagree' side. Are there other opinions that you want to put out there?"

There was an awkward silence in the room for a moment. Then Margaret spoke up from the "Agree" side.

"Bill, for me, there are lots of variables," she said calmly. "At what level of adolescence are we speaking? Are we talking about a thirteen-year-old girl choosing to have sex with a forty-year-old male? Are we talking about a sixteen-year-old boy choosing to have sex with a twenty-year-old female? Or are we talking about two fourteen-year-old girls or boys exploring each other's bodies? The ages and genders of the adolescents make a difference to me. And there are other factors too."

"Like what, Margaret?" asked George.

"If the twenty-year-old female is the sixteen-year-old's teacher or guidance counselor, I have trouble with it. If the two fourteen-year-olds are siblings, I have trouble with it. And I can't imagine when I wouldn't have trouble if it was a thirteen-year-old girl and a forty-year-old male."

"What about a thirteen-year-old boy and a forty-year-old male?" asked Dom.

"I can't think of circumstances that would make me comfortable," Margaret answered solemnly.

"Even if the thirteen-year-old was the aggressor?" Dan asked.

"Oh, good grief," Dom sighed with exasperation.

"I'd need to have you help me understand how it could be okay, Dan," Margaret said with a nod and half a smile.

"Good discussion," Bill said enthusiastically. "Let's see how you do with the third statement."

The third statement questioned whether complete sexual freedom undermines the stability of the individual, family, and society. We then explored whether we felt that people entering the field of sexuality should be encouraged to experience themselves in a variety of sexual situations. Extramarital sex and its impact on marriage was another issue, as was bisexuality. Finally, we decided if it was important for a HIV-positive person who always employs safe sex practices to tell his or her partner about their HIV status.

When we were finished and had settled back into our chairs, Bill asked us how we felt about the experience.

"It was *really* hard," Sr. Annette replied. "I found myself very torn, especially as I listened to other people's perspectives."

"I found myself getting angry at people," confessed Wendy. "I had to fight myself from putting them in boxes, and deciding I didn't like them anymore."

"I hope you won't put *me* in a box," said Tonya nervously. "I kept shocking myself with how I was voting. I'm much more conservative than I thought I was, or than I think I want to be."

"Anybody else," Bill asked as the room grew quiet. Both Dan and Dom had their arms folded and were staring at the floor.

"I felt a little lonely, sometimes," offered Gina. "And angry. I wanted more time to explain my view in the small group. And then, sometimes, like Annette, I felt confused."

"That's good," said Bill. "I suggest that our confusion results from the fact that we're often operating from more than one value system. One time, after the SAR, many years ago, a man came up to me and said 'You've just trampled all over my values.' I was horrified because, as I said earlier, I hold everyone's sexual values to be sacred. So I started doing a lot of thinking and research about our sexual values, and I've come up with a model that I think you'll find useful."

Several participants now reached beneath their seats for their packets, and pulled out paper and a pen or pencil.

"Theology's purpose," explained Bill, "is to give *meaning* to our lives. And theology guides the creation of our value systems. There are three basic theological systems, I believe, and I have labeled them simply 'A,' 'B,' and 'C.'

"Sexual Theology A, with which most of us were raised, is based upon the primacy of the male sperm," he said as he wrote the words "Male Sperm" in big letters on the whiteboard. "It says that the male sperm, in and of itself, is *life*, and that males are the 'givers' of life. Many of you heard this theology as children when your parents were explaining to you where you came from. They said that 'Daddy planted his seed in Mommy's tummy and it grew up to be you.' Right?"

"Right," Thomas affirmed.

"There are two functions of the male sperm, according to Sexual Theology A," Bill continued as he wrote. "One is for 'procreation,' and the other is for 'the upbringing of offspring.' If it's for 'procreation,' then it requires 1.) coitus, 2.) with another person, 3.) of the opposite sex, and 4.) in the appropriate manner. This, of course, therefore prohibits masturbation, bestiality, homosexuality, and any sex other than in the 'missionary' position. 'For the upbringing of offspring' eliminates the possibility of abortion. Basically, this is Catholic Canon Law from 1918, and the most articulate spokesperson for Theology A is Pope John Paul II.

"Sexual Theology C," he said as he continued to write on the board behind him, making long lines to delineate A, B, and C, "is *not* based on the primacy of 'male sperm,' but rather on the primacy of *relationships*. It says that the value of all sexual behaviors is to be judged against whether or not the behavior *enhances* relationships. Unlike Theology A, Theology C questions the motives and the consequences of the acts, and the criteria for decision-making. It's interested in research and experience. It seeks to help people with decision-making skills. Do you see the difference between the two?" he asked, and then continued. "The most articulate spokesperson for Theology C, in my opinion, was Pope John XXIII. Theology C is best summarized in the book *Human Sexuality: New Directions in American Catholic Thought* which was commissioned by the American Catholic bishops, and was edited by Tony Kosnik.

"Theology B," he concluded abruptly, "is a combination of Theology A and Theology C. That's where I think most of *us* fall, and that's why sometimes it can feel so confusing as we attempt to identify our values, and justify our judgments. One bumps up against the other.

"Let me tell you a quick story if I can," he said as he checked his watch for time. "Many years ago, I was approached by a man and his wife who asked me to help them arrange for an abortion for their 13-year-old daughter. He told me that under the circumstances, they felt they had no other options. The girl, he said, was extremely gifted, and that her life would be ruined if she had the baby. Furthermore, he explained, there was no telling who the father was, as she had sex with several boys on the same night. I told them that I would help, and he said, 'There's something else you should know. The reason that this is so very hard for us is that I'm the head of the "Right to Life" committee in this state, and I firmly believe that abortion is wrong. When this is all over, I will continue to work against others having abortions.'"

Many of the participants gasped. Several others shook their heads in disgust.

"Here's an example," Bill said solemnly, "of a person whose conflicted values fall into Theology B. It is often difficult for many us to respond with certainty to situations as they arise, because though we may feel as if our sexual values are set in stone, they often bump up against a reality where they just don't work for us. This week, I'd like you to keep close track of how you're feeling about the various topics that are presented, to ask yourselves 'why' you're feeling what you are, and then whether or not you're comfortable with your reactions." With that, he smiled with delight and sat down.

"Thank you, Bill," said Alison as she jumped to her feet. "We're going to take a quick, fifteen minute break, then come back to be assigned to our SAR discussion groups, and have our first small group meetings."

As Bill anticipated, the "values clarification" discussion continued during the break.

"Hi," Annette said softly as she stood over Dan. "May I sit with you?"

"Sure, Sister," he said.

"Please, it's Annette," she replied.

"Annette," he repeated with a half smile, and then turned back to look at the lake from his perch on the grassy hilltop.

"Are you okay, Dan?" she asked cautiously, reaching out and gently touching his shoulder.

"Me? Oh, sure. I'm fine. Why?" he asked.

"I don't know," she said. "Maybe it's *me* that's not okay, and I've come to get some help from you."

"What's up?" he asked.

"Sex with a priest. It makes me a little crazy. I'm sorry. Can I talk with you a bit about it?" she replied.

"Sure," he said. "Fire away."

"My cousin was very involved in the Boston ..." she hesitated, looking for the correct word.

"Hysterical witch hunt?" he offered.

"No, not witch hunt," she countered seriously. "Boston trials."

"Was he a priest or was he a so-called 'victim'?" he asked.

"Neither. She was a prosecutor," she explained.

"Ooooh," he said as he started pulling grass up in small handfuls. "So, Annette, how can I help you?"

"You said inside that you weren't molested, Dan. Help me understand how it can be that you, as a teenager, weren't molested by an adult male who had power and influence over you?" she asked. "You seem so at peace about the whole thing. Help me understand how, please. I really want to know."

"You're making all kinds of assumptions," he said.

"I am? Like what?" she asked.

"Like that he had power and influence over me," he replied.

"He didn't?" she asked.

"No. He was the son of a neighbor," Dan explained, turning his head briefly to make eye contact. "He was in his mid-twenties, and he used to visit his parents a lot. I was a horny sixteen-year-old who thought he was gorgeous. I flirted with him every time I got around him. He was really handsome, very athletic, and a nice guy. He used to jog through our neighborhood, and then around the track up at the high school. I'd run out and ask him if I could join him on the run. So, we'd run together. We'd get all hot and sweaty, and then we'd go for a swim. His folks had a pool, and I'd ask if I could come over to cool down afterwards. I'd horse around with him in the pool. I knew that he liked me but he was shy and I wasn't. I seduced *him*, Sister. He didn't seduce me. We had sex a few times, and it was great. It was mild stuff. Nothing heavy. Mutual masturbation. A little oral sex. Then he told me that he needed to break it off because he didn't think it was healthy for me to be spending so much time with him. I think he had fallen in love with me, and it freaked him out. He wanted me to spend more time with people my own age. So, Sister, I had sex with a priest, but I *wasn't* molested."

"Hmm," she sighed as she looked thoughtfully out over the mid-afternoon reflections on the hillside. "You're right. I *was* making assumptions. But Dan, a priest has so much power and influence. Even if he wasn't your pastor …"

"Pastor?" he exclaimed. "Sister, I'm not a Catholic."

"Well, there go those assumptions, huh?" she said. "But, Dan, help me out here, please. Don't you agree that a priest should never have sex with an adolescent over whom he has influence, either as a pastor or as a teacher? Don't you agree that regardless of the age of the young person, or the sexual orientation of the young person, or the 'horniness' and seductiveness of the young person, the priest who is the adult, and in a powerful position, is the one who has the responsibility to say 'no.'?"

"I think that *any* person who is in a position of influence over another is the one who has the responsibility to say 'no'," he answered. "I'm also saying that a lot of priests got railroaded in that whole 'pedophilia' scare, that a lot of the so-called 'victims' weren't victims at all, and that there's a big difference between an adult male having sex with a child, and an adult male having sex with a horny, teenage gay kid who won't take 'no' for an answer."

"Celibacy aside," she added.

"Celibacy?" he said. "Celibacy is a *Catholic* issue, not a civil issue. It has nothing to do with the priest scandal. Those priests didn't go to prison because of celibacy. That priest that was viciously beaten to death by his cell mate didn't die because he wasn't celibate. Or maybe he did. You Catholics have really been off the wall lately. "

"I'm sure it seems like that to a lot of people," she laughed. "And it often does to me too. Okay, Dan. Thanks. I need to think about this some more. This is a really difficult issue for me. I don't know if you've made it harder or easier, but I'm grateful that you took the time to talk"

"My pleasure, Sister," he said, and then corrected himself, "Annette. Thanks for asking. Really. I respect that."

As Annette got up, brushed off the bottom of her khaki shorts, and headed toward the door to Ridings, she heard Carol calling her from the sidewalk.

"Hi Carol," she replied. "What's up?"

"Can I talk with you for a quick second in private?" Carol asked.

"I'm all ears," Annette said as she walked down the hill a bit and over to the side. "What can I do for you?"

"Would you be willing to switch rooms with someone?" Carol asked. "It sometimes happens that I miss the mark in putting people together. You're with Tonya, and I was wondering if I could switch you into a room with Betty, and have Leona move in with Tonya? But before you say 'yes,' I need to explain my reasons."

"There's no need," assured Annette with a broad smile. "I'll miss my roommate Tonya, but if it's okay with her, and if it's okay with Betty, I'd be happy to switch. Have you spoken yet with Tonya?"

"Yes, I did a few minutes ago," said Carol. "And she said that she'd miss you too. But, Annette, before we make the switch, I want to talk with you …"

"About Betty being a transsexual?" Annette asked.

"Yes, but how did you know?" Carol said with some surprise.

"She said on the first day that there had been a major shift in the course of her life. It started me thinking. There were a few other clues. Anyway, it's not an issue for me. I have a dear friend who is transsexual back at home," Annette said. "And, Carol, I also know that Betty is a lesbian. She doesn't hide that. I'm very comfortable with both."

"Thank you so much," Carol said over the sound of the ringing bell. "I'll tell Betty and Leona. You're the best," she whispered as she gave Annette a big hug.

Chapter Fourteen

The SAR Group Forms

By the time it came to announcing my list of participants, everyone already knew who was in my group.

"Last, but certainly not least," I said as I rose at Alison's request, "the following people are in my SAR group: Kevin Brooks, Margaret Johansson, Leona Mills, Dom Paluzzi, Beatrice Ramos, Maggie Sutherland, Charlie Tatewell, and Wendy Taylor. We'll be meeting in the living room of Higley, which is the staff dorm."

"Thank you, Brian," Alison said with a nod. "Now, everyone should be in a group. Is there anyone whose name was not called? Good. Okay then. You all know the locations of your SAR group meetings. Please go there now. You'll be in session until 4:30."

The staff members then stood, and headed toward the door, signaling that it was time to move. All of us were aware that there were participants who were pleased, and others who were disappointed, with their assignments to small group. I noticed, for instance, that Maggie gave George the pulled fist sign of victory. Leona, on the other hand, sighed deeply when her name was called.

Wendy and Beatrice were the last to arrive in the living room in Higley. They entered the door laughing and with cold drinks.

"Oops! Sorry," Wendy said as she saw that we were all seated and waiting for them. "I didn't know that you were already here. Sorry." She and Beatrice quickly took the two open seats in the circle.

"That's okay," I said. "Welcome everyone. I really look forward to a great week together. I hope that you'll find this room to be a safe and comfortable space. It's my favorite place at Thornfield to meet. A lot of growth has happened in this room. I hope that's your experience here too. Incidentally, a quick housekeeping note, the bathrooms are right through those swinging doors. Yes, Maggie?"

"Were you in this same room last year?" she asked. "I mean, did your SAR group meet here?"

"Yes, I think we were," I said with a smile, and a nod that acknowledged my understanding of why it was important to her.

"I know that you all received in the mail Bill Stayton's article about the goals of the SAR," I continued, looking around the room at the others, "and that you have in your participant packet the 'SAR Goals and Group Norms.' Let me start, though, by briefly saying that the goal of the SAR is to enable us to reflect upon our sexual attitudes, values, and feelings, and to become more aware and accepting of the sexual attitudes and values of others. We're going to meet in this room two or three times a day from now until the end of the week to talk about the feelings and insights that are generated in us by the films and presentations. In order to do so comfortably, we all need to trust that we can speak without being put down for our thoughts, and we need to believe that everything we say here stays here. Please don't share with your roommates, colleagues, or new friends anything specific about what we're doing here, nor allow them to talk with you about what's happening in their groups.

"Assignment to the individual SAR groups is random, but care is taken to assure that couples, as well as people who work together, are separated. If you feel that you won't be able to be honest with your feelings because of your relationship with another participant in this room, please speak to me immediately after this session.

"Okay, in a minute we're going to go around the room, learn a little bit more about one another, and check in on how we're feeling, but let me first establish a couple of group norms. First, we will *not* start a session until everyone is here. So, please, be here on time. If, for any reason, you feel that you can't make a session, or that you're going to be late, you need to come and speak with me in advance. There is an expectation of commitment on all of our parts to the entire process. Secondly, everyone is expected to participate but *you're* responsible for choosing what, when, and how much of yourselves you want to share. My job is to keep the discussions focused, and to keep us all out of our heads, meaning that we'll be talking about our *feelings*, and not about our thoughts. We'll be talking about our *lives*, and not about our work.

"I think you'll find that the small group discussion is the richest experience of your week," I continued. "This isn't a therapy group. I'm not a therapist. Nevertheless, it provides us all a rich opportunity for personal growth. So, have fun. Be respectful. Have a good sense of humor. And, as you'll hear us say repeatedly, 'trust the process.' Any questions? Yes, Charlie?"

"I've never done anything like this before. Well, I guess I did a men's discussion group once, but I was wondering if anyone besides Brian has been through a SAR before?" he asked.

"Have any of you been through a SAR before?" I repeated to the group.

Leona and Kevin were the only ones to raise their hands.

"Looks like you're in the majority, Charlie," I said. "But, tell us how you're feeling about beginning the SAR process? Do you mind starting? Tell us all a little bit about yourself that you haven't already shared in the large group, and then talk a bit about your feelings right at this moment."

"Oh sure, pick on me because I opened my mouth," he said with a big smile.

"You don't have to start," I offered.

"No, I'm fine," he said. "Can I talk about my work?"

"Sure," I replied, "but only in this first go around."

"Okay. My name is Charlie Tatewell. As I said in the large group yesterday – gosh, have we only been here one day? Yikes. Well, anyway, I'm a Methodist minister. My wife, Cindy, and I live in Oklahoma City with our two sons, who are both in their late teens. Lyle is nineteen, and Kevin is seventeen. I'm not from Oklahoma City originally. I was born in Lockport, Illinois. Cindy and I met at the University of Chicago, just prior to me going into the seminary. We moved to Oklahoma City when the boys were young. It was quite an adjustment for all of us. Cindy's mother moved in with us shortly after we arrived because her husband, who was Cindy's stepfather, had just died of emphysema, which is a really awful way to die. Anyway, …"

"Charlie?" I interrupted.

"Yes? Am I doing it wrong?" he asked with a nervous look.

"No, not at all," I said. "But this first time around, let's just say a few words about ourselves. There will be lots of opportunities for us to talk at length about our journeys. I want to make sure that everyone gets a chance to speak."

"Oh, right. Sorry. Well anyway," he continued, "Cindy and I moved to Oklahoma City about fifteen years ago. I'm the pastor of a small church there. We have about two hundred members. It's a young church. Young not because the people who come are young, but because it's a fairly new congregation. The members are older, and a bit conservative in their theology. I don't know if you know much about Oklahoma City, but it can be very conservative."

"Yes, it can be," I interrupted. "I've done some work there. So, Charlie, say a word or two if you would about how you're *feeling* right this minute."

"My feelings. Okay," he said with a thoughtful sigh. "I guess I'm feeling a little anxious. As I said, I participated in a men's discussion group a few years ago, but we met only once a week, and we obviously weren't with each other all day like we are here. So, that was different. But I'd say, hmm, how am I feeling?"

"So, a little anxious, huh?" I said. "That's really normal. Thanks, Charlie. Okay, who's willing to go next? Just a word or two about yourself, and what you're feeling."

"I'll go next," Margaret offered.

"Good, Margaret. Thank you," I said.

"I'm Margaret Johansson. As you may recall, I'm a retired United Church of Christ minister from Indianapolis. I'm sixty-nine years old. My husband and I have been married for forty-six years. I'm still feeling a little anxious, but less so than I did yesterday when I arrived. How's that?" she asked.

"That's great," I said. "And if I remember correctly, you've just taken over the youth group in your church, and you're a practitioner of Buddhist meditation."

"You saw me on the lawn this morning," she said with a nod.

"Yes, and yesterday too. I'd love to sit with you at some point during the week," I said, to which she raised her hands in the prayer position, and bowed slightly with a warm smile.

"So, who's next?" I asked.

"Okay, I'll go," said Maggie, taking a deep breath. "I'm Maggie Sutherland, and I'm feeling a little freaked out knowing that my husband was sitting in one of these chairs at the same time last year. He came home from here and told me that he's 'gay.' I came here this year hoping to find out what happened to him. I'm really glad that I got assigned to Brian's group. I was hoping it would happen. You were Barry's SAR group leader."

"Yes, I was," I nodded and smiled at Maggie and at Margaret, who had reached over to squeeze Maggie's arm. "I'm glad that you got assigned to this group too, Maggie. Was there anything more you wanted to share with the others at this time?"

"No, that's enough for now," she said.

After a few seconds of silence, I continued. "Dom, we don't have to go in order, but we seem to be. Are you ready to go next?"

"Sure," he said, sitting up in his chair. "I'm Dominic Paluzzi. My friends call me Dom. As I said yesterday, I'm a football coach in Dayton, Ohio. I've been assigned to teach a class in family life to juniors and seniors. I'm hoping to get a lot out of my workshop at the end of the week with Carol and Pam. I'm not much of a talker, unless I get mad, which unfortunately has already happened a couple of times here already," he laughed. "Anyhow, I've never done anything like this small group meeting. If I don't say much it's not because I'm not listening or not interested."

"Dom, did you say you've gotten angry a couple of times already in this group?" Maggie asked a bit shocked.

"No. No," he said nervously. "I've gotten mad a couple of times since I arrived at Thornfield. But that's about something else. No. I haven't felt *any* anger in this group."

"Would you mind telling us what you've gotten angry about since you arrived?" asked Leona. "It wasn't the song was it? Or your roommate?"

"I, uh, I'd rather not say," he said. "Do I have to talk about that?" he asked me.

"You don't have to talk about anything you don't want to talk about," I assured him. "None of you do. But you do hate the song, don't you?" I said like a courtroom attorney.

"Actually, I kind of like the song," he laughed. "I've got a lousy voice, so I mumble, but I like it."

"Good," I sighed with feigned relief. "Me too. So, Leona. You're next. How about you? What are you feeling?"

"I'll pass," she said with a big smile.

"Okay," I said. "We'll come back to you. Kevin?"

"Hi everyone," he said with a bit of a shaky voice, straightening up in his chair, and leaning back. "I'm Kevin Brooks. This is my third or fourth SAR group, I guess. I've been coming here for a couple of years. I learn something new every time I come. Like, Dom, I don't say much. I'm really shy. But, I'm feeling fine, and I'm glad to be in Brian's group."

"Thanks, Kevin," I replied. "I'm glad to have you in our group. And he knows not to worry about being shy with me," I said to the other participants. "He knows I'll get him talking." To which he laughed.

"Well, I think I'm next," said Wendy. "Again, I'm sorry for being late. I promise to be on time from now on."

"Please, don't apologize," I said. "But, tell us something about yourself, Wendy, and about how you're feeling."

"I'm feeling *great!*" she said enthusiastically. "I'm glad to be out of Cleveland. I'm glad to be away from work. I look forward to a great week. And I'm glad to be in this group!"

"That's great," I responded with equal enthusiasm. "Is there anything more you'd like to tell us about yourself?"

"I'm a lesbian. I'm single. And Dom and I want to know when you're running tomorrow," she answered.

"Seven a.m.," I said with a wink. "But, how about if we talk more about that after this session? And Beatrice, that leaves you, and Leona, of course."

"My name is Beatrice Ramos," the pretty young woman said as she looked around the room and smiled at each of the other participants. "I live in Philadelphia at home with my parents. I have a younger sister and a younger brother. I'm in the graduate program in human sexuality at Widener University. Bill Stayton encouraged me to come to Thornfield. I either want to teach sexuality or be a sex counselor. I've never done a SAR. I'm not shy but I'm afraid that I won't have much to say because my life is pretty dull."

"Dull can be good," I said smiling. "Thank you, Beatrice. And now, Leona, how about you?"

"You first," she said.

"Okay," I said. "My name is Brian Robert Michael McNaught ..."

"You remember your Confirmation name?" Dom asked with delighted surprise.

"Of course I do," I replied proudly, and then continued. "I'm the middle child of seven Irish Catholics, and the product of sixteen years of parochial education. My life partner and spouse's name is Ray. You know from earlier introductions what I do for a living. But, I too am feeling a little anxious at this moment because I want very much to be the best group facilitator that I can be. I want to serve you well, but I also know that I can't do this job alone. I'd really like your help. I invite each of you to act as co-facilitators in this group. Please help one another and me stay focused on our feelings. That will be our key to success this week, and we will get out of these sessions what we put into them. And now, without further ado, I give you Leona Mills."

"Okay. Okay," she said with a sigh of resignation and a bright smile. "I was just wanting to see if I really could pass, and whether you were going to share anything personal about yourself. I'm Leona Mills. I've worked for the past year in pregnancy prevention for Planned Parenthood in Washington, D.C. My director sent me to Thornfield. She told me that I would really 'profit from the experience' in my work. I thought, 'Okay.' So, I came here thinking that I was going to some fancy, professional conference center. To say the least, I was *shocked* to arrive and find that I had to make my own bed, *and* that I had to share a room! Then I find out that my roommate is a ... Well, anyway, let's just say that this is *not* what I expected. I've been through a SAR before but it was just a weekend thing they did without any films. It happened right after I arrived. It kind of freaked me out, but I learned some things that were helpful."

"And how are you feeling?" I asked.

"I'm feeling like I have a couple more things to say about myself, but it won't be my consummation name, or whatever it was," she said with a bob of her head and a quick smile, and then turned her back to me, and spoke to the others. "I am *not* shy, and getting me to talk won't be an issue, but I'm not sure how I'm feeling. A piece of me wants to head back to DC after dinner, and then another piece of me wants to stay and see what it's all about."

"I hope you decide to stay," Margaret said. "I like your energy, Leona, and I'm interested in your perspective."

"Me too," said Maggie.

"We all hope you commit yourself to the process, Leona," I said with an affirming nod. "Now, we've got about twenty minutes to go before your break, and in that time I'd like to start talking about the issues of ignorance, secrecy, and trauma. But before we do, I'm going to tell you briefly about a homework assignment that I'd like us all to do.

"Please give some thought in the next day or so to your life's journey toward sexual health. I want you to focus on four or five significant events in your life that have impacted, positively or negatively, your sense of yourself as a sexual person. And when you think of yourself as a sexual person, please use all of the circles of Sexual Beingness that Pam described earlier – sensuality, intimacy, sexual identity, sexual health and reproduction, and sexualization. What has happened in your life that you see as being important moments in your developing sense of self? Now, once you have identified four or five events, I'd like you to take a large sheet of paper from the pad over there, and use whatever colored markers you prefer, and then illustrate your journey, including those events that you feel comfortable sharing with the group.

"By 'illustrate,' I mean use stick figures or symbols or elaborate drawings, whatever suits you," I continued. "At some point this week, we each will be invited to share the illustration of the journey with the group. Each person will be given a half-an-hour to themselves to speak. Remember, don't put anything on the paper that you don't want to share. Also, know that you can pass. This assignment is merely an aid to help you think about your sexual feelings and values, and the life that you have lived, and would *like* to live. And we'll use these maps in group only if the discussions we're having about the topics of the SAR run out of steam. I think you'll love the exercise. Do you have any questions?"

Chapter Fifteen

Prayer in the Woods

A chipmunk scurried across the altar in the woods behind Ridings, dodging, as it went, a wicker basket and the large vase of wildflowers that had been borrowed for the event. Flaming coals in the grill, next to the tree-trunk-and-plank altar, filled the air with the smell of charcoal starter fluid. As George stood with his eyes closed in silent prayer before the small group of staff and participants that had assembled, he was aware of the sound of many voices coming up from the direction of the beach. After a few moments, he opened his eyes, smiled, and began.

"Friends, we come together this week to understand, and to celebrate our sexuality, and that of each other. Many of us do so as people of faith. As such, we often bear horrible wounds from our struggle to harmonize our sexuality and our religious beliefs. With frustration, we ask for ourselves, and for the multitudes who can't comfortably bring themselves to this table, 'How did we get to this place?'

"We recall with ecstasy the great Song of Songs," he said, reaching for his Bible, "in which we are told, 'My lover is radiant and ruddy, he stands out among thousands. His head is pure gold, his locks are palm fronds, black as the ravens. His eyes are like doves beside running waters … His arms are rods of gold … His body is a work of ivory … His legs are columns of marble … His mouth is sweetness itself … My lover has come down to his garden, to the beds of spice, to browse in the garden, and to gather lilies. My lover belongs to me and I to him.'

"So says the Word of God. And yet, the word of man tells us a different story. The poet William Blake ventured to the same garden and wrote, 'So I turned to the Garden of Love, That so many sweet flowers bore. And I saw it was filled with graves, And tombstones where flowers should be; And priests with black gowns were walking their rounds, And binding with briars my joys and desires.'

"How did we get to this place?" he asked again, and then, closing his eyes, and lifting his arms up, he said, "Let us pray.

"God, as we know you and name you, we ask you to be with and bless us as we gather this week to take important steps toward our sexual/ spiritual health. We ask you to guide the work of the staff as they lead us on this journey. We ask that you fill us all with your Spirit and its gifts of wisdom, understanding, and fortitude, so that we might each celebrate our bodies as perfect reflections of you, and courageously confront those attitudes that separate us from ourselves and from others. We thank you, God, for our senses and for our emotions. We especially thank you for our sexuality, for it too allows us to know you, and to participate in you. As we gather together this week, we affirm as good the multiple expressions of sexuality that reflect love, which is to say, reflect you."

Opening his eyes again, and dropping his arms to his sides, George smiled warmly as he looked around at the circle. "Join hands with me for a moment, won't you?" he asked as he reached his left hand out to Maggie and his right to Margaret. The others did the same.

"We begin this sexual/spiritual trek by offering up to you, with hope and compassion, those things which we have identified as impediments to the success of our journeys," he said. "It is with hope that we sacrifice what is at the end of our ropes because we seek to be free of all roadblocks to our growth and sexual health. But it is also with compassion, as we know that we can never fully be free from that which binds us, only less attached. We also know that we ourselves, in some manner, are what is at the end of another's rope. Accept the burning of these words as an indication of our desire to free ourselves and others through you."

Letting go of both Maggie and Margaret's hands, George stepped over to the wicker basket, picked it up, and walked to the side of the grill. There he lifted the basket with both hands to the tree tops, lowered it to his waist, and proceeded to throw into the flaming coals the folded pieces of paper that had been gathered from the participants on the first day. They burned quickly and smoked heavily.

Stepping back into the circle, and taking back into his hands those of Maggie and Margaret, George said, "We now, God, offer our individual petitions to you as a community of brothers and sisters, black, brown, and white, gay, straight, and bisexual, male, female, and transgender, adherents of theology A, B, and C, who acknowledge and celebrate by our presence your role in our lives." And then to the others he added, "Please, let this be a time for quiet personal reflection, and then let's make known our individual petitions."

For several minutes, the small group stood in silence, their hands now freed and hanging at their sides. Most kept their eyes closed. Bill was the first to speak.

"I'm *so* glad that we're doing this," he said enthusiastically but with great seriousness, "because, for me, there is such an intimate link between my sexuality and my spirituality. They just can't be separated. How I feel about myself, about my body, about my wife Kathy, about my orgasms is how I feel about God. This is such a holy week for me because it is a time of celebrating the very things which make me human, which are the very same things which make me divine."

Bill smiled as he looked around the group in silence. As his eyes began to tear, he looked to the ground, and wiped them with his arm. Thomas smiled back with tear-filled eyes of his own. "It can be very lonely, can't it?" he whispered.

"And Jesus wept," Annette said nodding at the two of them. "The incarnated life of Jesus as a man who had beloved friends over whom he cried, who ate and drank, and saw fit to have his first miracle be the turning of water into wine for the sake of a celebration, who defended and befriended Mary Magdalene, who comforted the afflicted, and charged us to do the same, that is the clearest and most pressing case I have for embracing the physical as divine. May my vow of chastity always be seen by me and by others not as a repudiation of the sexual, but as an affirmation of it." With that, she smiled warmly at the others, one by one, and then gazed at the ground.

Joe looked up toward the sky with a smile of contentment on his serene face. He closed his eyes, and breathed in deeply the warm, pine needle and smoke-scented air. Upon lowering his eyes, he paused, and then said softly, "I stand in awe of that which dares to be fully human, and in sadness for the many times that I have feared to be. I'm very grateful to have this moment with each of you, and I hope that I will have the courage to respond with vigor to the opportunities that are provided me this week to be honest."

Again, it was silent for a brief period before the next person spoke.

"Saint Iraneus of Lyon once said that 'The glory of God is man - and I'd add *woman* - fully alive," said Carla a bit nervously but with a laugh, "and I'll drink to that."

"Me too," added Maggie. "I ask God to bless us all as we come here to find what we're looking for."

George then looked with a smile and raised eyebrows of encouragement to those members of the group who had not spoken.

Thomas responded. "My folded piece of paper identified my HIV status as what was at the end of my rope. As I watched the smoke go up, it occurred to me that it's also the bridge that I'm crossing, or need to cross, to get me to a life that is more authentic. We've only known each other for a day but I somehow feel safe in your company, and I'm *very* grateful to have this opportunity to explore my sexuality and spirituality with you."

Catherine looked over at Thomas, nodded, but remained silent.

Sensing after a few moments that there were no further petitions to be offered, George said, "Again, God, we thank you for the gift of our sexuality, and for your presence in it. We ask that all members of our community, both present and not present for this simple gathering, might this week know true liberation from the effects of ignorance, secrecy, and trauma, and experience the joy of a healthy sexuality." Turning to the others, he said, "Thank you for joining me for this."

"Thank you for suggesting it," said Margaret.

"Yes, thanks," added Thomas. "It was good. See you at dinner."

As the others moved slowly and reflectively away in a variety of directions, George said to Maggie, "There's probably still time for a quick swim. I'll walk down with you if you'd like."

"No, thanks, I think I'll go to my room and lay down for a few minutes," she replied, and then added with a look of concern, "Are you okay? You look a little down."

"I'm not down," he assured her. "I'm just a little deep in thought, I think. I'm in such awe of people who are able to embrace the sexual as the spiritual."

"And you can't?" she asked incredulously. "Your prayers sure sounded as if you can."

"Thanks. It all makes sense up here," he said pointing to his head, "but I haven't gotten it all together down here," he added, pointing to his heart.

"And you think *they* all have it worked out?" Maggie asked, nodding her head in the direction of the departing group. "You don't give yourself enough credit."

"Maybe so," he said, deflecting her compliment. "See you at dinner?"

"Wouldn't miss it," she said as she stepped forward to give him a hug.

A short distance from the site of the service, Peter was sitting alone on the lawn, reading a book.

"What are you reading?" Catherine asked as she approached from behind.

"Nothing special," he said as he turned the book over face down on the grass. "How was the service?"

"It was okay," she replied with a shrug and a look of indifference. "It wasn't as Christ-centered as I'd hoped it would be, but it was fine. You could have been there without feeling awkward. I missed seeing you there. Are you going to the dinner meeting?"

"I wasn't planning on it," he said with a grin. "And you?"

Chapter Sixteen

The Dinner Meeting

"Are you *sure* that allies are welcome at the meeting?" Charlie asked over the food serving counter as he helped himself to some more broccoli.

"Absolutely," said Thomas as he eyed the offerings of haddock, and vegetable lasagna. "The more the merrier."

"You're *sure*," Charlie persisted. "I came here to learn more about gay issues, so I'd love to come, but I don't want to make anyone feel uncomfortable."

"Why don't you just come and listen, then?" Thomas replied kindly. "Don't ask questions about homosexuality. It's not that kind of a meeting. It's just a social get-together so that we can all connect. But come and be a part of the group."

"I think I might, if it's okay," said Charlie.

By the time Charlie arrived on the patio of Higley, having stopped to talk briefly with Tonya at the juice bar, the two picnic tables that had been joined were nearly filled. Wendy, Gina, and Lisa were sitting together on one side of the first table, next to George, Maggie, and Lloyd. Across from them were Dan, Carla, Kevin, me, and Thomas.

Behind Charlie, Carol and Betty were walking quickly with their trays. "Got room for a couple more?" Carol asked.

"Always," replied Thomas. "Will someone please give me a hand with another table?" he asked.

"Sure," I said as I rose and helped lift a third table to join the others.

"I should have called in a reservation," Carol laughed as she headed to the spot next to Lloyd. "Come on, Charlie, sit across from me," she invited.

"If you're sure it's okay," said Charlie.

"Why wouldn't it be?" asked Betty, sitting next to Thomas.

"No reason. I'm just blabbering," Charlie replied nervously.

"Wow! What a great looking table," Thomas said in a voice that could be heard by all as he stood and eyed the diners. "I'm glad that we could do this. I don't have an agenda other than giving us a chance to come together as a group, and deciding if we'd like to do anything this week beyond just having dinner together tonight."

"What do you have in mind?" Dan asked in a seductive voice, to the appreciative claps and exaggerated gasps of shock from others.

"Well, let's just see what comes up?" Thomas responded playfully, and then quickly looked embarrassed by the reply.

"Ooh, baby!" Lloyd added.

"You guys are such pigs," Gina said with a laugh.

"Okay. Okay," pleaded Thomas. "Let's get serious."

"I *am* serious," joked Dan.

"Let's just go around the table," Thomas continued, ignoring the remark, "and introduce ourselves, maybe say something about ourselves, and say what, if anything, you'd like to do as a group this week."

"I'd like to have Carla dress Dan up," said Betty from her end of the table.

Laughter and strong applause, particularly from the women, greeted her suggestion.

"I'd be delighted," cooed Carla, "but I'm afraid that with all of his big muscles he'd ruin my outfits. Now, make-up I can do. How about it, Dan? Do you want to look pretty?"

"He's already pretty," mumbled Kevin to himself.

"Ooh, Kevin here says that you're *already* pretty," Carla announced playfully to Kevin's complete embarrassment, and to Dan's amusement.

"Way to go, Kevin," encouraged George, to his continued horror.

"How about an informal discussion group that meets a couple of times during the week?" I suggested, hoping to change the subject, to which Kevin shot back a quick smile of appreciation.

"That would be cool," replied Gina, "but I'd kind of like to have a meal or two just with other lesbians. You guys don't mind, right?"

"Not if you don't mind the guys meeting by themselves sometime," replied Lloyd.

"Like at night, in the woods?" Wendy offered with a big grin.

"Yea, we'll beat drums, and do manly things," said Dan with a wink at Kevin.

"Ooh, I might just slip back into butch attire for that one," laughed Carla, "but, then again, forget it. A bunch of guys dancing around a fire beating their chests sounds boring."

"Not to me," said Lloyd enthusiastically.

"I'd also like to have a meeting of trannies, if anyone is game," said Carla without looking in any particular direction.

"I'll be glad to meet with you," Betty replied with a strong voice. "Okay. Announcement to those of you to whom I haven't talked," she continued as she stood. "I'm Betty. I'm a lesbian *and* a transsexual."

"Hi Betty," several at the table replied with grins in traditional Twelve Step manner.

"Nice going, Betty," Carol said from across the table.

"And I'm Carol," she continued in a louder voice as she stood. "I'm a lesbian *and* the proud mother of a beautiful daughter named Kerrigan."

"I'm Lloyd. I'm gay," Lloyd popped up in response.

"I'm Maggie, and I'm married to a man who says he's gay," Maggie said as she rose. "I'm also an ally."

"I'm George. I'm glad to be gay," George said, giving Maggie's hand a gentle squeeze.

"I'm Lisa, and I'm questioning exactly *where* I fit in," Lisa said a bit nervously as she stayed seated.

"I'm Gina, and I'm not questioning. I'm very much a lesbian," Gina said standing.

"I'm Wendy, and I'm a lesbian," Wendy said smiling as she waved at the others down the table.

"I'm Dan, and I'm queer," Dan said seated.

"A pretty queer," George added, nodding to Kevin, who blushed and looked down at the table.

"I'm Carla," she said standing, and turning her smiling head in both directions. "And I'm a pretty cross dresser."

Applause from all members of the group affirmed her.

Waving and smiling shyly, Kevin half stood and said, "I'm Kevin, and I'm gay."

"Yea, Kevin," I cheered, then added, "I'm Brian. I'm gay, and it feels *great* to be at this table."

"I'm Thomas. I'm gay, and I too am a proud father," Thomas said rising from his seat with a gentle smile.

Betty, who had already introduced herself, turned to Charlie.

"Hi everyone," he said with a big wave, and a nervous smile as he stayed seated. "I'm Charlie, and I'm here to learn. I'm an ally."

"Welcome, Charlie," Carol and I said in unison.

"Let's dress Charlie up!" Carla said to Betty with excitement.

"Yes, we'll do it for the celebration!" exclaimed Betty with a mischievous grin.

"No, I don't think so," said Charlie laughing.

"Oh, but you'd be so pretty," teased Carla.

"You guys are awful," said Maggie with feigned disbelief.

"No, it's fine," Charlie assured her. "It makes me feel welcome."

"Good for you, Charlie," George said.

"Speaking of the celebration," Carol piped in, "you all may want to do something as a group."

"Like what?" Gina asked.

"Like anything," Carol replied. "A song, a skit, some readings. Why don't you check out the photo albums in the lobby to see what people have done in the past?"

"Does anyone want dessert?" Kevin asked as he stood with his tray. "I'm going up, and I'm glad to bring some extras back."

"What's for dessert again?" asked Wendy.

"Chocolate éclairs," George replied.

"Sure, bring a whole tray," Dan said.

"Okay, great," Kevin answered him as they made eye contact and each smiled.

Individual conversations began around the three tables as Kevin excitedly headed to the dining room.

"It sounds as if you're having a lot of fun down there," Martha said from a picnic table outside of Huntington where she, Beverly, and Leona were having coffee.

"Yea, it's great," replied Kevin with an appreciative smile.

"Boy, get over here," Leona said with a summoning gesture and big grin, to which he complied.

"It's none of my business, but is *everyone* at that meeting gay?" she asked.

"Not everyone," he answered. "Some are allies."

"So, Kevin, tell me the truth, you cute thing. What are *you*?" she asked.

"I'm gay," he answered seriously.

"Oh, Kevin, don't tell me that," Leona said with furrowed brow, and shaking head. "What a waste!"

Chapter Seventeen

Body Image

"It's a hot summer day, and we're going to take an imaginary trip to a beach," I explained to the participants who had gathered in the downstairs room of Ridings for the evening session on Body Image.

"When we arrive, we see that the beach is crowded. Please take a moment and reflect on what feelings come up for you about this trip to the beach. What preoccupies your thoughts? In a minute, I'd like those of you who think you would immediately strip down to your bathing suit to gather as a group in that corner of the room," I said pointing to the area near the door that led to the back patio and picnic tables. "I'd like those of you who would first wait to see how your bodies compared to the others on the beach before you disrobed to meet as a group over by the big screen TV, and those of you who would keep your outer garments on for the entire time at the beach to meet as a group over by the elevator."

"Is this a gay beach or a straight beach?" Lloyd asked.

"Good question," I replied. "Choose the scenario that's most challenging for you with regard to your body image."

"What about those of us who wouldn't go to any beach in the first place?" asked Catherine.

"Everyone's free to pass on any exercise," I said smiling, "but if you'd like to participate, pretend that your friends have coaxed you to come. What would you do? Now, before you move into groups, this is what I'd like you to do once you get together. First, ask yourself about how you feel being in the group that you're in. Second, ask yourself if you've *always* been in this group, and, if not, what were the circumstances that prompted you to move from one group to another? And, finally, talk with each other about why you are where you are. Remember, this is about you and where *you* feel most comfortable, not about where you think someone else belongs. Ready? Okay, please move into your group."

With some sighs, but mostly with shrugs of acceptance, the participants moved into one of the three groups, and after a moment of silence the room was filled with the buzz of conversation. Five minutes later, Carol, who was co-facilitating the session with me, called the room to order.

"So, what was that like?" she asked.

"Kind of hard," Tonya offered. "I was self-conscious about where I was heading. I was thinking maybe others in the group didn't think I should feel so comfortable about going to Group One."

Affirming laughter greeted her observation.

"I was a little afraid that because of my size the folks in Group One would think that I didn't belong," said Marjorie, "or that the folks in Group Three might feel betrayed in some way, but you said it was about what we think, and not what others think about us, and I'll be damned if I'm going to cover up at the beach for one second longer than I have to."

Applause erupted from several people in Group One.

"Anyone else?" Carol asked.

"At first I found myself looking around to see where other people were going just to see where *I* belonged," Beatrice said. "And I knew that was nuts, so I moved to where I felt most comfortable, which was here in Group Two. I'd love to say that I'm comfortable with my body, but I'm just not."

"Honey, if I had *your* body, I'd be showing it off *all* of the time," exclaimed Carla from Group One. "I'm here not because it's my *body* that I want to show off. I'm here because I'd be dying to show off the gorgeous *swimsuit* ensemble that I had put together."

"I used to worry about not having a more muscular body," Ben said from his wheelchair in Group One after the applause and laughter had subsided, "but losing the use of my legs changed that. Priorities changed."

"So, some of you have been in different groups than you are now," Carol said. "Ben said that losing the use of his legs changed his perspective. What else can change one's perspective?"

"Gaining weight," offered George from his place in Group Three.

"Losing weight," countered Lisa in Group Two.

"Deciding you don't give a damn anymore," said Margaret from Group One. "Weight or wrinkles shouldn't matter. Or maybe, I should say that they don't now matter to me."

"Did anyone notice anything about the make-up of the groups?" Carol asked.

"Yea," Lloyd replied. "The straight men and the lesbians were mostly in Group One. The gay men and straight women were mostly in Groups Two and Three."

"Surprise. Surprise," said George.

"It's an interesting observation," Carol said, looking at her watch, and then nodding to me, "and one that we should talk about again at another time."

"That's good," I said in affirmation of the process. "Good work. Thank you. Let's now go back to our seats, and we'll continue to explore this issue."

After the participants had returned to their seats, Bill moved to the back of the table containing the video equipment, Carol walked over to the light switches, and I continued to set the scene for the viewing of the first films.

"When Pam guided us through the five circles of Sexual Beingness and discussed 'body image'," I said, "we brain-stormed about the different issues of concern to society, from white teeth to muscle tone. We also talked about how our attitudes toward our genitalia can impact our ability to celebrate our sexuality, and to give ourselves to others. These first films help us explore our feelings about genitals, ours and those of others."

With the lights turned off, and the speakers filling the room with the sound of orchestra members tuning their instruments, the extra-large video screen was consumed with the image of a chorus line of naked women of all shapes, colors, and sizes. *Grand Opening* was the first film, and it provided an intimate, playful, and exhaustive look at female genitalia in its multiple manifestations and uses. With the music shifting back and forth from classical to show tunes, we first learned all of the slang and the proper terminology for the vulva, the vagina, and their components. We watched as beautiful photographs of orchids and iris, and cut melons and peaches, morphed into labias. "I Feel Pretty," from the musical *West Side Story* accompanied photographs of pubic hair in curlers or adorned with tiny flowers. A fast-paced tune set the tone for a presentation on masturbation with a vibrator. We then followed the course of menstruation, with many people laughing at the silly lyrics to the background music. Finally, with the majestic and powerful "Hallelujah Chorus," the participants watched the birth of a baby girl, and moaned in appreciation of the close-up of the infant's vulva, and the words "The Beginning."

With only a moment's pause, the music shifted and the second film began with an intimate look at male genitalia and its uses. Once again, a variety of sizes, shapes, cuts, and colors were presented with thematic music that underscored both the power of the phallic symbol in history, and the importance placed on size. Several people laughed as a "Peter Meter" was introduced by men on the screen to measure their prowess. The lamenting song in the background was entitled the "One Inch Blues." Penises were also presented playfully in this film, entitled *Exhibition*, as were the testicles and scrotum. Loud ringing church bells provided the music when there were close-ups of a man's balls. "Reveille" accompanied the presentation of penises becoming erect, "The Flight of the Bumble Bee" made clear the often frenzied nature of male masturbation, and "Taps" prompted laughter for the refractory period.

The "dirty" movies had begun, and though the participants began the process with breath-held silence, most of them were laughing and sighing with relief that it hadn't been as scary or as provocative as they had anticipated.

"So, how was that for you?" I asked as Pam turned on the overhead florescent lights and Carol stepped forward to join me.

"I was grateful for the variety of shapes and sizes," Marjorie said. "The bodies weren't all perfect by the culture's standards."

"Good. Anyone else?" I asked.

"They were funny," said Tonya. "I didn't think I'd be laughing, but I was glad to be able to."

"I liked all of the images that were presented for the vulvas," said Lisa a bit nervously. "I hadn't seen anything like that before."

"I hadn't seen female genitals before," Dan said.

"Good for you, Dan," I replied. "When I saw these films for the first time, I had never seen female genitals before either."

"Hadn't you ever seen a *Hustler*?" Curtis asked in amazement from the back of the room.

"No, my dad bought *Playboy*," I answered. "Going back to Bill's comments about ignorance, secrecy, and trauma, I was thrilled to be able to see female genitals for the first time in the safety of this group, and I compliment Dan on acknowledging that he had never seen them before either. Did anyone else have a reaction they wanted to share?"

"What was that scene where there was a string coming out the lady's vagina?" asked Lloyd.

"Great question, Lloyd," Carol said with a big smile and nod of affirmation. "That string was attached to a tampon that is inserted into the vagina to internally catch menstrual flow. The string allows the woman to remove the tampon. Does that make sense?"

"Yea, thanks," he said.

"I'm proud of you for asking. One year … Can I tell this story?" Carol asked, turning to me.

"Sure, go ahead," I said.

"One year, Brian asked me," she said.

"In seeming confidence," I laughed.

"Whether a woman has to take out a tampon to pee," Carol continued. "It was a *great* question! And the answer is 'no,' the urethra is not in the vagina. But how can we learn if we don't ask questions?"

"So, please don't be embarrassed to ask questions this week or to acknowledge that you didn't know something," I added. "We're now going to move forward on our journey of looking at our sense of our bodies, and at what stops us from fully accepting them. Ben told us earlier that his sense of self changed after he lost the use of his legs. He's agreed to briefly share with us more of his insights about the process of embracing one's body as it is. Ben?"

To looks of surprise from some participants, and delight from others, Ben maneuvered his wheelchair to the front of the room, and faced the participants with the video screen at his back.

"Hi everyone," he said with a half smile. "When Carol and Brian asked me about the possibility of sharing my story, I jumped at the chance. Well, to be truthful, I didn't 'jump,' but I said 'yes' quickly. I don't want my disability to come between me and a full life, and I don't want my chair to come between me and other people. I can manage the first part by myself, but I need your help with the second. In order to get past my chair, you need to know the person in it.

"I wasn't born with this disability. Until I was eighteen, I had full use of my legs, and I used them a lot. Particularly to dance. I loved to dance. Then one late Saturday night in June, after a day of beer drinking to celebrate getting out of high school, I went charging down a dock at a friend's cottage and dove into the water. I remember thinking that maybe it was a stupid thing to do because I had never been in the lake, and didn't know how deep it was at the end of the dock, but I was sort of drunk and showing off. I woke up a couple of days later without the use of my legs."

As Ben told his story, I watched the expressions on the faces of the participants. Emotions ranged from sympathy, to admiration, to embarrassment at being told such personal information.

"After I got past being grateful for being alive, I started thinking about what the rest of my life was going to be like. Would I ever get married and have kids? What woman would ever find me attractive? Would I ever have another orgasm? I thought my sex life was over," he said. "I was a horny, heterosexual teenager who had yet to have many sexual experiences, and I was sure I never would." Then, looking around the room slowly with an emerging grin, he said, "Suffice it to say, I was wrong."

After the applause and supportive laughter subsided, Ben continued. "As you probably already know for yourselves, the biggest sex organ in our bodies is located between our two ears. The *Readers Digest* version of my life is that once I started thinking of myself as *capable* of experiencing sexual pleasure, I started *experiencing* sexual pleasure. It isn't in the same manner that I did prior to my accident, but it works well for me, and apparently for my partners. Not only have I learned how to pleasure myself, but I've also learned how to pleasure them. I've learned how to ask questions about what feels good, and to feel free to say what feels good to me. I'm not sure how long that would have taken me to learn had I *not* had my accident."

Following a brief period of discussion in which Ben offered himself as a resource throughout the week to people with questions, Carol thanked Ben, and led us in a hearty round of applause as he maneuvered his chair to the side of the room. Then, without further explanation, I dimmed the lights and Bill began the film *Active Partners*.

The story began with a man in a wheelchair answering questions in a group not unlike our own, and then fighting uncooperative elevator doors to exit the building. His handsome female partner was frustrated by his late arrival at their designated meeting place, and let him know it. After he explained the problems he had encountered, he said, "You know what I'd *really* like to do? I'd like to go shopping and buy something nice for dinner, including a good bottle of wine. Then I'd like to go home, relax, and make love."

We watched the happy couple shop, unload groceries, and pour wine. Our participants laughed with them during the playful banter, and then grew silent as they moved into the bedroom and began to undress. I reminded myself that it wasn't Ben that we were watching without permission but a couple of people who had volunteered to help others better understand the sexual options available to a person with a disability.

The couple on the screen moaned, giggled, sighed, and smiled throughout their love making which included oral sex and manual stimulation of both penis and clitoris, as well as of nipples, ears, arm pits, and any other body part that was sensitive to touch. Each had their orgasm, neither with obvious ejaculation. And then they cuddled.

With only a moment of dark silence, the screen was then filled with the familiar face but contorted body of Whoopie Goldberg, entertaining and educating an audience with a comedic routine about a severely disabled woman who is courted by a reporter who wants to take her disco dancing and swimming. In the midst of her story, Whoopie's character relays a recurring dream in which her body unfolds from its withered state, her head is able to straighten, her voice box is freed, her lungs are able to fill fully with air, and she is finally capable of dancing, and doing exercise with Richard Simmons, and waving at two people heading off in separate directions at the same time. And then she reports, as always, she wakes up, and her body is the same disabled one she took to bed the night before.

Like Ben, and the man with the disability in the previous film, Whoopie's character testifies to the need not only to see beyond your own fears and seeming limitations, but also to trust that others have the ability to love you for who and what you are. At the end, she invites the audience to her wedding to the handsome, young reporter. It's going to be a disco pool party, she advises.

As happens each year, the room in Ridings was filled with grateful laughter and applause. The lights came up, and we closed.

"As we head off tonight, let's keep reflecting on this concept of 'body image'," I said, "and to ask ourselves again, what, if anything, is stopping us from embracing our bodies as good, lovable, and useful in experiencing and expressing our sexuality. It's 9:30. Remember that we need to keep all the noise down after 10:00 p.m. For you night owls, Bill is going to be showing a couple episodes of *Sex in the City*, tonight and every night at the end of the program. If you don't know the show, it's a fun and provocative story from HBO of four women who are best friends, and who share with each other reports of their sexual explorations."

"Thank you, Brian," Alison said, standing from her seat in the back of the room. "If I can also please remind you to keep all of the doors to these buildings closed at night, and the last one out should turn off all of the lights. We don't want bats or raccoons greeting us in the morning."

"And for those of you who have already seen or don't care to watch *Sex in the City*," Dick said in his strong voice from the second row, "I'll be going swimming tonight and would welcome company. Any takers?"

"I'll go, Dick" said Thomas.

"Is it a skinny dip?" asked Marjorie.

"I didn't hear that," Alison said with a laugh.

"And so it begins," announced Betty.

Chapter Eighteen

The Campfire

"Doing homework?" Dan whispered into Peter's ear as Peter took a seat to watch *Sex in the City*.

"Screw you," Peter said without looking up.

"Ooh. You say when and where," Dan replied seductively, and then turned to head out the door.

"Pay no attention to him," Dom advised as he leaned forward from his seat behind Peter. "He's an asshole."

"I don't pay attention to him," Peter lied.

Besides Peter and Dom, the carpeted upstairs room in Ridings where Bill had set up a TV monitor and VCR was filled with a large group of participants. About half of the full number had decided to stay and watch the two episodes. The others were either heading down to the beach, were out for a walk, or had gone back to their rooms.

Ben maneuvered his wheelchair out of the elevator and toward the back of the room where Beatrice was leaning against the door frame.

"Are you planning on staying for this or would you like to go for a roll around the driveway?" he asked with a big smile.

Turning to face him, she replied, "I'm sorry, I wasn't paying attention. Did you ask me something, Ben?"

"Yea, I was going to go look at the stars and get some fresh air. Did you want to watch these shows or are you up for an adventure?" he said.

"An adventure sounds good," she replied. "I've seen most of the series anyway. Do I need a sweater?"

"Maybe," he said, "but I doubt it if the others are out there skinny dipping."

"Where do you want to go?" she asked as she held the door from Ridings open for him. "Oh, gosh, look at those stars!"

"Beautiful aren't they?" he said. "I thought I'd head toward the driveway. It's a big loop up to the main road. We could go as far as the road and turn back or we could venture out on the road and pick up the other part of the driveway that loops back. It doesn't matter to me. I just wanted to get outside, and to spend a little time with you. So, tell me about yourself," he said as he continued to guide his wheelchair down the asphalt path from Ridings to the driveway. "And know in advance that I don't completely trust your judgement. Anyone with your beautiful body who puts herself in Group Two can't be fully trusted to see things clearly."

"What a sweet thing to say!" she said as she reached for the back of Ben's neck and squeezed it gently. "But remember, they told us it was about how *we* saw ourselves, and not how others saw us. Thanks, though, Ben. That was very nice of you."

"It wasn't nice at all," he protested. "You're *beautiful*. You also strike me as very sweet. So, you want to be a sexuality teacher or a sex counselor, and you're a student at Widener University in Bill's graduate program, right? You wanted to stand in the middle of his 'Value Clarification' exercise rather than at 'Agree' or 'Disagree,' and you're in Brian's SAR group. What else can you tell me?"

"My goodness," she said as they approached the beginning of the long, wide, tree-lined driveway, "you *are* observant. I still can't keep people's names straight, much less what they do professionally. Do you remember that much about *everyone* here?"

"Heck no," he answered. "Just you, I admit."

"Ben, I'm flattered," she replied. "Gosh is it dark out here, or is it just me?"

"It's very dark," he said. "It's the tall evergreens. Do you want to take my hand?"

"Hey, Dick," Ben and Beatrice heard from behind them in the direction of the participants' dorm, "you got a flashlight?"

It was Charlie, clad in a baggy bathing suit, a towel draped around his neck, hollering to the tall, skinny shadow that was carefully descending the hill from the staff dorm to the lake.

"He didn't hear you," Leona said from her perch outside of Peabody.

"Hey, Leona," Charlie said. "Have you already seen *Sex in the City*?"

"I don't need four white girls talking to me about being *sexual*," she said. "And I'm *not* going swimming because it's a lame excuse to get naked."

"Aw, come on," Charlie countered. "Don't sit there alone. Come down with me, and help me make a bonfire. It'll be fun."

"Where's your wood," she asked, "in your suit?"

"No, I'm just glad to see you," he replied.

"And where's your matches?" she asked, ignoring his joke.

"They're actually in my suit," he laughed.

"You're a *crazy* man," she grinned as she sighed, feigned reluctance, and got up to join him on the trip to the lake.

Laughter from the beach, and singing from the raft guided their steps down the grassy incline.

"Who's that?" a voice called from the beach.

"Who's that who says 'who's that'?" replied Leona.

"It's Wendy, Lisa, Gina, Betty, and Carla," the voice replied.

"Oh, geeze," Leona sighed heavily but inaudibly. "I'm going back," she said to Charlie.

"No, you're not," he said, gently taking her elbow. "It's Charlie and Leona," he hollered back.

"Oh good," a woman's voice said. "Dan, Kevin, Lloyd, George, and Thomas are down here too."

"It's a goddamn homo convention," Leona whispered to herself.

"Who's on the raft?" Charlie asked as he approached the group.

"The staff, Annette, and Maggie, I think," Wendy answered. "It's too far to see clearly. They just started singing oldie goldies like 'Let Me Call You Sweetheart'."

"How about a fire?" Charlie asked.

"Did you bring matches?" Betty replied excitedly. "We stacked some wood with some newspaper but no one thought to bring matches."

"I got 'em," Charlie said.

"In his swimming suit," announced Leona as she walked over to where the gay men were sitting at a picnic table. "You all clothed over here?" she asked.

"It's safe, unfortunately," replied Dan.

"Safe for whom?" she asked.

"I'm going swimming," Dan announced, ignoring her question. "Anyone else?"

"I'm going," said Thomas as he stood, joined Dan in the shadows near the edge of the water, and dropped off his swimming suit.

"Ooh, baby, even from here I can see that thing," Leona said with a laugh.

"Whose thing?" Thomas asked with feigned indignation.

"The shadow knows," Leona replied to a chorus of laughter from the women and men.

"Come on, Kevin," Dan called from the water a moment later where he was now laying on his back. "Come on in. The water's great."

"A little later," Kevin replied with an unseen blush.

A few minutes later, Charlie had a roaring fire going in the stone-encircled hole in the ground, and the people on the beach had formed a circle on the grass around it. Wendy and Gina had brought blankets from their rooms, and the women were stretched out on them. Carla, now in shorts, flip flops, and a long-sleeved top, had stretched out, her hands behind her head, and was admiring the multitude of stars.

"I don't recall ever seeing so many stars," she said.

"It's the absence of lights," Charlie explained. "A setting like this is the best place to see them."

The sight of the fire ended the singing of songs on the raft, as both the group there, and the one in the water, headed for the bright sign of heat on the beach. We all toweled off quickly, and slipped into the pile of sweatshirts and shorts that we had worn down. We then each found an open spot in the circle. Dan wedged in next to Kevin, and snuggled closer to him for warmth.

Carol was still in the singing mood, and started swaying back and forth next to me, humming the tune to "Edelweiss." Annette was ready to join in with the words, as was Betty, so the song took off without difficulty. Three or four songs followed, but by the third, most people seemed tired, or tired of singing, and it ended.

"It's getting to be my bed time," Pam said as she rose. "Good night, everyone. This was lots of fun. I hope you all have a really good night."

"I'm heading up myself," bellowed Dick from where he was standing in the back. "I'll escort you up."

"Me too," I said. "You all have a good time."

"Was it my singing?" Carol asked with a teasing look.

"I *love* your singing, Carol," Alison said as she rose. "I love all of your singing, but I want to be bright and ready to go in the morning."

"Oh, okay, I'm coming too," Carol said with playful exasperation as she left the circle.

"Good night, staff," Betty said as we headed up the hill.

Shortly afterwards, the group grew very small as people made their way back to their dorms two or three at a time. From my bedroom window, I could hear a handful of voices at the lake laughing and talking until I fell asleep around 11:30. At around midnight, I woke up suddenly in response to the shaft of bright light that was pouring into my room from the Higley living area.

"Psst. Brian, are you awake?" I heard whispered from the silhouette at the door.

"Yea, is everything okay?" I answered back.

"Can I come in?" the now familiar voice asked.

"Sure, come in, Kevin, and close the door," I replied.

"He kissed me," he said as he sat beside me on the bed.

"Dan kissed you?" I asked. "That's great. How do you feel?"

"Like I can't sleep," he said. "Everyone but Dan and me, and Wendy, Lisa, and Gina, had left to go to bed. He said that he needed to go to bed too, so I walked up the hill with him. Halfway up the hill, he stops and turns to me, leans down, and gives me this gentle kiss on the lips. So, I kissed him back. It was great."

"I'm glad for you. Thanks for telling me, Kevin," I said. "And you promise me that you'll take it slow, right? Enjoy it, but don't read too much into it, okay? I don't want to see you hurt."

"I won't," he said.

"Do you think you can sleep?" I asked. "If you want to stay pretty, you need your beauty sleep."

"Yea, I can, I think. Thanks," he laughed softly as he quietly left my room.

Chapter Nineteen

MONDAY

The Run

Dom was waiting for me outside of Huntington at 7:00 a.m. Wendy was nowhere in sight.

"Good morning," I said in a hushed tone as I approached in T-shirt, running shorts, and shoes. "You look wide awake. Did you get a good night's sleep?"

"Yea. Thanks, better than most, I think," he replied. "I don't think Wendy's going to make it this morning. Marjorie there says she heard her come in at 1:30."

"Good morning, Marjorie," I said to the cigarette-smoking woman in the pink floral bathrobe sitting outside of Peabody.

"Good morning, Brian," she said as she exhaled smoke.

"Let's give her five minutes," I suggested, "if it's okay with you."

"That's fine," he said. "How far do you run?"

"About five miles," I replied. "It's a nice run, Dom. There isn't much traffic on the road. The scenery is nice, and, if we're lucky, we'll see a deer getting a drink at the pond at the end of the road."

Five minutes later, we were off, heading down the driveway in silence as we each sought to find the other's pace.

"How's this for you?" I asked.

"It's fine. If I need to slow down, I'll just drop back. Don't change your run on my account," he said.

After a mile of running in single file against the sparse but fast-moving, early Monday morning traffic, I pulled back from the lead and ran side by side with Dom so that we could talk. If he couldn't comfortably talk, I knew that I needed to slow down the pace.

"So, how's the week going for you so far?" I asked.

"Pretty good," he said on his exhale.

"You said in the SAR group that you've gotten angry a couple of times already. Is that at Dan?" I asked.

"He can be an asshole," Dom said between breaths.

"Have you figured out what about him pushes your buttons most?" I asked.

"I don't know," he said. "He's angry, and he's cocky. He's sort of 'in-your-face,' don't you think?"

"Like all of us, I think he's a mixed bag," I replied, and then pulled ahead to make room for an oncoming truck. We continued the run in silence until we came to the pond, where I spotted a doe and three fawns getting a drink of water.

"Dom, on your left at about 11 o'clock. Do you see them?"

"Well, I'll be. You said we might see deer," he replied. "Look at the size of the little ones. The mother's keeping an eye on us, isn't she."

A half of a mile further up the road, we turned around and headed back. The deer were gone when we passed the pond, but we soon came upon Wendy, running toward us on the other side of the road.

"Sorry, guys," she said with a wave and a look of disappointment as she approached us. "I overslept. I'm glad you didn't wait. I'll see you at breakfast."

"We'll run together on Wednesday," I assured her as we passed each other. "Keep your eyes open for deer."

Dom and I ran to the furthest entrance to Thornfield and continued with our pace down the driveway until we reached the cement walkway to Huntington. I waved to Mary Lee and Susan as we passed their trees on our right, and slapped hands with Dom when we finished.

"Quick swim?" I asked.

"Sure, why not," he replied. "You know, I just want to make sure that you know that my negative feelings about Dan aren't about him being gay. I have no problems with the gay thing. I enjoyed our run. I like Kevin. George is funny. I think I even have a cousin who's gay. It's just that Dan is *so* gay, and so *confrontational* about it."

"Hey, you two," Betty called out from a picnic table in front of Higley where she sat with Carla. "Have a good run?"

"A great run! Thanks, Betty," I replied.

"So the anger that you mentioned having is about Dan being too confrontational about being gay?" I asked.

"That and his defense of pedophile priests," he said.

"Dom, I didn't hear him defend pedophile priests," I said. "I heard him say that based on *his* experience not all sex between a priest and a younger person is harmful."

"I don't want to argue. Let's not talk about that anymore," Dom said as he pulled off his sweat-soaked T-shirt. "How about a quick swim, and then get to breakfast? I'm starving. Maybe we can talk later."

"Have you been in the lake yet?" I asked as I stripped down. "It's a little mucky on the bottom but the water feels great!"

When I reached the raft and turned around to face the shore, I saw Kevin sitting on a picnic table. He waved when he saw that I had noticed him.

"Be right in," I hollered as I swam in his direction.

"Morning, Kevin," Dom said as he left the lake before me, and scraped the water from his head and hairy body with his hands. "Have we missed breakfast?"

"No, they're still serving," he replied. "You've got plenty of time. You guys have a good swim?"

"Hey, Kevin. What's up?" I asked as I stepped onto the beach.

"You got a minute?" he asked.

"Sure. See you up at the dining room, Dom?" I asked.

"That's where I'm heading after I shower. I'll save you a seat," he replied. "Thanks for the run."

"So, did you get any sleep last night?" I asked after Dom was out of earshot.

"Not much," Kevin sighed. "I'm feeling really nervous."

"I know. I understand," I said. "That's a normal feeling. But remember, no matter what happens, you are one hell of a catch. If someone doesn't

143

see that, it says more about him than it does about you. Have you seen Dan since last night's kiss?"

"I saw him head into the dining room the same time I saw you head down here," he said. "He was walking with Carla and Betty."

"Well, let's go up," I said, taking his hand. "I need to take a quick shower. Why don't you go into the dining room and plop yourself at his table. I'll check in with you before the first session."

"Okay," Kevin said.

"And Kevin, remember," I said as we got to the top of the hill and I headed toward Higley, "he came on to you. You didn't come on to him. And no one can take that kiss away from you."

Upon entering Higley, I found Dick examining the day's schedule, Alison and Bill discussing the format on the "Self-Pleasuring" program that was scheduled for that morning, Pam ironing a pair of white shorts and a colorful blouse, and Gail chatting away as Carol stood before the mirror in the women's bathroom curling her blond hair.

"Have you already eaten?" I asked.

"We're on our way," Carol replied. "How was your run?"

"Good. I'll tell you about it later," I said. "Who's doing the morning exercise?"

"You are," Alison called out from the living room.

"Oh, I think I'll do the 'Car Wash'," I said very seriously.

"You do, and you die," Carol shot back.

Most of the participants had eaten by the time I made it into the dining room. Dom was true to his word and had saved a clean place setting for me next to him at his table, where he sat with Chuck, Gina, and Wendy, whose hair, like mine, was wet.

Kevin was nursing a cup of coffee at another table with Dan, Carla, and Betty. Carla looked up and smiled warmly as I entered. I now observed that she was dressed neatly but casually in a bright pink cotton blouse, white shorts, white sandals, and a white and pink polka dot scarf that tied up her ponytail. I gave her the "thumbs up" sign as I headed to the serving counter. Kevin smiled weakly and shrugged his shoulders to indicate that he was up in the air about how to handle Dan.

"What's up for this mornin'?" Chuck asked as I sat with a half of a toasted bagel, a banana, and a glass of orange juice.

"Masturbation," Gina answered.

"Self-Pleasuring," I corrected with a smile.

"That's a good way to start the day," Chuck observed, and then quickly added with a blush, "I mean, having the first session be on 'Self-Pleasuring'."

The banana and bagel were only half-eaten when Gail began ringing the school bell from the other side of the lawn.

"We'll wait with you," Dom offered.

"Thanks. I'll take it with me," I replied. "I'm up this morning."

As we all headed across the grass toward Ridings, I watched Kevin follow Dan like a lost puppy.

"I'd like to get back to our discussion at some point," Dom said quietly to me with a nod.

"Is it something you'd feel safe doing in our SAR group?" I asked.

"Maybe not yet," he said.

"Well then, know that I'm happy to go for a walk any time you'd like," I replied.

We entered Ridings to the sound of the introduction to "I Love Myself." Each of us found an opening in the circle of standing participants. Most of the group still relied on the printed words, but some, such as Annette and Thomas, felt bold enough on this third singing of the song to do it unassisted. Remarkably, two or three others had progressed with the accompanying sign language better than the staff who had watched Gail interpret for years. At the beginning of this second full day of the workshop, there seemed to be a surrender by the majority of the participants to the song and the process. Leona's body language suggested that she still had reservations, as did Catherine's.

"Good morning!" Alison said with characteristic enthusiasm at the end of the song as we each found our seats in the upstairs room. "I trust that you all had a wonderful evening, and that you got a good night's sleep. We'll be moving downstairs in a moment for our presentation on 'Self-Pleasuring,' but first, I've asked Brian to lead us in a wake-up exercise. Brian?"

"Thank you, Alison," I said as I stepped forward. "Good morning, everyone. In our continued effort to get to know each other better, this morning's exercise has us taking turns identifying ourselves and then naming something we most like to do. But when we name our favorite pastime, we're going to briefly act it out and have everyone else join us in doing the same. For instance, my name is Brian and I like to run." At this, I ran in place for a few seconds with my arms and legs exaggerating the jogging motion.

"Okay. Come on. Join me as you're able," I said. In response, everyone but Ben ran in place. Ben moved his wheelchair back and forth in place.

"Good! Okay, Margaret, you're up!" I said.

"I'm Margaret, and I like to cook," she said on cue, as she held an imaginary big bowl in her left arm and vigorously stirred the contents with a spoon in her right hand.

Catherine then identified herself as a golfer and led us in a power drive. Dick announced that he was a gardener as he stooped down to dig in the dirt. Thomas said that he loved to play the piano, and so we animatedly tickled the keys with him. When it was Ben's turn, he reminded us that he loved to dance, and so we closed our eyes, threw back our heads, raised our arms, and moved them rhythmically in the air. Beatrice, who was standing next to him, smiled and said that she loved to go for walks under star-filled skies, so we again pulled our heads back, but this time with our eyes open, and pretended to walk slowly for a couple of steps. We had several golfers and runners and a couple of people who loved to fish. Leona announced that she loved to sleep, so all but Ben dutifully joined her on the floor for a three-second nap. He nodded his head in a simulated doze. Marjorie said her favorite pastime was taking her cocker spaniels to dog shows, so she showed us by raising and lowering her outstretched arm how to indicate "lay down." We danced again with Beverly and Martha, who stood side by side in the circle and illustrated the proper island swing of the hips. Carla then announced that she loved music, and we all joined her in the strumming of a guitar.

"Did you bring your guitar?" Carol asked.

"I did, and I'll play at the celebration if you'd like," she replied to a smattering of applause.

"Carol was going to tell you, Carla, that if you didn't bring your guitar, she was sure that Carl did," I said.

"Very funny," Carol replied, swatting my arm.

Dan smirked when it was his turn to introduce his favorite pastime but then eyed Sr. Annette smiling at him and changed his mind. "I like to *protest*," he said, and we all then followed his lead by raising and lowering imaginary protest placards.

Finally, Paula announced that she liked to give and receive massage, which was, of course, a big hit as we all turned to our right and began working on the neck and shoulders of the person in front of us.

"Good job!" I announced amidst the groans of pleasure.

"I'll say it was," confirmed Alison. "What a wonderfully diverse and talented group we are! Now, if you'll all take your seats for just a moment, I want to see if there are any announcements. Yes, Brian?"

"I'd like to meet for lunch today with the people who are in my 'skill building' workshop. That's Grace, Gina, Carla, and Lloyd," I said. "Let's meet with our food at a picnic table outside of Higley."

"Thank you, Brian. Anyone else?" Alison asked. "Let's do it quickly so that we stay on schedule. Yes, Gail?"

"I found a blanket down on the beach this morning," she said to hoots and hollers from some of the participants. "If you take blankets or pillows out of your room, please take them back to your room at the end of each day. Otherwise, we're going to hear from the staff of the center."

"That's right. Thank you, Gail. Speaking of the staff, I remind our staff that we have a meeting during the break this morning. Okay, if that's it, let's move downstairs."

As we exited the room, Ben moved his wheelchair toward the elevator. Beatrice walked behind him carrying both of their folders.

"Do you want me to go down with you?" she asked.

"I'd *love* you to, but unfortunately there's no room," he said with a frown. "How about if you meet me at the other end?"

Downstairs, the first couple rows of chairs were the first to be filled for the films on masturbation. Kevin sat next to Dan in the third row, behind Betty and Carla.

"Can you see?" Dan asked, his arms around Kevin, as he nodded toward Betty's tall stature in front of him.

"I can see fine," he said. "Besides, I've seen these before."

"Comfortable?" Dan grinned.

"Very," Kevin smiled back.

Dom and Chuck sat together on the opposite side of the room from Dan. In front of them sat Catherine and Peter.

"Are you going to be okay watching these films?" whispered Catherine as she squeezed Peter's knee.

"I don't see why not," he whispered back. "But, thanks for asking. If I get too uncomfortable, I'll get up and go to the bathroom."

Chapter Twenty

Self-Pleasuring

Following Jerry Seinfeld's whimsical introductory monologue, the scene before us opened with the television characters Jerry, Elaine, and Kramer listening with bemused shock at George's promise that he would never again pleasure himself after having been caught by his mother masturbating in her bathroom. The four friends then entered a bet to see who could remain for the longest period of time the "master of his domain," or the "queen of her castle." In other words, no self-pleasuring. It was a classic *Seinfeld* episode in which the words 'masturbation,' 'beating off,' or even 'self-pleasuring' were never used, only implied. Our workshop participants and staff laughed loudly along with the show's studio audience, despite several of us having seen the episode many times before.

Throughout the comedy sketch, the four abstaining friends were shown tossing and turning during sleepless nights. As each succumbed to temptation, he or she was seen finally sleeping peacefully.

The lighthearted and positive approach taken to self-pleasuring in this current-culture presentation was then contrasted with the attitudes toward masturbation that dominated the past, as Dick, our octogenarian, stood to read sections of books written about masturbation during his childhood and beyond.

"Now we come to the problem that is really serious," he read with gravity from *Safe Counsel*, a book written in 1922 by P.G. Jeffries and J.L. Nichols. "The boy who forms the habit of self-abuse is as unwise as a man would be if he were to break into his own house, rob it of its most precious goods, and throw them into the fire."

The laughter and groans that greeted this statement did not alter Dick's serious rendering. "There are at least three physical results that will show the gamut of self-abuse," he read. "The first of these is a retarded development of the body ... The muscles will tend to be less strong than they would have been if the body had not lost so much of the liquid of the testes ... Another mark of the damage that is done by this secret habit is the weariness of the boy. He does not respond to his work in school or to his play with the snap that is the sign of virility ... Another result of the abuse of the body is the weakening of nerves so that they are not steady and responsive as they ought to be.

"The human race is growing weaker year by year," he said, stopping briefly to look around the room with great concern. "...Secret sin ruins more constitutions every year than hard work, severe study, hunger, cold privation, and disease combined. Boys, the destiny of the race is in your hands ... "

When the laughter subsided, he continued. "Curative treatment of self-abuse: Bandaging the parts has been practiced with success. Tying the hands is also successful in some cases ... A remedy that is always successful in small boys is circumcision. The operation should be performed by a surgeon without administering an anesthetic, as the pain attending the operation will have a salutary effect upon the mind, especially if it be connected with the idea of punishment. In females, the application of pure carbolic acid to the clitoris is an excellent means of preventing the occurrence of the practice. Probably no single agent will accomplish more than electricity when skillfully applied."

Though the reading was funny by comparison, it was also shocking and sobering. Dick allowed for a moment of silent reflection and then offered an amusing sidebar.

"So concerned were the leaders of the day in stopping this practice," he said, "that an inventor by the name of J. Kellogg created a breakfast cereal made of corn flakes believing that if young boys would eat natural grains, as opposed to animal by-products, they would be less likely to engage in this unmentionable, animal-like behavior." Graham Crackers too, we were told, were created by a Methodist minister named Graham to achieve the same effect.

Without discussion, though following many groans of disapproval and disbelief at such seemingly primitive thinking, the lights were again dimmed for the showing of the film on male masturbation. In it, four men were presented talking about and illustrating the pleasures of masturbation. Three of the men were white, one was black, three were in their twenties, and thirties, and one was in his fifties. Most of the men were physically attractive by traditional cultural standards, and only one, I deduced, was gay. Each masturbated to the point of ejaculation.

Remembering my aroused response to the film when I saw it for the first time many years ago, I watched the faces of the participants I imagined might be struggling. Peter immediately came to mind. He, I noticed, sat stone faced, often looking toward the ceiling or the floor. Catherine patted his knee in support. There was, in fact, a stony silence in the entire room, as each of the featured men told his story of discovering the pleasures of masturbation, and how he worked through guilt, if indeed, he ever felt it. Though silent, some participants, such as Dan and Thomas, communicated with peaceful smiles that they were very comfortable with, and affirming of the message.

The man in his fifties was the first person featured. He masturbated stretched out on a sofa, looking at an erotic magazine, with his trousers and underwear pulled down to his knees. The second man was in a bathtub, filled with warm sudsy water. He explained that as a teenager he had continually frustrated his parents with his long, leisurely baths. "What are you *doing* in there?" he quoted his angry father saying as he pounded on the other side of the bathroom door. The black man, who lounged comfortably naked on a waterbed, stroking the back of his Siamese cat, spoke of the necessity for him of setting the right atmosphere with candles and soft music. He initially only used masturbation as a substitute for sex when his girlfriend was away, but he learned that it could be a wonderful activity in and of itself for him. When he pleasured himself, he did so not by just touching his penis, but also by gently stroking other sensitive areas of his body, such as his face, nipples, and underarms. The last person presented lay naked on his bed surrounded by pictures of the women he had dated. These he used to create exciting and pleasurable fantasies. Sex for him was recreational. He claimed to have had hundreds of sexual partners in his life, and said that learning to please himself through masturbation was what enabled him to learn to better please them.

The women, whose stories were told in the next film, were as varied in age and race as the men but more uniform in the leisurely time they took to reach orgasm. There were five women, but only four were shown masturbating with vibrators, pillows, or with their hands. The fifth was the narrator, a black woman, who spoke painfully of how much difficulty she has in feeling good about pleasuring herself, this despite her profession as a sexuality educator. She feared that her negative attitudes had already had an adverse effect upon her children and their sense of themselves as sexual beings. Each time she felt inclined to masturbate, she would say to herself, "No, not tonight."

One of the four other women was Chinese, one was Scandinavian, one was blind, and the last was an older white woman. The latter told of never feeling any sexual pleasure during intercourse with her first husband. Sex was something that she "endured." When she began to masturbate, she explained, she learned how to pleasure herself, and was then able to teach her second husband how to do the same. The clitoris, she discovered, had only one purpose, and that was sexual pleasure. She found this to be a most remarkable thing, as did I.

Though the room was as quiet during the second film as it had been during the first, the participants seemed less tense during the segment about the women, except during the sequences on orgasm. When the women and the men began to groan with pleasure, there was an awkwardness that I could relate to from my initial feelings of intruding upon a private moment. And yet, that was the purpose of the exercise: To witness this private moment so that it would generate thoughts and feelings about our own experiences with masturbation.

"All right," Alison said standing as the overhead lights were turned on in unison with the rolling of the film's credits. "It's time for our small groups."

"So, let's check in," I said ten minutes later as Leona sauntered in with a glass of lemonade, and took the last remaining chair in the circle. "How's everyone doing?"

Kevin smiled back weakly at me. Dom, Wendy, Beatrice, and Maggie nodded that they were fine. Charlie raised his eyebrows. Leona shifted positions in her chair.

"Any reactions to the films you just saw?" I asked.

"*Seinfeld* was funny," Dom said. "I hadn't seen that episode."

"You hadn't? It's one of my favorites! It was hilarious," affirmed Maggie, "although I can't believe how self-centered that whole group is."

151

"That's what makes it so funny," Dom replied.

"The segment was funny," I said, "but how did it, or the readings, or the films we watched on male and female masturbation make you *feel*? Did any feelings come up for you?"

"I felt a little put out that the one black woman is the one with the hang-ups," snorted Leona indignantly, "and that the black dude tells us that he started masturbating when his girlfriend got sent *back* to reform school. He did, however, have the biggest thing among the men," she laughed, "but then, that's another stereotype too, isn't it."

"The films are imperfect," I acknowledged, "but did they, or the readings, bring up any feelings about your own sexual journey with regard to masturbation?"

"Brian, may I say something?"

"Please, Margaret," I said. "And the rest of you, jump in when you have something to add."

"I could really relate to the readings that Dick shared with us," Margaret said as she looked around the room. "I know that my mother and father read literature such as that, as did I, though perhaps mine was a *little* less extreme. But not much. I never masturbated as a young woman growing up. None of my friends spoke of it, and I thought of it as just a male activity. I regret that. I could identify a great deal with the older woman at the end of the second film who talked about not enjoying sex with her husband until she discovered masturbation. I could also identify with the black narrator who worried about how her negative attitudes toward masturbation had impacted her children. So many times I have wanted to turn back the clock and start fresh with my children. I know that my mother and father did the best job they could with me, given their education on this issue, and I know that I did the best job that I could, given my lack of education, but how I wish I could have been a more positive influence on my children's attitudes toward their sexuality."

"Thank you, Margaret," I said. "That was a gift."

She smiled back. "You asked about what feelings came up. I felt sad and angry, but also very grateful that I had finally learned how to pleasure myself. I don't think that everyone has to masturbate in order to have a full, healthy, and happy life, but it sure made a difference in my life, and I have no desire to be the queen of my castle if it means that I can't enjoy my reign."

"All right! You go girl!" Leona said raising her hand to give Margaret a "high five."

Margaret giggled, and blushed slightly, and then raised her eyebrows and smiled.

As the animated laughter and chatter subsided, Beatrice leaned forward from her chair and said, "Margaret, may I ask you *how* you learned about masturbation, and how long it took you to become comfortable with it?"

"That's a very good question, Beatrice," Margaret replied with a warm smile. "I got involved in the women's movement in my late forties. I was drawn to it because of my association with the United Church of Christ. It was in a women's discussion group that I first got confronted with my conflicted thoughts about masturbation. On the one hand, I affirmed other women's rights to pleasure themselves, and on the other, I was aware of the guilt and shame I felt about never having masturbated. So, as is my style of learning, I did a lot of reading initially. Betty Dodson's book was particularly helpful to me. After getting everything together in my head, I took matters in my own hands, so to speak. I can't believe I just said that. But my, it feels good to be able to do so. Hmm. At any rate, I started practicing on my own at home. Initially I just used my fingers, and then a friend from one of my discussion groups took me to a store, and helped me buy my first vibrator. Like the woman in the film, I became best friends with my clitoris, and soon introduced my husband to it. It's been a wonderful friendship that they've both enjoyed."

"Dom, what are you thinking?" I asked. "You've got a big smile on your face."

"I can't believe I'm sitting here listening to a retired woman minister talk about making friends with her clitoris," he laughed. "It's blowing my mind."

"In a good way?" I asked.

"Oh, yea, in a good way," he replied. "Are they talking like this in the other groups?"

"My guess is that they are," I said. "But tell me, what feelings came up for *you* with the presentation on masturbation?"

"Well, for one thing, it made me remember my eighth grade nun, Sr. Mary Raphael. She was a big woman, and this was in the days when they wore the old habits. She used to come bounding into class in the afternoon to teach religion, and she'd say in this really loud and accusing voice, 'You boys with your hands in your pockets, I *know* what you're doing. MASTURBATION!' It used to freak me out. First, I didn't know the word, but I figured out what she meant, and I knew *never* to get caught with my hands in my pockets."

"You didn't know about masturbation in eighth grade?" Wendy asked above the laughter.

"I didn't say that," Dom replied. "I said I didn't know the word *masturbation*. My buddies and I didn't walk around talking about 'masturbation.' We talked about 'beating off' or 'whacking off.' Who heard of 'masturbation'? Master who?"

"Did you grow up in a home in which you could 'beat off' without guilt?" I asked.

"What? Are you kidding me?" he replied. "I grew up Italian Catholic. It'd kill your mother if she found out, like George's in *Seinfeld*, though she was Jewish. You grew up Irish Catholic. Was it different for you?"

"No. Pretty much the same," I said. "The first time I masturbated, I thought I had broken something, and that I was going to need medical attention. I was having a pleasant same-sex fantasy, and was rubbing back and forth on my stomach. Suddenly, there was this explosion. I reached down and felt this sticky fluid I had never touched before, and I thought, 'Oh, God, now you've done it. You broke something, and they're going to ask you how you did it'."

"I thought you came from a big family?" Leona said. "Didn't you have an older brother that told you about it?"

"I did have an older brother, but he was out on his own by this time, and he had never clued me in," I replied. "You didn't talk about sex in my family. I have a younger brother, Tom, and we shared a room. I never said a word to him about it either. Not only did I learn to masturbate on my stomach rubbing up and down on the bed, but I also learned that if I was fast enough, I could put my finger over the end of my penis and stop the semen from shooting out. When I was sure my brother was asleep, I'd sneak into the bathroom and release the semen into the toilet. One time my mom said to me, 'Do you know why your brother's sheets are stained?' I said 'I have no idea.' I'm embarrassed to say that it wasn't until I was in college that I actually talked with my peers about masturbation. I was in a fraternity and three of us shared a room. One night, when the lights were out, we were talking about masturbation, and I said something like '99 per cent of all men masturbate,' and this friend of mine from South Charleston, West Virginia, said from his side of the room, 'Brian, that's impossible. More than 1 per cent of the population is missing their hands.' And I thought to myself, '*Hands*? What do *hands* have to do with it?' But I didn't say anything because I was so unsure of myself. Ignorance, secrecy, and trauma!"

"I learned about masturbation while sliding down the banister in my grandmother's house," Leona said with a chuckle. "My older sister and her friend knew what they were doing and they said, 'Leona, slide down that banister. It feels good. Try it. You'll see.' So I did what they did and it *did* feel good. I did it over and over again, and my sister started laughing at me, making fun. And I remember feeling a little embarrassed, but mostly upset because we didn't have a banister in our house, and I didn't know when I was going to get back to my grandma's."

"Did you tell your sister that?" I asked.

"Not just then," Leona said, "but a couple days later she said, 'You know that good feeling that you had sliding down the banister? Well, you can have the same feeling whenever you want it by just rubbing yourself with your arm or your pillow like this.' Then she showed me how to do it."

"Weren't you lucky!" I said. "What a great older sister you had."

"I still do," she replied, slowly nodding her head.

We sat silently for a moment, and then Charlie spoke up.

"When I was a kid, touching yourself was equated with homosexuality."

"What?" asked Maggie incredulously.

"You're probably too young to remember Bromo Seltzer," Charlie said, "but they had this commercial that said 'Take Bromo Seltzer, and wake up feeling yourself.' Well, the guys changed it to 'Take Bromo, homo, and wake up feeling yourself.' You'd never admit to anyone that you touched yourself. They'd say you were a homo."

"Did that stop you from touching yourself, Charlie?" I asked.

"No, but it made it impossible for me to tell anyone," he replied.

"Can I say something please?" Maggie asked.

"Absolutely," I said.

"Are those statistics right? That 99 per cent of all men masturbate?" she asked.

"Oh, I don't know," I said. "I was very sure of myself in my twenties, but I don't know what the accurate number is, Maggie. I think it's safe to say that the overwhelming majority of men have masturbated."

"What about women?" she asked. "What's the percentage of women who have masturbated, do you think?"

"I couldn't say for sure, but my guess is that it's not as high. But the percentage is climbing," I said. "Why?"

"Hmm. It's just that I've *never* masturbated, and I'm feeling a little like a freak in this discussion," she said.

"I apologize if you've gotten the impression from me that there is something wrong with you if you *don't* masturbate. The purpose of the discussion," I said, "is to evaluate our *feelings* about masturbation. If we don't masturbate, and we don't want to masturbate, then this isn't an issue that should make us feel self-conscious. On the other hand, if we'd like to sexually pleasure ourselves but don't because of fear or shame or ignorance, then it's an issue we might want to take a good look at. And, finally, if I may, if we have strong negative feelings about masturbation, we need to be aware that we're probably communicating those to our clients and/or our children, and we need to decide if that's the message we *want* to be sending. Does that all make sense?"

"Yes, it makes sense," Maggie replied, "but I don't think it's fear, shame, or ignorance that stops me from masturbating. I just think it's *selfish*. Isn't sex about pleasing another person?"

"Can't you do both?" asked Leona.

"I suppose, and maybe it's just me, but I find it a little selfish to masturbate. It's like, why not wait?" she said. "But then, I find it easier, and it makes me happier, to buy a present for someone else than to buy a present for myself."

"Girl, don't you buy presents for yourself?" Leona asked. "Don't you ever go get your hair done just because it makes you feel good, or have your toenails done, or haven't you ever bought yourself a chocolate sundae just because it sounded like fun?"

"Not really," Maggie said. "I can't afford to eat the chocolate sundae, and I don't think I've ever had my toenails done. Is that freaky?"

"It's not freaky," Margaret said. "I think it's quite typical of the attitude of American women. We aren't encouraged to think of ourselves. We're raised to always first think of others, our husbands, our children ... "

"Our lovers," Wendy interjected.

"Our lovers," Margaret repeated with an appreciative smile. "I can relate to what you're saying, Maggie. Have you ever read the books *Co-Dependent No More* or *Women Who Love Too Much*? They helped me a lot."

"Maggie, I can relate completely to what you're saying," said Beatrice. "I've been sitting here feeling like a freak too. It was a long time before I ever masturbated, and I still feel guilt or shame when I do it. I was really uncomfortable with the movies because I felt I was watching something that the people in the film wouldn't want others to know they were doing. And then I realized, of course, they didn't care. It was *me* who cared. I don't want people to know that I masturbate."

"Why?" asked Leona.

"Because I think it makes me seem like less than a 'good' girl," Beatrice replied. "Intellectually I know that isn't true, but emotionally, deep down inside, I think I feel like 'good girls don't masturbate'."

"So, what happens if you end up being a counselor, and you're working with some girl who tells you that she masturbates?" asked Dom.

"That's a good question," said Beatrice. "I guess that's why I'm here."

"That's why we're *all* here," I affirmed. "Kevin, we haven't heard anything from you. Anything to add?"

"No," he said with a weak smile. "I just want everyone to know that just because I don't say much doesn't mean that I'm not interested. I really like the conversation, and I appreciate everyone being so honest."

"Did the films bring up any feelings for you, Kevin?" I asked.

"Well, I found myself attracted to a couple of the guys," he laughed with a blush.

"Which ones?" Leona asked.

"The guy in the bathtub, and the guy at the end with all of the women's pictures on his bed," Kevin said a bit reluctantly, and then added, "but the guy at the end is straight, and I'm not really interested in straight men."

"Wendy," I interjected before that conversation took off on a tangent, "Anything that you'd like to share regarding your feelings about masturbation?"

"Well, I found myself attracted to a couple of the women in the film," she laughed. "I guess I relate most to what Margaret and Leona said. Masturbation has never been a big deal for me. I learned about it really young. I didn't have an older sister, like Leona did, but I had a girlfriend who taught me about it when I was pretty young. For me, it's very natural. It's not a substitute for sex. It's just something I do for myself when it sounds good, like having a chocolate sundae. And I just want to say to Maggie that before the end of the week, we're going to do your toenails!"

"I've done my toenails before," Maggie protested amidst the laughter and clapping.

"No," Leona corrected, "*we're* gonna do your toenails."

Chapter Twenty-One

Staff Meeting

"Are you free to talk?" Dom asked in a hushed tone as the others in our SAR group left to enjoy their scheduled hour break. "Or is this a bad time?"

"I'd love to talk, Dom," I said, "but I've got a damn staff meeting scheduled for the break. The others will be showing up here momentarily. I can get out of the meeting if this feels urgent. Otherwise, let's set up a time to meet."

"Oh, no, it can wait," he said assuredly. "Anytime. Really. We just started talking this morning, and I didn't want to leave it hanging. How about at lunch?"

"I'm meeting with my 'skill-building group' at lunch," I said, looking at the day's schedule. "How about after the next SAR process group? We have an hour break before dinner."

"Sounds good," he said as he moved toward the door. "I'll catch up with you then, but if something comes up, it's no big deal. By the way, do you guys talk about us?"

"You mean the staff?" I asked.

"Yea. Do you talk about what's said in the groups or in private conversations?" he said.

"We check in with each other on how our groups are going," I replied, "and we offer input if we think it would be useful. Your and my conversation will be confidential unless you say otherwise."

"Okay. Thanks," he said as he headed out the door with a casual military salute.

With Dom's departure came the arrival of Alison and Pam, then Bill, and finally Carol. Each went to his or her room to drop something off, and then found a living room chair in the circle.

"Can this be a quick meeting?" I asked, as they were accustomed to having me do. "Someone wanted to meet with me, and if it's too late for that, I'd love to get in a quick swim before lunch."

"I don't see why not," Alison responded chirpily. "How is everyone's group going?"

"Great!" Carol answered enthusiastically. "I've got a *great* group. I love Thomas."

"Who's Thomas?" Bill asked.

"The gay man with three daughters, he plays the piano, and is HIV-positive," Carol replied quickly.

"Oh, yea," Bill said with a smile of recognition. "I like him too. He's in your group? I wanted him in my group."

"How's your group, Bill?" Pam asked.

"It's an interesting mix," he said seriously. "I've got Ben - in the wheelchair - he's great. He's right out there with his feelings. Paula, the sex therapist from Arizona with the gay son, she's got some issues but she hasn't revealed much yet. And then there's Chuck, the coach from Mississippi with the great sense of humor. I think this whole thing is blowing his mind, but he seems like he's really ready to learn. He keeps telling us that this is *not* what he expected, but that he's learning a lot."

"How's your group?" I asked Pam, and then looked over to Alison, her co-facilitator.

"Pretty good, wouldn't you say, Alison?" Pam replied. "We've got an interesting mix too. We've got Peter, which is really new for me with his 'ex-gay' stuff, but he seems to be doing okay in the group. He said that he's glad to be in *our* group, and not in Carol's or Brian's because he thinks it will be easier to be taken seriously in our group. We assured him that he would have been very comfortable in either one of your groups."

"I'm glad you got him," I said. "I think he'll feel safer with you, and he can do great work in your group. Who else is in there with him?"

"Grace, the corporate diversity manager," Pam said.

"How's she doing?" I interrupted.

"She's doing great," Pam said. "We've also got Lloyd, who's a sweetie, Marjorie, who's very good on 'body image issues,' Curtis ... "

"You've got the two smokers," I said.

"You used to be in that group," Alison said.

"We both did," I replied.

"Who else, Alison? Help me out," Pam said.

"Annette, the nun," Alison said. "She's very serious."

"I love her," Pam said. "I think she's going to be a great asset."

"Who's in your group?" Carol asked, turning to me.

"Kevin, Leona, Dom, Maggie, Wendy, Beatrice, Margaret, and ..." I hesitated, knowing that I was forgetting someone.

"Charlie," Carol added.

"Yea, Charlie. Thanks. How did you know?" I asked.

"I know everything," Carol laughed. "Charlie told me last night that he was in your group. He likes being in your group."

"How's Leona doing?" Pam asked.

"She's a challenge," I acknowledged. "I don't think she wanted to be in my group. She needs a lot of attention. Does she really work for Planned Parenthood?"

"Yes, why?" Alison asked.

"I just would have thought that someone from Planned Parenthood would be more of a team player," I said.

"She was sent here by her director because they feel she has a lot to offer but also because she's a little rough around the edges," Pam explained. "I know her director. She asked me if I thought this would be a good place for Leona to come. I, of course, said 'yes.' I think she wanted to be in my group. Give her a chance. I think that she'll come around."

"This isn't what she expected," added Carol, "and she got off to a rough start. I had her rooming with Betty and that freaked her out. I had assumed that because she was with Planned Parenthood, and had indicated on her application that she had been through a SAR, that she would be comfortable in that setting."

"Going through a SAR is no guarantee that someone will be comfortable with all of the issues," Alison said. "And, from what I understand, it was an abbreviated version of a SAR, with no films."

"I had a long talk with her," Carol said. "I agree with Pam. Give her some time. I think it takes her a long time to trust. She tends to criticize things as a defense mechanism. I'll bet you end up loving her."

"We'll see," I said. "By the way, I'm a little concerned about Kevin."

"How come?" Bill asked with surprise.

"He's falling pretty hard for Dan," I replied.

"Dan who?" Bill said. "Who's Dan?"

"Dan 'Fuck' Schemp," Carol answered.

"Who?" Bill asked with a look of bewilderment.

"Dan, who says he's 'queer,' and that he had sex with a priest. The hunky one," I said.

"I thought he was 'ex-gay'?" Bill said with a laugh.

"Oh, Bill," Alison said with frustrated amusement.

"Not him. The 'ex-gay' one is Peter. He's lean and handsome. Dan is the muscular one who seems so angry," Pam explained over our laughter of exasperation.

"Oh, *him*," Bill said with a big grin. "What about him?"

"Kevin has a crush on him," I said. "I'm afraid he's going to get hurt."

"There does seem to be a little romance blooming," Pam said.

"Speaking of romance," Carol interjected, "has anyone noticed that Ben and Beatrice have become very friendly?"

"They have?" replied Bill, and then with feigned befuddlement asked, "Who's Beatrice?"

"She's in your program at Widener, Bill" I responded with exaggerated patience, as if talking to a confused child.

"Oh, *that* Beatrice," he laughed. "What about her?"

"Is this meeting over?" I asked. "The lake is calling to me."

"Is there anything else?" Alison asked. "Is anyone having any difficulty that we can help with, or is there anyone else that we need to be aware of?"

"Whose group is Catherine in?" asked Pam.

"She's in mine," Bill said more seriously. "She's going to be a tough nut to crack. She's very smart, but she's *very* rigid. Scripturally, she's really conservative."

"She and Peter have been hanging together," Pam said. "Is she a lesbian?"

"If she is, she's not saying anything about it," I said. "She didn't come to our dinner meeting."

"Well, that's no indication," Carol said. "Peter didn't come either."

"Are we all set for this afternoon?" Alison asked.

"All set," Bill said. "I've got the film *Gender*."

"I've got the words to 'What Makes a Man a Man?'" said Carol.

"I think it's going to blow some people away," Bill said.

"I know it is," I nodded.

Chapter Twenty-Two

"A Trip to the Zoo"

"Such a small lunch," I commented when Carla joined our group at the picnic table for our "skill-building" workshop meeting. "Will just a salad tie you over until dinner?"

"A girl's got to do what a girl's got to do," she nodded with a knowing smile to me, Grace, Gina, and Lloyd as she straightened her back, and lifted her fork. "Besides, turkey tacos don't much appeal to the hungry man in me."

"If Carl was sitting with us, what would he be eating?" I asked.

"Wow! What an interesting question," Gina observed before taking a large bite of the turkey taco salad she had concocted. "Do Carla and Carl have different appetites?"

"Isn't your appetite affected by your moods?" asked Carla with a raised, plucked, and penciled eyebrow. "Mine is affected by a variety of factors, including whether I'm in a dress or sweats."

"Mmm. Good stuff," I said. "I hope you incorporate some of that into your presentation to us on Friday, Carla. But let's, if we can, get focused for a minute on your observations of the staff so far this week. Remember, I asked all of you to wear two hats while you're listening to the presentations. I'd like you to listen as participants who want to grow in your personal and professional understanding of human sexuality, and also listen as professionals who want to build skills as presenters. Did any of you have any 'ah ha' experiences?"

"I did," said Grace, opening her packet and reaching for her notes. "I went through the 'Guidelines for Trainers' that you gave us, and I saw how the staff really personifies a lot of the points you made. For instance, I've been impressed with how prepared, and yet flexible you all seem to be. Bill, for one, is very organized, but he's also very comfortable letting a discussion take a different turn. Pam did the same thing. She seemed to know where she wanted us to end up, but she was comfortable when the conversations got sidetracked. She just kept bringing us back. I'm not sure that I'm able to be that laid back."

"It comes with time, Grace," I said. "When I first started out, I was very rigid. I had everything neatly laid out in my mind as to how things needed to go in order for the presentation or workshop to be a success, and if anything or anyone interrupted the flow, I'd panic, and get upset, and worry that I'd failed. With time, I started to relax. Working with people who had more experience than I did helped a lot. I'd watch them stay cool in the worst of circumstances, and I learned that sometimes those unwanted interruptions are the best things that happen in a workshop. They can become the 'teachable moments.' So, I'm really glad that you observed it in the staff, and that you related it to your own work. And I promise you that with time you'll roll with the unexpected too. Anyone else?"

"I like the humor," Carla said strongly. "Bill is a very smart man but being smart doesn't make you a good presenter. I feel so relaxed with him because he seems so relaxed with himself. He makes me laugh every time he wiggles his butt. Actually, sometimes I think to myself 'We've got a budding transvestite here.' But I do find that I pay real close attention to him not just because I want to learn new things, but also because I don't want to miss something funny that he says."

"I agree," said Gina. "You and Carol, for example, are always going back and forth, and it doesn't stop you from being taken seriously. I like the playfulness, especially here. I'm not sure though how much of it would work outside of here. Does Bill wiggle his butt when he's talking to professionals?"

"We're professionals," Lloyd spoke up.

"Yea, but you know what I mean," Gina replied. "Like business executives or politicians or people like that?"

"It's a really good point, Gina," I said. "We have to know our audience, and speak to our audience in a way that works for them. I'm more playful with some groups than I am with others. I always use humor, but with some groups I use a lot less. Some audiences want lots of facts. Some want you to be very dressed up. Others want you to be dressed casually, and some want you to speak very personally. That's why it's so important to know your audience."

"How do you get to know them?" Lloyd asked. "How do you know when you need to be funny and when you need to be serious?"

"Well, first of all, the thing you need to be is *yourself*," I said. "If you're not naturally funny, don't try to be. But, going back to the guidelines I gave you, you remember that I recommend that you learn as much about your audience in advance as you can prior to going in to speak. Ask lots of questions of your host. Ask about what programs have been most successful with the group. Ask if the group is traditionally interactive. Ask if the attendees will be required to be there, or will they be freely signing up for the presentation. Ask about their religious backgrounds, their job descriptions, the climate in the site. If they're going through a major downsizing in the company, be aware and sensitive to that. Also, once the program begins, read their faces. Watch their eyes and their body language. If humor seems to loosen them up, keep using it. If they don't smile, change tactics."

"I noticed that all of you seem to make a lot of eye contact," Lloyd said. "You all look around the room a lot."

"And how do you feel about that?" I asked.

"I like it," he said. "I feel like you care about me."

"That's the feedback I get, Lloyd," I said. "People tell me that they like the fact that I made eye contact with them because they felt as if I cared about their reaction to what I was saying. It's an important thing to do, but a word of caution. If you see someone who refuses to look back at you, or whose body language is telling you that he or she is disinterested or angry, don't stay focused on them. Let go of them. If everyone is giving you the same nonverbal feedback, then pay attention to it, but if it's just one or two people, let go of them. I used to become preoccupied with them, like a moth drawn to a flame. I felt as if I needed to win their approval. What I didn't realize is that once I started focusing on that one person, I abandoned everyone else. I left the majority of the group in order to win just the one. Many of us seem drawn to negative criticism."

"I can relate to that," Carla said. "That's why I'm here, and that's why I want to start talking about transgender issues. I'm sick of being afraid and needy of approval. I'm a pretty man in a dress. Get over it."

"You go, Carla," Gina said.

"The messenger *is* the message," I said. "Do you hear the strength in Carla's voice? That's what people will pick up. Beyond any facts and figures that she shares with them — and facts and figures are important, and they need to be current and accurate — what her audiences will walk away with is the image of a confident cross dresser who isn't asking for permission to be herself. That frees them up from thinking it's a problem they have to solve. They just need to know that she's out there, and that she wants to be treated with courtesy and professional respect."

"Amen," said Carla.

"And if we're not telling our own story?" asked Grace.

"You *are* telling your own story," I replied, "you're just not doing it as the affected subject of your talk. But you *are* telling them in your demeanor, and in your words, how you, as a privileged white heterosexual woman, grew to understand and become comfortable with your subject matter. They walk away from their meeting with you, Grace, with a role model for their own behavior. Watch Bill in the next presentation. He's not transgender, but he's so comfortable with the topic that sometimes people wonder if he is."

Carla smiled at me with a nod of recognition.

"He role models for the rest of us how *we* can respond to the issue," I continued.

"And how did he get so comfortable with the issue?" asked Carla.

"Like all of us," I replied, "through personal contact. Bill's got his doctorate in human sexuality, and he works as a therapist with transgender people, but I'm sure that it's his personal interactions with transgender people that have changed his life. That's true for the whole staff. You'll have a profound effect upon the participants this week, Carla, just by being yourself as you eat meals, sit by the campfire, and share in groups."

"Well, I'm not sure I want to be a 'trip to the zoo'," she said.

"But you *are*, Blanche, you *are*," Lloyd replied in a decent impersonation of Bette Davis with a line from the film *Whatever Happened to Baby Jane?* "We *all* are."

"Such wisdom from such youth," I said. "He's right. We *all* are. When we decide to go out and tell our stories as diversity educators, we are 'a trip to the zoo' for many of the participants. They're seeing and learning about something that they don't have much access to in their daily lives. I'm a gay, white, middle-aged, Irish Catholic male. Lloyd's a gay, black youth. Gina's a young, white lesbian. Grace is a white, female, heterosexual ally. You're a cross dresser."

"A pretty cross dresser," Carla added.

"A pretty cross dresser," I affirmed.

"A pretty cross dresser who'd like to powder her nose before the next session," she insisted.

Chapter Twenty-Three

Gender Identity & Expression

The scene before us on the screen was that of a beautiful, blond woman taking off her makeup as she sat in front of a dressing room mirror. As she did so, she sang a sad song, the words to which were passed out by Carol at the beginning of the afternoon session. The lyrics detailed the many challenges she faced trying to find a niche for herself in a cruel and judgmental world.

Given the topic of the session, it undoubtedly came as no big surprise to our participants when the woman removed her wig to reveal a neatly cropped haircut, and later removed her underwear to reveal a penis. "Tell me if you can," he queried as he threw a feather boa over his muscle T-shirt and tight jeans, "what makes a man a man?"

Bill repeated the question when the lights were turned back on. "What would you say makes a man a man? Or, more precisely, what is a *male*?" he asked in a serious tone with raised eyebrows as he looked around the room. "Anyone?"

After a silent minute, Maggie volunteered "a penis?"

Bill smiled back with a questioning tilt of his head, and stayed silent. "Chromosomes," shot out Marjorie.

Again, Bill smiled silently and looked to the others for more input.

"Attitude," announced Dan. "It's what's between his ears, not what's between his legs."

Bill looked at him with an expression of interest but kept the floor open for other thoughts.

"All of the above," said Paula with uncertainty.

After a long period of silence, with Bill just smiling at us, Lisa said in frustration, "Tell us!"

"What we're going to discuss this afternoon is the question of 'What is a "male," and what is a "female"?' To do so successfully, we're going to need to make some distinctions," Bill finally replied with a grin as he flipped pages of newsprint on one of the easels. "Pam outlined for us some of those distinctions in her presentation yesterday on the five circles of 'Sexual Beingness.' During that, she talked about the differences between 'Biological Sex,' 'Gender Identity,' 'Gender Role,' and 'Sexual Orientation.' I want to make some further distinctions. And let me just say as we head forward, that at this time, there isn't complete agreement in the field about terminology. But these are the terms and the definitions that we, at Thornfield, have agreed upon. By the way, you may want to take notes."

As he said this, the majority of participants reached for their packets, and pulled out writing paper and a pen.

"When we talk about 'Biological Sex,' and ask the question, 'What is a male?' we're asking about it chromosomally, hormonally, gonadally, as well as with reference to the internal and external genitalia, and to brain dimorphism," he said, writing the words on the whiteboard at the front of the room. "Chromosomally, we are talking in terms of xx equaling a girl, and xy equaling a boy. Hormonally, we're talking in terms of estrogen for girls, and androgyn or testosterone for boys. Gonadally, we're talking about ovaries for girls, and testicles for boys. With regard to internal genitalia, we're talking about the Mullerian Structures for girls, which are the upper vagina, fallopian tubes, and uterus, and the Wolfian Structures for boys, which are the prostate, seminal vesicles, and vas deferens. Externally, we're talking about the clitoris for girls, and the penis for boys. Brain dimorphism refers to the differences in the male and female brains. The problem with all of this is that not all girls are xx or boys xy, we all have the same hormones but in varying levels, we're not all born with clear gonadal or genital differences, and brain dimorphism isn't a reliable indicator. So the question remains, '*What* is a male?'."

"Can you run that by me again?" Chuck asked, scratching his head.

"With chromosomes," Bill continued, smiling at Chuck, but undeterred in his efforts to stir the pot, "the male sperm determines the outcome. What happens, however, if instead of adding an 'x' or a 'y' chromosome to the female's 'x,' that the male shoots a blank sex-determining chromosome and the child is born 'xo'?"

"Turner's Syndrome," Marjorie answered with confidence.

"That's right!" Bill said appreciatively. "It will be a female. She may have some webbing in neck, fingers, and toes. She will generally be short, often not over five feet, one inch, and she won't be able to conceive. One out of every 1600 births are 'xo'. You can also get 'xxx,' which will be a female, but there are a significant number who may have mental retardation. You can get an 'xxy,' which often will be a tall, infertile male who frequently has difficulty in relationships. We call this Klinefelter's Syndrome. You can get an 'xyy,' which is commonly seen in a significant number of recidivists in prisons, and you can get an 'xxyy,' which is a pure, bilateral hermaphrodite."

"Slow down a minute, will you, Bill?" Grace asked as she wrote furiously.

"And you can get an 'xyxo,' which will be a short male whose gender and orientation may be up for grabs. That's called Noonan's Syndrome," he continued.

"Stop!" pleaded Maggie.

"The point is," Bill said with a satisfied look, "that nature is *not* neat. Biological sex is not an easy issue. Further, when we talk about 'male' and 'female,' we're talking about 'sex,' 'sexual identity,' and 'sex role.' When we ask the question, 'What is a "male"?' we're not just asking about chromosomes, hormones, gonads, genitals, and differences of the brain. We're asking about sexual identity and sex role. We're asking both about the sex of assignment and rearing, as well as gender identity differentiation. In other words, is a person male who has 'xy' chromosomes, is raised male, but sees self as female?"

"What was that about sex role?" Beatrice asked.

"What 'sex role' does a female have that a male does not have, and vice versa?" asked Bill.

Again, the room was silent.

"Females lactate, gestate, and menstruate," he answered. "Males impregnate. That is how the two sexes are distinguished by their 'sex roles.' But what if there is no ability to lactate, gestate, menstruate, or impregnate? How do you answer the question 'What is a male?'?"

"This is confusing," Maggie said.

"Good," said Bill with delight. "And we haven't even started talking about gender role and sex-coded role. Where before we were asking the question 'What is a male?' we now ask the question 'What is "masculine" and "feminine"?' and what is the difference between a man with a feminine sex-coded role and a man who is gay?"

"Can you stop there for a minute," Beatrice asked. "Sex-coded role and sexual orientation?"

"Good. You ready for a couple more definitions?" Bill asked. "Sexual orientation is about our erotic potential. What turns us on erotically?"

"Is that the same as 'sexual lifestyle'?" asked Grace.

"No," he replied. "Sexual lifestyle refers to the patterns around which we organize for daily living. For instance, open marriage would be a sexual lifestyle."

"What's an open marriage?" Maggie asked. "Is that like 'swinging'?"

"No, they're different. We'll talk more at the end of the week about the various options for sexual lifestyles," Bill said. "But let's get back to *my* question. What's the difference between a man with a feminine sex-coded role and man who is gay? First, what's our 'sex-coded role' or our 'gender-coded' role?"

Again, silence.

"Sex-coded roles, or gender-coded roles, terms which I use interchangeably, are those attitudes, roles, and behaviors that we find *appropriate* for ourselves. These we label as 'positive.' They are also those attitudes, roles, and behaviors that we find appropriate for the *other* sex. These we label as 'negative.' It all happens for most of us by age two and a half. Deaf and autistic children code later."

Bill now drew two large circles, side by side, that touched on one outer edge. He labeled one "masculine" and the other "feminine."

"As a male, I might label masculine gender roles as 'positive,' and feminine gender roles as 'negative'," he said. "For instance, I might *hate* doing dishes, and label it as 'feminine' and 'negative.' My whole life, I'd hate doing dishes. That doesn't mean that I *couldn't* do dishes. I just wouldn't feel *natural* doing them. I might even be a dishwasher by vocation, but I would always have to go against my nature to do them. Yet, another male might code doing dishes as 'positive.' He might *love* doing dishes. Now, remember, this says *nothing* about our erotic potential. In other words, it says nothing about our sexual orientation. It's just about doing dishes. Do we label doing dishes as 'positive,' or as 'negative.'

In today's world, as a result of the women's movement, and the men's movement, there's a lot of overlap in what is labeled 'positive' by the sexes. Boys are raised to have less negative feelings about doing traditionally feminine things, and girls are more able to acknowledge their positive feelings about doing traditionally masculine sex-coded behaviors. Would you agree with that?"

"Of course," Marjorie said. "Men are more able to show their emotions. Women are admired for being assertive."

"Sometimes," Pam interjected.

"Okay. Now. Moving on," Bill said with a look of satisfaction and excitement. "How would you label a man who codes 'positive' for masculine-coded gender roles, and 'positive' for feminine-coded gender roles?"

"Transgender," offered Carla with confidence.

"Exactly," said Bill. "More precisely, 'transvestite,' although I acknowledge that there is a lot of debate in the transgender community about terminology. 'Transvestite' has fallen out of favor."

"Would the word 'bi-gendered' work here too, Bill?" Carol asked.

"It's a new term but I like it, and I think it works," he responded. "Now, how would you label a man who codes 'negative' for masculine-coded gender roles, and 'positive' for feminine-coded gender roles?"

"Transsexual," answered Betty after a few seconds of silence.

"Correct," said Bill with a proud and affectionate smile. "A transsexual is a person who has his or her entire life coded as 'positive' for themselves the gender role of the other sex, and 'negative' for themselves the gender role of their biological sex. And the answer to the question 'What's the difference between a man with a feminine sex-coded role and man who is gay?' is that the first is an example of 'gender identity,' and the second is an example of 'sexual orientation,' or erotic attraction. There isn't a comparison to be made. For the record, most transvestites, bi-gendered people, and transsexuals are *heterosexual* in their sexual orientation, but some of them are gay."

He now drew a line indicating the "Transgender Continuum." The name "Joe" was written at the far left end, and "Joanne" at the other end. In between the two he wrote the words, from left to right, "traditional male," "transvestite," "transgender/bi-gendered," and "transsexual."

"At this end of the continuum," he said, pointing to the word 'transsexual', "Joe becomes Joanne. There are one thousand surgeries a year from male to female, and 500 a year from female to male."

Stopping, and standing still and quiet for a few seconds, Bill smiled warmly at all of us. "I think that the most important message that we can get from all of this is *diversity*. Gender is on a continuum. Orientation is on a continuum. *Everything* is on a continuum. That's the major message of nature! It is *diversity*.

"I know that this is a lot of information given to you in a very short period of time," he continued, "but I wanted to offer you a quick framework for the next segment of our time together, which is to put a 'face' on transsexuality. Are you ready to move on? What if I told you that one of our participants had made such a transition in his or her life, and was willing to talk with us about it now?"

To this cue, many of the participants smiled, and offered looks of support to Betty, who smiled back appreciatively, but with a slow nodding back and forth of her head indicated that Bill wasn't talking about her. Leona, as many others, looked confused.

"Kevin," Bill said with a big grin, and with his right hand outstretched, "will you come up and share with us your very important story?"

Chapter Twenty-Four

Kevin's Story

Kevin wrung his hands slowly as he sat in the chair at the front of the room, next to Bill, who was beaming.

"For some of you, I know this comes as a big surprise," he said in a nearly inaudible voice, soft and low in his nervousness.

"A little louder," Bill whispered as he put his arm around Kevin's shoulder and squeezed it.

"I know that this comes as a big surprise for some of you," Kevin repeated more clearly as he raised his head and looked at nearly everyone but Dan, who sat with a pleasant smile but gently crossed arms.

"It's hard to keep something like this to myself, but I've learned that it helps to have people get to know you a little before you tell them that you're a transsexual," he explained.

"And we on the staff have asked Kevin to wait until today to share the information, even with his SAR group," Bill interjected in a strong, declarative tone. "We, too, feel that it's important for us all to experience the person before we explore the labels. I'm sorry, Kevin, please continue."

"Anyway, Bill and the staff have asked me to share my story with you. I've been doing this for the last couple of years, and I do it for Bill in his class at Widener," Kevin continued. "Nevertheless, I'm really shy, and speaking isn't easy for me.

"I've known that I was different for as long as I can remember, but I didn't know why. I was born a girl in a large, close-knit family. I've got two older sisters and two younger brothers. I always wanted to play with my brothers, and not hang around with my sisters, which was fine with each of them. I was your typical tomboy," he smiled. "I'd climb trees, and play sports, mostly baseball and touch football, and I'd *always* wear jeans or cut offs. I'd never wear a dress. *Never.* I couldn't stand wearing girls' clothes. I felt like a freak in frilly things. So I wore what my brothers wore. This worked okay for me until I entered puberty, and my body started to change. I really started to *hate* my body then. I hated the fact that I was getting breasts, and that boys were looking at them. I hated getting a period. I thought it was awful and I'd just cry. My mother and my older sisters tried to help but I didn't want their advice. I used to pray at night that I'd wake up a boy in the morning. Sometimes I'd even dream that I *was* a boy, that I had a penis, and hair on my chest, and that I was this really cool James Bond kind of guy. I liked James Bond. He was confident and masculine without being super macho.

"My parents quit trying to get me to like girl things like Barbie dolls and little Betty Crocker ovens," Kevin said smiling to the very quiet and attentive participants. "My favorite Christmas present was a football that my younger brothers pitched in and bought me. My parents sort of decided I was a tomboy, and that I'd eventually grow out of it. I think they thought I might be a lesbian because I didn't date boys. That's when things really started to get complicated for me, during my teenage years. I didn't want to go out with guys because I didn't want them touching my breasts. I had kind of big breasts, and, as I said, they got a lot of attention. I liked being with guys who didn't care about my breasts, and they turned out to be the guys who were gay. I really didn't know who I was attracted to. I worried that I was a lesbian because having women attracted to you sort of fit my James Bond image, but I wasn't really interested in having sex with a girl. I just think I liked the idea that I *could* have sex with her if I was a guy. I don't know if that makes any sense, but that's what I was feeling at the time."

Sighing, Kevin looked up at the ceiling for a few seconds in silence and then continued in a softer, more serious voice. "I really *hated* my life," he said. "I hated my body. I hated being a girl. I hated the attention I got from other boys. I hated my confusion about my sexuality. I just wanted to die. If I couldn't just fall asleep and wake up a boy, I wanted to die so that I didn't have to live my whole life feeling so confused and miserable.

I thought about taking pills. I also thought about running away but I didn't know where I'd go. I wrote a couple of suicide notes but I ended up ripping them up. I remember trying to say in them that my parents shouldn't feel bad because they didn't do anything wrong, that I was a freak, and they were better off without me.

"I didn't do very good in school," he continued, still avoiding eye contact with Dan. "I was pretty good at sports, but I didn't get very good grades. Everyone else in my family was smart, and I felt stupid. A teacher in high school got me interested in photography. I took a lot of the pictures for the yearbook. I liked working in the dark room, dipping the photographic paper in chemicals, and seeing an image appear. I liked knowing that I could capture things with my camera just as they are, or I could shoot something at a different angle, and capture it in a whole new way." Here he chuckled softly at his own efforts at philosophy. "Maybe it's because I wanted others to see me in a whole new way," he smiled.

"At any rate, I graduated just barely from high school, and I got a job at our local community newspaper as a photographer. I didn't have many friends. I lived at home. And I was *really* depressed," he said, raising his eyebrows to indicate his frustration. "And then one night, while I was at home alone watching television, I was channel surfing, and I came upon this program on 'transsexuality.' It was on a cable station, and they were interviewing all of these people who had sex-change operations. The first people I saw were people who were born male and had transitioned to female, but then they interviewed some guys who had been born female and they talked about their experiences, and I thought, 'That's me! That's me!' I got up out of my chair and started pacing around the room, and I kept saying 'That's me! That's me!' I was shaking, I was so excited and so nervous. Then I sat down and started listening again, and I noticed that the guys who had the operation were really good looking guys. You could *never* tell that they were once girls. And I thought 'I could look like that!'

"At the end of the program," Kevin said with a big smile, "I wrote down the information they gave on who to contact if you had any questions. It was for the Harry Benjamin Association. I wrote them this long letter the next day explaining to them all about me. I waited and waited for the reply. I thought, 'They're not going to answer me. They think I'm a nut. They're going to contact my parents or call the local mental hospital or the police. I'm going to end up in a straight jacket.' But then, the reply finally came, and they referred me to Bill Stayton because he was the closest professional to where I lived. So, I called Bill the next day from a pay phone several miles from my house. He wasn't in, and his secretary said he would call me back. I hung up and kept calling him until he showed up at the office. I know I drove your secretary crazy," Kevin said with a smile at Bill. "But finally we connected, and then my life changed forever. Why don't you take over for a minute? I need a break."

"When Kevin called me," Bill said, not missing a beat, "I arranged for him to come in and talk about his feelings. He fit the profile of a transsexual perfectly. We then spent a lot of time together talking about his options. I provided him a lot of literature about transgender issues and had him come and sit in on a weekly group I run for transgender people. There he met people from the whole transgender spectrum, including a man who had transitioned from being a biological female."

"That's where I met Betty," Kevin piped in, smiling broadly at Betty. "She was *great*! She took me under her wing right off the bat. I was a little afraid of the guy who had transitioned. He seemed a little grumpy to me at first. But Betty was really cool. She made sure I felt at home."

"You were *adorable*," Betty said from her seat. "Scared like the rest of us when we first started our journeys, but adorable. And you still are!"

Kevin blushed as Bill continued his description of the process.

"We brought Kevin's parents into the process pretty early in the game," Bill said. "Though Kevin was an adult, he still lived at home, and wanted and needed the support of his entire family. He suspected that his younger brothers would be okay, but he feared that his mother and father and his sisters would have a hard time with it. He was right."

"Everyone blamed themselves," Kevin said, "and everyone blamed Bill. Initially, Mom and Dad insisted that I see a psychiatrist, which I did, and she told them that I was a classic transsexual, and that I was very lucky to be working with Bill Stayton. So then they started talking about me just being a lesbian, and how that would be okay with them. But, I said I didn't think I *was* a lesbian. It took a lot of time before they could get on board. My mom had a harder time than my dad, especially when she started thinking about how my grandparents and my aunts and uncles might react. In the beginning, they asked me to keep the whole thing to myself."

"That's pretty hard to do," Bill spoke up, "because before a surgeon will perform reconstructive surgery, the transsexual candidate has to live for a year as the sex to which he or she is being surgically assigned. That meant that Kevin was required to take testosterone and to live as a male every day, all day, for an entire year."

"Which meant coming out to my boss at work and telling him what was going on," Kevin said. "He was pretty cool about the whole thing, and since we were a small company, the bathroom issue was no big deal. We had a men's room and a women's room but they were single occupancy, and no one seemed to mind that I used the men's room. We were a small staff, so the editor called a staff meeting, told everyone what was going on, asked me to talk about why I was going through it, and gave everyone the chance to ask questions. People sort of took their lead from him. My parents, on the other hand, asked me to move out of the house and into an apartment of my own. They helped me with the rent. Mom just wasn't ready to have someone drop in and see me. She didn't know what she would say. So, I moved into my own place, and saw my family at designated times, which usually didn't include the holidays because those were always big family events. My mom made up stories for my grandparents and aunts and uncles about why I wasn't home for Thanksgiving and Christmas."

"Kevin's surgery involved a radical mastectomy, a hysterectomy, and genital reconstruction surgery," Bill said. "It's expensive and most insurance companies don't cover the costs. Not every person who is transsexual opts for surgery. Some can't afford it, and some don't see it as necessary for themselves. There are some people in Kevin's position who take testosterone, have their breasts removed, but don't go any further."

"I wanted the full program," Kevin said, "and I was lucky. I needed to have some surgery done that my insurance company was willing to cover, and I got my doctor to do it all at one time, at least in terms of the hysterectomy and the radical mastectomy. The genital reconstruction was another matter. There are a couple of different ways you can go with the reconstruction surgery. Some guys opt for a 'phalloplasty,' which is to have a penis constructed from skin and fatty tissue that's taken from the stomach, the inner thigh, and the forearm, then rolled, and attached to the groin area. This penis doesn't get erect, but you can opt for a device that allows you to pump it up or you can have an implant that makes it erect. Other people choose to have a 'metaoidioplasty.' With this surgery, the clitoris is freed so that it will be more prominent. It has already been enlarged and elongated through testosterone therapy. The metaoidioplasty procedure allows the clitoris to be easily seen and stimulated. It also involves creating a scrotum from the skin of the labia majora and inserting testicular implants. All of this is for the psychological benefit of the individual. The female to male transsexual, or FTMs, can't create semen or ejaculate through the constructed penis. You can, however, pee through the penis that is constructed through phalloplasty, which is very important to some people who want to be able to pee standing up. With metaoidioplasty, you can opt to have the urethra extended, but it's expensive and a bit complicated. I didn't bother with that procedure.

"I had my genital reconstructive surgery done in Colorado," he continued. "There are three or four places in the country that are well-known for this type of work. I decided in favor of utilizing my own clitoris as my sex organ. So, my penis is bigger than my clitoris would have appeared otherwise, but it's not a 'big' penis. If you remember Pam's story about being in Trinidad, my penis is what you'd call a 'zut'."

"It's not the size that counts," Bill said with a smile and a nod of affirmation, "it's how you *use* it." Then, looking at his watch, he said, "Why don't we stop now, and see if there are any questions?"

In response, several people began to clap enthusiastically for Kevin, who smiled appreciatively back. Within seconds, the room was filled with the sound of strong applause, and whistles, and hoots of support. When it was quiet again, Maggie raised her hand, and asked, "Kevin, did your family ever come around?"

"Yea, they're pretty good now," he said. "My sisters and brothers came with me to Colorado for the operation, which was very cool. From the very beginning, they called me 'Kevin.' My dad did good in not calling me by my birth name, but it took him a long time before he could call me 'Kevin.' My mom called me by my female name for a really long time. I kept asking her not to. She said that I was still her little girl, and nothing was going to change that. But now, they're all pretty good. Everyone calls me 'Kevin'."

"And do you go home for the holidays?" Maggie asked.

"Yea, now I go home for holidays," Kevin said.

"Tell them what happened to change things," Bill egged Kevin on.

"Well, my younger brother Tim, who I was always pretty close to, when he got married, he asked me to be his best man," Kevin said in a voice that suddenly cracked with emotion. "My mom went ballistic at first, but Tim said that I was going to be his best man and that if anyone didn't want to come, that was their business. That's when my mom and dad started telling all of the relatives so that they would be prepared. I was a nervous wreck, but almost all of my relatives, including my grandparents, were great. They all told my mom that they loved me, and they didn't care what I called myself, and that if *I* was happy, they were happy for me. So, there I was, standing on the altar at the church, in my tuxedo, next to my brother Tim. It was a really great experience."

"And tell them about the reception," Bill said with a nudge.

"Well, as you know, the best man is supposed to make a toast," Kevin said. "So I stood up, clinked the glass to get everyone's attention, and then made this short but nice toast. So, then my brother Tim stands up, clinks his glass, takes the microphone, and says that he wants to toast me, his brother Kevin, who was truly the best man at the wedding. Well, I started to cry, and my brothers and sisters stand up and applaud, and then a bunch of my cousins stand up, and my Aunt Connie, who's my mom's sister, and then my grandma, and then probably half the crowd, but I don't think that most of them knew what they were clapping about. But since then, things changed with my parents."

"That's great!" Maggie said.

"Kevin," Leona called out from her seat.

"Yes, Leona?" he replied.

"Thank you for telling your story," she said. "You're a *very* brave person. But can you clarify something for me? What's your sexual orientation? Didn't you tell me that you were gay? How did you end up gay in all of this? If you liked girls before, I thought you'd end up being straight?"

"That's a really good question," he replied with a nod and a smile that affirmed her bewilderment. "It's real clear to me now that I'm attracted to men. I don't know if I always was but never thought about it because I didn't want to be seen by them as a woman, or if I'm bisexual and have just become aware that my homosexual feelings are the stronger of the two, or if the testosterone had some effect, or if I was out of touch with my sexual orientation because I was so focused on my gender identity. I don't know for sure what the answer is. I know, though, that it would be easier if I *was* heterosexual. To begin with, it would have been a lot easier dealing with my family. Me being both transsexual *and* gay was a lot for my mom and dad to cope with. They asked 'So, if you were going to end up being attracted to men, why didn't you stay a heterosexual woman?' Doctors used to ask the same question and for years, many of them wouldn't perform reconstructive surgery on a gay person. They were obviously confusing two different issues, 'gender identity' and 'sexual orientation.' But I didn't want a sex-change operation because of who I was attracted to. I wanted it because I was completely miserable in a female body. Eventually the doctors figured that out, and with a lot of help from Bill, so did my family."

Here Kevin paused, stared at the ceiling for a moment, sighed, shot a quick look at Dan, and then faced Leona. "And last but not least, it would be easier for me if I was heterosexual because I think there are more women out there who would be comfortable with my body than there are gay men. I think penis size is a lot less of an issue for women. But, I'm *not* heterosexual. I'm gay."

"Not just *gay*," Carla piped in, "a handsome, sexy, fun gay man with a killer smile!"

To that, Bill winked appreciatively and again put his arm around Kevin's shoulder and said, "We've run out of time, but I just want to say that Kevin is a gift to me and to my students at Widener. He has opened more eyes with his honesty about himself. It's now time to go to our process groups, but before we go, how about giving Kevin another round of applause."

Once again, the room filled with strong applause that instantly became a standing ovation. Kevin smiled shyly in response. Several people, including Maggie, Thomas, Betty, Carla, George, and Annette rushed forward from their seats to give Kevin a hug, to touch his arm, to kiss his cheek, to shake his hand, to pat his back, or to offer a few quick words of appreciation. As Kevin scanned the room, which stayed full of participants talking with enthusiasm to each other about his story, he spotted Dan, who nodded, gave him a "thumbs up" sign, and slipped out the door and up the stairs.

Chapter Twenty-Five

Dan's Reaction

"You look as if you've just lost your best friend," Peter said as he approached Dan, who was sitting on the lawn outside of Ridings.

"Fuck off," Dan replied after noting who had made the comment.

"Why are you so damn hostile?" Peter asked, still standing.

"Because you're a fuckin' phony," Dan replied, focusing his attention on the lake at the bottom of the hill.

"*I'm* a phony?" Peter said. "Who just ducked out on his new boyfriend because he found out he was born female? You walk around here like Mr. Gay Liberation, or rather, Mr. *Queer* Liberation. Who's a bigger phony?"

"Fuck you!" Dan said. "Why don't you and that closeted dyke Catherine go hold a prayer meeting, and ask Jesus to save you from your desires?"

"And why don't you ask Him to save you from yourself?" Peter replied as he walked away toward Huntington to get a drink before the start of his SAR process group meeting.

Dan stood and felt himself swell with rage, and the desire to grab Peter from behind and throw him down the hill. Yelling out, "Eat shit, you closet case," was his next best response.

"Well now, that's quite a strong statement," Alison said as she left the group with which she was walking, and put her hand gently on Dan's shoulder. "Anything you want to talk about?" she asked as she rubbed his back and smiled warmly.

"Sorry," Dan said. "He and I have a few differences of opinion."

"That's why we're here, to sort them out," Alison comforted. "Tell me, Dan, how was that last session for you?"

"Kevin was great," he said, looking away. "He did great."

"Yes, he did," she replied, "but how was it for *you*? I suspect that Kevin hadn't shared with you that he was transsexual. That must have come as quite a surprise."

"Yea, it did. It came as quite a *big* surprise," Dan said, focusing his eyes again on the lake. "I had no idea. It's really remarkable when you think about it."

"Yes, it is," Alison affirmed, "and besides admiration for Kevin, how did his story impact you? What feelings came up? Did you feel sad, angry, happy, confused?"

"Yes. Yes. Yes. And yes," Dan said, finally smiling. "I felt a little 'set up,' to tell you the truth. We've been hanging out a little together, and I just wish I had known his story, that's all."

"Do you understand why Kevin doesn't start off with his story when he meets people, particularly handsome young men such as you that he hopes might be attracted to him?" Alison asked kindly.

"Yea, it all makes sense, but it doesn't mean that it's right," he replied. "There are two people involved. Two sets of feelings."

"Yes, there are. It's a little like revealing your HIV status right off the bat isn't it?" she asked. "It's not a perfect analogy, but you get my point. Some people who are HIV positive want to have the other person get to know them before they decide they can't handle it."

Dan turned and looked at her intently. Finally he smiled. "You're a very smart lady," he said.

"I don't know about that," Alison replied. "I just know that it's complicated. Nothing is neat. Everything is gray, including our sexual orientation identity. 'Queer,' 'ex-gay,' 'closet case,' are just words that reflect the gray of perception. Perceptions change. Words change. What matters is what works for the person."

"Maybe," he said. "I need to give that some thought. Peter's as 'gay' as I am. It makes me really crazy when people pretend to be something that they're not."

"We all do it at different times in our lives, Dan. *Why* we do it is the important question for us," she said. Then, looking at her watch and the empty grounds around her, she exclaimed, "I'm sorry. Can we continue this at another time? We're both going to be late for our group meetings if we don't hurry. And *I'm* the one who harps on punctuality!"

"Yea. Sure. And thanks," Dan said as he leaned down and kissed her on her forehead. Not being able to help himself, he then added, "But it *still* pisses me off that Peter is lying about being 'ex-gay,' and I'm *not* sure what to do with my feelings about Kevin."

"Talk about it in your group, dear," Alison said as she hurried off. "Stay in touch with your feelings, and trust the process."

Chapter Twenty-Six

Maggie's Map

Kevin slumped in his spot on the sofa, looking exhausted, but smiling with accommodation to the affirming statements of our SAR group members as they entered Higley.

"Nice job, Kevin," Beatrice said. "I was *really* proud of you."

"Me too," added Margaret as she took the seat to his right, and patted his knee. "You did well."

"Alrighty then," I said in an undistinguishable Ace Ventura impersonation, "let's begin with Kevin. How are you feeling?"

"I'm glad it's over," he said with a half laugh, and weak smile.

"How do you think you did?" I asked.

"I did okay," he grinned back at me. "I think it went pretty well."

"Me too," I winked, smiling.

"You were *awesome*," Maggie said.

"Great job, Kevin. You blew me away," added Charlie.

"Thanks," he said, and sat silently with us for a moment or two.

Then, sitting up straight with a pained look on her face, Leona asked, "Kevin, can I be perfectly honest with you?"

"Sure," he replied.

"I'm feeling overwhelmed right now, and I don't know what to do with all of my feelings," she said with a deep sigh. "From the moment I laid eyes on you, I thought you were the cutest thing I had seen in a long, long time. I was *so* disappointed to hear that you were gay, but I got past that. I thought, 'Well, it's not my thing and I don't fully understand it, but if that's what he is, that's what he is.' But now, to learn that you were born a girl is just blowing me away. I keep thinking, 'What if he was *my* child, *my* daughter? What would I do?' I like you, Kevin, a whole lot, but I need you to know that I do *not* know what I would do if you were my child, and I don't feel good about that."

"Feel good about what, Leona?" I asked gently, sensing her vulnerability.

"Feel good about the way I *feel*," she replied with angry exasperation.

"I understand," Kevin said in a low voice as he held Leona's gaze.

"I'm glad that *you* do, because I sure as hell don't," she said, shaking her head slowly.

"It's all new to you," Kevin comforted with a supportive smile. "Give yourself a break."

"Yea, give yourself a break," echoed Charlie.

"But I'm supposed to be more *accepting* than I am, and I think more accepting than the rest of *you*. I work for Planned Parenthood," Leona said, her voice cracking. "*Planned Parenthood*! I'm real good at pregnancy prevention. Real good. Those kids think I'm very cool. But I tell you, I feel like I am flunking every challenge thrown my way here at Thornfield. I feel like I have wandered into 'Bizarro Land.' Is it just *me*, or is anyone else feeling like this too?"

"I'm sure we're all feeling a little challenged, but I agree with Kevin, Leona," said Margaret as she leaned forward, and reached her hand across the circle to touch Leona's knee. "This is new for a lot of us. Don't beat yourself up for taking some time to think it through. My guess is that Kevin's not personalizing our confusion. He's undoubtedly run into it before, and will again."

"And I'd like to say that working at Planned Parenthood doesn't mean that you're going to be comfortable with *every* sexual issue," Beatrice added. "You're human. You're learning like the rest of us."

"I don't think anyone would want their child to be gay or transgender," Maggie said. "I don't know how it all happens, but once it does, I'm sure it takes some getting used to. Why do you think it should be easier for *you*, Leona, than it might be for *me*?"

"Okay. Enough attention on Leona. I've said my piece. Let's move on," Leona said to me, gesturing like a cop who was directing traffic.

"Thanks for putting yourself out there, Leona," I said. "I hope you heard the affirmation from the others in the group that a lot of this is challenging for them too."

"Yes. Thank you. Let's move on," she replied with raised eyebrows and a sigh.

"Gotcha," I smiled sympathetically. "Does anyone else have anything they'd like to share about this afternoon's presentation, either Bill's or Kevin's? Yes, Wendy?"

"I just want to say how much I admire you, Kevin. You sure have a lot of courage," she said.

"Thanks," smiled Kevin.

"Anyone else before we move on?" I asked.

"Can I ask something?" Dom interjected.

"Sure," I answered.

"It's about something else," he said.

"Go ahead," I replied.

"What's with Dan yelling at Peter out on the lawn as we were coming over here?" Dom asked. "I was glad to see Alison walk over to talk to Dan. I thought what he said to Peter was inappropriate. Was it all in reaction to Kevin's talk?"

"I didn't hear it," I said honestly, "but let's assume that Dan and Peter are each dealing in their own SAR groups with their feelings about Kevin's presentation, and about their verbal exchange. The question that comes up for me, Dom, is what feelings did it bring up for *you*?"

"You mean Kevin's talk?" he asked.

"That or whatever happened between Dan and Peter?" I replied.

"I felt good about Kevin's presentation," he said. "Like Leona here, I don't know what *I* would do if a kid of mine ever said they were transsexual, but I learned something new, which is why I came here in the first place. And I admire Kevin's courage. I don't think I could do the same thing if I was in his position."

"Any feelings about Dan and Peter's exchange?" I asked.

"Will someone *please* tell me what happened with Dan and Peter?" Leona said.

"Dan yelled at Peter saying that he was a 'closet case'," Maggie said.

"How is that about Kevin?" Leona asked.

"I didn't say that it was," Maggie said. "Dom did."

"I didn't say that it was. I *asked* if it was," Dom replied.

"We're getting off track here," I interjected. "What happened between Dan and Peter is their business. The only purpose that it serves to discuss it here is how it made *us* feel. Stay with your own feelings. Dom, did you have feelings about their exchange that you want to share?"

"No," he said.

"Kevin," I said, "you've been brought into this discussion. Any feelings that you'd like to share?"

"No," said Kevin.

"Anyone else?" I asked.

Silence.

"Okay, then, if it's all right with you, I'd like to move on," I said. "We can come back to this any time that you'd like, but I want us to start the process of sharing our personal journeys. My hope is that most of you have finished writing them up. Is anyone ready to share with us his or her map of their sexual journey?" I asked.

"I feel like I've already done mine," Kevin laughed.

"You did a lot of yours, Kevin, and it was great, but there may be more that you'd like to share with this group. Let's keep that option open," I replied. "But how about the rest of you? Anyone ready?"

"I am," said Maggie, "but I think most of you know what's on my map already."

"Good, Maggie. Thank you for volunteering. You go first. You can use the coffee table to display it, if you want. We'll pull our chairs forward," I said, doing so.

Maggie's sheet of newsprint was filled with brightly colored stick figures. There were five groupings.

"Do you want me to go through it?" she asked.

"Yes, please," I replied.

"Okay. Well, this is me when I was 13-years-old," she said, pointing to one of the four figures with curly orange hair in the upper left-hand corner of the sheet. "I'm here in the middle. That's my mom, and that's my older sister, Ginny, and my younger sister, Patty. My dad died in an automobile accident, and this is all of us after he died."

Turning to me she explained, "You said to put four or five events in our lives that impacted us positively or negatively with regard to our sense of self sexually. My dad's death, I think, had a really big impact on my sense of *family*."

"Tell us how you feel your dad's death impacted you, would you Maggie?" I asked.

"I don't know how it did completely, but I know that when I think about my life, that's the first big memory that jumps out at me," Maggie said. "We all sort of pulled together. It was hard on all of us. Mom was faced with raising three daughters and having to make a living. Ginny became our 'mom.' I helped take care of Patty. It made me grow up really fast, I think. It was a sad time. That's why there are frowns on all of our faces. But we pulled through.

"This picture," she said, pointing to the upper right-hand corner of the sheet where there were two, broadly smiling stick figures, a curly orange-haired one with green eyes, and another with dark black hair and blue eyes, "this is Barry and me on our wedding day. It was a *very* happy day for me. We were high school sweethearts. We met freshman year and dated nonstop. In senior year, I was the homecoming queen. He was class president, and he crowned me. It was very *romantic*. We both went to the University of Wisconsin, and got married right after we got out of college. My mom and sisters love Barry, and his family loves me."

Here Maggie sighed deeply, teared up, and sat silently for a moment. Beatrice grabbed the box of Kleenex from the floor, and handed it to Maggie.

"Thanks," she said as she pulled out two, and dabbed at her eyes. "I'm sorry. I promised myself that I wasn't going to cry."

Taking a deep breath, she continued. "Barry and I decided to stay in Racine near our families. He got a good job at S.C. Johnson, and I stayed home to take care of our first born, Sean Patrick. That's us standing together at his birth eleven years ago," Maggie said, pointing to the picture in the center of the page that depicted her holding a baby, with Barry standing by with a big smile.

"Here we have me holding Mary Louise. She's nine-years-old now. And then, this last picture," she said, pointing with a sad sigh to the one in the lower right-hand corner, "is Barry and me after he came back from Thornfield last year. That's when he told me he was 'gay.' I put frowns on both of our faces because he's as sad about all of this as I am. I know he loves me, and I know he loves the children and he doesn't want to lose any of us. Neither one of us wants the family to be pulled apart. That's why we're in therapy. But I know that I'm losing him. I can feel it. Anyway, that's my map. How did I do? Did I pass?"

"You did a *great* job," I replied. "There's no test. But before we see if anyone has any questions or comments, Maggie, can you talk for a minute about how it was to do the map, and how it felt to share it?"

"Sure. Doing it wasn't real hard, at least in terms of coming up with the five points," she said. "I suspect that if you did the map more than once in your life, different things would appear, but for me, these are the five 'biggies' right now. I felt sad as I drew the pictures. I cried a little when I put the frowns on Barry's and my faces at the end. I don't cry or feel sad about my dad's death anymore because it was so long ago, but right now my whole world seems torn apart because of Barry being gay, and it feels real fresh. One day, I suppose, I won't cry when I think about it, but that feels like a long time off."

"How did you feel sharing it with the group?" I asked.

"Fine," she replied. "I think everyone knew about Barry anyway. It wasn't like I was revealing any deep dark secret. I feel comfortable with this group."

"Brian, may we ask questions of Maggie?" Margaret inquired.

"Absolutely," I replied, "and Maggie is free to not answer if she so chooses."

"It's actually more of an observation than it is a question," Margaret said, smiling at Maggie warmly. "In looking over your drawings, I noticed that the beginning and the end are similar in many ways. In each, there is an end to the way things were. Someone has left, or appears to be leaving. The figures in both are frowning. The children are nearly the same ages. Have you and your mother talked about this?"

"She knows that something is going on," Maggie replied with a weak smile. "She caught me crying a couple of times, and asked me what was up. I just said that Barry and I were going through some challenging times. I haven't wanted to be specific, and Barry's not ready to tell anyone in the family that he's gay. Sometimes I really want to talk with her about it, but I respect his need for privacy. It's just that besides our therapist and Barry, I don't know who I can talk with about it."

"And the children don't know?" asked Beatrice.

"No. They know that Mommy and Daddy aren't as happy as before, but we keep assuring them that we love them and that we love each other," Maggie said.

"How does he know he's gay?" Leona asked. "Maybe he's 'bi.' Maybe it's just a phase."

"That's what I was hoping too," Maggie answered with a nod and smile. "He assures me that it's *not* a phase, that he's felt like this his whole life. That's the hard part for me. Why didn't he tell me back in high school? Why did he wait until now? Sometimes I feel so duped, and that's when I get really angry. I could have made different choices. Had I known what he was feeling, I could have married someone else. Oh, geeze, what am I saying? I wouldn't have wanted to marry someone else. He's my soul mate, dammit."

Chapter Twenty-Seven

Dom's Uncle Murray

Seeing that Kevin wanted to talk with me, Dom exited Higley with the rest of our SAR group, and waited for me at the nearest picnic table. I waved appreciatively, and indicated with outstretched fingers that I needed five minutes.

"So, how are you doing?" I asked Kevin, who had stayed seated.

"Do you have time to talk?" Kevin replied with an expression of concern on his face.

"Dom and I are scheduled to meet now, but I've got a few minutes," I said. "He'll wait for me. Tell me how you're doing."

"I'm okay, I guess. Did you see how Dan sort of fled the room?" he asked.

"I noticed that he didn't hang around. You didn't tell him before the session, did you?"

"I wanted to. I just ran out of time. Everything happened so quickly," he said. "When was I supposed to tell him?"

"How are you feeling?" I asked.

"I'm upset. I *hate* this. Just when I think everything is going great, it all seems to fall apart. It wears me down."

"I understand," I said. "But don't jump to conclusions. You don't know how Dan feels. You don't know for sure what he felt *before* your talk, and you don't know what he feels now. Why don't you go search him out, and ask him how he feels?"

"Yea, I know," Kevin replied. "What do you think I should say?"

"Say what you're feeling. Say 'I'm sorry that I didn't tell you about me before I told the whole group. I was afraid that you'd reject me, and I felt that you were getting to like me. Everything happened so fast that I didn't know when to do it.' Then I'd ask him to talk about *his* feelings. When he talks about them, just listen."

"God, I hate this," he said.

"I know. I hate it too. But are you up for it?" I asked.

"Yes. I can do it. I *need* to do it. You going to be around later?"

"Sure. Dom and I are going for a walk. We'll certainly be done by dinner. Come tell me how it went."

"Okay. Thanks," he said.

"How about a hug?" I asked.

"I need one badly," he sighed as he got up, stepped forward, and allowed me to pull him to me for a good, long embrace.

"I love you, Kevin," I said.

"I love you too," he replied.

The three pats on my back let me know that it was time to end the hug.

As Kevin meandered down toward the lake, Dom followed my lead as I walked toward the driveway.

"I thought we'd just go for a walk if that's okay with you," I said.

"Sounds good," he said. "Are you *sure* that this is a good time?"

"It's great," I replied. "I've been looking forward to talking with you. I think we left off with you saying that you don't feel you have an issue with a person being 'gay,' but that you're turned off if the gay person is confrontational. Does that sound right?"

"You've got a good memory," he said smiling. "I don't really know *why* Dan pushes my buttons, but he sure gets to me. I've wanted to belt him a couple of times. What's with that guy?"

"What is it about him that bothers you the most?" I asked as we walked past Huntington, and onto the long right leg of the U-shaped driveway.

"He's cocky. He's angry. He's foulmouthed. He's obnoxious. How's that for starters?" he asked.

"But why does any of that push *your* buttons?" I asked. "I sort of figure that if someone else's behavior makes me crazy, it's a good indication that I need to take a look at myself. The same person is not prompting the same reactions in all other people. Kevin, for instance, is attracted to Dan. So Dan provides you an opportunity to look at yourself, Dom, and figure out what's going on in you. Are you with me?"

"You lost me. I think lots of people here are turned off by Dan. Do you like him?" he asked.

"He pushes some of my buttons too, but they're *my* buttons," I replied. "There are things about him that I admire. But, again, the issue isn't Dan. He's our teacher. Our feelings about him allow us to take a look at *ourselves*. For instance, Dom, do you see yourself as 'cocky'?"

"No more than most guys I know," he said. "I don't see myself as 'angry,' 'foulmouthed,' or, what did I say, 'obnoxious,' either."

"But you *are* angry," I said. "You're angry at Dan. You're angrier at him than he is at you. Wouldn't you say?"

"I feel like you're defending him," he said. "I think this was a mistake."

"I'm sorry that you feel like that, both that I'm defending him, and that talking about your feelings was a mistake," I said, stopping and looking at him. "I'm not defending Dan's behavior. My opinion of Dan's behavior is irrelevant. It certainly is irrelevant to Dan. He's not going to change his behavior because it pushes my buttons. He *can't* change his behavior to please me. He can only change his behavior if *he* wants to change. So, for me, when you get angry at Dan because of his behavior, the issue isn't Dan, it's your *feelings* about Dan. Dan didn't ask me to go for a walk. You did. Why should you and I waste our time talking about Dan's behavior? We can't change it. We can only change our *expectations* of him, and understand our *reactions* to him. Does that make sense?"

"Yea, I guess," he said with a sigh. "So you're asking me to think about *why* he makes me angry."

"Yes, because when you understand *why* you are reacting the way you are, you can change the way you're reacting," I said as I started walking again. "For instance, one question that I would have for you is, 'If Dan was straight, would his behavior make you as angry as it does?' Another question would be, 'Does Dan *remind* you of anyone in your life?' You may want to also ask, 'Has anything Dan's said triggered painful memories for you?' Again, Dan's your teacher here, Dom. He's unknowingly giving you the opportunity to take a look at yourself. At the end of the week, when you both head in different directions, the angry feelings you have won't disappear. Someone else will come along who triggers the same reactions unless you take the time to figure out why you're reacting the way you are."

"I get it. I get it," he said with a laugh. "Okay. One at a time. Would I be as angry at Dan if he was straight? Probably not. To be honest, I don't think I expect gay people to be as ... "

"Self-affirmed?" I asked.

"Hmm. I'm not sure that's the word I would have chosen," he said.

"Dom, I think it's great that you're even thinking about it," I replied with excitement. "Do you remember when some white people talked about black people being 'uppity?' It's the same thing. It's threatening to people in the majority when people in the minority speak up for themselves without embarrassment. In this case, it's called 'heterosexism.' It's nothing to be ashamed of. We're *all* heterosexist, just as we're all racist and sexist. But it *does* impact how we react. It's like people thinking that gay people holding hands in public is 'flaunting' their sexuality when the exact same behavior by a straight couple wouldn't raise an eyebrow. It's a double standard."

"I've got to think about that one," he said. "I'm not sure it's the same, but I'll think about it."

"I admire your willingness to do so. It will serve you well in your work, and in your personal life," I replied. "So, how about the question on whether Dan's behavior reminds you of someone in your life?"

"If we're talking about 'angry' and 'abusive,' there are some candidates, but the one question you asked at the end is the one that I wanted to talk with you about," he said. "My younger brother and my cousin were both molested by a friend of the family when they were little. The guy used to take them to the ballpark, buy them candy, go to the zoo. I never thought a thing about it, except to be a little jealous of the attention they were getting. The guy was like an uncle. Then we find out that he's feeling them up at the pool, telling them that it's 'normal,' that it's okay because he's a friend of the family. He tells them it's just 'horseplay.' My brother spills the beans one night while we were in bed. He doesn't even know that anything's wrong. He just starts talking about how Uncle Murray gets erections when they go swimming. I tell my pop, and all hell breaks loose. My brother starts crying. Somehow word gets out, and kids at school start laughing about it. My brother and my cousin's friendship ended. It was a mess."

"And you heard Dan defending Uncle Murray?" I asked.

"Yea. That's right. He didn't know he was talking about Uncle Murray, but that asshole did a lot of damage, and anyone who defends it is just as responsible," Dom said angrily.

"Dom, I didn't hear him defend pedophiles," I said cautiously. "I heard him say that not *all* sex between a priest and a young adult was molestation. He said that *he* had sex with a priest, and that it wasn't a 'bad' experience. He wasn't defending the abuse of your younger brother and your cousin by Uncle Murray."

"Say what you think," he replied dismissively.

"Again, it's not about Dan and his opinions. It's about *your* reaction to the issue, your feelings about what happened to your brother. And one of the questions that you'll need to ask yourself is, do you see Uncle Murray as a 'homosexual' or as a 'pedophile'? Or, are they the same thing?"

"I'm not saying that most homosexuals are pedophiles, but wouldn't you agree that most pedophiles are homosexuals?" he asked.

"No, I wouldn't," I answered. "I think that *you* know that most of the children who are abused are young girls who are molested by adult men that they know. And that's not even the issue here. The issue that you might want to take a look at is how did what happened to your brother color your feelings about gay men?"

"I've been wrestling with that one for a long time. If you think I'm angry today, you should have seen me a few years ago. I'm good compared to what I was like. I never would have been able to go for a run with you like I did today," he said. "And I had a good time, incidentally."

"And I didn't try to molest you," I said with a grin.

"And you didn't try to molest me," he laughed.

"You doing okay?" I asked.

"Yea, I'm doing fine," he said. "Thanks for listening. I appreciate it. I don't know what's different, but I'm glad we talked."

"Still want to punch Dan?" I asked.

"Sure. That hasn't changed, but I agree with you that it's my issue, not his."

Moments later, Dom and I headed into dinner. On the other side of the dining room, Leona summoned Dan as he and Kevin headed with dinner trays down the hill toward a picnic table in front of Higley. Walking back to the door of Huntington where she was standing, he asked, "What's up?"

"You be careful on how you treat him, that's what's up," she replied with raised eyebrows in a look of warning. "And you *know* what I'm talking about, so don't act dumb."

"Yes ma'am," he said with a bemused smirk as he turned, and joined Kevin at the table.

"What did she want?" Kevin asked, smiling politely at Leona who was waving at him from the dining room door.

"Just wanted to check in," he said as he shook pepper vigorously over his plate of macaroni and cheese.

Inside the dining room, Pam sat at a table with Lloyd, Thomas, Beatrice, and Ben.

"So, come on everyone. Fess up. How's it going with all of you?" she asked. "You glad you came?"

"Oh, yea. Everything's been great so far," Thomas said grinning. "I'm learning. I'm making new friends. I've got a *great* roommate," to which he lightly punched Lloyd's arm. "I'm confronting some of my own issues. I'm growing. All positives. 'A-plus' for me."

"I'm so glad to hear that," Pam said with genuine enthusiasm, as she reached over and stroked his hand. "And how about you, Lloyd? Same thing?"

"Pretty much," he replied as he poked with his fork at his salad. "It's a *lot* of work, though. Besides all of these sessions, I've got to be working on my presentation for Friday."

"What's that about?" Ben asked. "What's happening on Friday?"

"The 'skill building' workshops," Pam answered. "You in Brian's group?" she asked.

"Yea, and he's a *slave driver*," Lloyd whispered, "but don't tell *him* I told you that."

"I'll bet you get a lot out of it," Pam smiled. "And Beatrice. How about you? Too much work, or does it feel about right to you? How are you doing?"

"I'm doing great," she said, discretely reaching under the table to gently squeeze Ben's knee, as she nodded slowly in affirmation. "I'm really glad that I came."

"I'm glad that you came too," Ben said, smiling at her.

After a few seconds of awkward silence, Ben offered, "Tomorrow is the big day!"

"What's tomorrow?" Lloyd asked nervously.

"Oh, come on, you don't know about tomorrow?" Ben responded playfully.

"No, what's happening tomorrow?" Lloyd asked, turning to Pam for help.

"Oh, nothing," Ben sighed in feigned disappointment.

"Oh, let us in on it," Pam begged in animated excitement. "What's special about tomorrow?"

"Tomorrow is when I go into the *water*," he said with a big grin.

"Really, Ben? That's great. But tell me more," Pam said.

"He hasn't been in the water since his accident," Beatrice explained with a serious look, and then with a broad smile added, "There's a long break between lunch and the afternoon session, so we're going to head down the hill in his chair and get into the water. A couple of people – Maggie and Peter — have offered to help."

"I want in," said Thomas.

"Me too," said Pam and Lloyd in unison

"Well, show up at 1:30 and be ready to get wet," Ben advised with a sly smile. "It's not going to be a 'graceful' entry, I assure you. But who cares? Right?"

At a table across the room, Catherine and Peter both sat down with hair wet from their swim, and with dinner plates only half-covered with food.

"Mind if we join you?" Peter asked as Annette and Joe looked up with welcoming smiles. Dick acknowledged them with a nod but continued to make his point.

"As I say," he said, clearing his throat of phlegm, "I've seen Kevin blossom here at Thornfield. It's a matter of finding fertile ground for growth, I'd say. But that's true for all of us, don't you think?"

"It's true for me, Dick," Annette said as she cut into the small, thin pork chop that waited as the last item on her plate to get attention. "I wasn't always a Sister of Loretto. I was with another religious community for nearly twenty years, and I came to believe that I was dying emotionally. When I indicated my interest in working with people with HIV and AIDS, I was told that such a ministry wasn't within the 'realm' of their mandate, which was to teach. I didn't see myself as a teacher anymore. I felt called to advocate for, and to minister to, people with AIDS. We butted heads about it for a year, and I finally decided that I needed to find a different group of women to grow with. It was hard, because I had to say 'good-bye' to a lot of very good friends. But, as you say, I needed 'fertile ground' in which to grow."

"I admire your courage," Joe said. "It wasn't easy pulling up stakes after all of that time, and relocating in another community. Were there hard feelings?"

"Some members were angry with me for abandoning them," Annette replied. "But most people knew that I needed to make the change and move on. It was hard at first, but nothing to compare to what Kevin went through. Talk about courage."

"It's a shame, I think, that he had to go through it at all," said Catherine. "It surprises me to hear that they've had no success in helping people learn to accept the sex with which they were born. If this phenomenon does occur in humans with any consistency, then there must be thousands of people who have lived before Kevin who learned to live full and happy lives with the conflict Kevin described. I think maybe Kevin's life might have been less painful if he had been able to accept that he was female. I know that he said he didn't identify with being a female, but I'm not so sure that with time and therapy he might not have changed. And his poor parents and siblings. What *they* must have gone through."

"I feel differently, Catherine," Joe replied. "I think it's a *blessing* that Kevin lives in an age in which it's possible to bring harmony to his life. We can only speculate about the painful lives people like Kevin have lived throughout history. Perhaps many of them took their own lives rather than live with such conflict. I can certainly sympathize with Kevin's parents, but, as you well know, life is filled with disappointments, particularly if we have preconceived notions and expectations of how things should be or go. At least, that's been true in my life. Is there anything in your life that makes you feel otherwise?"

Catherine looked at Joe for a few quiet seconds and smiled politely.

"I'm happy for Kevin," Peter said, pulling attention away from Catherine. "He seems very happy, especially compared to how he once felt about himself. That's my criteria. If it doesn't work, figure out a way that you can *make* it work. And yes, that's based upon the experiences of *my* life. Being 'gay' didn't work for me. I've found a way of being in the world that does."

"I'm so glad that you've brought that up," Annette said with excitement. "Ever since I heard you say that you were 'ex-gay,' I've wanted to talk with you, and the time has never seemed right. Can I ask you a couple of questions about it?"

"Sure," Peter said.

"Thanks," said Annette. "Peter, I know lots and lots of gay men who *love* being gay. What didn't you like about it? Why didn't it work for you? And, if I may, when you say that you're 'ex-gay,' does that mean that you're functioning now as a heterosexual?"

'Well, first, I'd want to question your gay friends who say that they're 'happy'," he replied. "Quite frankly, I've *never* met a gay man or lesbian who was truly happy."

"I'm sorry to hear that," said Joe. "I know several."

"Who *say* that they're happy," Catherine piped in.

"I trust that they are," said Joe. "All evidence would support it being true."

"I think Brian and his partner Ray are *very* happy," added Dick, "as much as one could be happy being a homosexual in this culture. I've been with them on many occasions, and I'd say they're as happy as any heterosexual couple I know."

"I don't know Brian and Ray as a couple so I can't comment," Peter said. "All I'm saying is that *I* have yet to meet a gay man or lesbian who was happy. I wasn't. I was miserable. Everywhere I went, everything revolved around *sex*. Sex, sex, sex. That's what my friends talked about, thought about, and lived for. It was boring! And it was cruel. I found gay men particularly to be petty, mean, immature, deceitful, and obsessed with their bodies and the bodies of everyone else. Relationships were anathema. I found nothing of substance in the gay community. No consideration for the plight of other groups, no aspirations to improve themselves except financially and physically, and a complete contempt for anything spiritual. I hated being 'gay,' just as Kevin hated being a female. So, like him, I changed. I found a group named Exodus that I read about in a gay magazine. I started going to meetings. I found support among conservative Christians. I joined a church and got involved in youth work. And I'm much happier."

"Peter, thank you," said Annette with a kind smile, and a soft touch of her hand on his arm. "I'm sorry that you had such a bad experience in the gay community. My guess is that there are some heterosexuals in the singles bar scene who might say the exact same thing about the people they meet there. But you say that you're happier now, and I'm glad for that. None of us should be miserable. St. Catherine of Sienna said, 'The road to heaven *is* heaven.' I want your road to be heaven too. But I'm curious, are you happy now as a man who no longer associates with gay people, or as a man who is now 'heterosexual'?"

"What does it matter?" asked Catherine a bit impatiently. "He's away from the people who made him feel less good about himself, his life, and his relationship to God. As a Catholic nun, Sister, I'd think that would be the important issue."

"Oh, it is, Catherine," Annette said. "And please call me 'Annette.' Be patient with me. I'm here to learn. I've heard the term 'ex-gay' before, and now I have the opportunity to learn what it really means. Peter, if I'm not prying too much, what does the term say about your sexual feelings of attraction?"

Sighing slightly as Catherine rolled her eyes, Peter replied, "Do I find myself occasionally attracted to other men? Yes, I do. Do I ever see myself acting on those feelings? Never again. Am I dating a particular woman? No one yet, but I've been out on a couple of dates, and have had really fun times. Am I a heterosexual? I think that's God's intention for all of us, just as I think God intended for Kevin to be male. It didn't work out that way. Who knows what went wrong with either of us? It doesn't matter. What matters is that we're finding a way to be who we think we were *intended* to be."

"Well said," Catherine chimed in proudly.

From across the lawn, everyone's attention was drawn to Gail's clanging of the school bell, announcing that it was time to begin the evening session.

"Oh, dear, I have so many more questions, but thank you, Peter," said Annette as she gathered her dishes and searched for her schedule. "What's tonight's topic?"

"Hurdles to sexual health," Joe replied with a smile and raised eyebrows to Catherine.

Chapter Twenty-Eight

Hurdles to Sexual Health

"The topic of tonight's discussion," Carol said beaming as she stood erect in her "Queen of Everything" T-shirt, "is 'Hurdles to Sexual Health.' Brian and I are going to brainstorm with you about those things in our lives that prevent us from being sexually healthy people."

"Carol, may I please ask a question?" Catherine said, standing up in the back row of chairs. "Will you remind us of how you are *defining* sexual health? And, secondly, who's the doctor? In other words, who are you suggesting determines if a person *is* sexually healthy?"

"*You're* the doctor," Bill Stayton said, standing in his place in the second row. "May I?" he asked Carol and me.

"Please," we replied in unison.

"It's an excellent question, Catherine," Bill said as he walked to the front of the room. "What *is* sexual health? Back in 1975, the World Health Organization defined it as, 'the integration of the physical, emotional, intellectual, and social aspects of sexual being, in ways that are positively enriching, and that enhance personality, communication, and love.' They also said that it was 'freedom from fear, shame, guilt, false beliefs, and other psychological facts that inhibit sexual response and impair sexual relationships'," he quoted by rote.

"The definition of sexual health that I most love, perhaps because I had something to do with its writing," he laughed, "was in Surgeon General David Satcher's 'Call to Action to Promote Sexual Health and Responsible Behavior' back in 2001. Unfortunately, I don't have it memorized, and I don't have a copy with me. "

"I have one on the resource table," Alison said excitedly as she left her seat, and headed to the long table at the side of the room that she had covered with books, pamphlets, and fliers on sexuality and organizational resources.

"You do?" Bill replied with obvious pleasure. "Will you please go to the beginning where it talks about 'sexual health,' and read us the second paragraph? That's a real gem, I think."

"The part that begins 'Sexual health is inextricably bound to both physical and mental health'?" Alison asked, standing at the side of the room, holding the booklet.

"Yes. That's it! Jump to the middle of the paragraph if you would, Alison."

"Let's see," she said, pulling her half glasses to the end of her nose. "It reads, 'Sexual health is not limited to the absence of disease or dysfunction, nor is its importance confined to just the reproductive years. It includes the ability to understand and weigh the risks, responsibilities, outcomes, and impacts of sexual actions, and to practice abstinence when appropriate. It includes freedom from sexual abuse and discrimination, and the ability of individuals to integrate their sexuality into their lives, derive pleasure from it, and to reproduce if they so choose."

"Isn't that good?" Bill asked with a face-filling grin. "So, that's a couple of definitions of sexual health, and as I think you noticed, they were *very* similar. Another source of input comes from SIECUS, the Sex Information and Education Council of the United States, for which Pam, Dick, and I have all served as board members. It has offered us a good list of the characteristics of a sexually healthy person. Like signals to the medical doctor, these would be signs that one's sexuality is in good working order. And remember, when we talk about 'sexuality,' we're talking about *all* of the components that Pam outlined for us on Sunday, such as 'Sensuality,' 'Intimacy,' and 'Sexual Identity.' So the question becomes, is our sexuality *in all of its components* enhancing our lives in productive ways?

"The characteristics of sexually healthy people include the appreciation of one's own body, the ability to interact with both genders in appropriate ways, the affirmation of one's sexual orientation and respect for the orientation of others," Bill explained. "It also includes developing and maintaining meaningful relationships, avoiding exploitative or manipulative relationships, and seeking new information to enhance one's sexuality. Pam, Dick, help me out. Name some of the others?"

"The ability to express love and intimacy in appropriate ways," Pam offered. "Taking responsibility for one's own behaviors, and living according to one's values."

"Enjoying and expressing one's sexuality *throughout* one's life," Dick said enthusiastically to a spattering of applause and laughter. "Expressing one's sexuality while respecting the rights of others. Enjoying sexual feelings without necessarily acting on them. It's a long list and I recommend that everyone read it through completely."

"We planned on handing out copies of the list on Thursday, but we'll make sure they're available tomorrow morning," Carol said.

"Many of the characteristics describe people who not only enjoy a full and satisfying sexuality themselves, but who also engage in behaviors that enhance the sexual health of *others*, such as promoting the rights of *all* people to accurate sexuality information, and demonstrating tolerance for people with different sexual values and lifestyles." Bill continued. "And, going back to Catherine's second question, I believe that the ultimate determiner of your sexual healthiness must be *you*, just as the ultimate determiner of your spiritual healthiness must be you. Others can have opinions on your healthiness, and may give you feedback on what they see or hear, but you're the one who has to decide if your life is working for you. Am I right?" he asked as he looked from face to face. "Catherine, does that answer your question?"

"Yes, thank you," she replied with a polite smile of acceptance.

"Okay. Sorry for the interruption, Carol," Bill said, taking his seat.

"No. That was great, Bill. Thanks," Carol said.

"So, going back to Bill's presentation on Sunday when he introduced the SAR, who remembers the three things which he identified as obstacles to sexual health?" I asked from my place next to Carol.

"Ignorance, secrecy, and trauma," Marjorie called out with certainty.

"Right! Thank you, Marjorie. Ignorance. Secrecy. Trauma," I said as I wrote the words out on the large whiteboard behind me. "Tonight, we'd like you to give some thought to how *your* sexual health has been impacted by ignorance, secrecy, and trauma. We'd also like you to think about the roadblocks that might prevent another person from experiencing sexual health. To begin the process, we're going to break up into groups of three, and take ten minutes to talk about the hurdles to sexual health. When we're finished, we're going to list the hurdles on these easels, and then focus on one or two of them, time permitting. As always, please try to sit and talk with people whom you don't know well."

The participants then stood and turned their chairs, or pulled them across the linoleum floor. After twelve minutes of what seemed to be engaged participation, Carol gave a "two minute warning." Five minutes later we brought the discussions to a close by asking people to pull their chairs back into place, and to give us feedback on the process.

"How was that for you?" Carol asked.

"We didn't have enough time," Maggie whined. "It was good, but we ran out of time."

"We were just getting started," Dom agreed.

"Sorry about that," I said. "Our goal was just to get us focused on the topic of 'hurdles.' We figured that the really heavy-duty conversations on the obstacles that you face in your own lives will take place in your SAR groups. If anyone here started to open up about a personal hurdle and felt cut off, please be sure to keep the discussion going in your small group, which meets at the end of this session. So tell us, what topics came up? What are some of the hurdles to sexual health that you identified?"

"AIDSphobia," said Thomas strongly and eagerly from his seat.

"Thank you," Carol said, as she wrote the word on the first flip chart.

"Thomas, say a little more about that if you would," I asked. "Explain how AIDSphobia is a hurdle to sexual health?"

"Gladly," he said as he stood up. "And, for the record," he continued, smiling and making earnest eye contact with as many members of the group as he could, "I speak about this personally. For starters, if you're fearful or hateful of your own HIV status, it can stop you from having a positive body image. You can feel dirty, diseased, and ashamed. As you might imagine, that certainly can prevent you from feeling good about your sexuality, and it most *definitely* can eliminate the possibility of freely and joyfully reaching out sexually to others," he explained. "If you feel shame, you can feel unworthy of respect, and if you hide your status from others, even when you practice safe sex, you can feel selfish and dishonest about the sex you had. Let's just say that the sex doesn't linger in your mind as *love making.* I've spent too many years of my adult life struggling with shame and fear. From the other side of the issue, if you're terrified of HIV-positive people, you really risk losing a rewarding, loving relationship with someone who might be perfect for you. I know a lot of guys who say that they quit dating someone when they found out he was HIV-positive, and now they're kicking themselves, particularly because HIV has become such a manageable virus, and HIV-positive people are capable of living such full and ordinary lives. I'm a long-term survivor, and I've had more than one potential partner walk away when he found out about my HIV status. Initially, I secretly supported their decision. It made sense to me. More recently I've come to decide they were the losers, not me."

"Right on," yelled Annette from her seat, followed quickly by a smattering of applause led by Lloyd and George.

"How was that?" Thomas asked.

"That was good. Thanks, Thomas," I said. "That was *really* good. How about someone else? What are some obstacles to sexual health?"

"Sexual abuse," said Gina.

"Definitely," said Carol as she wrote down the word.

"Good, Gina," I said. "What else?"

"Homophobia," said Dan.

"Heterophobia," said Peter.

"Okay," I replied. "Homophobia and heterophobia. Anyone not understand how these could be obstacles to sexual health? Lisa?"

"Define 'heterophobia' again," she asked with a befuddled look on her face.

"Well, if 'homophobia' is defined as the fear and hatred of homosexuality and gay people, then 'heterophobia' must be the fear and hatred of heterosexuality and of straight people," I explained. "Right, Peter?"

"That's what I had in mind," he said as Dan shook his head slowly in disgust.

"If you say so," he mumbled.

"And how is that an obstacle?" Lisa asked.

"That attitude would make it difficult to be tolerant of people with different sexual values and lifestyles," I replied. "A heterophobic gay person could be just as blocked from sexual health as a homophobic straight person, or a homophobic gay person for that matter."

"Hear! Hear!" affirmed George from his seat next to Maggie.

"How about alcoholism?" Curtis offered as a question.

"Absolutely," I said. "Also speaking as one who knows," I smiled at Thomas, "when you rely on alcohol or drugs to build up sexual confidence and deaden guilt, it can become an enormous obstacle to experiencing sexual health. As I recall, Bill, one of the characteristics of a sexually healthy person is his or her ability to practice effective decision-making, and to make informed choices."

"That's right," he said.

"There's also something on that list about engaging in sexual relationships that are characterized by honesty, equity, and responsibility," I continued. "Being drunk or stoned makes it really hard to make informed choices, or to engage in honest and responsible sex."

"You can say that again," said Lloyd with a loud sigh.

"But when you're condemned by the culture and religion for being who you are, you do what you can to numb your feelings of shame or guilt," George called out. "That's one of the reasons that there tends to be a higher rate of alcoholism in the gay community than in the general population."

"I agree," I said. "One person or group's lack of sexual health, such as *not* respecting the orientation of others, can have a major impact on the sexual health of the others. But let's keep going. What else? What are some more obstacles to sexual health?"

At the end of another ten minutes of brainstorming we had a long list of hurdles that included a lot of "isms" such as heterosexism, racism, sexism, able-body-ism, ageism, and look-ism, as well as emotional abuse, disability, body image, religious upbringing, family of origin, culture, race, ethnicity, politics, age, economic status, education, geography, and the influence of organized religion in the culture.

"In the time that we have left," Carol said as she looked over the list for possible misspellings and glanced at her watch, "we'd like to focus our attention on just one of these hurdles, and that is 'sexual abuse'."

"There's been a lot of attention given recently to sexual abuse of children, particularly of young boys by priests," I said. "As a survivor of sexual abuse, I found the intense media attention to the topic both liberating and deeply disturbing. It was liberating in that most discussion about abuse in the past has focused on the sexual abuse of young girls by adult men that they know. It was affirming to me to have some recognition that boys are abused too, although much less frequently. One the other hand, all of the lurid descriptions of the abuse that took place, and the repetition of all of the 'lines' used by the abusers to make the boys feel safe, brought back really disturbing memories for me. But though it was very painful, it was also really helpful."

Putting her arm around my shoulder, Carol said, "Many of us have been abused. Given the high incidence of sexual abuse in this country, we suspect that there are several people in this room who as children were inappropriately touched by adults. For some of us, particularly those who suffer in silence, that touch or those sexual activities can be permanently damaging, preventing any possibility of experiencing sexual health. Others of us have found our voice, have named what happened to us, and have been able to work through the multiple issues in our lives. We've come to see ourselves as *survivors* of abuse as opposed to *victims* of abuse. Tonight, we have a film that we'd like to show you that all of us will find very disturbing. It's about the sexual abuse of a young girl by her father."

"The film is from a television special done by Oprah Winfrey," I explained. "We show it with the hope of generating some reflection and discussion in our SAR groups about how trauma in general, and sexual abuse in particular, can create significant obstacles to sexual healthiness. Pam, if you'll turn off the lights please."

Chapter Twenty-Nine

Beatrice's Map

We sat in silence around the living room in Higley for two or three minutes. There had been little chatter as the members of our SAR group entered the building. The film on abuse had its expected effect.

"Let's begin with reactions to the film," I said, "and then we can talk about other hurdles to sexual health. As time allows, we'll do another one of our sexual journey maps."

Still, the room remained quiet.

"I had the biggest urge to knock that guy into next Tuesday," Dom said, shaking his head with disgust. "How could he hurt his little girl like that? His own *child*? I just don't get it."

Everyone remained silent in reflection. Many in the circle stared at their feet, picked lint from their clothing, or gazed out the windows into the dark.

"He said he was abused himself," Charlie said softly.

"Then he should have gotten help," Dom snapped angrily.

"I'm not defending him," Charlie protested. "I'm just saying that most people who abuse children were abused themselves as children."

"Maybe. But that doesn't mean that everyone who *was* abused *will* abuse," Dom replied less harshly. "Some people get help."

"Dom, why don't you talk about your feelings?" I asked. "What came up for you as you watched the film?"

"My little brother, of course," he said, locking my eyes with a stare.

"Do you want to talk with the group about that?" I asked. "You can certainly pass."

"No. It's okay. I'll talk about it," he said with a slight smile. "As I told Brian this afternoon on our walk, my little brother was molested by a guy who was like an uncle to us. It happened a long time ago, but I've still got a lot of strong feelings about it. Seeing how the abuse impacted the girl in the film made me think about my brother, and started me wondering about how the abuse had impacted him."

"Well, that makes sense," Maggie said relieved, and with a tone of reassurance. "No wonder you want to knock that guy into next Tuesday."

"I was wondering if maybe that's why his daughter ended up a lesbian," Dom said, raising both hands in a questioning manner.

"I don't understand the lesbian thing, as most people know," Leona said from her place next to me on the sofa, "but I *do* know that being abused as a child doesn't turn you into a lesbian. At least not everyone."

"I don't think it does for *anyone*," Margaret offered. "You either *are* a lesbian, or you *aren't*. I think his daughter would have ended up a lesbian even if she *hadn't* been abused."

"There's no documented connection between abuse and sexual orientation," I said. "But, let's get back to our feelings. Does anyone else want to talk about what feelings came up for them? Wendy, you look as if there's something on your mind."

"I don't know if I should say it," she said, shaking her head in disgust. "I don't want to cause any bad feelings."

"What is it?" Beatrice asked kindly. "It seems like you're *very* upset."

"It makes me *really* angry that people keep talking about being gay as if it has to have been caused by something awful, like sexual abuse," she said with obvious frustration. "It's *not* a disease. It's *not* a curse. I'm a lesbian. I *like* being a lesbian. I was *never* abused. I don't *hate* men. And I get sick of hearing the same shit, pardon my French, over and over again. I'm sorry. I do. I thought the guy in the film was a real creep but I felt sorry for him. He was *sick*. He turned my stomach, but he was sick. People who sexually abuse children are sick. They need to be punished, but they're sick. And I didn't see his daughter as a victim. I saw her as a *survivor*. She was strong, and appropriately angry, and she was really clear about her boundaries. She *inspired* me. She didn't take any crap from him. She was wounded by the abuse but it also made her strong and self-sufficient. I'm sorry for running on like this, but I'm so tired of hearing people talk about being gay as if it was the result of some awful tragedy in a person's life. Being gay is *not* a tragedy. For me, it's a *gift*."

Kevin clapped twice instinctively.

"You liked that, huh, Kevin?" I asked playfully.

"I did," he said seriously. "And I just want to say that being *transgender* is no tragedy either. It's not always easy, but it's no tragedy."

"Wendy, I'm sorry if I offended you," Dom said as he turned his body toward her, and worked hard to make eye contact. "I'm really ignorant about this stuff, which is why I came here. I need to learn. Forgive me if I hurt your feelings."

"You didn't hurt my feelings, Dom," Wendy said with a weak smile. "Thanks for apologizing. It's not about *you*. It's about *me* being tired of listening to the same old stuff coming up over and over and over again. I'm just a little tired of explaining myself to people."

"I'd like to say something," Charlie said.

"What's that, Charlie?" I asked.

"I know someone who was touched as a child by an adult, and he spent the longest time worrying about it," he said. "He felt like maybe it was wrong, and that he was responsible. And because he *enjoyed* what happened to him, he didn't think of it as abuse."

"What do you mean 'he *enjoyed* what happened to him,'?" Maggie asked.

"According to him, it felt good," Charlie explained.

"Is he gay?" Dom asked. "Or did I just put my foot in my mouth again by asking that question?" he added nervously.

"Charlie said he 'enjoyed' it, Dom, which would suggest to me that he was either gay or bisexual," I said.

"Okay. Thanks," Dom said with relief.

"He's *not* gay," Charlie said with certainty. "If he's anything, he's bisexual."

"I can relate to that," I said. "When I was abused, I didn't think of it as 'abuse.' What happened to me wasn't heavy duty, and I mostly enjoyed it. So I was pretty confused, particularly when later I started thinking about how I had been manipulated, about how *I* was the child and *he* was the adult."

211

"That's what happened to my brother!" Dom said excitedly. "He was *manipulated*. He didn't make a big deal out of it at the time. *I'm* the one who made a big deal of it. And he was pissed at me for doing that. But the kid was being manipulated by an adult who took him fun places and bought him nice things."

"Dom, have you and your brother ever talked about this as adults?" Margaret asked.

"No. Never," he answered. "The whole thing got dropped. I sort of picked up that I wasn't supposed to bring it up again."

"Dom, is your brother gay?" Maggie asked.

"Maggie, why would you even *ask* that question?" Wendy said with frustration.

"Because he said his brother got angry with him for making a big deal about it," Maggie protested. "I don't know."

"No, he's *not* gay," Dom said without doubt. "He's definitely *not* gay."

"Okay. We've established the fact that Dom's brother is not gay, and we've made the point that there's no connection between sexual abuse and sexual orientation," I said, sitting up straight. "Does anyone else have a reaction to the film that they'd like to share? If not, let's move on to some other obstacles or hurdles to sexual health. Did any of you have any feelings in the session about the hurdles that we surfaced?"

"Yes, I did. I was moved when Thomas talked about his HIV status," said Margaret. "I thought it was a very brave thing to do. Each morning we go over to the big room in Ridings and we sing 'I Love Myself' in front of that panel from the Quilt. I look up and see all of those names of people who've died of that awful disease. When Thomas spoke up tonight and told us that he was HIV-positive, I thought about how he's been singing 'I Love Myself' in front of that AIDS Quilt every morning with us. Having him say that he'd lived with shame for so many years, and was not going to live like that anymore, made me teary."

"Me too," Maggie sighed. "Of course, I immediately started thinking of Barry, my husband, and how I don't want to think about him ever getting AIDS."

"I'm sorry, Maggie, but why *would* he?"asked Wendy a bit impatiently. "I mean, I know that there's a higher incidence of HIV in the gay male community in the U.S. than there is in the general population, but that doesn't mean that he's going to expose himself through risky behaviors.

Most of the gay men who are getting HIV today are young blacks and Latinos."

"And who gets teary for them?" Leona asked flippantly.

"Oh, Leona, I think that's unfair," Margaret said, slowly shaking her head. "If Thomas was black and made the same speech he did tonight, I'd be just as moved."

"No offense. I'm not saying that you wouldn't. I'm just asking if anyone cares as much about a young black kid getting AIDS as a young white kid?" Leona said.

"It would help if black ministers cared about it," Wendy replied. "There's so much damn denial in the black community about AIDS because of homophobia. Black gay men often get more sympathy in the white community."

"I won't argue about the denial," Leona said.

"May I ask a question?" Beatrice interjected with a look of alarm.

"Please," I replied.

"Is this kind of back and forth going on in the other groups? This seems kind of intense. I'm getting a little uncomfortable," she said.

"We've all been asked to talk about our feelings, and I think we're doing a great job of it," I said. "I'm sorry that you're feeling a little uncomfortable, Beatrice. But I do expect that they're having as much back and forth in the other groups. If they aren't now, they will be. Remember that the SAR is about assessing our attitudes and values. That includes our personal feelings about how homophobia and racism color issues. Your willingness as group members to speak up and talk about unpleasant feelings is our key to success. That, of course, means doing so in a way that is respectful. Trust the process. I'll step in if I feel we're off track. You okay with that?"

"Yea, okay. If this is the way it's supposed to be," she said. "I didn't grow up in a family that argued, so it's sometimes hard for me to sit through what feels like fighting."

"We're not fighting," Leona said lightly. "Does anyone feel like I'm *fighting* with them? They better not, or they'll soon discover what a *real* fight looks like."

"Not me," said Dom holding up his hands to push away the question. "I'm not taking you on, Leona."

"Not if you know what's good for you," Leona laughed.

The tension in the group dissipated in the laughter, and we continued to talk, mostly in cautious ways, about the kinds of hurdles people can face on their life journeys to sexual health.

"Okay, before we run out of time, let's move onto our maps," I said. "Is anyone ready and willing to share with us their sexual journey? Wendy, how about you?"

"Not tonight, okay?" she answered. "I'm already self-conscious enough about coming on so strong in the group. It's not like me ..."

"Hey," I interrupted. "Don't back off from it. I was *proud* of you tonight. You said clearly what was on your mind. But we'll give you a break. You don't need to do your map tonight. But who? Beatrice, that looked like a nod of 'yes' to me. Will you go?"

"I knew I shouldn't have made eye contact with you," she laughed. "Okay. I'll go. I warn you in advance, though, it's *boring*. Boring. Boring. Boring. There's nothing about my sexual journey that's interesting."

"Tell that to Ben," Leona quipped, with immediate recognition by laughter from Charlie, Kevin, and Maggie.

"Hey, what is this?" Beatrice protested with a slight laugh and significant blush.

"And don't you be laughing, Kevin," Leona warned. "I'm looking for a report tonight about you and Dan."

"Don't wait up," Kevin replied.

"Okay. Okay. We'll get back to *The Dating Game* in just a moment, but first this word from Beatrice about her sexual journey," I said in a television announcer's tone. "Beatrice, please, unfold your map on the coffee table, and guide us through it. Leona, behave yourself."

"You wish," she said.

"Okay," Beatrice began. "I was inspired by Maggie's drawings, and her great use of color, so I redid mine. Here it is, 'Beatrice Ramos's Sexual Journey.' Ta da."

Her story wasn't boring. It was merely without apparent major conflict. She told us, as she had before, that she was the oldest of three children. Her figures were drawn with love, indicating to me the care that she had for her parents, younger sister, and younger brother.

"Here I am in Catholic grade school, dressed up as St. Theresa for 'Saint Day'," Beatrice explained. "That's a halo, not a doughnut, over my head. I put this in because I feel as if I was heavily influenced by early messages about purity. Do you see this picture here where I've got a big frown and no halo? That's the day that I masturbated for the first time. My feelings of guilt left a big impression. As you recall, I'm still not all that comfortable with it, but I know that's my issue."

To the right of the picture of the frowning girl was a bed with two figures, a male and a female, reclining. "That's Peter and me. It was at the end of junior year in college and it was my first sexual experience with another person. It's when I lost my virginity," she explained. "We had dated for about a year and a half, and I felt very self-conscious that we hadn't done anything other than some heavy petting. I think that all of my girlfriends had sex by that time. They teased me a little about being a virgin at twenty-one. Peter was really patient with the whole thing, but I know that he was getting teased by his friends too. So, one night, we just decided to do it. I wish I could say it was romantic, and everything that I dreamed it would be, but it wasn't. It was fun, and a little scary at the beginning, but then it hurt. I remember that it hurt, even with him being as gentle as he was. He knew more about sex than I did. I didn't ask him to stop, but he could tell it wasn't all that pleasant for me. Anyway, Peter and I broke up in senior year. I don't think it had anything to do with sex. I think we both sort of decided that the relationship had run out of steam."

"Do you wish that you had waited?" Dom asked.

"I'm sorry," Beatrice answered.

"Do you wish you had waited to have sex until you got married, being Catholic and all?" he asked.

"No, I think if I had waited, I would have been even more disappointed," she laughed.

The final drawing was of a female figure and a male figure, standing side by side, him holding a book with a cross on it. They were both smiling broadly.

"Who's that?" Leona asked. "It looks like a minister."

"It is," Beatrice said with a smile to match the one in the drawing. "It's Bill Stayton. I wrote to him after I read an article in a Philadelphia magazine about him being both a theologian and a sex therapist. I was intrigued with how he brought those two worlds together, and I asked him to send me some information about his work at Widener. After a letter and an e-mail back and forth, he and Kathy invited me to their house for dinner one night. She's *amazing*. When they invited me over, I thought 'What kind of people have perfect strangers over for dinner?' When I got there, I met a woman who was living with them on weekends because she was in Bill's graduate class, and couldn't afford room and board too. You can get your sexuality degree in a part-time program where you take classes on the weekends," she explained.

"At any rate, meeting Bill and Kathy had a big impact on my sexual journey," Beatrice continued. "I'm not clear yet what I want to do with a graduate degree in human sexuality. I've thought about teaching or being a counselor. I've just started the program, so it's early. Anyway, that's what I came up with for my sexual journey so far. Does anyone have any questions?"

It was perhaps the hour, or the fear that any questions might spark more controversial discussions, but the others just smiled appreciatively at Beatrice and joined in with Kevin when he began a slow applause.

"Really boring, huh?" she said to me.

"Not at all," I assured her. "It's nice to hear a story that seems free of major trauma, which is not to say that you haven't faced hurdles to your sexual health. I think everyone's a little pooped, but as you're willing tomorrow, or sometime before we break up on Thursday, Beatrice, I'd love it if you'd talk with us further about how you feel your religious and cultural heritage has impacted your sexuality."

"Sure," she said.

"Thanks," I replied. "That's it for the time we have. Don't forget that you have optional films tonight being shown over in Huntington. Bill will be showing more episodes of *Sex in the City*, probably upstairs, and downstairs we have the film *Hairspray*. Have a good night, everyone. And Kevin, if you've got a minute, I'd like to talk with you."

"Wouldn't we all?" quipped Leona as she gathered her things, and headed out into the cool night air.

Chapter Thirty

Alone on the Beach

"So, what happened in your group?" Gina asked Wendy as they left the dorm with Lisa, pillows and blankets in tow, on their way to watch *Hairspray*. The chill in the air made the idea of wrapping up in covers very appealing.

"Don't ask," she replied with an exaggerated frown. "I sort of lost it. I'm feeling a little self-conscious."

"What happened?" Gina asked excitedly. "Tell us."

"I sort of blew up when some people started associating 'abuse' with being lesbian or gay," Wendy explained.

"Who said that?" Lisa asked incredulously.

"I'd rather not say. You know, 'What's said in the group, stays in the group.' They didn't mean any offense. I just get really tired of hearing it, that's all," she sighed.

"I know what you're saying," Gina said as she slung her free arm around the shoulder of her new friend for the walk over to Ridings. "But it was Leona, wasn't it?"

Ahead of them walked Betty, Annette, and Carla, also with pillows and blankets under their arms. As she turned back to see who was behind them, Betty exclaimed, "A pajama party!"

217

"I've *always* wanted to go to a girls' sleep-over," Carla said. "Here's my big chance."

"They'll be *guys* there," Betty said, pretending disappointment.

"We'll just ignore them," Carla giggled.

From the top of the hill, it was apparent that not everyone had decided to watch *Hairspray* or *Sex in the City*. Through the trees, it was easy to see the orange-yellow glow of a campfire on the beach.

"Do you want to change your mind, and go to the beach?" Gina asked Wendy and Lisa.

"No," Wendy said. "I want to see the movie. You guys can go. I'll catch up with you later. I haven't seen *Hairspray*."

"We'll stick with you," Gina replied. "I've seen the movie before. It's a blast. We can go down later."

At the bottom of the hill, a handful of people huddled in silence around the crackling fire, watching a stream of smoke and cinders flow upwards toward the star-filled sky.

"God, it's cold. How did it get so cold so quickly? We were swimming last night," said Charlie.

"Oh, you're not going to let a little cool air discourage you, are you?" asked Dick with a chuckle. "There has to be *one* hearty soul among you who will join me for a skinny dip tonight? What's happened to the youth of America?"

"I'll join you, Dick," Dan said.

"He said *youth* of America," George jabbed.

"Fuck you," Dan laughed.

"You're all 'youth' to me," Dick asserted as he carefully rose to one knee and then straightened himself up. "At least in body, if not in spirit," he added as he disrobed in the shadows. Dan followed suit and joined him naked in the water. Dick paddled around some near the shore as Dan swam the short distance to the raft.

"Who's in the water?" asked one of two figures who stood at the bottom of the path, having just descended the hill.

"It's me, Dick," he responded. "Whoever you are, come on in. The water is wonderful."

"It's me, Peter, Dick. I'll be right in."

"And it's me, Dan. Yes, do come in. We're skinny dipping."

After a moment of silence, and then a muffled exchange between Peter and his companion, Peter said, "Dick, I think I'll take a pass. Catherine and I are going to go up and catch the film. I'll take a rain check. Maybe tomorrow night."

"Chicken," yelled Dan as he watched Peter and Catherine depart.

"Lead us not into temptation," mumbled George to himself at his place by the fire.

"Shush," Maggie elbowed.

Within minutes, both Dan and Dick were fireside, each dressed and wrapped up in a towel or blanket. "That was invigorating," Dick proclaimed. "You don't know what you missed."

"I'll take your word for it," said George, "but I've decided I want to be like you when I grow up, Dick."

"And that would be *when*?" Dan poked.

"Ooh, what a bitch," George replied, and then wished his response had been less predictable.

The banter among those gathered around the fire for the next half an hour covered a range of topics, from early recollections of skinny dipping to their feelings about the superb job Kevin did in giving his talk that morning. Dick offered his theory on why society was so prudish about nudity, and then excused himself with the acknowledgment that he was getting a bit cold and besides, he wanted to catch at least one episode of *Sex in the City.*

Soon after Dick departed, Kevin joined the group, and was greeted with a warm smattering of applause and a nod of Dan's head, indicating that he wanted Kevin to sit next to him. As he began to sit down, Dan extended his right arm and enveloped Kevin in the blanket that covered his body.

Kevin smiled a bit nervously at the others but edged his body as close to Dan's as he could, and wrapped his left arm around Dan's waist.

"You went in the water?" Kevin asked Dan as he felt the dampness of Dan's shirt.

"Yea, it was great! Maybe we can go for a swim together a little later," he replied as he pulled Kevin closer to him and began slowly but firmly massaging his neck.

In the next hour, the site at the beach was visited by an array of participants. Some joined in the circle around the fire, but most came down to check out what they were missing, and then proceeded back up to their dorm and to bed.

"Come sit with us," George implored Martha and Beverly, who stood close to the fire for warmth.

"It's too cold," Martha explained. "It looks like you're having a good time though. We'll see you all in the morning." As they headed back up the hill, guided by the glow of their small flashlight, Maggie commented, "I really like those women. I wonder if everyone from Trinidad is that nice."

Leona was the next one down the hill. She stood alone, eyeing the crowd, and then focused her attention on Dan and Kevin. She smiled slightly and nodded her head up and down in recognition.

"Come join us, Leona," Charlie invited.

"No, child. It's looks *real* cozy, but this girl needs her beauty rest," she said with a laugh. "I just came down here to make sure you all were staying out of trouble. So far, so good." And off she went.

Following the end of *Hairspray*, a steady stream came down the hill, including Thomas and Lloyd, Wendy, Lisa, and Gina, and Carla and Betty.

"Why, it's a gathering of the gay, lesbian, bisexual, and transgender campers," announced Betty. "And *friends*," she added with an appreciative smile to Maggie and Charlie. "We're just missing a couple of people. Brian and Carol …"

"And Peter and Catherine," added Dan.

"Ouch!" said Betty. "Don't be a bad boy, our little *queer* activist."

"Why are you so *mean* to Peter?" Maggie asked Dan. "Why can't you give the guy a break? And who says that Catherine's a lesbian? She hasn't said anything about it, has she? Why would you say that she's a lesbian?"

"How many people here feel that Catherine is a dyke?" Dan asked, looking around the campfire. Wendy, Gina, Betty, and Carla raised their hands.

"The rest of you disagree or are you just not voting?" Dan asked.

"Not voting," he heard in response.

"Well, I don't think we should be gossiping about someone who's not here to speak for herself. But answer my question," Maggie persisted. "Why are you being so mean to Peter? What has he done to you?"

"I'm not being mean to Peter," Dan insisted. "I'm just calling him on his charade. There's no such thing as an 'ex-gay.' The boy's *queer*. Saying that he isn't makes life harder for him, and for the rest of us."

"How?" Maggie asked.

"You tell me," he said with raised eyebrows and a slight smile, and then looked away.

"Why do you think he decided to come to Thornfield?" Carla asked. "He had to know from reading the web site that this place was gay-positive."

"Maybe he thought he could convert us," offered Lloyd.

"He could convert *me*," said George. "Man, he's easy on the eyes."

"*Convert* you. Not *insert* you," Dan replied.

"Oh, you *are* a bad boy," Carla chirped.

"I think that like the rest of us, he's on a journey," Thomas said thoughtfully. "I hope he finds what he's looking for here. I hope the same for all of us."

After a minute or two of awkward or reflective silence in the group, Thomas looked at his watch, and said, "Oh, gosh, it's nearly midnight. I'm getting out of here before I turn into a pumpkin."

"Me too," said Wendy as she got up, and was joined by Gina, Lloyd, and Lisa.

Charlie followed soon after, yawning and complaining of being sleep deprived. He walked up with Carla and Betty. Soon, there were only Dan and Kevin.

"Good night you two," said George as he took Maggie's arm, and headed up the hill. "See you in the morning."

"So, do you want to swim?" Dan asked as he leaned over, and kissed Kevin on the neck, "Or do you want to just sit here and make out?"

"Making out sounds good," Kevin said as he turned his head and kissed Dan gently, and then more firmly on the lips.

They kissed like that for several minutes, each softly moaning with pleasure, occasionally pulling back to look into the other's eyes, and gently touching one another's face. Finally, Dan slowly fell back and brought Kevin with him to the ground. As he kissed Kevin's entire face, and pulled gently with his mouth on Kevin's ear, his hands began to explore Kevin's lean, muscular body. Kevin did the same, reaching his hand up under Dan's shirt and eagerly playing with the rings on his erect nipples.

Dan's left hand explored Kevin's entire upper torso, from his finger tips down his arms, past his nipples to the stream of fine, soft hair that led from his chest to his hard, flat stomach, and to the unbuttoned opening of his jeans.

Their tongues explored each other's mouths, eagerly inhaling each other's scents, as Kevin's hand slid down to check on Dan's level of excitement. The bulge in Dan's jeans was long and hard. Kevin unbuttoned them, slipped his hand into Dan's jockey shorts, and gently but firmly stroked his penis.

When Dan's hand began to enter Kevin's jeans to do the same, he felt Kevin suddenly tighten up, and Kevin's hand pull quickly out of his underwear.

"Relax," he said as he kissed him on each eye, and then on his neck. "Lay back and let it happen."

Kevin apprehensively followed his orders. He laid back, closed his eyes, and allowed Dan to explore his genitals. Once Dan's hand reached Kevin's erect penis, he touched it cautiously, probing its width and length and then gently feeling the texture and size of the scrotum that hung beneath it. He did this for only a matter of a few seconds. Then his hand stopped. It lay perfectly still on top of Kevin's genitals. It stayed there motionless as he continued to kiss Kevin gently on the forehead, mouth, and cheek. Gradually, Dan withdrew his hand from Kevin's pants and brought it back up to further explore Kevin's chest and arms.

"You've got a great body," he whispered.

"So do you," Kevin replied smiling as his hand headed back into Dan's pants. He could feel Dan pull back but he persisted until he found what he suspected. Dan was now flaccid.

"You okay?" Kevin asked.

"Yea, but I'm pretty tired, and a little cold," he answered as he kissed Kevin again on the forehead. "You mind if we continue this at a later date? I'm really bushed. How about you?"

"You sure that you're okay?" Kevin repeated as he pulled back and buttoned up his jeans.

"Sure. This was fun. You're a very sexy man, and I enjoyed making out. But, aren't you tired too?" Dan asked.

"Yea, sure," Kevin said. "Let's head up."

"You were awesome today," Dan said as they stood up, pulled together the blanket, and started up the hill.

"Oh, thanks," Kevin replied. "I'm glad you liked it."

Chapter Thirty-One

TUESDAY

Signs of Trouble and of Community

"Can I ask you to do something really gross?" Lloyd said to Thomas after exiting the bathroom, wrapped in a towel.

"You can ask," Thomas replied as he continued to make his bed. "What is it?"

"I want you to look at my butt."

"And why would *that* be gross?" Thomas laughed.

"I don't go around asking people to look at my butt every day, but I think I've got what I hope is just a pimple near my anus, and I thought it might gross you out to have to look."

"Not at all," Thomas said, turning and giving Lloyd a reassuring squeeze of his shoulder. "Now, turn around, and spread those cheeks."

When Lloyd did so, his roommate carefully examined the inflamed area.

"I don't think it's a pimple, buddy," he said. "It looks to me to be something else. It looks like a little ulcer. It's about the size of an eraser on a pencil. Is it tender?"

"No, it doesn't hurt. I just knew something was there when I was showering. I don't remember feeling it yesterday."

"I suggest that you have Dick take a look at it," Thomas advised. "He's a doctor and he'll know more than me, but my guess, my friend, is that you've got syphilis."

"Damn," Lloyd said with exasperation. "That's what I was afraid of. I've been waiting for signs of the flu, thinking that I probably got infected with HIV. Then, when I felt that bump, the first thing I thought of was 'syphilis.' There's a damn epidemic of it going around out there. Fuck me."

"Hey, if I'm right, and it *is* syphilis, it's treatable. But first you've got to find out what it is. As I say, Dick will know more than me, but I'll bet that he's going to have you get your blood tested as soon as you get home."

"I am such a fuck up," Lloyd said. "What the hell was I thinking? I hand out condoms for a living, for Christ's sake. But when *I* have sex, no condoms for me! What a goddamn fool."

Though he was thinking the same thing, Thomas said, "Hey, roomie, quit beating yourself up. You made a mistake. You won't do it again. Now, first things first. Get dressed, and we'll walk over and get some breakfast. Then talk to Dick. There's nothing more that you can do right now."

Thomas and Lloyd were soon hurrying past Marjorie and Curtis, who were perched in their usual spots outside of Peabody, having their third or fourth smokes of the day.

"You've got plenty of time," Marjorie called out to them.

The guys weren't the only ones who arrived in the dining room late. Wendy wandered in, sweaty from a run, grabbed a cup of coffee and a bran muffin, and hustled back to the dorm for a very quick shower. Leona sauntered in, surveyed the food that had been sitting in the steam trays for a half an hour, rolled her eyes, pulled an orange out of the fruit bowl, and walked out. Carla and Betty came in together, made a bee line for the coffee machine, and hurriedly popped sliced bagels into the toaster. Charlie stretched and yawned at the door to the room, and then got in line behind Thomas at the serving table. "I need more sleep," he moaned.

After scooping some scrambled eggs onto his plate, and forking two sausage links, Lloyd spotted Dick at a picnic table outside of Higley, excused himself, and headed outside empty handed. A moment later, Thomas watched Dick and Lloyd walk into the staff dorm. By the time he and Charlie had finished their waffles, Gail was ringing the school bell, announcing the beginning of Tuesday's program.

As he headed out the door, Thomas spotted Margaret, Joe, and Annette each getting up from their spots on the lawn, brushing off the seat of their shorts, and collecting their packets. "Meditation," he correctly surmised. Tonya, Judith, and Paula were walking quickly from the beach, dumping coffee from their mugs to avoid spills. He waved them on, like an encouraging fan at the finishing line.

When he entered Ridings, Thomas walked to the table that displayed the vase of wildflowers, and deadheaded several day lilies. After tossing them into a trash can by the door, he directed his steps to where Carol stood at the front of the room and moved in close to her as we formed our circle to sing our opening song. His eyes were trained on the entrance to the room for Lloyd's arrival. When he saw him enter with Dick, he gestured for him to come join him.

"What did he say?" he whispered.

"What we suspected," Lloyd sighed.

"I love myself, the way I am," we sang as people continued to stagger in. Looking around the room, I spotted Margaret taking in, once again, the sight of Thomas standing in front of the AIDS Quilt panels, this time with his arm around Lloyd's shoulder. When she noticed me watching, she smiled and winked.

On the other side of Carol stood Kevin, and then me. Kevin made a point of reserving the chair between Carol and me when he walked into the room earlier.

"Good morning, handsome. How are you doing?" Carol asked.

"I'll survive," he said with a faint smile, and then, turning to me, whispered, "Be grateful I didn't wake you up to talk. It didn't go so well at the beach last night."

"I'm sorry," I said. "Let's talk later."

Dan stood across the room, mumbling the words, his eyes rarely leaving the song sheet he held in his right hand. When he did look up, he tried to make eye contact with Kevin. It happened once, and he gave Kevin a reassuring smile. Kevin smiled back politely.

"I love you, the way you are, there's nothing you need to do," we sang.

Gail stood to my left and one step into the circle. Her dependably cheery disposition and enthusiastic sign language interpreting of the song provided an anchor to each day's beginning, regardless of what was going

225

on. Alison, Pam, and Bill, lined up next to Gail. They, too, were "steady Eddies." The team functioned like a well-tuned machine, each member clear on his or her responsibilities, and fully supportive of the others when it came time for them to perform.

Continuing my perusal of the circle, I observed that the room that was filled with strangers just two and a half days ago was quickly being transformed, as I trusted that it would, into small groupings of kindred souls. Community was forming.

Maggie and George stood together, as always, and shared a song sheet, a few playful elbows to the side, and grins of appreciation. Peter and Catherine were side by side too, not sharing a song sheet, but clearly taking comfort in each other's presence. Beverly and Martha, despite their desire to stay separated for the week so that they could meet new people, generally found themselves, like sisters, in each other's company. Carla, dressed today in pretty blue and white polka dots, seemed also to have found a sister in Betty, who towered over her, dressed in wrinkled beige shorts and a well-worn, plain white v-neck T-shirt. They couldn't be more different in stature or in expression of their femininity, but they had found their common ground.

Curtis and Marjorie didn't generally sit together but always exited at the same speed and to the same spots for their smokes. What more, I wondered, did they have in common, if anything? Dom and Chuck also didn't make a point to sit together, but were usually in the same area of the room and could usually be spotted drinking coffee together at one of the picnic tables during the day. They were likewise faithful viewers of the evening airings of *Sex in the City*.

Beatrice and Ben now seemed inseparable. Each glowed in the other's presence. So too did Gina and Wendy, though I didn't suspect there was anything romantic about their friendship.

Most of the other participants appeared to still be loners at this point in the week. Dan, Leona, Charlie, Joanne, and others whom I still struggled to connect with names, wandered in and out of groups, though Charlie and Leona seemed to be getting close.

"Behind your fears, your raging tears, I see your shining star, and I love you, just the way you are."

It was Bill's turn to lead us in a warm-up exercise. When the music ended, and at Alison's invitation, Bill stepped forward to explain the principle behind the "Whoosh" exercise. We stayed standing, closed up the gaps in the circle, and were instructed to raise our hands high above our heads and bring them down in a big arc to the floor with the loud, verbalized sound of "whoosh." If we did it sequentially, going clockwise around the room, we would create a wonderful wavelike phenomenon.

Dick's "star" truly shined in this exercise, as he had the least inhibitions about making large sweeping gestures with his long, lanky arms, and loud, guttural "whooshing" sounds. Standing tall in his Planned Parenthood T-shirt across the room from me, he smiled expectantly as the wave approached him, and he gave the swell a major boost with his deep, toe-touching feat.

Three times we went around the room before Bill thanked us, and Alison had us take our seats for the morning announcements.

"Are there any needs that we can address for you this morning?" she asked with her now familiar welcoming tone and smile. "Does everyone have everything that they need to feel comfortable?"

"Can we get fresh towels?" Curtis asked.

"Yes, indeed," she said. "Fresh towels will be put out by the housekeeping staff both today and on Thursday. Please help yourselves. Anyone else?"

"Can we get more fresh fruit during the breaks?" asked Paula.

"Yes. Certainly. I'll speak to the chef at the first opportunity. Anyone else? No? How about announcements then? Yes, Bill?"

"Tonight's film is called *The Lovers*," he said with a little wiggle of his butt and raised eyebrows of excitement. "It's a fantastic film by Candida Royalle that pulls together some of the themes of the day. I think that you'll like it a lot."

"Bill, why don't you explain who Candida Royalle is?" Pam suggested.

"Oh. Okay. Candida Royalle was a porn star who decided that there weren't any good commercially-erotic films from a feminist perspective, so, she started producing them. Come see for yourselves. As I say, I think you'll like it."

"Thank you, Bill. Anyone else? Yes, Carol?"

"Alison, why don't you say something about our guests tomorrow."

"Right you are," she smiled appreciatively. "Tomorrow's program is dedicated entirely to gay, lesbian, and bisexual issues."

"We call it 'Gay Day'," Carol interjected playfully.

"Traditionally, we have guests who spend all or part of the day with us because it's a topic that touches their lives quite personally," Alison continued. "It won't be a large group but I'd like us all to welcome them warmly. One of the people coming tomorrow is Michael's mother," she said turning and pointing at the name "Michael" on the AIDS Quilt. "All of the names on these panels represent people who lived and died in the Syracuse area. Virginia Montgomery, Michael's mother, helped us secure this section of the Quilt as our backdrop for the week. She and some members of the local AIDS support group will be here in the morning, along, perhaps, with one or two old friends and former Thornfield campers. Thank you for reminding me, Carol. Is there anything else? If not, I have an announcement. The staff is reminded that we have a meeting during the break this afternoon. That's at 1:30."

To this, Pam quickly rose from her seat beside Alison and whispered in her ear.

"We need to change that," Pam explained. "Some of us have committed to be with Ben when he goes for his swim. How about if we meet briefly over lunch?"

"Thank you," whispered Alison. "A change in plans," she announced cheerily. "The staff will meet over lunch. Without further ado, let's proceed then downstairs for our first session, which is on the 'Sexual Response Cycle'."

As the participants and staff rose from their chairs and headed for the stairway, I pulled Kevin back to me.

"It didn't go so well, huh?" I asked.

"It did for a while," he smirked with raised eyebrows of appreciation. "But then he stuck his hand down my pants and freaked, I think."

"Did he say anything that hurt your feelings?"

"No. He was good about it. He said he was 'tired'," Kevin said.

"You sure he wasn't?" I asked.

"He went from being really hard to really soft as soon as he touched my penis."

"You announced you had a 'zut.' What did he think he'd find?"

"I don't know," he sighed. "Too bad. It was going good. I tried to prepare myself, like you said, but it's always a letdown. I keep hoping it'll be different."

"One of these days," I said.

"I know. I was just hoping it was *this* time."

Chapter Thirty-Two

The Big "O"

"You all recall," Pam said, "when we talked on Sunday about 'Sexual Beingness,' we spent a little bit of time on Masters and Johnson's 'Sexual Response Cycle.' We're going to spend a little more time this morning examining that model, and expanding upon it."

As Pam turned pages of newsprint on the easel back to her diagram, several of the participants began filing through their packets in search of the notes they had taken two days before.

"The sexual response cycle refers to a series of stages that individuals go through in sexual pleasuring," Pam explained. "Masters and Johnson identified four stages: 'Excitement,' 'Plateau,' 'Orgasm,' and 'Resolution'."

The diagram before us looked like a small, hilly mountain, with the ascending line on the left labeled "Excitement" and the peak of the mountain labeled "Orgasm."

"There are two important physiological processes that both men and women experience during sexual response. Remember, *vasocongestion* refers to increased blood flow into organs such as the penis and clitoris, and *mytonia,* refers to muscle contractions," Pam said smiling as she sought to make eye contact with all of the participants. She then described the remarkable changes that take place in the body during "Excitement" and "Plateau" and moved into a description of "Orgasm."

"For men, there is a point in the cycle just before orgasm that is called 'ejaculatory inevitability.' This is the moment when contractions in the prostate gland and seminal vesicles force fluids into the urethra and the man gets a sensation that says, 'I'm about to come.' I know you men in the group are wondering how I know this," Pam joked.

She went on to describe the stage of 'Orgasm' for both men and women. "Orgasm is a reflex that occurs after a build-up of excitement. While much of the response cycle is similar for men and women, one difference for men is they experience a 'refractory period.' Once a man has an orgasm, there is a period of time that must go by before he can have another orgasm. This period of time varies by the age of the man and the circumstances. Women, on the other hand, have no refractory period, and therefore have the capacity to have multiple orgasms."

"Right on," Wendy said to appreciative applause and laughter from many of the other women in the group.

"There have got to be *some* advantages," said Marjorie.

"There are *lots* more advantages than just multiple orgasms. Trust me," assured Betty to more applause.

"Okay, my sisters," Pam said laughing but ready to bring the room back to order. "We don't want to make these guys *too* jealous. And, by the way, some men report having a kind of multiple orgasm where they experience orgasmic contractions at different points before actually ejaculating."

Pam spent her final minutes talking about individual variations in how women and men experience the sexual response cycle, including a lively discussion of the G-spot and female ejaculation. In closing she said, "Bill is going to come up now, and expand upon Masters and Johnson's model, focusing on the psychological component. Bill?"

Pam sat as Bill stepped over to the whiteboard and quickly duplicated Pam's drawing from the easel. "We start here with 'Excitement,' then move up here to 'Plateau,' then on to the big 'O,' and then down the hill with 'Resolution.' I now want to add two very important components to this model. The first comes to us from Helen Singer Kaplan, formerly a sex therapist in private practice in New York, who, despite her strange and regrettable lapse into homophobia," he smiled accommodatingly at me, "offered us an invaluable insight by focusing our attention on the stage that should precede 'Excitement,' and that is *Desire*. Once she said it, it made perfect sense to everyone that prior to our engaging in sexual activity, there needs to be 'desire.' If you don't have sexual desire, you don't have the rest of the cycle. Some people have *no* sexual desire. Finding out 'why' is essential for the therapist in helping them have satisfactory sexual relationships with their partners.

"The second invaluable contribution to this model comes to us from David Reed, a marriage and family therapist, who added the notion of ESP, Erotic Stimulus Pathways," Bill continued as he wrote the words, drew an arc above the Masters and Johnson model, and then, with three vertical lines, divided both the arc and the "mountain" into four quadrants that he labeled "Seduction," "Sensations," "Surrender," and "Reflection."

"Reed reminded us that 'Seduction' is what traditionally precedes the sexual experience," Bill said with wide eyes of excitement. "So what's 'seduction?' Seduction is two things. It's how we get ourselves interested in sex, and it's how we get someone else interested in having sex with us. Do you remember in our films on masturbation how one of the men talked about lighting candles and putting on soft music in his room prior to masturbating, and how the woman told us how she would draw a warm bubble bath? That's seduction! It's putting you in the mood for the sexual experience. It's one partner bringing home the other's favorite flowers. The other partner prepares a really nice meal. The lights are turned down. A fire is lit. Their favorite music is selected. They turn off the phone. If they have kids, they've been dropped off at the grandparents' house. The mood is set. For Reed, 'Seduction' is the emotional correlate to the 'Desire' and 'Excitement' stages in the Kaplan, and Masters and Johnson models.

"Next, you have 'Sensations,' which are essential to the 'Excitement' and 'Plateau' of the sexual experience. Sex at its best involves *all* of our senses. It involves what we see, what we smell, what we taste, what we hear, and what we feel. Right? The sight of a person's face, their chest or breasts, their genitals, these are what turns many of us on. The smell of a person's body, their hair, their genitals. The taste of sex. The sounds of sex. The feel of their skin on our skin," Bill said with a swooning voice that brought claps of affirmation.

"And then, of course, we 'Surrender' through 'Orgasm' to this experience," he said, pointing to the appropriate spot on both curves. "And finally, we 'reflect' on what has just happened in our period of 'Resolution.' If what happened during the sexual experience is recalled during 'Reflection' as very satisfying and pleasurable, we are set up psychologically to enthusiastically begin the process the next time around with desire. If, on the other hand, our reflection of what transpired is not so positive, we're a little less inclined to feel the same level of desire.

"Now, quickly, because we're going to run out of time, what do you think the first thing to go is in most marriages?" he asked with a mischievous smile.

"Sex," bemoaned Chuck in a drawl that created two syllables.

"Yes," laughed Bill, "but before that? In Reed's model, which area is the first to lose attention?"

"Seduction," the majority of women answered at once.

"Right," he said appreciatively. "Seduction. You quit bringing home flowers. You eat frozen pot pies in front of the television. You don't bother with the music, and you leave the phone plugged in. Sex is relegated to the end of a long, busy day. It becomes orgasm-oriented. And as seduction goes, the sensations go. Instead of using all five senses, we decide that we really don't want to smell or taste the body. The negative messages of the culture about body odor and genital smells begin to block the excitement of discovery that we once had. Next, you get quiet and want your partner to be quiet because rather than being *stimulating*, the noises are now *irritating*. Then we decide we want the lights off because we accept the cultural message that naked bodies, particularly when they're not trim and muscular, are 'gross.' Finally, we try to squeeze the whole experience into the commercials during *The Tonight Show*. Upon reflection, the sex wasn't all that much fun, so we're not in such a big hurry to do it again!"

After the applause of recognition subsided, Lloyd announced from his seat, "That is *not* something that I look forward to."

"It doesn't have to be that way," assured Bill. "If you want to get the magic back, you can. But you have to be *aware* of what you're doing. You have to *want* to have more satisfying sex, and you have to be aware of *how* you have dropped seduction and closed down your senses. The fewer the senses we utilize in sex, the less satisfying the sex will be. Many people, particularly those in long-term relationships, forget that the senses are nature's 'aphrodisiacs'."

"Is that why gay men keep moving from partner to partner, so that the experience stays exciting?" asked Tonya.

"*Some* gay men," Thomas gently reminded her. "Lots of gay men are in long term relationships, and many of them could identify with Bill's description of what happens when sex with their lovers loses its magic."

"But some queer men *do* move from sex partner to sex partner because they want to keep the sex fresh and exciting," insisted Dan.

"And a lot of those men go from partner to partner because they're afraid of commitment," George said.

"Well, so do a lot of straight men," said Paula.

"And a lot of straight women," added Alison.

"It's not about sexual orientation," said Bill. "We've opened up a whole new category with this discussion on orientation, and Brian's going to be covering some of it when we come back from the break, but let's be clear that Reed's model applies to *everyone*, and everyone is capable of losing excitement in their sexual experiences. Everyone's also capable of getting it back!"

"You promise?" asked Maggie.

"A quick ten minutes to use the bathroom," Bill cautioned. "You'll get a longer break after the next session."

Fifteen minutes later, we were sitting in the dark, watching a beautifully photographed, choreographed, and edited film that presented four people – two men and two women – lovingly, erotically, and pleasurably having sex with one another in sets of two.

Responding it was called, and 'respond' is what they did to each other in every combination conceivable. Man to woman. Woman to woman. Man to man. The same four people were coupled in the total possible number of pairings and positions. With soft, classical music in the background, we watched a woman lovingly perform fellatio on a man. The camera drifted to his face that was peaking in pleasure. It then drifted slowly back to his penis, which was now in the mouth of the other man. The two women kissing tenderly transitioned into one of the women kissing with equal tenderness one of the men. Touching breasts became touching chests. Heterosexual intercourse fused into gay male body rubbing, or 'frottage.' Anal sex was anal with a male partner, and anal with a female partner. The film was brief but the message was clear and powerful. No more guessing. In this montage of sexual activity, it was quite apparent that the sexual activity engaged in by homosexuals was the same as engaged in by heterosexuals with the exception of penile-vaginal intercourse.

"The focus of our time together is *sexual orientation*," I explained, pointing to the word at the bottom of the newsprint. "As Pam discussed on Sunday in her presentation on 'What is Sexuality?' we make a distinction between four components of 'sexual identity' which are often confused. They are 'Biological Sex,' 'Gender Identity,' 'Gender Role,' and 'Sexual Orientation.' Bill spent time with us yesterday elaborating upon the differences among the first three categories, all of which have to do with 'gender.' What then is *Sexual Orientation*? Sexual orientation is our core sense of erotic and affectional attraction. Everyone has a sexual orientation. We are either 'heterosexual,' 'homosexual,' or 'bisexual.'

"And when we discuss being heterosexual, homosexual, or bisexual, we do so with reference to our 'Orientation,' our 'Behavior,' and our 'Identity.' Our 'Orientation' is what we *feel* sexually. Our 'Behavior' is what we *do* sexually. And our 'Identity' is how we *identity ourselves* sexually both to ourselves and to others. Sometimes these three elements are in sync, but often they are not. For heterosexual people they are almost always in sync. They feel attracted to people of the other gender. They have sex with people of the other gender. And they comfortably identify as heterosexual to themselves and to others. For homosexual and bisexual people, it is generally more challenging. We feel attracted to people of the same or both genders, but we're reluctant to act upon our feelings, and we have a great deal of difficulty acknowledging our feelings to ourselves and to other people, particularly when we are young. Our sexual orientation, however, isn't determined by what we do or by what we call ourselves. It's determined by what we *feel*."

"But feelings change," asserted Catherine from her seat in the second row. "Doesn't that mean that a person's sexual orientation changes also?"

"Do feelings change or does our *awareness* of our feelings change?" I asked. "Using Kinsey's model, Catherine," I said, pointing to the graph on the second easel, "we think of sexual orientation on a continuum. As many of you know, Alfred Kinsey was a biologist at Indiana University who surveyed nearly 12,000 Americans in the 1940s about their sexual behavior. He plotted out their responses on this seven-point grid. If their orgasms post-puberty had been exclusively with people of the other gender, he placed them in the '0' category. If their orgasms post-puberty were exclusively homosexual, he placed them in the '6' category. People with equal amounts of experience with both genders were '3's,' whom he called 'bisexuals,' and the others fell into categories '1,' '2,' '4,' and '5,' according to the percentages they represented. A Kinsey 1 had 'incidental' homosexual experiences, but predominantly heterosexual experiences. A Kinsey 2 had 'significant' homosexual experiences but, again, the majority of their post-puberty orgasms were with people of the other gender. At the other end of the continuum, a Kinsey 5 had 'incidental' heterosexual experiences but was predominantly homosexual in their post-puberty orgasms, and a Kinsey 4 had 'significant' heterosexual experience, but again, was predominantly homosexual.

"We use Kinsey's Scale today to discuss all three categories of 'Orientation,' 'Behavior,' and 'Identity.' Every person in this room can place him or herself on the continuum in each area. For instance, I'm a Kinsey 6 in *orientation* because I'm incapable of creating erotic feelings of attraction for women. I love women. I find them beautiful, but I'm not able to be turned on by them, this despite years of therapy, prayer, and sexual experiences with women. My *behavior* would be categorized as a Kinsey 5 because of the incidental heterosexual sex that I've had in my past. My *identity* today is as a '6' but it wasn't always. Initially I told myself that I was a '0' or a '2' or '3' at the most. Finally, I came to the point in my life that I acknowledged that I was a '6,' but I told everyone else that I was a '0.' And then I 'came out,' and began telling the truth to others about myself.

"You haven't answered my question," Catherine said.

"I'm getting to it," I replied smiling. "You ask if people's orientation changes because they experience a change in sexual feelings. I suggest that how they *label* themselves changes. In other words, their *identity* changes, but their orientation can't change. A true Kinsey 0 and a true Kinsey 6, by definition, can't have changing feelings of attraction. Bisexual people, which in today's thinking covers categories '1' through '5,' might become aware of same gender or other gender feelings later in life, but that doesn't mean that they've *changed* their orientation. It means that they've discovered their bisexuality. There is no evidence of a Kinsey 6 being able to *change* his or her orientation, only their behavior and identity."

"So you say," said Catherine.

"So says the bulk of research from the American Psychiatric and Psychological Associations," I replied. "But I'm the first to admit that we're in the cave with a candle on this. We know more about sexual orientation than any previous generation, but we're still putting pieces of the puzzle together. Let's acknowledge that we don't know everything, and that we're perhaps on safer ground acknowledging that there are *heterosexualities, homosexualities,* and *bisexualities.* We don't know, for instance, what exactly causes sexual orientation, but we know that homosexual behavior has been witnessed in every species of mammal. Thus, it is 'natural.' We don't know why there seems to be more women who identify as 'bisexual' than there are men. Is it cultural influence, hormonal, left brain versus right brain differences? And, we're not sure we're all talking about the same thing when we talk about erotic and affectional attraction. Two young women kiss one another today in front of men and correctly see it as a turn-on for some heterosexual men. Is there erotic or affectional attraction involved? Are they both heterosexual? Is such kissing 'sexual' at all?

"And what do we call a man who uses a woman sexually for his own pleasure but doesn't care what she feels sexually, and who prefers to spend all of his social time with other men? Is he heterosexual if all of his needs for intimacy are met by other men?"

"You call him 'Frank,' my former husband," Marjorie said to laughter and applause.

"He has many names," I said when the room quieted down. "The point is, the words and concepts that we use today to describe our experiences of feelings, behavior, and identity are limited and will change. What doesn't seem to change, however, is a person's core sense of attraction. Let's talk now about what we *do* know about the causes of sexual orientation."

For the next several minutes I enumerated the variety of scientific studies that strongly suggested the influences of "nature" as opposed to "nurture" on our sexual orientation. It included reports on the differences in brain mass between gay and straight men, the high incidence of correlating sexual orientation among identical twins, the National Institute for Health study on genetic markers, and the impact of testosterone in early brain development.

"Regardless of whether you accept or don't accept the validity of the research," I said, "the most important element that I think we bring to this discussion is our view of God's or nature's *intention* with sexual orientation. Just as Bill explained how our sexual values are determined by whether we think the purpose of sex is for 'procreation' or for 'relationship,' so too is our approach to heterosexuality, homosexuality, and bisexuality impacted by what we see as 'normal.' *Heterosexism* is a term that is used to describe the attitude that only heterosexuality is intended by God or by nature, and that anything else is an 'aberration,' or a poor substitute. Not unlike racism and sexism, it's a *value* system where one erotic attraction is valued over the other.

"If you believe that heterosexuality is the *only* noble and legitimate way to yearn another, you are likely to say things such as, 'What did I do *wrong*?' when you find out that your child is gay. Or, you comment, 'My cousin *admitted* to me that he was gay.' You don't *admit* that you've been to Europe or that you've won the lottery. You 'admit' to something bad, such as breaking the lamp, stealing the money, or not being heterosexual. A television talk show host asked me once, 'Brian, if I could give you a pill that would make you a heterosexual, would you take it?' His question reflected his bias that it's more desirable to be a heterosexual. My answer reflected my bias too. I told him, 'If you had offered me that pill when I was seven, eleven, fifteen, or twenty-one, I would have taken it because I didn't *want* to be gay. But I wouldn't take the pill today, even if there was such a pill, which there isn't. I *celebrate* being who I am. It's all a matter of perspective."

Looking at my watch, and realizing that we were running out of time, I reminded everyone that we would have lots of time tomorrow to discuss this further. "But, before we move on, I want to make sure that I have answered your question, Catherine."

"Not entirely," she said. "I understand where you're coming from. I'm just not sure that I agree."

"Fair enough," I replied. "We don't have to agree on this or anything else presented here this week. What's important is that we individually come to understand what it is we feel, and why we feel the way we do about the full range of human sexuality. Knowing our biases will make us more effective educators, ministers, counselors, etcetera. Now, though, we need to move on. We have a short film on 'bisexuality' that you all may find interesting. Pam, the lights please."

Kinsey 3 was an audio-accompanied slide show in which a travel agent named "Brian" told us of his bisexuality and of his simultaneous relationships with his girlfriend "Sharon" and with his boyfriend "Frank." According to Brian, both Sharon and Frank were content to share him with the other. We watched Brian and Sharon shop and dine out together, and Brian and Frank read the Sunday paper and cook together. Each person had his or her own apartment and life. Brian found the situation ideal because both Sharon and Frank met unique needs in him, emotionally and sexually.

Brian enjoyed each of their bodies. He learned from performing oral sex on Frank what Sharon was feeling when she did the same for him. Having Frank penetrate him anally allowed him to feel the fusing of the bodies that Sharon felt when he penetrated her vaginally. Back and forth between scenes of intimate sexual activity we went, with Brian's voice matter-of-factly describing the advantages to his life in this arrangement.

When the slide show ended, and the lights were turned up, Bill jumped to his feet to explain, "Incidentally, I know all of the people in this film. Brian and Sharon eventually got married and recently celebrated their 20th anniversary. And Frank is still part of Brian's life. Okay. Off to your process groups."

Chapter Thirty-Three

Dom's Map

"Okay. I've got some questions," Leona said as she walked through the door into Higley, her participant packet in one hand, and a glass of lemonade in the other. "What's with that bisexual guy running back and forth between lovers and not using a condom? And were all of those people having sex with each other in that other film 'bi,' and where were their condoms? And how come Bill says that sex therapist who talked about 'desire' was a 'homophobe'?"

"A-plus for paying close attention, Leona," I said as she and the others took their seats in the circle.

"I was wondering the same thing about the condoms," Charlie said.

"Well then, 'A-plus' for you too, Charlie," I grinned.

"I saw it too," said Wendy smiling and waving her hand for recognition.

"Looks like everyone gets an 'A'."

"Not me," Margaret said. "I'm ashamed to say I didn't even *think* about condoms. I just thought the first film with the four people making love was *beautiful*. I was less impressed with the bisexual travel agent. What was his name? 'Brian'? He came across as a little too self-absorbed for me."

"A 'little' too self-absorbed?" Leona replied in astonishment. "Honey, that man was a *mess*. I'd just like to see him try to get away with that with me. He wouldn't know what hit him."

"We know he wouldn't," I confirmed. "Okay, Leona, let's start with the first question about condoms. The films were made in the seventies before we had any knowledge of HIV. People didn't really talk about 'safe sex' back then. We show the films because they're the best we've got. Ideally, they'd all be using condoms. If you hadn't caught it, I would have brought it up. Your second question was about the four people in the first film. You wonder if they're 'bisexual.' It would appear that they are, given the pleasure they seem to be getting out of having sex with both genders, but they could also be actors. As we know, gay actors and straight actors regularly pretend in films to be experiencing sexual pleasure. I don't know what the orientations of the people in the film are, but I liked the fluid back and forth scenes where the genders kept changing. I, too, thought it was beautiful, and it made the intended point that there isn't an awful lot that's different about gay and straight lovemaking."

"Everything happened so fast, I didn't get the chance to look away," Dom said. "If the whole thing had been about two guys going at it, I probably wouldn't have watched it."

"What would you have done?" Maggie asked.

"Like I say, I would have just looked away. But if I wanted to watch men having sex with women …"

"Or women having sex with women," Wendy interjected.

"Yes, that too," Dom acknowledged, "then I had to watch the whole thing."

"Did the man-to-man lovemaking disturb you, Dom?" I asked.

"Not like I thought it would," he said. "It's clearly not my thing, but I got through it."

"Were there any surprises for you?" Beatrice asked.

"What do you mean 'surprises'?" he replied.

"You know, any 'ah has?' Things you didn't expect to see, or reactions you didn't expect to have?"

"Naw, not that I can think of."

"What about with the film on bisexuality, *Kinsey 3*?" she asked.

"Oh, well, he was a jerk," Dom said. "I didn't like him at all. I can't believe his girlfriend married him, especially since he's still with his boyfriend."

239

"But what about the sex in that one?" Wendy asked. "Did you look away with that one?"

"Hey, I'm starting to get a little self-conscious here," he protested with a slight laugh. "I don't remember what I did. I think I watched most of it. I'm here to learn. Sometimes my own shit – oh geeze, sorry," he said with a wincing look at Margaret. "My own *stuff* gets in the way, but I'm here to learn."

"I liked the film on bisexuality," said Charlie.

"Which one? The first or the second?" asked Maggie.

"Both of them. I thought the first was really cool, and I thought the guy in the second one had a lot of courage. I don't think most people who are bisexual have lives that look like that, but I liked his honesty and I learned something new."

"Like what?" Leona asked.

"I was impressed with his desire to know what Sharon felt when she was performing oral sex on him, and he also wanted to know what she felt when he was inside of her. He learned that from his sex with Frank. He seemed really open to me, like he wasn't afraid to have a sexual experience if it was going to teach him something. I didn't find him as selfish as everyone else did."

"I hadn't thought about that," Beatrice replied. "I just kept thinking that it wouldn't be an arrangement that *I'd* agree to."

"I wonder," said Maggie solemnly. "I've lay awake at night thinking that maybe I could keep Barry in my life if I was able to give him that kind of freedom."

"Did you see yourself in that film, Maggie?" I asked.

Sighing deeply she said, "It really freaked me out. I hated Frank. I felt like he was the 'home wrecker.' And then when Bill said that Brian and Sharon were married, and that Frank was *still* hanging around, I thought, 'Get a life!'."

"He *did* have a life," Charlie said softly. "With Brian, the travel agent. Why be angry with Frank if everyone involved agrees with the situation?"

"It's not about Frank, Charlie," Margaret said. "It's about Maggie and Barry."

"I know," Charlie said.

"Is your husband bisexual, Maggie?" Dom asked gently.

"He says not. He says he's gay. I'm not sure he knows *what* he is, and I'm not sure that Catherine wasn't right. If your feelings can change, then maybe your orientation *does* change. And if it does, then maybe it can change back."

"Do you believe that?" I asked.

"I *want* to believe it," she said softly."I don't know what I believe. I'm so confused."

"And in a lot of pain," I said, reaching over and taking her hand.

The silence that followed was broken by Maggie's assurance of, "I'm fine. Let's talk about something else."

And so we did. We spent a lot of time talking about "Seduction" and how everyone could relate to the important role it plays, or played, in their enjoyment of sexual activity. Each offered examples of things that they, or their sexual partners, had done to help create feelings of excitement and "specialness" prior to lovemaking.

"I always knew my wife was in the mood when I'd come home and find candles lit on the dinner table," Dom laughed.

"My wife had a special perfume that she knew I liked," added Charlie. "If I smelled it when I walked in the door, I knew that 'tonight's the night'."

"If the television *wasn't* on when I came into the bedroom, that was my indication my husband was in the mood," Margaret said laughing.

The emotions in the room covered the range from revelry to regret. Generational differences were obvious, as were those created by relational status. Members of couples who had been together for many years often spoke in past tense about seduction. Single people, such as Wendy, Beatrice, and Kevin listened to the expressed regret but couldn't come up with their own examples of things they no longer did to create the erotic moment.

"How about you, Leona?" Maggie asked. "You haven't said much about 'seduction.' Were there special things that you did, or that you do, with your partner?"

"That was a long time ago," she said with a laugh to Maggie. "Besides, I don't want to go getting into my story and then not have anything to say when it's my turn. You're just going to have to wait for the juicy details. But before we go any further, will you answer my third question?" she asked, turning to me.

"What third question?"

"Why did Bill say that lady was a 'homophobe'? The one who talked about 'desire'?"

"Oh, sorry. Helen Singer Kaplan," I said. "She came on pretty strongly that gay people could change their orientation."

"That made her a 'homophobe'?" Leona asked.

"No, it wasn't her position so much as the manner in which she argued her point. Homophobia really refers to the attitudes and behaviors of people who make the effort to create a hostile or unsafe environment for gay people and their family members," I replied. "I'll be saying more about this tomorrow, but you and I can meet to talk about this later if you'd like."

"No, that's okay. I got it," she said.

"Okay, well, we've got about twenty-five minutes left," I said. "Why don't we do another map of our sexual journeys? You want to go now, Leona?"

"No, I'm not quite ready," she said.

"Okay. How about someone else? Who's ready to share with the group the important points in your sexual journey?"

"I'll go," both Margaret and Dom said in unison, and then laughed.

"You go," Dom said.

"No you, please," Margaret replied.

"Dom, why don't you go since we've had a couple presentations by the women in the group so far?" I said. "It's the guys' turn."

"Okay," he said as he opened his participant folder and withdrew a folded piece of newsprint. "But, like Beatrice said, I think you'll find my map really boring. Besides, I think I've already told you about most of the highlights anyway." Spreading it out on the coffee table, and smoothing out the folds with his large hands, he began.

"I've never done anything like this before, so bear with me."

Dom followed the pattern set by the others in the group, and used stick figures to make his point. The biggest difference on his sheet was the lack of color. Everything was marked in black.

"Here's 'Nona'," he said pointing to the first stick figure, labeled "Nona." "She's my mother's mother, and she lived with us. If sexuality is everything that you say it is, like our values, our sense of ourselves, our feelings about 'family,' then Nona had a *really* big impact on my sexual journey."

"How so?" I asked.

"She was full of life. She was very religious, and by today's standards, you'd probably say that she was 'prudish,' but she loved to laugh, and she enjoyed her vino. She also was an incredible cook. The kitchen in our house was the most wonderful place in the world. There was always something in the oven or on the stove. Whenever I smell onions and garlic cooking in olive oil, I get this warm feeling that I always had with her in the kitchen. She was a little bit of a thing but she had a strong hug, and she really loved me and my brothers. So, that's Nona.

"Here you have a cross for the Church," he continued. "The Church was everything. St. Charles Borromeo parish was our whole lives. If any of you are Catholic, you know what I mean. During the weekday, you'd be in the Catholic school, on Saturday, in confession, on Sunday, in church. Even if I disagree with stuff, I know that all of that Catholicism had its effect on my sexuality. Well, here's a good example. I already told you about Sr. Mary Raphael, our eighth grade nun who scared the bejesus out of us with her squawking about masturbation. How could you *not* feel guilty after getting that message twenty-four hours a day?

"And down here," he said, pointing to three small stick figures and one larger one, "is me, my brother Peter, and my cousin Vinny. The tall one is Uncle Murray, the slime ball. Enough said about that. Over here's me and my wife Terry, Dominic Junior, Tony, and Sophie. That's the family. The kids are all grown and out of the house. Sophie's a senior at the University of Dayton, another good Catholic college. And finally, down here, you've got some goal posts, which represent my life as a coach, and the school, Liberty View, where I'll be teaching the class in human sexuality, which is why I'm here. How's that?"

"It's good. You did great," I replied. "How did it feel putting it together, and how did it feel sharing it with the group?"

"Sharing it was pretty easy. As I say, it's pretty boring stuff, and most of the things I put down there I've already talked with you about. It was kind of interesting putting it all down on paper though. It made me think about a lot of things. I liked thinking about Nona, and about how she influenced me. Good feelings came up. I wish my own kids could have known her. The Church stuff was really clear as far as how it impacted my values. You notice I don't work at a Catholic high school? I got myself worked up this week about old Uncle Murray. I have a lot of unfinished business with that whole thing. And it felt good to draw my family and label them. I'm proud of my kids and I feel good about my marriage, though I have to go home and talk to Terri about that 'seduction' stuff. She hasn't lit candles on the table in a long while. And she just gets flowers on Mother's Day, Valentine's, and her birthday. Anyway, I think we've run out of time."

"No, we've got time," I said. "Does anyone have any questions for Dom? Yes, Wendy?"

"Dom, thanks for sharing your map. I was just wondering though. There's nothing down there about your 'first' sexual experience and how it felt. I remember that you asked Beatrice if she wished that she had waited until she got married before having sex. I was wondering if you waited until you got married, and if you didn't, do you wish that you had?"

"Who, me?" he laughed. "No. Let's just say that I had sufficient experience before I got married, and that I sure knew what I was doing."

"Do you think that your discomfort with the male sexuality in the films comes from your bad experience with Uncle Murray, or your Catholic upbringing, or what?" she asked.

"I think my feelings are pretty *normal*," he answered a bit defensively. "I don't know where they come from. I don't have anything against homosexuals. I think I even have a cousin who's gay. It's just that I'm not all that comfortable watching two men go at it, that's all. Maybe it's being Catholic. Maybe it's being Italian. I don't know. What do you think?"

"I'm sorry, Dom, I'm not wanting to argue," she said moving forward in her chair. "It's just that you've asked the others in the group some good questions when they did their maps, and I wanted to do the same with you."

"Go ahead," he said.

"Well, when Beatrice said she had a problem with masturbation, you asked her how she was going to deal with that if someone came to her for counseling and talked about it. I was wondering how you feel you'll handle gay kids coming to you for help, if you think that they might?"

"I don't know," he said. "I don't know if they will. I *hope* they will think that they can. A couple of years ago, I had a kid on the team who I suspected might have been homosexual. Some of the guys talked as if there were rumors about it. I just left it alone."

"You didn't speak to him about it?" Wendy asked.

"No. Do you think I should have? He didn't bring it up with me. I thought it was best to just leave it alone unless someone made a big deal out of it."

"I can understand your feelings, Dom," Margaret said, "but I wonder if we shouldn't step forward and initiate a discussion when we suspect that a child is gay, especially if we hear others talk about it."

"What are you supposed to say?" asked Leona. "Are you gay?"

"No, but you could create an opportunity for him or her to share the information," Margaret replied.

"To do that, you have to have established some credibility with them in advance," Wendy said. "They have to know they can trust you on this issue. You've got to speak up when you hear anti-gay comments or when people use derogatory terms to describe gay people. The gay kids need to know where you come down on the issue before they're going to come out to you. I had this great teacher who *never* laughed at an anti-gay joke, and who always called the kids in class on their anti-gay remarks. Guess which teacher I decided to come out to?"

"You were lucky," Kevin said.

"I *was* lucky," Wendy affirmed.

"This is a great discussion. You've all brought up a lot of really important points about sexual orientation, our comfort level with people who are different from us, and how we communicate to others that we want to be seen as 'approachable.' We need to stop though," I said. "I see that the other groups have broken up, it's lunch time, and I've got a staff meeting. But, we can continue the discussion the next time we meet, which is at 5:00 p.m., right after the presentation on 'heterosexuality.' Dom, thank you for sharing your map. Thank you, everyone, too, for sharing in the group."

Wendy lingered in the room as the others filed out.

"You look a little unhappy," I said.

"I thought he was dishonest," she said with exasperation.

"How so?" I asked.

"He played the whole thing safe. He didn't tell us anything about himself that we didn't already know. The women are telling the intimate details of *their* first experiences. Dom said nothing. The only traumatic thing that he mentioned happened to someone else, his brother and cousin. It angers me that he's not being more honest."

"But maybe he's being as honest as he's capable of being at this moment," I said. "This whole thing is voluntary. I trust that people will share as much as they feel comfortable sharing. I don't want people to go past their boundaries. Trust the process, Wendy. I think Dom's getting a lot out of this."

"Okay. You asked what was wrong. That's just how I'm feeling."

"And I'm glad that you told me," I said. "One thing I'd like *you* to think about if you would, though, is what's going on that's pushing *your* buttons? Is it Dom or is Dom prompting some resentments that have built up in you about someone or something else? Does Dom being 'heterosexual' or being 'male' trigger a stronger response in you than you'd have to

245

Margaret if she told us her story, but wasn't as forthcoming as the others? Do you see what I mean? It's a great opportunity just to think about where our feelings come from."

"I'll think about it," she said as she offered a half smile, grabbed her packet, and added, "See you later."

Chapter Thirty-Four

Ben's Swim

"If no one has anything else to report or any problems that need our attention, we'll end this meeting," Alison said. "I understand that some of you are heading to the water for Ben's swim. I wish I had known about it earlier. I agreed to go into Cazenovia with a group that wants to shop. And I know that some others are planning on a volleyball game. When and where does this begin, and is Ben going to be disappointed that not everyone will be there?"

"We're meeting at Peabody in a few minutes," Bill replied. "But the whole thing has just been by word of mouth. That's the way he wants it. Our entire SAR group is going to be there because he talked in group about how meaningful this event is to him. He's both excited and frightened, but he's not expecting or wanting a crowd."

"We'll tell him you wanted to be there, and we'll give you a report," Carol said.

"Thank you, again, though, Alison, for having the meeting during lunch. We really appreciate it," Pam said as she stood and tried to organize the dirty dishes and cafeteria trays that filled the coffee table in Higley.

"I'll help you with that," I said to Pam. "But let's get our suits on first so that we're not late. We can get this stuff when we get back."

Three minutes later, I was in my swimming suit walking into Pam and Alison's bedroom, with a beach towel over my shoulder. "Are you ready?" I asked.

"One minute, sweetie," she replied. "Where's Carol? Is she coming?"

"She's already heading for the cafeteria with an armful of dirty dishes. And, she's got her suit on. What takes you so long?"

"Just one more minute. Okay, how do I look?"

"Great as usual."

"Brian, I wanted to talk with you about Kevin. Is he doing okay?"

"Yea, I think so. He's feeling a little let down about what happened with Dan at the beach last night, but he's doing fine. Why?"

"How many people know about what happened with Dan and Kevin at the beach last night?" she asked as we walked to the large windows of Higley that looked out over the lawn, and saw that Ben had yet to exit his dorm.

"I don't know. Probably just us. I think we're the only ones he's talked to. Why?"

"I'm really wrestling with how I feel about it," she said.

"Like how?"

"Well, to begin with, I don't know that it's healthy for Kevin to set himself up for disappointment so quickly. He just met Dan three days ago. It seems like it all moved pretty quickly."

"Maybe for some people, but not for them. I think we've got our classic difference here between how a man might approach sexuality, and how a woman might approach it. A lot of guys think about sex as recreational. Three days may feel like a long courtship to them. If this was about them deciding to buy china together, then I'd agree with you. But, that's something different. Here, you're talking about two gay men who found each other attractive. Kevin enjoyed the attention he got from Dan. He knows he runs the risk of rejection because he's transsexual. Dan knew Kevin's story. Kevin thought maybe this time it would be different."

"But I feel terrible for him. He must be hurting so badly. I just wish he could find the right guy, and not have the heartache," she said.

"He's disappointed but he's not devastated, Pam. One of these days, if that's what he wants, he'll fall in love with someone who's in love with him. But that's *not* what was going on at the beach. One's 'love,' the other's 'lust'."

"I know. I know. It doesn't compute with me, but I understand. How do you feel, though, about Kevin being on staff?"

"He's *not* on staff," I said. "He has no power or authority with the participants other than that which comes from him telling his story. But, there's Ben. Can we continue this later?"

"Sure. I don't know that there's anything more I have to offer. I've just been wrestling with it, as I said."

"Okay, but *I'd* like some time with you," I said as I held the door for her, and we walked to the cafeteria with the remaining dirty dishes, "to talk about Leona. I saw you go for a walk with her. I need some guidance on how best to work with her."

"I'd be happy to, sweetie," she said.

A large group of participants and staff, all clad in bathing suits, formed a loose circle around Ben. Hoots and whistles greeted him as he maneuvered his chair through the door of Peabody, which Beatrice proudly held open.

"Get a look at Ben!" Leona gasped with delight. "My Lord, child, where have you been hiding that body?"

"Give him room. Give him room," George said as he waved an opening in the circle. "Okay, Ben, what are our instructions?"

Ben grinned up at George from his chair, where he sat dressed in a bright red pair of boxer-style swimming trunks. His legs hung down, lifeless and without apparent fat or muscle. His skin, from the tips of his toes to his neck, was a pasty white. Ben's arms, though, like his face, were well tanned and highly muscled. His neck, shoulders, upper back, and chest were "buff" by any standards. A fine layer of chestnut-colored hair covered his legs, arms, and chest.

"Thank you all for joining me for my inaugural swim," Ben said. "I'm psyched. I've waited way too long to do this, and I can't think of any better group than you sex-crazed maniacs to do it with. Peter's got my inner tube that I brought for this occasion. If you'll give me some room, I'll line this thing up with the beach, and start it on its way. That's a really steep hill, though, with no steps. I've never taken this chair down such a deep incline. I'll need someone good and strong behind the chair to grab it if it starts to roll too fast. I'm also going to need a lot of help getting back up the hill. Do I have any volunteers?"

"I'll do it," I said.

"He *said* 'good and strong," Carol smirked.

"Ha. Ha," I replied.

"Get out of the way. I'll do it," Betty said, as she nudged me with her hips, and moved into place. "Come on, Carla. You can help me."

"I'd love to," she said, "but I'm not that strong."

"I'll do it," said Chuck. "Move over there, little lady."

"Well, that's one of the *nicest* things anyone's ever said to me," Carla chirped.

Carol and I looked at each other with big eyes, and smiles of amazement.

"George, you're in charge of crowd control," Ben said. "Can you handle that?"

"Okay, everyone in Ben's SAR group who doesn't have a job, come out here and form a line on both sides," George said. "Catherine, you go there. Paula, next to her, Beverly, you're next. Gail and Joe go on the other side. Bill, you too. You're the official color guard. The rest of you, if you would, please walk ahead of us and keep your eyes open for rocks, sticks, ruts, or anything else that could make this trip down the hill more challenging than it otherwise will be."

"The staff will go down and make sure the beach area is free of debris," Carol said. "Come on, Brian and Pam. You too, Dick."

The weather was perfect for the event. The deep blue sky was dotted with billowing, creamy-white clouds. The hot sun warmed us as we waited for the arrival of the procession.

"So, what about Leona?" Pam asked as we stood by ourselves ankle-deep in the water. "Is there a problem in your group?"

"No, not really," I said. "But I think that she has an effect on people that I'm not quite sure how to handle. She's sassy, which I like. I actually think she's very funny. But, she pretends as if she's above what's going on. She withholds information about herself, and yet, sometimes she's very vulnerable, and lets us know it. She seems really flustered by the content of the material. She thinks that because she works for Planned Parenthood that she should be more comfortable with some of these issues. As you know, she's not all that comfortable with transgender issues, and she has a lot of trouble with homosexuality. Or so, she says."

"Brian, you hit the nail on the head when you said she's *vulnerable* underneath the sassiness. Culturally speaking, it's challenging for her here. She feels really lonely and isolated some times," Pam said. "Think about it, sweetie. The only black man here is gay. The other two black women are from a completely different culture, and I'm not all that accessible because I'm on the staff. I understand that she's a dynamic educator, but she's new to Planned Parenthood. They sent her here because they knew she needed to do some work in the areas she's having the hardest time. I know that she wanted to be in my group, but I think it's great that she's in your's. Be patient with her. I think she's getting a lot out of this week."

"Did she say anything to you that might be helpful for me to know?" I asked. "Oh, never mind. We'll talk later. It's swim time."

"Make room. Make room," George ordered as the procession reached the beach, and we formed a semicircle around Ben. "Okay, Ben. What now?"

"Now we move the chair as close to the water as we can," he replied. "Then, I need a couple of you to lift me out of the chair and carry me into the water. Once I'm in the water, I'll grab the inner tube and paddle around. That'll be it. No synchronized swimming or fancy dives from the raft. You ready? Wait a second. Wait a second. How's the water?" he asked Pam and me.

"It's nice," we both replied.

"Here, let me put a handful on your feet," I offered, cupping my hands and dripping water slowly onto Ben's feet. "Can you feel that?"

"Oh, yea, that feels good. Okay. Chuck? Betty? You ready? Lift away."

Chuck and Betty moved to the sides of Ben's chair, looked at each other with a little apprehension, reached down and put one arm beneath Ben's legs and the other behind his back.

"On the count of three," Chuck said. "One, two, three."

Together they lifted Ben up as George and Maggie pulled his chair back.

"Watch the stones," I advised. "It can be tricky walking in."

"Now you tell us," Chuck said with a grunt. "You okay over there, Betty?"

"I'm fine. You just hold up your side," she shot back with a grin.

Slowly, they inched forward with Ben seated in their arms. The group on the beach applauded.

"Careful now," Beatrice pleaded.

"Son of a *bitch*!" Chuck cried as he jerked to one side, sending Ben and Betty into the water. "I stepped on something sharp. A damned log or something," he explained as he quickly moved forward to grab Ben, who was now splashing his arms in the water, attempting to get off of Betty who was submerged beneath him.

Screams and yells of panic accompanied the abundance of advice that came from the beach. "Grab Ben." "Pull Betty up." "Bring him back to shore." "Is he okay?" "Where's the inner tube?" "What did he step on?" "You guys need help?" "There's too many people involved."

As Chuck and I pulled Ben off Betty, and cradled him in our arms in waist-deep water, Betty pulled herself up with the help of Carla and Pam, who both had frightened looks on their faces.

"What in the *hell* happened?" she coughed. "Is everyone okay?"

"Are *you* okay?" Chuck asked. "I stepped on a damn sharp stick or somethin'. I'm sorry. Are you okay?"

"I'm fine," she replied, standing straight up, and wiping the water off of her face. "Ben, are you okay?"

"Is he crying?" Catherine whispered to Maggie when she saw Ben's head hung down and his shoulders shaking.

"Is he okay?" Peter asked in a loud voice as he waded into the water with the inner tube.

"He's *laughing*!" Chuck announced. "You mind telling me what's so damn funny? We could have had a serious accident here."

"I told you it wouldn't be pretty," Ben laughed. "I told you all that you'd get wet. Betty, you sure you're okay?"

"I'm fine, doll. The question is, how are *you* doing?"

"I'm greaaaat!" he exclaimed. "I'm better than great! I'm fucking *wonderful*! Thanks everyone. Thanks a lot. Hey, Bea, where are you? Get in here. The water's great. Guys, let go of me. Turn me around and let go."

"You sure?" I asked.

"Come on. I know what I'm doing. If I sink, pull me up."

"Letting go on three," I said. "One, two, three."

When Chuck and I let go, Ben began to sink. He moved his arms wildly in an attempt to stay afloat. He was in fairly shallow water, so he didn't sink far.

"Okay. Okay," he said. "Pull me up. I need the tube. Is this great or what, though? Bea, where are you? Oh, there you are. Once I grab that tube, let's float out to the raft. What do you say? God, thanks everyone. This is great. This is *really* great! I *love* the water. I love the feel of it on my body. I'm *never* coming out of here. You'll just have to have the next session on the beach. What are you all waiting for? Get into the water!"

Within a couple of minutes nearly everyone was waste deep in water, splashing one another, and moving close to Ben with big grins of admiration and appreciation on our faces.

"I feel so *blessed*," Joe whispered to Bill as they stood together smiling on the shore.

"Me too!" Bill gushed. "I wouldn't have missed this for the world. But I'm getting in the water. How about you?"

Chapter Thirty-Five

Heterosexuality

"Would everyone please take a minute and look around the room at some of the faces in our group?" Pam said with delight, as she stood beside Bill in the downstairs meeting room. "I mean, have you ever seen such big smiles? For those of you who missed out on the excitement, Ben here took his first swim in many, many years, and he had an army of very excited supporters cheering him on. So, tell us, Ben, how was it?"

"You mean after I nearly drowned Betty?" he laughed.

"I nearly drowned you both," Chuck objected.

"It was *great!*" Ben said. "I just want to say 'thank you' to everybody once again. You all were wonderful. I'll never forget it."

"You going skinny dipping tonight?" George asked.

"Hey, if there's any skinny dipping, I don't want to hear about it," Alison chided with a stern look, and a grin.

"You going skinny dipping tonight?" George repeated in an exaggerated whisper.

"Congratulations, Ben," Bill said. "We're all *very* happy for you," to which the room responded with enthusiastic applause.

"Okay," Pam said, bringing our attention back to the subject at hand. "This afternoon, Bill and I are going to lead you in a discussion of 'heterosexuality.' We have a beautiful film to show you, entitled *Going*

Down to Bimini, but first we want to focus our attention on three areas that we feel can cause difficulty in heterosexual relationships."

"It's been my experience, that the biggest issue facing heterosexual couples in their sexual relationships is *communication,*" Bill said as he wrote the word on the whiteboard.

"I'll second that," Pam said.

"We're simply not brought up to communicate effectively with members of the other gender," Bill continued. "A second area that causes trouble is that though we're born sexual and sexually responsive, we're not born *lovers.* Third," he said as he wrote the word "lovers" on the board, "men are brought up with the message that they know what to do sexually, and that they're *not* to ask for guidance from their partners. They have the false impression that they're born lovers, when they're not, and because they don't ask, they don't know any better. As a result, many men don't have mutually-satisfying sexual relationships with their female partners. They concentrate on the big 'O' rather than on *love making.* Lovemaking is seen as merely a means to an end."

"My former husband, Frank," Marjorie dryly reminded us.

"Well, my wife Kathy would have said the same thing about me," Bill said, prompting laughter with his gesture of inserting his finger into the imaginary middle hole and tickling.

"To address these issues, I have the couples who come to me for counseling do two things. The first is to talk about *everything.* Talk about what turns them on. Talk about what turns them off. Talk about the fears they have of not knowing what the other wants. Open and honest communication is essential to having and maintaining a healthy, happy sexual relationship with one's partner.

"Secondly," he said, "I have the couples engage in a *sensate focus.* In other words, I have them practice seeing each activity in lovemaking as an end in itself. Face caressing and kissing, non-genital pleasuring, eroticizing the entire body, and genital pleasuring are all experienced as pleasurable, and as *independent* entities. During one session of lovemaking, the couple will agree to only kiss. In another, they agree to only massage or only fondle. As they're engaged in this lovemaking, they talk about it. They give positive feedback and guidance. 'Yes, that feels good.' 'A little more gently, please.' It's amazing to see how this kind of an exercise can completely rejuvenate a couple's sexual relationship and the health of the relationship in general."

"It sounds good to me," Grace said as she looked up from the notes that she was diligently taking.

"It does sound good, doesn't it?" Pam affirmed. "I want to underscore Bill's reference to *positive* feedback. It can be a real 'turn off' to a man if a woman gives him negative feedback during sex. She can help him more successfully by gently moving his hand where she'd like it, and by making pleasurable noises when it feels good. Nonverbal guidance during sex is very helpful. So, I agree with Bill 100 percent. Couples need to communicate, which regrettably they don't get a lot of practice doing. So, now, we're going to give you all a chance to communicate with each other about yourselves as sexual beings, and as lovers. Bill said that we're not *born* lovers. We *become* good lovers through communication and through practice. We thought that since we don't have any heterosexual couples here to model this open communication, we'd give the men a chance to listen to the women talk about their feelings and experiences. Then we'll give the women a chance to listen to the men. And then, we'll give you *both* a chance to talk to each other. How does that sound?

"Now, I know that for those of you who are gay or lesbian, this exercise may not be as relevant because you're not in romantic relationships with members of the other gender. But I also know that some of you have had heterosexual experiences in the past that you can draw from. And I'm hoping that you'll all be interested in learning how to better support your heterosexual clients or peers in their relationships. So, please relate to this as you're able, and be allies to your heterosexual fellow participants in this exercise. You with me? Good."

Then, following Pam's instructions, the participants formed two concentric circles with their chairs, the women on the inside and the men on the periphery. Pam sat with the inner circle and said, "Okay, women, this is going to be a kind of 'myth-information' game. I want you to talk right from your heart and tell me if you think the following statement is a 'myth' or a 'fact,' and why. We'll get your answers and have some discussion. And if I have any information to add, I will. Guys in the outer circle, you're just listening. Make notes of any questions or comments that you want to make, but don't interrupt, please. So, here's the first statement: 'Women usually take considerably longer to get aroused and reach orgasm than men.' What do you say?"

"I'd say it's definitely a fact. Speaking for myself, I need time to build up my sexual excitement," Margaret said. "I want to be kissed and caressed. I want my husband to take his time. For me, if it's lovemaking and not just sex, I want to *feel* some love from him."

"Yea, I want to feel as if I'm not just a prop, like a blow up doll," said Tonya. "I want to know that it matters that it's me that's in the bed."

"Thanks," said Pam. "How about you, Leona?"

"Mmm. I want a man with a slow hand. I want a man with an easy touch," she sang, laughing in response to the applause she received.

"The Pointer Sisters knew what they were talking about, huh?" Pam replied. "Does anyone think the statement is a myth?"

"No, it's a fact. Men can be so orgasm-oriented," Joanne moaned. "Two kisses are followed by a grope of the breasts, and then it's right down to the genitals. Most women I know love to have their clitoris gently stimulated, but not in the first twenty seconds. Take your time. Give us some time to build up some excitement."

"Are there cultural differences that you want to bring into this discussion, Martha or Beverly? How do you think women in Trinidad would respond to the statement?" Pam asked.

"I think women in Trinidad would be saying very similar things," Beverly replied. "They want their male partners to hold them, like the story you told about the 'zut.' Women want to make love with a man who is sensitive, and who wants to satisfy them."

"Does that mean that women *never* want to have 'quickie' sex?" Pam asked.

"I think there are some women who are really excited by a 'quickie' from time to time, but not as a steady diet," Paula answered.

"I want to say something in defense of the men," Beatrice said. "Not *all* men are orgasm-oriented. Some men are *great* lovers."

Dom, Chuck, and Ben applauded their approval.

"Good point, Beatrice," said Pam. "When we say 'men do this' or 'men do that,' it sounds like we're talking about *all* men. We should say, 'some men' or 'in my experience.' What do you think makes a man a great lover?"

"They're focused on what makes *you* feel good. They ask questions. They let you know what feels good to them. They take their time," she replied.

"You got any telephone numbers that you'd like to share?" Leona asked.

The conversation continued for several minutes as various women in the group gave examples of their positive and negative sexual experiences with male partners.

"May I say something?" Carla asked, sensing that the conversation had run its course.

"Please," Pam replied.

"I don't want to interrupt this process if there's something more the others want to say."

"No, I think we're done with this statement. The group clearly thinks that it is a fact that women usually take considerably longer to get aroused and reach orgasm than men. So, please, Carla, what is it that you'd like to say?"

"Well, first of all, thank you for letting me sit in the inner circle. I would have felt really strange sitting on the outside dressed like this," she said gesturing to her brightly colored, lightweight cotton skirt and turquoise tank top. "And maybe I shouldn't say anything here at all, but I have a question. I think I might be a good lover because I do everything that we've been describing. I talk about what feels good to me. I ask about what feels good to my wife, Dianne. I have a slow hand. I take my time. I make love. So far, so good. But when I make love, I like it if I can wear a silky nightgown or stockings, just a little something to keep me in touch with 'Carla.' It's 'Carl' that's making love to my wife, which is what she wants and I want, but there's definitely something missing for Dianne. I feel that despite me being tender, attentive, etcetera, etcetera, that my wife would be more sexually satisfied if I was more 'masculine.' None of you have talked about that. Doesn't some of your pleasure come from your partner being more 'aggressive,' or more 'dominant'? I mean, this is about heterosexuality, so we're talking about being in bed with a *man*, right? So what *male* characteristics make sex pleasurable for a woman?"

"A penis helps," Leona replied to laughter.

"Right, but what else? Is it the penis or the person that you're in bed with?" Carla asked.

"I think it's a good question," Wendy said. "Let's assume that your partner does all of the right things. What makes being in bed with a man a 'turn on'? I can talk about what turns me on about being in bed with a woman, but that's tomorrow's discussion."

"For me, it's both. I find real pleasure in the male body," Judith explained. "I like my partner's penis, his hairy chest, and the feel of the muscles in his arms, legs and butt. I like the way he smells, and the warmth of his breath. But I'm also turned on by his self-confident walk, his sense of self."

"Me *too*!," said Dan.

"Me three," laughed George.

"Okay. You guys get your chance later. Let's hear from the women now," Pam said. "Who else? I agree with Wendy. Carla has asked a very interesting question. We need to wrap this segment up in just a minute, but does anyone else have anything to say?"

"I want my husband to take the lead in bed, just as he does on the dance floor," Margaret said. "There's something wonderful about that assertiveness, as long as it's done with grace and sensitivity to me."

"In other words, you don't want him stepping all over your feet or your feelings in the process," Alison said.

"Very good," Margaret replied.

"I take a little different approach," said Marjorie. "I know that I'm attracted to men who are self-assured, but what I am *most* attracted to in bed is a man who risks being passive. By that I mean, that he's not afraid to let *me* take the lead. It doesn't threaten his masculinity."

"Yes, I agree," said Martha.

"Well, that was a rich discussion with diverse perspectives. I hope it answered your question, Carla. If not, there'll be time when we break into small groups later," Pam said.

After giving the men a chance to ask questions or make comments, she continued the exercise. "Okay, now it's the guys' turn to be in the fish bowl. If the two groups will change positions, we'll go through the same process with the men. I'll read a statement and you'll decide if it's a 'fact' or a 'myth'. This time, the women just listen."

After the men had moved into the inner circle and the women had taken their places around them, Pam said, "Okay, guys, would you say that the following statement is a myth or a fact? 'It's a man's role to make sure his woman reaches orgasm.' What do you say?"

"Fact," said Charlie.

"Myth," countered Dom.

"It's her own responsibility," said Curtis.

"Exactly," said Dom. "A man's got to be sensitive to a woman's needs, and help her experience pleasure, but he can't be responsible for whether or not she has an orgasm. What if she doesn't *want* to have an orgasm, and he spends all of his time trying to make it happen? That can't feel very good for either of them. Right?"

"Right," said Curtis. "Most women probably have their orgasms after the guy rolls over, anyway."

"You've got that right," Marjorie piped in.

"Okay, ladies. It's the guy's turn," Pam gently admonished.

"I'd rather err on the side of caution," Charlie said. "Most women go to bed expecting that all the man cares about is his own orgasm. Why not have as the goal making sure she knows that your focus is her pleasure?"

"It can be your *focus* without it being your *responsibility*," Curtis said. "Is it *her* job to make sure *I* have an orgasm? Is it her 'responsibility'?"

"I can only speak for myself," Ben said, "and I know that my perspective's really different, but I go into lovemaking completely focused on the pleasure of my female partners. Is it my 'responsibility' that they have an orgasm? That's a really heavy burden, and I wouldn't want her faking it just to make me feel that I'd done my duty. But I get 'high' knowing that I'm bringing her pleasure. One of the things you learn really quickly when you sit where I'm sitting is that the biggest sex organ we've got is between our two ears. That's where the big 'O' happens for me, and I know that the best sex *I* have is when I feel that I'm participating in the best sex that *she's* ever had."

"Okay, girls, get in line," Leona said. "Beatrice, honey, you're going to have to wrestle me for him."

"Leona, you're the best!" Ben laughed along with the others.

"And you better be wearing that hot red bathing suit of yours when I come a calling," she added for good measure with a giggle.

A few minutes later, after she had brought the room back to some semblance of seriousness and had solicited opinions from Chuck and Joe, Pam gave the women a chance to ask questions or make comments on what they had heard. She then asked the men to turn their chairs to face the women and to talk in mixed groups of three or four people about any "aha's" they were taking away from the discussion. "What did you get from these conversations," she asked, "that might help you in your relationships with the other sex, either personally or in your work?"

"It's real easy to go along as if everything is working just fine," Chuck confided to Margaret, Gina, and Annette. "It's something else to go home and admit that you don't have a clue what your wife is thinking or feeling. I agree with everything I heard you ladies say, but I'll be damned if I know how to bring it up once I leave here. It's just so much easier to play dumb."

"Maybe you can bring up the issue sometime when you're telling her about your Thornfield experience," Margaret said, gently patting his hand. "I think she's going to love it that you care enough to ask about what pleases her, what feels good, and what doesn't."

"I agree, Chuck," Annette said. "I'm sure that she'll be so pleased that you want to make sure she's getting as much pleasure as is possible in your sexual relationship. And, who knows. She may want to know more about what pleases *you*, and then what a great conversation you'll have!"

"Why not just go home and say that one of the things you learned here was that men and women don't learn how to communicate with one another about their sexual needs, but that they *need to* in order to have a healthy, happy sexual relationship?" Gina suggested. "Then you could say, 'And I'd like us to feel that we could talk to each other openly about sex, and what is or isn't satisfying to us.' Do you think you could do that?"

"Yea, that sounds like a good approach," he said, and then leaning forward he asked in a whisper, "Did Carla *really* say he likes to wear a silky nightgown to make love with his wife?"

"She did," Margaret whispered back with a nod and affirming smile. "When she said it, I thought to myself, 'Well, why not? Many women think it's sexy to wear a man's pajama top to bed. Why shouldn't Carla wear something that makes her feel sexy?' To each their own."

Similarly engaged and open conversations took place for the next ten minutes in the small groups of participants clustered around the circle. Pam then announced a two minute warning.

"Okay, everyone," she said five minutes later, "let's hear a few of your 'aha's' in the large group and then we'll see our film." When two or three summarizing statements had been made, Pam introduced the film. "As promised, we have a film about a heterosexual couple who take a trip down to the beautiful island of Bimini. It's called *Going Down to Bimini*. Please pull your chairs back into place. Carol, if you would, the lights please?"

Chapter Thirty-Six

Margaret's Map

"Before we begin talking about the last session, I want to quickly check in to see how everyone is doing," I began as our SAR group members settled into their chairs. "Are there any pressing issues for any of you?"

My inquiry was greeted with silence, some repositioning in chairs, and one or two smiles of "I'm okay. No need to call on me."

"I wouldn't mind hearing why Kevin's been so quiet lately," Leona said with a sly smile.

"I'm always quiet," Kevin blushed.

"Maybe so, but I think that something's up, and we're not hearing about it," she replied in a tone that acknowledged the conversation was finished, at least for now.

"How about the rest of you?" I asked. "Anybody have any feelings that you want to share? No? Okay, then, how about talking in this group about any 'aha's' you got from the session we just did on 'heterosexuality'? Yes, Charlie."

"A lot of things came up for me," he said, "but I wanted to ask about the couple in the movie. I thought it was really cool that they were so free in expressing themselves sexually. It felt very intimate. But, I was blown away by them having anal sex and then oral sex. I mean, that can't be healthy, can it?"

"Good point, Charlie," I said. "Again, it's an educational film, probably made in the late seventies or early eighties. The intention of the director likely was to show the heterosexual couple enjoying all sorts of mutually-agreeable sexual activities. I suspect that it was assumed we knew that in between shots of him anally penetrating her and her orally stimulating him that they would have washed off his penis. But like the lack of condoms in the last set of films, it can send the wrong message to those who don't know better. On the other hand, there *are* some couples, both gay and straight, who would consider the exchange of all bodily 'fluids' to be an indication of true 'intimacy.' I'm glad, though, that you caught that, Charlie. Anything else?"

"Is anal sex among heterosexuals all that common?" Maggie asked. "I thought it was a gay male thing."

"Anal sex is a form of sexual pleasuring. Not all gay men enjoy it, and many heterosexual women do. Its popularity varies from culture to culture," I said. "In some cultures, anal sex is commonly used as a means of contraception. In the U.S., numbers-wise, there are more heterosexual people who have engaged in anal sex than homosexual men. But, we don't hear about heterosexual anal sex much, do we?"

"No, you sure don't," Charlie replied. "But it *is* unhealthy to go from one to the other, right? I mean, it's like rimming."

"What's 'rimming'?" Maggie asked.

"It's sexually stimulating a person's anus with your tongue," I explained.

"Oh, gross!" she replied, her tongue fully outstretched as if she were gagging.

"It's *not* gross for everyone," Wendy said. "It can be very pleasurable and safe, provided that proper precautions are taken."

"Like what?" Maggie asked incredulously.

"Like not inserting the tongue too deeply into the anus, and using a dental dam or Saran Wrap as a prophylactic," she explained. "Otherwise, rimming, like having oral sex after anal penetration *can* be risky. And it's not so much because of the fecal matter as it is the pathogens that live in the mucous lining of the anus. There's high probability of passing on bacteria, parasites, or viruses, such as hepatitis."

"How come you know so much about it?" Maggie asked.

"It's my job. Remember? I'm a HIV-prevention educator. I *need* to know this stuff."

"Doesn't douching or having an enema lower the risk of infection?" Beatrice asked.

"Not really. In fact, it can possibly increase it by bringing the pathogens into closer proximity to the opening of the anus. But, that said, good hygiene, such as douching, does lower the risk of making contact with fecal matter, which for most of us would be a good thing," she answered.

"How did we get on this?" Dom asked.

"I brought it up," said Charlie. "Anal and oral sex were in the film."

"And I'd like to add my two-cents worth," Leona said. "We're seeing an increase in anal sex and oral sex among young heterosexuals who are getting the message 'abstinence only until marriage.' They think that they're still virgins by engaging in anal sex rather than vaginal sex."

"I saw something about that in *Newsweek,* I think," Beatrice said.

"This is great, and a very informative discussion. Thank you, Wendy and Leona. But, I'd like to steer us back to our feelings, if I may. Did any *feelings* come up for any of you in the last session? Any more 'aha's' to share?" I asked.

"This came up in my small group, not in the large group," Dom said, "but we didn't get to talk much about what's sexually pleasing to a man. We spent a lot of time talking about what women want, which I'm glad we did, but we didn't say too much about what men want."

"Say more, Dom," Beatrice prompted.

"Okay. For starters, I'd say that most married men would like to have *more* sex than they're having. It seems like after the first few years of marriage, women are less interested in sex."

"It was the opposite for me," Maggie said. "It was my husband, Barry, who was less interested in sex."

"But that's different," Dom said. "Right?"

"Dom, besides wanting to have more sex, what would you say men want to happen in sex that they feel isn't happening? Give us an example," Beatrice continued.

"Well, for instance, I heard the women say that they don't like their partners to go straight for the genitals. I sort of knew that's how my wife felt but it was good to get confirmation. But just for the record, I *like* my wife to go straight for my penis. I don't really need a lot of kissing and playing with nipples. Some women seem to avoid the area as if it was something 'dirty,' or maybe they think it doesn't look good for them to be too interested in a man's genitals."

"I don't know that I agree, Dom," Beatrice said. "Maybe it's generational or cultural, but women I know never talk about *avoiding* a guy's penis."

"Well, maybe it *is* generational or cultural. All I'm saying is that it sure feels as if it takes a long time to get down to business."

"Are you talking about a hand job?" Maggie asked.

"No, not a hand job, although there's nothing wrong with that either," Dom replied. "I'm talking about touch. Just touch. Soft touch, firm touch, exploring touch. Show some interest. It won't bite you."

"Says you," Leona quipped.

"Now, I know you don't believe that," Dom said. "You're much too savvy a woman to think like that."

"I'm just having fun," Leona said. "He's right, though. I've heard some men complain that women take too long to touch them. The funny thing is, I think most women want to touch right away."

"Maybe it's because some women think that as soon as they touch the man's penis that foreplay will end," Beatrice said. "The kissing and the hugging will stop, and he'll take it as a sign that she's ready for penetration. Or maybe the women you're talking about just don't know. They assume that he feels the same way she does about going slowly."

"Women don't get any better education in being lovers than men do," Leona added, "and a lot of times they're no better at asking questions either. That's one thing that I really liked about Bill and Pam's approach is that couples need to *talk* to each other about what feels good, and they need to figure out when's the right time to do that."

"And just for the record, I'd like to say that lesbian and gay couples can have the exact same problems in communicating about sex," Wendy said. "We don't have the same Mars and Venus gender problems, but we're not born lovers either. We don't always know how and when to say that something's not working for us sexually."

"I'll second that," I said.

"Me too," Kevin added.

"Oh, he *does* speak," Leona said with a smirk.

"When I've got something to say," Kevin replied.

"Kevin, did you have any 'aha's' in the last session?" I asked.

"It wasn't so much a new insight as it was a reminder of a painful one," he said. "It frustrates me that talking honestly to each other is so hard, especially when you're shy. Not knowing when to say something, and how to say something, can be so frightening that you feel paralyzed. Or, at least I do. Sometimes it's easier for me to just not go there."

"There's a lot of risk in loving," Margaret affirmed, "and in *being* loved, isn't there? I think that the trick is in trying to let go of our ego. We worry so much about losing status or power or control, and that's all the ego. I get most frightened and paralyzed, Kevin, when I cling or grasp at something, like security, or perfection, or having things go my way. The more able I am to let go of my expectations, the freer I am to relax, and to experience the real joy of the moment."

"Apply that to what you experienced in the session on heterosexuality, if you would," I asked.

"Sure. On a very immediate level, it felt good to me to hear the women's voices so clearly and strongly talking without shame about what they wanted from men. When I'm surrounded by that sense of power, I find myself getting in touch with my anger and frustration with men for often behaving so insensitively with women. And I want to stay with those feelings. It feels good to own the anger, and to feel that it's 'justified.' My feminine ego is fully supported in those moments, and I want to cling to the feelings of empowerment that I have."

"I can relate to that," Leona said.

"Me too," Maggie added.

"But then," Margaret continued, "a little voice reminds me that I'm on shaky ground, and that I'm setting myself up for 'suffering.' It's my Buddhist practice. The more I want to feel strong as a woman and angry at men, the more I will see myself as 'different' from others. The more 'different' I feel, the more needy I am of affirmation of my 'uniqueness'."

"That makes sense, but what's wrong with wanting affirmation?" Maggie asked.

"Nothing's wrong with *enjoying* affirmation, it's when we *need* it that we get into trouble. The little voice also reminds me that the more I nurture my anger, the less available I am to experience my senses and my feelings in the present moment. Anger stops me from noticing the bird in flight, or the smell of the flower, or just the joy of being with new friends."

"So, what do you do to stop it?" Charlie asked.

"I *own* my anger at men, and I acknowledge that I wish to be free of it. I work at having a compassionate heart for men, reminding myself that they're just as much a product of the culture as I am. We are *not* different and separate. I then try to imagine and embrace *their* feelings of insecurity and fear, and I send out to them healing, nurturing thoughts of support. By the end of the process, I'm aware that I enjoyed the feelings of empowerment that I felt with the women, but I needed to let go of my anger so that I could hear the men with an open heart and mind. And, going back to your original question and to Kevin's comment about 'fear,' my 'aha' came from my awareness of my fear of being 'discounted.' I avoided feeling paralyzed by letting go of my expectations that men will know the right thing to do without me telling them."

"Wow!" Wendy said. "That was *great*! I need to talk to you later about the process you just described so that I remember it and use it. I know that I can get really angry at men. Dom, I think you push some of my buttons, not because of what you're saying, or because you're 'Dom,' but because I'm so frustrated with men not getting it, and frustrated with the power this culture gives to men. I don't like my feelings of anger. They don't help me in my life. They paralyze me, to use the word of the day. So, I really liked what you had to say, Margaret. And just so that we're all clear, I'm *not* a lesbian because I'm angry at men, and I'm not angry at men because I'm a lesbian. I'm angry at men because I'm a woman," she said with a smile.

"Thanks for saying what you did, Wendy," Dom said. "I didn't pick up that you were angry at me. I picked up that you weren't going to let me say things and get away with it, but I never thought you had angry feelings at me. Besides, you can't be angry with me. We're going running together tomorrow morning, aren't we?"

"We are," she assured him. "And I'm glad that you didn't feel any anger from me."

"Okay, Margaret," I said after we sat quietly in reflection for a moment, "I know that you probably feel that you've already been on center stage in this session, but unless someone else has something to say, I'd like to ask you to share with us your sexual map. Are you ready to do that with us?"

"Sure," she replied, "unless someone else wants to go before me."

"No, Margaret, it's your turn," Beatrice said with an encouraging smile. "Please."

After unfolding her piece of newsprint on the coffee table and moving forward in her seat, Margaret looked around the group and smiled. "I did mine a little differently," she explained. "I think I told you that the way I learn is first by *reading* about a subject. Given that, I thought it would be appropriate to use 'books' as the signposts of my sexual journey. This has been a fascinating exercise for me. I've loved doing it. The hardest part has been to limit myself to four or five significant events that impacted my sexuality, and to select only one book for each event. As you'll see, I wasn't completely successful in following directions.

"Though I know that my concept of myself as a woman and my sense of myself as a sexual being were heavily influenced by my childhood, my awareness of those influences didn't come to me until much later in my life. That's where the books come in. But, before I get to them, let me offer you a quick framework for my story. As you recall, I'm a retired United Church of Christ minister, and my husband Bruce and I live in Indianapolis. But I was raised Methodist in Muncie, Indiana, where I lived with my parents, my older brother and my younger sister. I joined the UCC in college because of a dynamic campus minister, who I suspect was gay, who made religion very relevant to my life. Bruce and I met in college, were married a year after we graduated, and we now have three wonderful grown children. That's the information that would appear in my obit. Here's the flesh on the bones, or at least some of it."

Margaret's map was presented as a winding road, drawn in red, that began in the upper lefthand corner of the paper and ended in the middle of the sheet, three-quarters of the way down. At periodic intervals there were drawings of books, each in a different color. The titles were neatly printed in black ink on each cover. The first was *Siddhartha* by Hermann Hesse.

"How I loved that book," she sighed with pleasure. "I read it in college, and it planted the seeds for my sense of self. It told me so clearly that in order to *know* truth, I needed to *experience* it. That was a challenging thought for someone who liked to learn about life from reading. I didn't stop reading, as you'll notice with all of the other books listed along the way, but I learned that in order to make what I read true for me, I needed to go see for myself if it was true. No blind obedience for this Methodist from Muncie.

"The next book that came to mind is *Adult Children of Alcoholics*, and I'm embarrassed to say I can't remember the author's name, but reading it shook me to the bones."

"Janet Woititz," Wendy offered.

"Right! Thank you! Janet Woititz wrote it, and, as I say, it really shook me up. I had created a wonderful fantasy about my family growing up in which we were the perfect family, and of course, I was the *perfect* little girl. The latter was true. I was a perfect little child, but it was in response to us being a very dysfunctional family. My dad was an alcoholic, a functioning alcoholic, but an alcoholic nevertheless. My mother was a tea-totaling Methodist, and we had a lot of tension in the house around Dad's drinking.

I was the peacemaker in the family and became very adept at anticipating people's moods and needs, and running interference so that conflict was avoided. I learned a lot from reading her book about how my sense of self had been impacted by the need for me to be an adult in my childhood. And then I read Melody Beattie's book, *Co-Dependent No More*. Wow! What an eye-opener, and so helpful in the healing process. And, as you'll note, I also put down here the book *Women Who Love Too Much*. I told you that I didn't do a very good job of limiting myself with examples. Forgive me.

"Okay, so here I am on the road, with a new sense of how my experience of life has been impacted by my obsession with meeting other people's needs, I get into a women's discussion group through my church, and I read *Our Bodies, Our Selves*. As the women in this group probably already know, that book allowed me to start focusing on my feelings, needs, and wants as a *woman*. It was unlike anything else I had read. Then I was introduced to Betty Dodson's book, *Liberating Masturbation - A Meditation on Self Love,* and I was on my way to claiming my body and my sexuality as my own. As I think I told you in this group, I could really identify with the older woman in the masturbation film who said that she didn't enjoy sex with her husband until she learned how to pleasure herself. That was certainly true for me.

"How's my time?" she asked.

"You're doing fine. You've got plenty of time," I replied.

"Thanks. Then moving right along, here I am, on the journey, knowing that I want to experience life on my own terms so that I can trust it, and knowing that I can't do it by counting on feedback from others that I'm 'okay.' I'm feeling very excited about discovering myself as a sexual person, but there's something missing. From the outside, it all looked perfect. There's that word again. I was an ordained minister and was doing work that I loved. I had a beautiful, healthy family. We had financial security. So, what's not right? It was my *spirituality*. I had this gnawing feeling that my religious beliefs lacked experiential evidence. And then I met Pema Chodron, or, I should say, a friend introduced me to her writings. Pema is a Buddhist teacher who writes about spiritual centeredness in a way that was very accessible to me as a Midwestern woman. The first book of hers that I read was *The Wisdom of No Escape*. Then I read *When Things Fall Apart, Start Where You Are,* and *The Places That Scare You*. I can't recommend them to you enough. They introduced me to a way of thinking and being that has made my everyday experiences meaningful and manageable. I can't do justice here to their impact on me, but it's right up there with all of the other important steps I've taken on my journey.

"Now, you'll notice that the road ends a little more than halfway down the paper. Given my age, I probably should have had it end a little further down because I'm well past middle age, but I wanted to indicate that the journey is far from over. Thank you for listening. Does anyone have any questions?"

"Margaret, thank you," I said. "Before we take questions, I want to find out how it was for you to present it to us. You said that putting it together was a wonderful experience for you. How about the process of explaining it. Any feelings?"

"It *was* wonderful thinking it through and putting it together," she replied. "Presenting it was fun because I felt as if I was introducing new friends to some of my dearest old friends. I suppose though that I'm going to think of things later that I wish I had said."

"You can always add a postscript," I assured her. "So, now, does anyone have a question for Margaret?"

"I do. How has your husband been with the different turns your journey has made?" Charlie asked. "Has he been threatened by them?"

"I don't think so, Charlie," she replied. "Bruce is my best friend, and I suspect that I'm his. We haven't always walked at the same pace on our journeys nor always headed in what felt like the same direction, but I think we've always trusted the love that binds us, and we've always wished for the other's happiness. In some ways, I wish Bruce was here this week. I think he'd really get a lot out of it. Selfishly, I'm glad that he didn't come, and that I have the week to myself. But, I think I'll try to get him to come next year."

"As long as he doesn't come home and tell you that he's *gay*," Maggie sighed as she rolled her eyes and laughed.

Chapter Thirty-Seven

Carla, Betty and the Tree

"This has been quite a day for you, Ben, hasn't it?" Joe asked as he reached for the salt shaker.

"It's been *very* special," Ben replied with a big grin as he cooled with his fork the small mound of turkey tetrazzini that sat in the center of his plate.

"I was really honored to be a part of it," Joe said.

"I wish I had known about it, Ben. I would love to have been there," Marjorie said, dipping her spoon into her bowl of minestrone. "We went into town, shopping with Alison."

"Maybe we'll do it again before we leave on Saturday," he replied. "Say, what did you all think about the session with Bill and Pam on 'heterosexuality'?"

"What did *you* think about it?" Beatrice asked.

"I thought it was great. I really liked hearing what the women had to say. I sort of knew most of it, but it was good to be reminded that we take so much for granted. Bill's right. We're *not* born lovers, and we're not raised to *admit* we need help in understanding what others want from us. I could really relate to that."

"I was impressed with what *you* had to say, Ben, about focusing on the pleasure of your female partners," Marjorie said. "I'm not used to hearing that. If it wouldn't be too much of an intrusion into your privacy, would you talk about how, if at all, having a disability affected your thinking? Or have you always had this approach to sex?"

"Oh, that's such a good question," Annette affirmed. "Please, Ben, unless we're getting too personal, would you talk about how you came to such an awareness? I'm learning so much this week. Aren't you all?"

"It's been a real eye opener," Joe said.

"To answer your question, Marjorie, my experience of having a disability has had a *profound* effect on my attitudes about sex, about asking for what I want, about finding out what other people are thinking, and a whole slew of other things. I was just a punk kid when my accident happened. I didn't have a clue about my own feelings, much less the feelings of women."

"Who does at that age?" Marjorie said.

"Well, I sure didn't. And, as I think I said when I spoke to the group earlier in the week, I thought my sexuality was over at age eighteen. To tell you the truth, though, it *wasn't* initially the biggest thing on my mind. First, I wanted to know if I was going to live. Then, I wanted to know if I was ever going to be able to walk. And how was I going to go to the bathroom, and where was I going to live, and what was I going to do to make a living? I had a thousand questions. It was only much later, when I began to settle down, that I started to focus on sex."

"Of course. Of course," Annette said.

"One of the hardest things for me to do in the early days, after my accident, was to *ask* for what I wanted," Ben continued. "I'd wait for people to ask me what I wanted, or to guess what I needed. I mean, I'd ask for the basics, but I wasn't trained or skilled at asking for what I really wanted. I had to learn the hard way."

"That makes perfect sense," Annette nodded.

"And, the more I thought about it, the more I realized that other people generally didn't know how to ask for what they wanted either," he said. "If I didn't, then they didn't. In the beginning, I didn't care. It was all about *me*, but then I started to think about how tired my folks must be, and how they felt too guilty to say they needed a break from the daily routine with me. And I started to imagine how scared my friends must have felt, not knowing what to say to me. Once there was this girl who worked in rehab who I thought was really beautiful, and I imagined how awkward she must have felt with my flirting. So, I started acting as if my sense of people's feelings was accurate, and that got me in all kinds of trouble. I pulled back from my folks, my friends, and the girl in rehab. It was my way of taking care of them all. Needless to say, it caused a lot of unintended hurt feelings. We finally started talking about it, and I learned that my folks *were* tired, but they didn't want a break from me. My friends felt awkward at times, but they never really felt scared, and the girl at the rehab place told me that she was flattered by the flirting, thought I was cute, and that if she didn't have a boyfriend, she might have flirted back. Okay, so lesson number one was that I needed to learn to ask for what *I* wanted, and lesson number two was that I needed to ask others what *they* were thinking, or what they wanted. It was good to be thinking about others, but not good to make *assumptions* about their needs. I know that I could have learned all of that without being in a wheelchair, but my disability sped up the process, I think."

"Not everyone learns those lessons," Annette said. "They're very hard lessons to learn."

"I'm not sure that *I* have," Joe sighed a bit mournfully.

"Anyway, I'm running on at the mouth, but you asked," Ben said.

"No. No. This is good stuff," Marjorie said. "So, when you had your *first* sexual experience after your accident, you brought to it all of the insights you gained from having a disability?"

"I wish *that* was true," he laughed. "My first sexual experiences were disasters! I did *everything* wrong. I forgot everything that I had learned. I wanted my partner to guess what I wanted without me asking. I was so focused on my needs that I didn't give much thought to hers, and when I did, I guessed what she wanted, and was afraid to talk about it afterwards."

"That sounds familiar," Joe said.

"What changed things for you, Ben?" Beatrice asked as she reached across the table and gently took his hand.

"Practice. Practice. Practice," he said grinning. "Seriously, I was ready to give up in the beginning. I was completely unsatisfied, frustrated, and feeling stupid. Then I put two and two together, and realized that what was true in the rest of my life was probably also true in sex. So, I just decided to start talking. It was either that or forget about it. I started explaining what felt good to me, and I started asking about what felt good to her. When we talked about it, she learned what my fears were, and I learned what her fears were. And the positive, nonverbal feedback I got during sex was really helpful. Like Pam said, the moaning and the groaning helped give me confidence that I was doing the right thing. Well, that changed everything. The moans and the groans started turning me on completely.

Soon, I found out that the more I pleased her, the more pleasure I was going to feel."

"You want to come home with me and talk with the young men and women in our peer sexuality program? You'd have quite an impact," Marjorie said with a big, warm smile.

"Thanks. That's a kind offer," Ben said. "My agency keeps me very busy here, but I'm flattered you asked."

"Does anyone want anything to drink?" Beatrice asked as she stood.

"Not me, dear. Thank you. I'm heading out for a smoke," Marjorie replied.

"All set," Joe, Annette, and Ben indicated with quick waves, winks or smiles.

"You are a *very* special man," Beatrice whispered in Ben's ear as she leaned over, gave him a gentle kiss on the cheek, and walked to refill her glass with water.

As Marjorie stood to depart, her chair bumped Betty's, who was also standing with hands full of dirty plates, silver, and crumpled paper place mat and napkin.

"Where are you heading?" Carla asked Betty, who was nodding "hello" to Marjorie.

"Oh, just for a walk. I need a little exercise to work off the tetrazzini. I thought I'd loop the driveway and then go sit by Susan's tree," she answered. "Want to come?"

"May I?" Carla asked with delight.

Fifteen minutes later they were sitting on the grass next to a small blue spruce, a few feet from the driveway. Betty sat with her legs crossed, Carla's were folded together at her side.

"Tell me about Susan," Carla said.

"Susan Vasbinder was on the staff when I came to Thornfield for the first time," Betty answered. "We ended up pretty close by the end of the week. She was a strong, proud lesbian who came from a similar blue collar background to mine. I was a little emotionally unstable that summer and she ..."

"I can't imagine that," Carla interrupted with an incredulous look. "You're so strong. So together."

"I appear to be, I know, and for the most part I am, but that summer I was having a hard time. Susan was my small group leader, and she watched me cry a lot."

"Do you mind me asking why?"

"No. I don't mind," Betty answered, reaching out and putting her long arm around the shoulder of her new friend. "I had recently broken up with a woman, and I thought I'd never be loved in the same way again. My self-esteem was at a really low point, and I was scared."

"Why? You're wonderful," Carla said smiling up at Betty.

"You're very sweet, Carla, but I had no delusions about being a pretty woman. I'm a tall, big-boned broad and, at that time, I had a face that didn't please me, and I feared wouldn't please anyone else either."

"I think you're *beautiful*! But, were you having doubts about transitioning?"

"Oh, hell no," Betty replied with a laugh, bringing her arm down to the ground. "I *had* to be a woman. There was no question about that. I just was having serious doubts about ever finding another woman who would love me, once Janey and I broke up. And Susan was there to assure me that whether or not I did, I could find happiness in just celebrating 'me.' The whole SAR group rallied around me that year. And it worked. I left here feeling a lot stronger. Susan told me I could call her at any time, and initially I did. Once I got myself together, we sort of drifted off into our own separate lives. On my desk at home, though, I have the picture that Carol took of our group at the end of the week. Susan and I are side by side. We're both grinning like fools. I've often looked to that picture for inspiration."

"And Susan died?" Carla asked.

"Yep, she did," Betty sighed. "One day, life became too much for her, and it makes me crazy that I couldn't have been there for her the same way that she was there for me. The staff planted this tree, like the one they did for Mary Lee over there. And, I come out here and I talk to her, and I tell her 'thank you,' and I tell her I'm sorry."

"Hmm. I wish I could have known her," Carla said, reaching up and gently touching the tip of a branch's needles.

"Hey there, Leona," Betty called out, with her arm raised up in a wave. "How's it going?"

"It's going good," Leona said with a smile as she gave a short wave, and continued more slowly on her walk down the driveway toward Huntington. "How's it going for you, Betty?"

"It's going good," she replied, also smiling. "We out of time?"

"We start in ten minutes," Leona said, looking at her watch.

"Thanks. See you there," Betty answered.

"I haven't spent any time with her. Have you?" Carla whispered.

"She was my roommate on the first day," Betty said.

"What do you mean she *was* your roommate?"

"It didn't work out. Me being a transsexual *and* a lesbian to boot was a little much for her, I think."

"How come you never said anything about it before this?" Carla asked.

"What's there to say? I wasn't shocked that it was too much for her. It would have been too much for a lot of people, especially on the first day. I'm sorry that she got such a rough start to her week."

"Have you two talked since then?"

"No," Betty grinned, "I thought it was best to cut her a lot of slack. When she's ready, *if* she's ready, she'll talk."

"Betty, I want to be like you when I grow up," Carla said.

"Thanks. But tell me, when you say that Carla, what do you mean?"

"I mean I want to be self-assured, wise, gracious. You're the most confident transsexual that I've ever met."

"Again, thank you, but I'd rather you thought of me as a self-confident *woman* than as a self-confident *transsexual*. I'd really like to move on from that."

"I agree, so how come you told Leona that you were transsexual?"

"Because I knew that it would come up this week, especially here, and I thought that she should hear it from me. In most situations, I don't raise the issue, as I'm sure you don't."

"No, I do. I get into a cab as Carl and I say, 'Hi. I'm a cross dresser. Take me to Victoria's Secret'," Carla laughed.

"Very funny."

"Betty, I've had a better time with you this week than I've had in a long, long time. I'm so glad you were here. I don't know what I would have done if you *hadn't* been."

"Kevin would have taken care of you."

"He's a doll," Carla said, "but it would have been very different. No 'girl talk'."

"What are you going to do when you go home, Carla? Do you think you're going to be content just cross dressing on occasion as you do now, or do you think you'll ever want to transition?"

"Why do you ask that? Right now, I can't imagine transitioning. Do you see something I don't see? Tell me!"

"No. No. It's not about you. It's just that I've known a lot of cross dressers who eventually decided that they had one foot into their female persona and the other foot on a banana peel. And then again, there are lots who are perfectly content leaving things alone. At any rate, we've got to get a move on. We're going to be late."

"As we walk," Carla said, standing up and brushing the grass off of her skirt, "tell me about your ring. It's beautiful, and it's *big*!"

"Yea, I know. But you know what they say: 'Big fingers, big ring.' It's the only 'fem' thing I've allowed myself. I'm not really into 'sugar and spice.' But it *is* nice, isn't it?"

Chapter Thirty-Eight

The Hand Exercise

"We're meeting upstairs for the first part of the session," Gail greeted each group of participants as she rang the school bell.

"What's this one about?" Leona asked.

"Touch," replied Gail with excitement. "You'll love it!"

"I'm just sure I will," Leona mumbled as she walked into the main meeting room and found a seat in the large semicircle.

"We're going to begin with an exercise that is my *favorite* exercise of all time," Bill said enthusiastically as the last of the participants took their seats. "And then, after the break, we're going to show you a film that, in my opinion, is the *core* film of the week. It doesn't have anything to do with 'sex,' but everything to do with 'sexuality'."

"You've got *my* interest," said Marjorie.

"Good," Bill smiled appreciatively. "Now, I'm going to describe exactly what we're going to do in this exercise, and then you can make a decision for yourselves whether you want to participate."

"Okay, Leona, this is when we all get naked," Dom teased from across the room.

"You first," she challenged with a grin.

"Oh, *that* could be interesting," Bill mused as he stared at the ceiling and scratched his chin as if seriously considering the possibility. "No," he said as if a decision had been made, "that comes *later* in the week."

"Very funny," Pam said to the relief of more than one participant.

"Now, in this first exercise, which Alison is going to guide us through, we're going to ask you in a moment to stand, as you're able, to close your eyes, and to mill around the room with your hands outstretched like this until you encounter another pair of hands."

"Then what do we do?" Tonya asked.

"Alison will give you instructions at that time," Bill replied, "but I really want to encourage all of you to participate. It's a lot of fun, and you learn a lot about the significance of 'touch.' However, if you'd prefer to pass, then we'll ask you to volunteer to stay on the outside of the group with your eyes open, and help us make sure everyone finds a partner. If that's clear, I need all of you to move forward into the center of the room. Those of you who want to watch, stay on the outside of the circle."

Ben decided for himself that his wheelchair might cause some damage if his eyes were closed, so he volunteered to be a 'watcher.' Catherine decided to stay on the sidelines too, as did Chuck, Curtis, Beverly, Lisa, and Grace.

"Come on, Lisa, get in here," Wendy implored.

"No, I need to keep my eyes open to make sure you don't walk into a wall," she replied.

"Okay, now I want all of the people in the center of the room to close your eyes," Bill instructed, "and turn yourselves around two or three times. Keep your eyes closed. It's *very* important to keep your eyes closed or it won't work."

"That means you, Brian," Carol said. "He always cheats," she explained to the others.

"Eyes closed, turn yourself around, hands outstretched, and now slowly move forward and find another pair of hands," Alison said. "Once you find your first pair of hands, and perhaps you'll wander in on more than one, I want you to get to know those hands. What do they feel like? Are they women's hands or men's hands? What's the age of the hands? Explore them."

George started walking toward the chairs and Catherine gently turned him around and headed him toward Joanne, who was also without a partner. As their hands met, they smiled and began the process of carefully feeling each other's fingers, palms, wrists, and the backs of each other's hands.

"Good," Alison said after a couple of minutes. "Now, say 'good-bye' to these hands, and move on to find another pair of hands. Once you do, get to know those hands too."

The room was quiet except for the shuffling of feet, kept close to the floor for the sake of balance. The words "sorry" and "excuse me" were whispered periodically as the temporarily blind participants groped in the dark for another set of hands. In addition, you could hear occasional soft moans of pleasure or giggles of self-consciousness. The volunteers, taking their assignment very seriously, kept a watchful eye on wanderers and stragglers.

Alison repeated the process twice more. Each time, the participants were allowed ample time to explore another's hands, and as she had predicted, it was at times a threesome that was formed.

"What can you tell from touching these hands?" she asked us to consider. "Are they soft? Are they working hands?"

By the third time through, most of the participants felt more confident, and more serious in their effort to truly have a sense of another's hands. The nervous giggles died out. An air of intensity replaced the initial giddiness.

"Once more, please say 'good-bye' to those hands, and move on to find another set of hands," she said. "Remember, no matter what, keep your eyes closed. It's *very* important that you do. You'll be told when to open them."

When it was clear to her that everyone had a partner or two, Alison continued. When she felt that they had sufficient time to get to know the hands of their partners, she instructed in an emotionally-compatible tone, "Now I want you to imagine that you've just received some very *sad* news. Communicate that to one another."

Annette took the hands that she was touching and held them still for a few seconds. She then began to gently pat them in a comforting, sympathetic way. Dom gave a firm squeeze to the hands that he was touching. Marjorie stroked her partner's hands, as if petting a puppy. Maggie held her partner's hands completely still for the entire time.

"And now, you've received some very *good* news," Alison said with excitement. "Express to your partner your feelings about this good news."

Thomas took the hand of his partner and gave it a "high five" slap. Marjorie and her partner began swinging their joined hands back and forth in play. Carol and her partner attempted to play 'patty-cake.' Beatrice and her partner brought their hands, palm to palm, high up above their heads. Kevin and his partner, the fingers of each hand entwined, pushed their hands back and forth toward each other, playfully keeping rhythm.

"But now something has happened, and you're very *angry* at the other. How do your hands express your anger?" Alison asked.

Peter pulled back from his partner's hands and refused to be touched. When his partner went looking for his hands with their own, Peter firmly pushed them away. Furrowed brows dominated the faces in the room as each sought ways to communicate their displeasure with their partner.

"Now, the anger is over," Alison instructed in a soothing voice. "You want to *forgive* the other and be forgiven. Communicate those feelings to your partner."

Peter's frown ended and his tightly-closed eyes softened into an expression of forgiveness. He reached out with his long fingers and found the hands of his partner who was eager to be reconciled. They warmly stroked each other's hands, and gently probed the tender areas between each other's fingers. Then they stopped, and just held one another's hands in peaceful and loving surrender.

"This leads you to want to play, so *play* with those hands," Alison instructed.

Many of the participants resumed the patterns they had employed to express 'joy.' Some swung their hands back and forth, a couple played 'patty-cake,' and some even snapped fingers to make the noise of play. Each, though, who played, did so with more depth than they had originally, even if they used the same technique to show it, because now they were playing after an awful argument, and it felt good. Kevin, for instance, had once again locked fingers with his partner and was pushing his hands back and forth in rhythm, but there was a new intimacy to the gesture.

"Okay, you and your set of hands have become very close through all that you have been through," Alison said. "You find that you're drawn to these hands *erotically*. Express sensually your feelings to these hands."

A series of low, pleasurable moans filled the room as the participants sought ways to express sensual feelings to their mates. Catherine, at this point, was pleased that she had decided against participating. Ben was wishing that he had been able, especially as he watched Beatrice caress Charlie's hands.

Some people very slowly stroked the back of the hand of the person with whom they were paired. Wendy made small circles with her thumb in the palm of her partner's hand. Leona used her fingernails to gently massage the wrists of her's. Maggie and her partner moved their hands around each other's as if they were carefully but softly washing them with soapsuds.

Peter and his partner began tentatively by just holding hands. The warmth felt very good to Peter. He sighed deeply as he held one of his mate's hands in the palm of his and then with his other began slowly pulling on each finger. His partner responded by gently stroking the back of the hand that was pulling. Peter then focused on just one finger, and moved his thumb and forefinger back and forth in a slow, rhythmic manner.

"It's now time to say 'good-bye.' Events have transpired that require that you leave, and you know that you will never experience these hands again," Alison explained. "Say 'good-bye' to your partner's hands, and then let your own hands drop to your side."

Peter didn't want to say "good-bye." Neither did his partner. Quickly and feverishly, they explored each other's hands, as if trying to remember every detail. Wrists, palms, fingers. Then they both stopped, held onto each other tightly for a moment, gently squeezed, and then very slowly let their hands fall to their sides. Both sighed in disappointment, and then smiled at the sound they heard from the other.

"But wait," Alison said excitedly. "Plans have changed! For some unknown reason, you can reconnect with those hands! Find those hands, and *celebrate* your reunion."

Peter and his partner reached up, grabbed each others hands, and squeezed excitedly. Both of them smiled broadly.

"Now," Alison said, "open your eyes."

Gasps of astonishment, laughs of delight, and words expressing a variety of pleased and awkward feelings filled the room. Peter and Kevin stared at one another in embarrassed disbelief. Then, following the lead taken by the majority of other pairs in the room, they hugged one another briefly, said "I had no idea it was you," and looked away nervously.

"Before we hear from those of you in the center of the room," Bill said, "let's hear from our volunteers. What was it like for you watching what was going on?"

"It was *awesome*," Ben said. "You guys should have seen your faces. If the feeling was 'joy,' you all were smiling. If it was 'anger,' you all were frowning. There was so much expression on your faces. It was really cool."

"Once the thing started, I wished that I had decided to participate," said Chuck. "It looked like a lot of fun. On the other hand, I had a good time just watching. Sometimes I had to put two people together because some of you were wandering around like a chicken with its head cut off."

"How about some reactions from the folks *in* the circle?" Bill asked. "What was it like for you?"

"It was really weird at first," Tonya said. "But then, it was like 'wow,' I'm really expressing feelings with just my hands, and it's real clear to me how my partner's feeling from what they're doing with their hands."

"What was the most difficult time for you in the exercise?" Alison asked.

"Having to say 'good-bye' to people," Thomas replied. "It was like, 'No, wait. Not yet. I really *like* this pair of hands. We've got something going here.' I didn't want to move on."

"Yea, it was saying 'good-bye'," confirmed Maggie. "Definitely."

"There's one pair of hands out there that I went looking for after we had to part," laughed Leona. "We were having a good old time getting to know one another when Alison said 'stop.' I know it was a man by the size of the hands. Whoever it was had a big old ring on."

"Betty has a big ring," Carla offered loudly from where she stood near Betty.

"Shush," Betty whispered with a shake of her head.

"I don't think it was Betty," Leona laughed with a convinced look, and then discreetly peered through the group to eye Betty's ring.

"It sounds to me as if you enjoyed the exercise as much as I do," Bill said with delight after fielding a few more comments. "Well now, we're going to take a real quick bathroom break, and then meet downstairs for the next segment of this workshop. No more than ten minutes, please."

Animated conversation then erupted between many of the pairs who had been joined at the end of the exercise. Kevin looked up and gave Peter a weak and embarrassed smile. Peter smiled back warmly, put his hand on Kevin's shoulder, squeezed it, and said, "Thanks, that was a lot of fun."

Meanwhile, Leona walked over to Betty and asked, "May I please see your ring?" Betty smiled back, lifted her hand, and watched as Leona closed her eyes and felt the ring. "Well, I'll be," she laughed, raised her eyebrows, patted Betty's arm, and walked downstairs.

Fifteen minutes later, we sat in rows, and many of the participants took notes as Bill drew a graph on the whiteboard to illustrate the findings of a study on "touch" done by Vidal Starr Clay for her doctorate from Columbia University. It suggested that there are two types of touch, *good touch,* which is the touch of "affection," and *bad touch,* which is the touch of "duty" — care-taking, control, and/or hostility. Bill's diagram illustrated Clay's conclusion that the good touch of affection from our parents decreases from a high point at our birth to a low point at the onset of puberty, just as the bad touch of care-taking, control, and/or hostility increases proportionately in the same time frame. In other words, as children become older, they generally receive much less affectionate touch, and much more controlling touch.

The good touch of affection can increase again in our romantic relationships with others, just as bad touch will increase with the diminishment of love in the relationship. The bad touch of care-taking, control, and hostility is likely to increase significantly again as we age and/or become infirm.

The "feel good" film that followed presented a variety of dramatized vignettes that helped illustrate the need for us all to be touched affectionately. Narrated by a grandmotherly-appearing social scientist named Jessie Potter, who was a strong proponent of "good touch," the film presented scenes from the entire span of human life. Without touch, we were told, infants will physically die. And, as we go through the other stages of life, we can also die emotionally without the benefit of touch. Human beings hunger for it, and need it, from birth to death.

The amount of touch and the type of touch we receive is heavily influenced by the culture, Potter explained. Little boys in the United States, for instance, are traditionally jostled by their parents, while little girls are cuddled. But even that touch stops at puberty, not only from parents but also from many others outside of the house. Doctors and other health practitioners, for instance, often refrain from touch, even when delivering life-shattering news.

Driven by the need to be touched, people can become creative in their methods of securing it. Children and some senior adults, for example, will often "act out" to get attention, even if it produces the touch associated with control and discipline. Many people buy pets to secure the affection they crave. Several people also find it by getting their hair shampooed and cut, or by paying for a massage.

Potter underscored the healing power of touch by showing how problem children and complaining adults who receive "good touch" generally change their behaviors. She said that in her own life, she makes sure that her grandchildren always know they can count on her for hugs and efforts at affection. This includes being greeted by Grandma after a bath with towels warmed in the oven.

Though the film was at times humorously dated, it nevertheless had an immediate effect upon many of the participants who throughout the presentation reached over and stroked the back of the person beside them, or forward to massage another's neck. When the lights were turned back on, there was a collective sigh of appreciation and applause.

"That's it for tonight," Bill said with a smile of self-satisfaction. "For those of you who want to watch the Candida Royale film, *The Lovers*, we'll take a ten-minute break, and then meet back down here. We'll be showing more episodes of *Sex in the City* upstairs in the small room, and Alison will be guiding an optional hand massage in the large meeting room for those of you who would like to participate in that exercise. Otherwise, you're free. Have a good night everyone."

"Peter," Catherine whispered as the other participants began to disperse, "you got a minute?"

Chapter Thirty-Nine

A Walk with Joe

"I know that this is none of my business, Peter," Catherine said as they walked slowly down the lawn toward the picnic tables behind Ridings. "So, please forgive me if I'm intruding where I'm not wanted, but I'm wondering if being in this place is threatening your resolve regarding your sexual orientation?"

"Hmm," he sighed as he tossed his head back and looked at the star-filled sky. "I appreciate your concern," he said.

"I'm not sure it wasn't a mistake for *both* of us to have come here," Catherine continued. "I'm thinking about heading home tomorrow morning."

"*Really?*" Peter replied with obvious shock and disappointment. "Is it *that* bad for you?"

"Well, the week is certainly *not* what I expected, and I'm not feeling particularly supported in my values," she said. "I'm not sure it's *healthy* for me to stay."

"Are you having a hard time in your SAR group?"

"Yes and no. Bill is evenhanded," she said, "but the group is *very* liberal, and I don't feel comfortable stating my opinion on many things. I especially dread tomorrow."

"What's tomorrow?" he asked.

"We spend the *whole* day on 'homosexuality'! My views wouldn't be very popular in *that* group, and I don't think I'm up for the fight."

"But why do you have to fight? Why not just state your views and see what happens? You're not *really* thinking about leaving tomorrow are you? I'd hate to see you go."

"Why don't you come with me?" she encouraged. "Maybe they'd get the message that their agenda here is too heavy-handed if we *both* left. Do *you* feel safe here, Peter?"

"I feel *challenged* here, Catherine," he said, reaching out to put his hand on her shoulder, "and often uncomfortable. That last session with the hands, for instance, shook me up a bit. I need some time to think about what happened in there. But I'm feeling a lot safer here than I imagined I would on the first day. Alison and Pam respect my space in the SAR group, and I'm learning a lot about how other people experience their sexuality. You've got to admit, there's lots of useful information presented here on a variety of topics. You're finding *some* of it helpful for the work you're doing, right?"

"I am," she conceded, "but I'm not sure I couldn't get it elsewhere. But, Peter, since you brought up the last session, I have to admit that I was watching you and Kevin in the hand exercise. It looked to me as if you were really enjoying what was going on between you. Doesn't that scare you a bit?"

"I *was* enjoying it, and it *did* scare me," he acknowledged, "particularly when I realized that it was Kevin."

"Well, that's what I'm talking about. Isn't staying here for you a little bit like a recovering alcoholic spending a week in a bar?"

"Maybe you're right," he smiled as he pulled his hand back from her shoulder. "But maybe it's a great opportunity for me to *test* myself."

"You could be playing with dynamite," she said.

"I know. I know," he replied.

"Again, it's none of my business, but are you praying for help? The help is there if you ask for it, Peter."

"I pray every day, morning, noon, and night," he replied. "I pray for guidance, and I pray for strength. You too?"

"Of course," she replied. "I couldn't have survived this long at this program if I didn't pray constantly. I pray especially during the films."

"Can I ask you a personal question? I know that it's none of my business, but you haven't said much about *your* sexuality to me. You've been very supportive of me being here as an ex-gay man, and I've really appreciated your friendship, especially at the beginning of the week when I was feeling so out of place. I haven't asked you about yourself because you seem so private, and I figured you'd tell me when you were ready. But, if you're really thinking about leaving tomorrow, I'd be honored if you'd feel comfortable telling me tonight where you are on the continuum."

"You're right. I *am* a very private person, and I don't talk with others about my sexuality," she said, carefully looking around to see if anyone else was within earshot. "I probably will stay, Peter, but I do feel that you deserve to know. I'm sexually celibate, and I have been for many years."

"You've *never* had sex?"

"I've had one sexual relationship in my life, and it just so happened to be with a woman," she whispered. "I've *never* talked about that relationship with others, and I feel very uncomfortable doing so now. I also feel very strongly that I'm *not* a 'lesbian,' and that I shouldn't have allowed the relationship ever to become sexual. But we were very close, and it's what she wanted. I believe that homosexual sex is completely contrary to the teachings of the Bible, just as heterosexual sex outside of marriage is. I've known several homosexuals in my life, and they all seem to be very sad people. I believe that with the help of God, they could successfully fight their homosexual feelings and find happiness. That's why I so admire you, Peter. You're a very courageous man."

"Thank you, Catherine, for telling me about yourself. I promise you that it stays just between us. I'm really glad that you felt you could trust me. May I ask you another question, though?"

"Certainly."

"The woman that you broke up with, you really loved her?"

"Yes," she sighed more audibly.

"And have you two ever talked about what happened?"

"We never spoke to one another again," she said with resolve.

"Huh. Okay. One last question before we head down to the movie. And this is based upon your professional perspective as one who has studied the Bible. I think I know what your answer will be, and I'm a little nervous about even asking the question, because I don't want to worry you, or give you the wrong idea, but all of that said, do you think that Kevin being born female would make a man's attraction to him technically 'heterosexual'? Oh, never mind. Forget that I asked. Let's go down and watch the film."

A couple of minutes later, as Catherine and Peter descended the stairs, they passed Joe on his way up.

"Better hurry," he encouraged. "They've started the film."

"Is it any good?" Peter asked.

"It's a matter of perspective," he replied. "I thought I'd try out the hand massage."

Alison had begun the optional hand massage, and was giving instructions to the eight participants who had joined her for the exercise. Thomas paired off with Lloyd, Carla with Betty, Ben with Beatrice, and Annette with Dick. Joe sat down with Alison, who took his right hand into her left and poured in a dab of oil. "Continue making small circles into your partner's palm and then work your way down each and every finger with your thumb and forefinger," she directed.

"That feels great," he said. "You're good at this."

"Thank you," she replied. "You'll get your chance to practice in a few minutes. I'm glad that you came up and joined us. I love giving a hand massage, and I also like *receiving* one. It's nice to have my own partner."

"Do you have a few minutes to talk when this is over, or would you prefer that we pick a time tomorrow or the next day to talk?" he asked after Alison gave the next set of instructions to the group. "I would really appreciate your perspective on something."

"I'd *love* to talk with you, Joe," she replied with a tilt of her head and a supportive smile. "Why don't we wait and see how we're both feeling at the end of this exercise, and we can decide then the best time to talk? How does that sound?"

A half an hour later, each person's hands had been thoroughly massaged. "You can start on the feet if you want," Alison encouraged. "Having your feet massaged is a *wonderful* experience. Just use the same technique we used with the hands. I'm going to sign off. Please be sure to clean up after yourselves. We'll be meeting in this room in the morning."

"Thank you, Alison," Beatrice said.

"My pleasure," she replied. "And now, Joe," she whispered, "how about we grab a cup of hot chocolate and take a nice walk around the driveway, under the stars?"

As they walked in silence with cocoa in hand down the path from Huntington to the driveway, Alison took a deep inhale of the cool night air and sighed with pure delight. "What a *beautiful* evening it is," she announced. "So what troubles you, my friend?"

"I suspect my wife is non-orgasmic," he replied directly. "I've been thinking about her and us all week, but particularly when the older woman in the masturbation film said that she did not experience an orgasm in sex with her husband until she learned to pleasure herself. I fear that Eleanor would say the same thing, except that I don't think she's ever learned to pleasure herself. All of the discussions about the need for communication, and the need for good touch, are making me feel very sad. Do you have any suggestions for an old guy who wishes that he was a better lover?"

"I'm *so* glad you asked to talk about this," Alison said looking up at him with a big smile as they continued to walk. "Your wife is a very lucky woman to have a husband who cares so much about her feelings."

"Oh, but that's the problem, Alison," he said with an exasperated sigh, "I feel that I *haven't* been attentive to her feelings at all. Don't get me wrong, I think I've been a good husband, and I love her very much. It's just that I've always taken for granted that she was getting the pleasure she needed in sex and I was getting the pleasure that I needed. But I don't think she has at all. I think she's just 'put up' with sex, and besides making me sad, it makes me very angry at myself for being such a complete boob!"

"Hey there, don't be so hard on yourself," she said as she reached over and rubbed his back with her free hand. "People from our generation received no education at all about sexuality or about being good lovers. Women my age were taught to cross our legs and don't jiggle. But fifteen minutes after our wedding we were supposed to suddenly have a sense of our sexuality and that of our partner. But tell me, Joe, how do you know that Eleanor doesn't enjoy sex with you? Have you ever talked with her about it?"

"Regrettably, never, Alison. We have sex, which I initiate, and then, and it's okay for you to laugh, I roll over and fall asleep. Watching the films and listening to the women here talk has driven home to me something I have suspected for a long, long time. I'm a *horrible* lover, and what frustrates me to no end is that I don't know how to change. I don't know if I'm even *capable* of changing. And if I can't, she's doomed, and I'm doomed, to second-rate sex for the remainder of our lives."

"Nonsense," she said strongly. "The fact that you're even *aware* that you're not the lover you want to be says that you're well on your way to *becoming* a better lover. Be gentle with yourself, Joe. You've done the best you know how, and now you know that you can do better. That's what's wonderful about this week. It can open our eyes to what's possible for us. On the other hand, it can also make us sad about what we've missed in our lives."

"But after I leave here, what do I do? What steps would *you* take to help improve our love life?"

"Well, the one thing you *don't* do is to go home and say 'Honey, our lovemaking is inadequate. I'm going to teach you what I've learned at Thornfield. Before I'm finished with you, you're going to have your first orgasm!'" Alison laughed.

"That wouldn't be my style, but I wouldn't mind some coaching about what I *should* say," Joe replied.

"You begin by asking her how her week was while you were gone. Let her talk first. Then, a little bit at a time, you talk about how the week impacted you. Talk about *your* feelings, not hers. And be careful not to overwhelm her. At Thornfield, we have the unique experience of talking intimately with one another after just a couple days of being together. Unfortunately, that's not the norm in the outside world, and we have to remind ourselves that our partners and our friends haven't had this experience."

"I agree," he said. "So, I begin slowly talking about my feelings. But then, do I suggest that she come here next year and wait until she's had the experience before we talk further, or do I recommend that she read a book? How do I get us on the same wave length about honest communication, asking for what you want, and all of the other elements of good lovemaking?"

"You can certainly recommend that she come to a program like the one we have here at Thornfield. That's a wonderful way to ensure that you're both on the same page, and I do have some books that I can recommend, if she's interested. Lonnie Barbach's book, *For Yourself*, is a 'must-read' for women. But, we're way ahead of ourselves. You don't want to go home with a knapsack of 'things to do.' The most important thing you can do is communicate to Eleanor that you're interested in her feelings and interested in knowing what gives her pleasure. A good lover is one who can communicate his or her real joy in learning the secrets of what pleases the other."

"What if she recoils at the very thought of having such a discussion? That's when I fear that I'll panic and go back to my old patterns of behavior. I'm quite shy to begin with, and I'm sure that I'm not going to be able to maintain the resolve that I'm feeling so strongly right now. See, that's what scares me, Alison. Everything seems so clear to me today, but I'm afraid of slipping back into our old routines at home."

"You may," she acknowledged. "That's when you pick up the phone and call someone from the workshop just to reconnect with the positive energy you feel here. So, if your wife recoils, you think to yourself,

'Maybe I'm coming on too fast or too strong. Maybe I need to back off and revisit this a little later.' But keep in mind, Joe, you can't *make* Eleanor experience sexual pleasure. You can't make her have an orgasm that she's not open to having. Your first obligation is to yourself. You need to know and to celebrate your own sexuality. Then you need to communicate your interest in knowing more about hers.

"For instance, you may want to ask her to talk about how she learned about her own sexuality, and perhaps about how she knows what feels good to her. She may not be ready to talk about it yet, but at least you've opened the door to honest communication. That's what makes you a good lover, whether or not she responds. She may not say anything to you right away because it all feels so new and possibly threatening to her, but you've planted the seeds, and she can't help but appreciate the fact that love is motivating your efforts."

"Thanks, Alison," Joe said as they neared the end of their walk.

"No, thank you, Joe. Thank you for asking for help. As I say, I think Eleanor is a very lucky woman. And remember, if anything else comes up for you that you'd like to talk about, please come back and we'll talk some more. That's why I'm here."

"This week is a real eye-opener for me."

"Good," she replied. "Then it's a success. Information is power. It allows us to make free, conscious, and informed decisions about our sexuality and that of others. By the way, I'm showing a terrific film by Betty Dodson Thursday night on women and their sexuality. I think you might want to come. She teaches a group of women to comfortably explore their bodies. They sit in a circle and examine their vulvas by looking into hand-held mirrors. Then they stimulate themselves with vibrators or with their fingers. You know, Joe, your wife may not know what an orgasm is. Many women my age don't."

"Is that right?" he asked incredulously.

"How would they unless they felt comfortable exploring their bodies on their own? And who from our generation got the message that it was okay to do that? That's what the woman in the masturbation film was saying. She didn't experience pleasure having sex with her husband until she learned to pleasure herself. That's why I like the Dodson film so much. It teaches women that their bodies are beautiful, that they were designed for pleasure, and that it's good, healthy, and fun to experience pleasure. If we think of sex as dirty, evil, and wrong, then we think of ourselves that way because we and our sexuality are inseparable. To love ourselves, we have to love our sexuality. Right?"

"Right!" he said with a smile and enthusiastic punch of the air.

"So, you think you might come?" she asked.

"I'll be there."

Moments later, as Alison parted and entered Higley, she saw Kevin enter my darkened room.

"Psst. Brian, are you asleep?" he whispered.

Chapter Forty

WEDNESDAY

"Gay Day"

"What are you doing up so early?" I whispered to Alison outside of our adjacent bathrooms.

"Carol and I are going off in search of more wildflowers. The arrangements are looking a bit sorry. What are you up to?" she whispered back.

"I'm going for a run with Dom and Wendy."

"You had a late night caller," she said.

"Who?" I replied looking confused.

"Kevin. He was heading into your room when I arrived last night. Did you have a good talk?"

"We didn't talk. He must have decided not to wake me. I'll go looking for him after the run and make sure he's all right."

Dom and Wendy were doing stretching exercises in the breezeway between Peabody and Huntington. Marjorie, in her pink floral bathrobe, was in her usual perch on the bench with a cigarette and a cup of coffee.

"Oh, to be young again," she sighed.

"We're the same age," Dom replied.

"Let it go, Dom," she said.

On our run down the road, we passed Thomas and Lloyd who were out for a brisk walk. A hundred yards ahead of them were Gina and George.

"What is this, 'Gay Exercise Day'?" Wendy said.

"Hey, what about me?" Dom asked with a grin.

"There's always hope," she replied.

As we approached the end of the driveway a half an hour later, I spotted Kevin sitting alone on one of the picnic tables outside of Higley. "Thanks, you guys," I said as I headed for the dorm. "Same time on Friday?"

"Good morning," Kevin said as I kissed the top of his head and sat beside him.

"I heard you came a calling last night. Sorry I slept through it," I said.

"It's okay. I didn't want to wake you. But, did you see who I ended up with in the hand exercise?"

"Peter. So, what happened?"

"I'm not sure, but I got the feeling he was really into the erotic part. Do you think he thought I was a woman?" Kevin asked with a look of concern.

"Not with those manly hands," I replied.

"No, seriously. He couldn't have thought I was a woman, so why do you think he was so into it? Do you think he thought he was touching Dan?"

"I have no idea what he was thinking. What were *you* thinking? Did you think it was Dan?"

"I kind of hoped it was."

"What did you think when you saw that it was Peter?" I asked.

"I freaked out. He's 'ex-gay'! I don't want to be involved with someone who's 'ex-gay'," he said.

"Kevin, you were doing the hand exercise. You aren't *involved*. But, let's just say, for the sake of discussion, that he comes up and tells you that he *really* enjoyed doing the hand exercise with you. Would you *seriously* feel that you couldn't be open to his interest in you?"

"I don't think I'd want to encourage the interest of someone who's not happy with his sexuality. He's very handsome, but I don't know. What do you think?"

"I understand what you're saying. I think you ought to leave it alone and see what happens. You don't know what he's feeling, and there's no sense in guessing. Now, I've got to get a move on because I'm on today, and I need to shower and have breakfast. Are you okay?"

"Yea, sure. I'm fine. Break a leg."

Pam was in front of the mirror in the women's bathroom blow-drying her hair when I stepped out of the shower across the hall.

"Hey, sweetie," she said with a big grin. "Good run?"

"Yes, great. Thanks. Where is everyone?"

"Carol and Alison are arranging their flowers, Dick is at breakfast, and Bill is having a talk with Catherine down by the water. You ready for today?"

"All set. Thanks. What's Bill talking with Catherine about?"

"How should I know? She came here this morning looking for him."

Breakfast consisted of a glass of orange juice and a muffin, which I quickly grabbed and took with me over to Ridings.

"We upstairs or downstairs for your session?" Gail asked me as I entered the main meeting room.

"Downstairs," I said. "I'm heading down now to make sure it's cleaned up and set up."

Ten minutes later, I was drawn to the first floor by the ringing of Gail's bell, and then the beginning sounds of "I Love Myself" on the boom box. Carol nodded me over to the space beside her. "You all set?" she whispered.

There were four new faces in the circle, one of which was very familiar and dear to me.

"Michael's here," I whispered to Carol as the group sang.

"He never misses it," she whispered back.

"Good morning," Alison said cheerily as we took our seats.

"Good morning," the participants replied with equal enthusiasm.

"My, aren't we bright-eyed and bushy-tailed this morning," she observed with delight. "Good! It's an important day, and we need good energy. In a moment, I'm going to ask Gail to lead us in a warm-up exercise, but before I do, I want to introduce our guests to you. Michael Crinnin is here. Michael is the executive director of Syracuse's AIDS Community Resources, a former Thornfield camper, and a friend of the staff. Raise your hand if you would, Michael. Thank you, dear. And this is Scott Meadows, and next to him is Gary Cousins, both of whom are from the area and volunteers at AIDS Community Resources. Finally, we have Virginia Montgomery, who, as you know, helped us secure this wonderful section from the AIDS Quilt, and who made this beautiful section for her son, whose name was also Michael. We welcome all of you. Michael, Scott, Gary, and Virginia have all accepted our invitation to join us at lunch, so they'll be available to talk to later. We're glad that you're here."

Warm smiles and applause affirmed Alison's welcome.

"Now, it's time for our warm-up exercise," she continued.

"Alison, before we do," interrupted Marjorie, "will Dick please stand so that everyone can see his T-shirt?"

"Of course. Dick loves unusual T-shirts with messages, don't you, Dick? What have you got on today?"

Dick stood up, smiled appreciatively, and stuck out his chest. "Sticks and stones," the shirt proclaimed, "may break my bones, but whips and chains excite me."

Laughter, some of it nervous, and a smattering of applause, greeted his display.

"Thank you, Dick," Alison said with amusement. "And now, if you would, please stand as you're able, as Gail is going to lead us in our wake-up exercise."

Following Gail's aerobic exercise, during which Martha and Beverly broke into an island dance which everyone subsequently followed, Alison called for announcements.

I asked for a dinner meeting of those people who were participating in my Friday workshop, Bill announced that the optional film would be *Sordid Lives,* to the appreciative hoots and hollers of Dan, Thomas, and Lloyd, and Carol called our attention to the fact that only two people had signed up to perform at Friday night's celebration.

"Does that include me?" Carla cooed demurely.

"You're my headliner," Carol replied enthusiastically.

"Very good!" Alison proclaimed, clapping her hands together once for attention. "We're right on schedule. Let's now move downstairs to begin our very exciting program on gay, lesbian, and bisexual issues."

Bill had exited quickly to ensure that the music of Holly Near and Meg Christian greeted us as we descended the stairs. He swayed enthusiastically next to the boom box as he inserted a video into the projector for the wide-screen T.V.

Our guests sat together in the back row, across the aisle from Dan who took his familiar perch in the rear. The majority of the other gay and lesbian participants, scattered around the room, seemed wide-eyed expectant. Catherine and Peter sat together in the second to last row, near the exit and stairs. They each smiled politely when I made eye contact and smiled at them.

"Good morning," I intoned as I nodded to Bill to turn off the music. "Today, we're going to focus on the journeys made by most gay, lesbian, and bisexual people, and, I suspect, by many transgender people too. We've talked a lot this week about the scientific research on sexual orientation and gender identity. Today, we're going to take a look at the *personal* side of the issue. This morning I'm going to offer you a framework for understanding the growing-up experiences of most gay people. This afternoon, Carol and I are going to introduce you to a model that helps us understand the psychological process that gay people go through from the initial *denial* of their feelings, to the *affirmation* of their identities. Along the way, we're going to put faces on the issues by telling you about our own journeys, and we invite you to do the same. Our time together will be far richer if we each share from our perspectives what we have observed in ourselves and in others who have come to know themselves as 'homosexual,' 'bisexual,' ' gay,' 'lesbian,' 'queer,' ' transgender,' or 'ex-gay'. All of that spectrum is represented in this room today. So too is the perspective of being a parent, sibling, child, or spouse of a gay person. Please feel encouraged to share those personal insights too."

Catherine and Peter's arms remained crossed but they each sat a little less rigidly in their chairs.

"As a reminder, we seek to understand the journey made by gay people toward sexual health because we're in the process of assessing our sexual attitudes. Our personal 'music' reflects our attitudes, and our attitudes reflect the ignorance, secrecy, and trauma in our sexual lives," I explained. "As we explore this issue today, we remind ourselves that we're not comparing or measuring one oppressive experience against another. We're simply seeking to understand why a person needs to tell us that he or she is gay, and what they mean when they tell us.

"The model that I'm going to present, which is not my own, helps us understand how the experience of growing up gay is different from growing up as another minority. In addition, I'd like to introduce the concept of 'psychological homelessness.' I suggest that the key factor separating gay children from black, Latino, Asian, or Jewish children is their experience of rarely feeling that they belong in their own families, in school, in church, in the neighborhood, or in the work world. Most gay people I know grew up feeling psychologically homeless. I certainly did."

The words "Being," "Swallowing," "Separating," "Building," and "Extending" filled the sheet on the easel to the right of the large television screen. On it's other side stood the large, empty whiteboard.

"'Being' in this model describes a brief period of time in each of our lives when we had no sense of being inferior or unwanted. Imagine, if you would, that all of us were born at the same time, and that we're all laying side by side in the same hospital maternity ward. If you look around, you'll notice that there are black babies, white babies, red, yellow, and brown babies among us. Some of us are right-handed and some are left. Some have been born to white-collar families and some to blue-collar families. Some of us have been born into the Christian faith, some of us are Jewish, some Muslim, and some have no faith heritage at home. Some of us are heterosexual, some are homosexual, and some are bisexual. Some of us will feel at home in our bodies, and some of us will feel terrible conflict. And for the briefest time in our lives, during this stage of 'Being,' none of us has a sense that our being born with a penis gives us more cultural status than had we been born with a vulva. It's an innocent time in which we don't fear, hate, or disrespect the differences between us because we're unaware of the differences and of the significance those differences are given by the culture at this particular time in history."

"And throughout history," Catherine shot from her seat.

"Yes, some attitudes such as the inferior status of women and the 'non-normalcy' of same-sex feelings have dominated many cultures, but joyfully for both of us, not all," I smiled back. "And when we were born, Catherine, we had no idea that your Church, for instance, found women unworthy of ordination, or that mine found the expression of my sexual orientation to be gravely sinful. How lucky for us to have been spared those attitudes, at least initially.

"And then, regrettably, we entered the 'Swallowing' stage. Our parents or primary caregivers picked us up and brought us home where we learned about how our families and friends valued the other babies in that hospital. We heard words such as 'faggot,' 'nigger,' 'cunt,' and 'kike,' and we believed what we were told about others and about ourselves to be true.

"The difference, however, between what a black baby heard and the gay baby heard at home is what separates the journeys we've made. While the black baby may hear awful comments about its skin color outside of the home, the gay baby is assumed to be heterosexual and often hears in his or her own home the poisonous words that they subsequently swallow.

The gay child hears from its unsuspecting family how horrible it is to be a homosexual.

"Help me, if you would, recall the words or expressions that gay, lesbian, and bisexual children might well have heard to describe homosexuals at home, in church, in the classroom, in the locker room, on the playground, or in their neighborhood," I asked as I stood next to the whiteboard with a black marker in my hand. "What are the words we *swallow* about being gay?"

"Homo," Chuck called out. "Thank you," I said as I turned and wrote the word "homo" on the board. "What else?"

"Fag" Thomas hollered.

"Thank you. What else?"

"Queer," Gina said.

"What else?"

"Fudge Packer," Dan yelled from the back.

"What else?"

"Abomination," Charlie said.

"Punk," Leona added.

"Muff diver," Wendy said.

"Sick," George sighed.

"Fairy?" Maggie asked.

"AIDS carrier," Carol said.

I wrote for nearly five minutes. The other words or expressions on the board included: he-she, shim, fruitcake, sin, corn-holer, cock sucker, light in the loafers, limp-wristed, child molester, immoral, pervert, dyke, three dollar bill, AC/DC, switch hitter, poof, maricon, mariposa, lisp, queen, Mary, Tinker Bell, predator, butch, and nellie.

"How about things that have been said to you directly?" I asked. "What have you heard about yourself personally? I'll start. One morning when I came down from my apartment on my way to work, I found a sign hanging over the mailboxes in the lobby that read 'Get out of town McNaught. I hope you die of AIDS'."

Carol stood and took the marker from me and said as she wrote the words of one student's parent, "How do we know what Ms. Dopp does behind closed doors with her students?"

George then stood, took the marker and said as he wrote, "We won't tolerate your kind in our seminary."

Gina then hurried up to the board to write "Women who love women should be shot."

The room sat in awkward silence for a long moment, and then Virginia Montgomery stood from her seat in the back, walked slowly to the board and wrote "We're sorry about what happened to your son, Michael, but it would seem that he reaped what he sowed."

"This was said to me at his funeral by a member of my church," she said with a sad shake of her head as she headed back to her seat. Again, we sat in silence for a long moment.

"Now, if you would," I said, "I invite those people in this room who grew up with an awareness that they were gay, lesbian, or bisexual, or who later in their lives discovered this to be true about themselves, AND who feel comfortable doing so, to stand, as you're able, to identify yourselves."

Carol stood on cue. She was followed solemnly by Betty, Kevin, Thomas, Gina, George, Lloyd, Lisa, Dan, and Wendy. Catherine's hand was on Peter's knee. A pensive look crossed his face, he smiled at her, shrugged his shoulders, and slowly stood with the others.

"The words on this board are the words that we all were expected to swallow about ourselves. Most of us believed them to be true," I said.

"Why can't the world allow these people to be themselves?" Dick pleaded in a cracking, strongly emotional voice as he shook his fist, and his red face registered his rage and pain. "What are we so afraid of?"

"Thank you, everyone," I said, scanning the standing participants with an appreciative smile and a gesture that invited them to be seated. "We're going to explore Dick's question when we come back from our very quick bathroom break."

Chapter Forty-One

A Face on the Issue

"Why did you stand?" Catherine whispered in an agitated voice when Peter returned to his seat. "That's what he *wanted* you to do!"

"He said to stand if we grew up feeling that we were homosexual. I did, so I stood," Peter replied calmly. "He didn't ask us to stand if we *identified* ourselves as 'gay.' I don't know if he's being clever or compassionate, but I'm giving him the benefit of the doubt."

"Not me," she said with frustration. "I think he's setting you up."

"Dick has asked us what we're so afraid of?" I said as the last of the participants took their seats after our brief and very quiet bathroom break. "I suggest that the answer is 'difference.' Ignorance is the parent of fear, and fear is the parent of hatred. These hateful words on this board reflect our fear of the unknown. But, what impact do you think all of these words have upon the gay, lesbian, or bisexual person who has swallowed them? The horror of growing up gay is the horror of having a secret that you don't understand, and that you're afraid to tell anyone for fear that they won't love or respect you anymore. The questions that I'd like you to keep asking yourselves as you look at the words, and at the films we're about to see, are 'If I was gay, how would I feel, and, who would I tell how I feel?'

"Imagine, if you would, being a 15-year-old boy, riding in the car with your dad, on your way to a ballgame. The talk show host on the radio makes a funny, anti-gay comment, and you look over to see Dad's reaction. He's laughing. He wouldn't laugh if he knew you were gay. I'm sure that if you were an adopted Vietnamese child and the joke was about the Vietnamese, Dad would turn off the radio, tell you that the guy who made the joke was a jerk, and that he loved you just the way you are. We hope he would also do the same if he knew that you were gay. But he *doesn't* know. Like the parents of most gay people, he expects or hopes that you're heterosexual. So he laughs. And you think to yourself, 'I can *never* tell him who I am. I want to, but if I do, he'll hate me.'

"The young girl rushes home to watch *Oprah* because she knows that Oprah Winfrey is going to have lesbian women on her talk show. You turn on the television, excited about the prospect of seeing what you might look and act like when you grow up, and then Mom walks into the room. She listens for a minute to the program, and then what does she do?"

"She turns it off," Lisa said with confidence.

"Right. She turns it off or she asks you, 'Are you watching this?' And what do you reply?"

"No, turn it off. I'm not watching," responded Wendy earnestly.

"And you say to yourself, 'I can never tell her who I am because if I do she won't love or respect me anymore.' We have a couple of short film segments that help us better understand the full impact of this 'Swallowing' stage. Alison, the lights please?"

Alison turned off the lights as a weary-looking woman named Mary Griffith made her way on the television screen toward the site of her son Bobby's grave. At age 20, Bobby committed suicide by doing a back flip from an overpass into the path of an oncoming truck. Mary introduced us to Bobby through childhood photographs, and growing-up stories of her exceedingly handsome, blond-haired son. She also shared pages of Bobby's diary in which he wrote in despair about what an awful person he was because of his homosexual feelings. He longed for freedom from thoughts and behaviors that his very religious mother considered an "abomination."

When she learned of Bobby's suicide, Mary confided that her first thought was a sense of relief. "Thy will be done," she said in heavy tears. It was only later, when she had come to better understand homosexuality, and to distance herself from her fundamentalist congregation, that she realized how wasteful and tragic Bobby's death had been. Where before she had been ashamed of her son, she was now ashamed of the way *she* had responded to the news of his homosexuality, and of his subsequent suicide.

I stood in darkness at the film's end, and explained that attempting suicide was not uncommon among young gay people. According to most studies, including one by the U.S. Department of Health and Human Services, gay youths are three times more likely than their heterosexual peers to take their own lives. "Why?" I asked, gesturing at the words on the whiteboard. "Because the horror of growing up gay is the horror of having a secret that you don't understand, and that you're afraid to share for fear that no one will love or respect you anymore."

Fifty percent of the kids who are on the street as runaways are there because they're gay, I explained. "Why? Because they have a secret they don't understand, and are afraid to share for fear that they will lose the love and respect of their parents, their brothers and sisters, their teachers, their pastors or rabbis, their coaches, and their friends.

"As we think about how we might feel in these situations, we need to remind ourselves that our experiences will be impacted by a variety of factors, such as our faith, our family's exposure to gay people, our race, and our economic security, among other influences. This next short segment is from the Academy Award-winning film by Marlon Riggs entitled *Tongues Untied.*"

The handsome black face on the screen explained that when he first played the game "Spin the Bottle," as a child he didn't know how to kiss, so his male friend taught him. They subsequently kissed passionately on a regular basis until his friend's older brother caught them and called them "homos."

"'What's a 'homo?' I wondered."

In a short time it became clear what was meant by "homo," and that his feelings of attraction for other boys made him one. He then moved to Georgia and was one of only a handful of black students to be in the honors class of one of the area's best white schools. "Uncle Tom" he was taunted by a large black male face on the screen. "Nigger, go home!" spat another that was white. Blacks hated him because he was a high achiever in a white school. Whites hated him because he was black.

"Punk." "Faggot." "Homo." "Uncle Tom." "Nigger, go home."

The repeated chorus of these poisonous words completely engulfed him and us. Finally, he explained, he ran as fast as he could away from his family, his home, his church, and all that was familiar to him.

As Alison raised the lights, I scanned the room for reactions. There were no smiles. Shoulders were slumping. Virginia Montgomery dabbed at her eyes with a tissue passed to her by Betty, who had stretched out her arm around Virginia's shoulders. Paula cried too for the loneliness that she imagined her gay son had endured. Charlie stared blankly at the floor. And Catherine glared coldly at me.

"I have an exercise that I'd like to take you through," I said softly as I smiled at as many participants as would make eye contact. "It's a 'guided imagery,' and I've found it to be the second most powerful tool I have in helping people understand the unique experience of growing up with an awareness that you're gay. The first most powerful tool is the telling of our stories."

For the next twenty minutes, the participants, with their eyes closed and with my guidance, imagined themselves attracted to people of the other sex but growing up in a gay family where being gay was honored and preferred. They grew to believe that if they hoped to ever be treated with as much love and admiration as their openly gay older sibling received, they too would eventually have to say that they too were gay.

At age fourteen, they found themselves on a bus driven by a gay bus driver, surrounded by gay friends singing popular gay songs, gazing at gay billboards, heading to a school run by a gay principal, home room teacher, coach, and guidance counselor. Everyone at school assumes that they too are gay, rather than the detested "breeder," a nasty term used to described people who were attracted to those of the other sex. Fearing social rejection, and possible violence, they go to their first "social" at the school with a same-sex date, dance to slow songs in the arms of their same-sex date, get their first goodnight kiss from their same-sex date, and are asked by their gay families at the end of the evening whether they had fun.

They reluctantly date same sex people for four years of high school, learn to kiss with "passion," hold hands in public, and pass love notes in class. They go on to college hoping that things will be different, but all of the popular kids in school are dating people of the same sex. Those who are attracted to the other sex are shunned and refused entry into most social groups. "Breeder" is scribbled across meeting announcements for the "Straight Pride" group. So, out of fear and the desire to be accepted, the participants in the guided imagery "fake it," and secure for themselves a steady gay romantic interest, surround themselves with gay friends, and, feeling social pressure, ultimately have their first gay sexual experience in their junior year.

As seniors, they happen upon a newspaper aimed at heterosexuals. They read it with excitement and terror, and before they hide it from their gay college roommate, they learn about a bar that caters to people just like them. Once they finally get up the nerve to go to this "straight" bar, they meet someone very special with whom they eventually decide they want to spend all of their time. Secretly, they rendezvous as often as is possible. Eventually, the two of them agree to rent together a two-bedroom apartment in which they pretend to be only "friends" so that gay family members can safely and comfortably visit.

At work, no one knows that they're "straight." They bring same sex friends to social functions. They refrain from making easily-heard personal phone calls to their significant others, and from placing photos of them in their work areas. The charade succeeds until their lifetime partner is critically injured in an automobile accident. After they eventually find the love of their lives in the intensive care unit of a local hospital, they must make a big decision. Do they notify the hospital's gay doctors and nurses of the status of their relationship, thereby alerting them that they are attempting to revive someone that they have been raised since childhood to hate, or do they keep it a secret, and sit quietly in the waiting room, hoping to be allowed to see their "friend"?

"How do you feel, and who do you tell how you feel?" I repeatedly asked throughout the guided imagery.

"Frightened." "Lonely." "Exhausted." "Angry." These and other words surfaced as we explored what feelings had come up for us during the exercise.

"How do you escape this nightmare?" I asked.

"You could kill yourself," George replied.

"Yes, you could," I said. "Bobby Griffith did that. But, what else could you do?"

"You could come out," Thomas said.

"You could start living life on your *own* terms," Dan hollered.

"That's right. You could. And that's what's represented by the next stage listed here, which is called 'Separating.' With 'Separating,' you decide to end the nightmare by pulling away from those people, institutions, and other influences that feed you poison. You 'run as fast as you can' away from them, as Marlon Riggs explained. And you purge yourself of the poison.

"And then, if you're lucky, you start 'Building,' which is the next stage listed here. In this important stage, you replace the poison in your system with good, nourishing, healthy input about what it means to be gay. You affirm yourself as good, as whole, as holy, and as worthy of love. You begin buying gay-positive books, and going to gay-positive films, and listening to gay-positive music, and surrounding yourself with fully-supportive people who nurture nothing but good attitudes toward your sexual orientation.

"And, finally, in this last stage of 'Extending,' you come to realize that *all* people face the exact same road that you have walked, and that just as others have fed you poison, you too, out of your ignorance, fear, and hatred of difference, have fed *others* their poison. The 'Extending' stage brings you full circle to the 'Being' stage, where we sit or stand or walk side by side without attitudes of superiority or inferiority.

"The two films that we're now going to share with you help us witness and celebrate the 'Separating' and the 'Building' stages. It is in these life-giving stages that we seek out our own community for the sake of friendship, of love, and of sexual intimacy. Alison, again, if you would, the lights please."

Two attractive young women pushed each other in park swings, canoed, and hugged one another playfully in the opening scenes of *A Special Place*. Their faces registered delight as they flirted, teased, and kissed to the background music of Cris Williamson's song, "Sweet Woman." Once inside their house, they undressed each other with loving care and walked naked to their bed. There they tenderly began stroking each other's faces, breasts, stomachs, and vulvas.

"Heaven," sung by Joan Armatrading, filled the room as the women stimulated each other with fingers, arms, and tongues to orgasm. The constantly changing photo montage allowed the participants to watch the women in a variety of sexual positions. Throughout the lovemaking, both women smiled or laughed with delight. They then headed for the bathroom where they showered together, continuing their playful courtship with shampoo and soap.

The mood in the room was upbeat as the film credits rolled. The pall that had been so palpable after the guided imagery had been lifted and replaced with more relaxed breathing.

Then *Vir Amat* began, and I sensed again that breaths were being held. Two good-looking men in their mid-to-late twenties played in the kitchen as they prepared a meal. Phil Collins sang "Groovy Kind of Love" as they started bumping butts, tickling, pecking each other lightly on the lips, and eventually heading toward the living room sofa. There, the kissing became more passionate and the gentle stroking of each other's faces and heads more intimate. "When I'm in your arms, nothing seems to matter, my whole world could shatter, I don't care."

Soon, one led the other to the bedroom where they carefully unbuttoned each other's shirts and jeans and interlocked their naked bodies in a huge, joyful hug on the bed as Elton John sang "How wonderful life is while you're in the world."

The primary means of expressing feelings for these two male lovers was kissing. They did so tenderly throughout the film. They also orally stimulated each other's penis and mutually masturbated to orgasm. The montage of their sexual activity was framed by Joe Crocker's hauntingly romantic lyrics, "You are so beautiful to me. You're everything I hoped for. Everything I dreamed …" Yet, even without such deeply-moving music, it would have been perfectly clear that what was transpiring before our eyes with these two men was "love making," pure and simple.

At the end, after they had carefully cleaned the semen off of each other's chests and stomachs, the men again kissed, and engaged in post-coital play. One comically stuck out his tongue and the other moved it from side to side by pulling on his partner's ears, and then retracted it by touching the tip of his partner's nose. They laughed with delight. "You are so beautiful to me."

When the lights came on, I watched Catherine dramatically shake her head disapprovingly. Charlie, who sat in the second row on the other side of the room was weeping softly. When our eyes met, his seemed filled with great sadness.

"Time for group," Alison announced from where she stood next to the light switch.

Dom and Chuck headed dutifully for the door, but many people stayed in their places. Thomas and Lloyd hugged one another in their seats. George, whose arms were around a very teary Maggie, mouthed the words "thank you" when he caught my eye. Betty was stroking Kevin's back. Virginia Montgomery was being strongly hugged by Paula. "I have a gay son, too," she said proudly.

"Are you coming?" Catherine asked with a pained sigh as she surveyed the scene.

"You go ahead," Peter replied. "I want to sit here for a minute."

When Catherine walked out, Peter sat alone.

Chapter Forty-Two

Charlie's Map

"Nice job," Margaret said in an exhausted sigh as she sat next to me on the sofa, and patted my knee.

"That was cool!" Wendy said as she plopped into an adjacent lounge chair with her glass of Diet Pepsi. "That was *really* cool. I'm ready to do my map now if no one else wants to go."

"Thanks, Wendy," I said. "But, let's first check in with everyone, and see what they're feeling."

Maggie walked into the room quietly with Kevin. Charlie was the last to join us, which he did without making eye contact. He took his seat gingerly, as if hoping to be invisible.

"Let's begin by hearing how everyone is doing," I said softly. "Do any of you have anything that you'd like to talk about before we move into our maps?"

"That was very heavy," Dom said. "I hadn't really thought about how lonely gay kids must be. I feel like I really want to do a better job being there for them. I'm not exactly sure how, but maybe you all can help me before the week is over."

"Thanks, Dom. It's wonderful to hear you say that," I replied. "It makes the whole thing worthwhile. Anyone else?"

"I was deeply struck by the *beauty* of the lovemaking, particularly by the men," Beatrice said. "It was so tender, and so caring. How could anyone object to those two men coming together to express their feelings for one another? It just makes no sense to me."

Maggie eyes teared up, and she reached for the tissue offered her by Margaret. "It *was* beautiful," she said, sniffling and rubbing her eyes, "and it made me so *sad*. Barry and I *never* made love like that. Never!" She stopped here, and began to cry. "It makes me so sad to know that's what he wants, and that I can't give it to him." After catching her breath, she whimpered angrily, "And he can't give it to me *either*! I deserve to be loved like that. I want it too!"

Margaret put her arm around Maggie, squeezed her, and kissed her on the side of the head. "Of course you do," she comforted. "And there's no reason why you can't have it in your life too."

"This 'gay' thing sure can complicate things," Leona mused lightly.

"Leona, stop it!" Charlie shouted angrily. "It's not a 'gay' *thing*! My heart bleeds for Maggie, but it's not Barry's fault that he's gay, and it's not something he chose to be in order to complicate Maggie's life. He is what he is, and he never should have gotten married. But he didn't know that, and I'm sure it's killing him that he's causing Maggie so much pain."

"I didn't say that he did," Leona shot back defensively. "I simply said that it complicates things. It does. It complicates things."

"Leona, you've just got this attitude about the whole thing that makes me crazy. I like you. I really do, but from the moment you arrived here, you've been bad mouthing being gay, and it's wearing thin," Charlie said.

"Where's all of that coming from?" Leona replied with shock. "I thought we were friends. We've been hanging out. I know, and I've admitted, that I don't fully understand homosexuality, but when have I given offense to you, Charlie, and why would *you* take it so personally?"

"This is making me very uncomfortable," Beatrice said softly to me.

"Let them talk," Wendy replied.

"Leona, do you remember walking down to the lake together the second night and how when you found out who was down there you mumbled something about it being 'a goddamn *homo* convention'?"

"I didn't think you heard that. I wouldn't have said it if I thought you'd take offense. I shouldn't have said it at all, but I was feeling a little overwhelmed and out of place here. I've never been around so many gays and lesbians before, or for that matter, so many white people in a long time. I shoot my mouth off when I'm afraid. It's how I cope. I've got a big mouth, and it gets me in trouble. But what does all of this have to do with you, Charlie?"

"Why does it have to have *anything* to do with him?" Wendy asked. "Couldn't he be offended by homophobia as a straight man?"

"He could," Leona said coolly. "But are you, Charlie?"

"No," he said with less anger. "I'm not. I'm not 'gay,' or at least I don't think I am, but I'm definitely 'bi,' and if you want to know the truth, it's why I came here, and it's eating me alive." Charlie sighed deeply, looked to me for support, and started crying.

"We're with you, Charlie. Stay with your feelings," I said. "Talk about what's eating you alive."

"I'm so *scared*," he cried. "I look at Maggie and I think of my wife, Cindy, and I think of my kids, Lyle and Kevin, and I don't want to *ruin* their lives. But all I can think about, all I've been able to think about for the past several years, is my attraction to men. I ache for the kind of connection with another man that I saw in that film. I want *my* life to have that, but I don't want to lose everything that I've got, and I don't want to cause anybody any pain. I'm so miserable. I don't know what to do," he pleaded.

Leona reached over and began stroking his back, gently rubbing it back and forth as Charlie buried his face in his hands and wept.

"Oh, God, this is *exactly* what Barry did last year, isn't it?" Maggie declared. "Oh my God, I can't believe I'm watching this, and that some poor, unsuspecting woman in Oklahoma is sitting at home having no clue what's going on here."

"What *is* going on here, Maggie?" I asked gently.

"Charlie's sitting here thinking about ending his marriage, and we're just listening, and not saying *anything* to discourage him."

"Is that what you imagine happened with Barry?"

"I don't know. Did you try to talk about what it would do to me if he came home and announced that he was gay?"

"Maggie, we didn't encourage Barry to go home and 'announce' that he was gay. Certainly not in the manner you've suggested. We sat here, as we're doing with Charlie, and tried to create a safe environment for him to talk about his hurdles to sexual health and happiness. For Barry, it was his secret homosexual feelings. But let's get back to us in the here and now. Is there anything that you'd like to say to Charlie at this time?"

"Yes, but I don't know what it is. Charlie, I can see how much pain you're in. I'm so sorry for it. I'm really glad that you're thinking about

Cindy and the kids. I guess I know that Barry did the same, and I know that it tore him apart to think about losing us all. I don't *want* you to be in so much pain. I want to comfort you, and tell you to be true to yourself. But I'm also feeling anger about the whole goddamn thing, and I'm scared to death for Cindy. Please, please, please don't go home and announce that you're gay. Please try to work it out in therapy. If you find that you really *are* more gay than straight, and that you can't stay married, then get into couple's counseling and please break it to her gently."

"Charlie, what feelings come up for you when you listen to Maggie?" I asked.

"I don't know. I'm feeling overwhelmed. I hear Maggie's concern for Cindy, and she's not telling me anything I don't already know. I wouldn't deliberately hurt Cindy for all of the money in the world. But it's not like I understand what's going on with my feelings. I know that I'm in the driver's seat, but I don't feel like I've got control of the car. I'm not planning on going home and announcing that I'm gay. I don't think I *am* gay. I don't know for sure what I am. All I know is that I'm terribly confused. I'm scared to death. And, yet, being here and meeting so many happy gay people, and seeing these films, as upsetting as it can be, is God taking care of me. I'm sure of it. I feel like I could be sick to my stomach at any minute, but I'm also very excited about being able to tell the truth about myself for the first time."

"Charlie, can I just say how sorry I am that I have been such a pain in the ass about this," Leona said. "I'm feeling confused as all get out myself but I sure as hell don't want to cause you or Wendy or Kevin, or even you, Mr. Group Leader, any more pain than you're already in."

"Thank you, Leona," Charlie's bloodshot and weary looking face smiled back

"I think that when it's time to do the maps, Charlie should go first," Wendy said.

"I second that," Leona said as she continued to rub Charlie's back.

"My map is one great big lie," Charlie said, shaking his head with disgust. "I did it the night you told us to start thinking about it. I was afraid to tell the truth so I came up with all this bullshit that wasn't really lies but sure as hell doesn't talk about what I see as the significant moments in my sexual journey."

"Will you show us," Margaret asked kindly, "and maybe tell us how you might change it today?"

"I feel like I've taken way too much time already," he sniffled.

"It's my job to monitor the time, Charlie," I said. "If you're up to it, I think this would be a good time for you to share your map. But before you do, let me just check in to see if the rest of you are ready to move forward. Maggie, do you want to say more about what you're feeling? We've got lots of time."

"No. I want to hear Charlie's map."

"Leona, how about you? Anything you want to say before we move on?"

"No. I want my friend Charlie here to talk."

"Okay, Charlie, it's unanimous," Dom said. "Let's see that map."

"I'm not going to want to leave this group at the end of the week. You know that don't you?" Charlie said smiling as he unfolded his sheet of newsprint onto the coffee table, and dabbed at his eyes with a tissue.

"I'm not going to want to leave you either, Charlie," Leona replied with a pat on his back.

"So here it is, my big lie," he said, smoothing out the paper with his hand. "Here's me with my parents and my younger sister, Patty. Here's me with Cindy when we met at the University of Chicago. Here's me being ordained as a United Methodist minister. Here's me with Cindy, Lyle and Kevin, and here's me with my little 200 member congregation in Oklahoma City. Obviously, all of these have been or are important pieces of my life. My folks had a happy marriage which gave me a model of what a marriage should look like. Dad sold cars and Mom stayed at home and raised Patty and me. Meeting and marrying Cindy was a big part of my sexual journey. I love Cindy. I've loved her since we first met. She makes me laugh. I make her laugh. We like the same music, and the same kinds of food, and going to movies. We both love our boys. She's been the perfect wife and mother. She's always been completely supportive of me, like moving to Oklahoma from Illinois for me, and me of her, like having her mom move in with us when her step-dad died of emphysema. We're a team.

"My ordination was the biggest and one of the happiest days of my life. I've always wanted to serve God as a minister. How could I separate that day from my map? And, of course, the boys here are the highlight of my existence. I love them so much. And all of these people in the pews, here. I do good work with them. I really do. They like and respect me, and appreciate how hard I work at being a good minister to them."

"So, Charlie, where's the lie in all of this?" Margaret interrupted with a look of concern.

313

"It's what I left out, Margaret. What you see here is what people know of me. Good old Charlie, responsible husband, loving father, a pillar of his community."

"And you're not?" Margaret gently prodded.

"How long do you think I'd last in my church if they knew that I find myself attracted to one of the single members whom I'm sure is gay? Or that I go on-line to gay chat rooms and give a phony name so that I can just talk to gay people? Or that I'm here weeping because I found the gay male lovemaking film so beautiful?

"Back here, where I drew the picture of myself with my parents, how proud do you think they would have been of me if they had known that when I was away in church summer camp as a teenager, I climbed in bed with one of the counselors late one night and that we explored each other's bodies for hours? I'm sure Cindy would have really wanted to marry me if she had known that I couldn't take my eyes off her cousin Greg at our wedding. And," he said with a weakened and shaky voice, "how proud would my boys be to know how much I envy that travel agent Brian in that film on bisexuality? I want to be with a man so badly that I ache, and yet, I know that I don't want to leave Cindy or my boys.

"What makes me and Barry different, Maggie, is that I'm not 100 percent gay. I'm 'bi,' I think. Well, maybe he is too. I don't know. All I know is that I like having sex with Cindy, but at the same time most of my fantasies are about sex with men. I cherish the memory of being in bed with my camp counselor. Some of you may think that was 'abuse' because he was older, but he's been my secret fantasy friend since I was fifteen. He's probably married with kids of his own now, but being in bed with him stays in my memory as one of the most important and happy moments in my sexual journey. Anyway, I'm rambling on, as usual. But that's why my map is one big lie, and why I took your comments so personally, Leona."

"How are you feeling, Charlie?" I asked.

"Really confused," he said with a deep sigh, "and a little scared. I hadn't intended to say all of this to the group."

"Are you sure, Charlie?" Margaret asked. "I wonder if that isn't exactly what you hoped to do this week. It's completely understandable to me that you would want to, and I'm really very pleased that you decided to. But don't you feel, deep down, that this was your mission this week? That God brought you to this point for a purpose?"

"Yes, I do, Margaret. I've been playing games so long that it's hard to sit still with the truth. I've wanted to tell you all what I've been feeling since our first session but I'm so accustomed to being cautious. I thank God for those films and for that guided imagery thing you did, Brian. I needed to be pushed, and Leona, thank you for helping to push me too. Getting angry helped me say something. In fact, all of you have helped me more than you'll ever know."

"You're glad, then, Charlie, that you have talked with us truthfully about your journey?" I asked.

"Yes, but I'm no less confused about what to do."

"Maggie offered you some good advice when she suggested counseling for yourself, and for you and Cindy. What do you feel about that?" I asked.

"She's right. I need to talk to someone. The problem is finding someone supportive and discreet."

"Charlie, I'm sure there are all kinds of resources for you in Oklahoma City," I said. "There's a book out called *Gayellow Pages* that lists resources city by city. I'll help you get a copy, and you'll certainly find a supportive and discreet professional listed there."

"Why does the person have to be gay?" Maggie asked. "What about a straight counselor? Won't a gay therapist be more likely to convince Charlie that he's gay and needs to leave his marriage?"

"*Gayellow Pages* may send him to a straight therapist, Maggie. The first criteria is that the person be a supportive and knowledgeable *professional*, but, quite honestly, my bias is that a gay therapist is more likely to understand the intensity of Charlie's feelings, *and* the ramifications of his decision, one way or the other. There are also books and organizations available for people in Charlie's situation, and books and organizations available for their spouses too."

"Barry was good about giving me a list of those resources," Maggie acknowledged. "There is a lot out there, but that doesn't mean that Cindy is going to be ready to read it or join it."

"Charlie, I want to support what Maggie said about breaking this news gently to Cindy. However, I do feel that it's something that she has the right to know," Margaret said. "As your soul mate, friend, and mother of your children, as well as a woman who deserves a fully satisfying sexual life of her own, she needs to know the full truth about the man to whom she's married. Couple counseling is critically important."

"I agree. I agree," Charlie said. "This is the work that I do, but it's a lot easier to give others advice than to do what you think is right."

"What about this guy at church that you're attracted to, Charlie? That doesn't sound healthy or wise," Wendy said.

"I know. I'm keeping my distance from him. I mentioned him only to help you understand how big an issue this is for me."

"What are you going to do about your boys?" Dom asked.

"I don't know. I'm scared to death of losing them."

"Tell them," Kevin said.

"Are you sure?" Charlie asked.

"Yes. Tell them. Even if you decide to stay in the marriage, keeping such important secrets makes it impossible to be close. I kept hearing 'Don't tell your father. Don't tell your brothers and sisters. Don't tell your grandparents.' When I finally did tell everyone, they wondered why I hadn't told them before. 'Didn't you trust that I'd love you?' they each asked."

"I don't know, Kevin. I think it's different. These are my kids, not my siblings."

"Well, all I know is that you'll never have an honest adult relationship with them as long as you lie about who you are."

"Silence equals death," Wendy said.

"That's a little dramatic, isn't it?" Dom asked.

"No, it's not!" Wendy replied strongly. "We've just been told that one possible result of gay kids keeping secrets is suicide. You asked earlier about doing a better job responding to gay kids because your silence can mean death, if not physical then certainly psychological for the kids. Charlie being silent about his bisexuality could kill his relationship with his sons. They'll learn about it one day and then they'll question all of the years that they thought they knew their father. Better he should say something now, even if it's to tell them that he's confused about his sexuality."

"But not without Cindy's knowledge," Margaret insisted. "This is a family issue. And the boys shouldn't be told as if it was a problem they needed to solve. Charlie shouldn't say anything to them until he's comfortable with it himself. Otherwise, he's asking them to respond with solutions they won't have to offer. I think that if Charlie and Cindy go into couple's counseling over this, which I trust they will do, that one of their primary tasks is deciding how to tell the boys."

"Did you and Barry talk with your children, Maggie?" Beatrice asked.

"No, but they're a lot younger than Charlie's sons. They know something is going on. They just don't know what. But I really agree with

Margaret. Cindy has got to be involved in any decision to talk with the boys. She's the one they're going to go running to."

"What do you think, Brian?" Charlie asked.

"I'm not sure you're clear yet on what it is you'd want to talk with your sons about, Charlie, and until you are, I'd not spend too much time thinking about it. The more important challenge facing you right now is coming to terms with your feelings and deciding how you want to manage them. That's where the therapist can help.

"I think it's great that you've been able to acknowledge your homosexual feelings, and how those feelings are causing pain in your life. I suspect that your wife, children, and parishioners have experienced your 'confusion' but haven't figured out what's wrong. For your sake and for theirs, it's important that you come to terms with your bisexuality. And that doesn't mean you have to *act* upon your feelings. Feel your feelings, but choose your behavior. You *may* decide that your happiness depends upon you acting on your attraction to men, but you don't have to, Charlie, in order to be 'bisexual.' Remember the differences between 'orientation,' 'behavior,' and 'identity.' Only you can decide what's right for you. Once you have, and you've come to peace with it, you need to decide if it's information that needs to be shared with others.

"I'd certainly bring Cindy into the discussion if there's *any* possibility that you may choose to act on your feelings or to not stay in the relationship. If your attractions to men are so strong and not acting upon them causes you so much stress that you can't function happily as husband, father, and minister, then you need to work with Cindy on finding a solution. There are lots of options, but only you and your wife can decide on what works best for the two of you. *Then* the question of telling your sons becomes relevant.

"As excited as you are about naming your bisexual feelings, Charlie, I urge you to pace yourself. I agree that silence equals death. But, now's the time to patiently and lovingly get to know that side of you that you've kept a secret for so many years. And I'll be glad to help you find a therapist in Oklahoma City who can guide you in the process.

"I feel as if you've all been wonderfully supportive of Charlie in this session. A lot of personal issues came up between us, and we didn't stop to address each one because it felt right to stay focused on Charlie. This afternoon, Carol and I are going to be going through the stages of 'Homosexual Identity Formation.' I think all of us are going to find it helpful in addressing some of the issues that were raised in this session.

When we reassemble as a group, we'll be revisiting some of those topics. And Wendy, if you're up to it, we'd love to have you do your map at that time.

"Nice job, Charlie."

Chapter Forty-Three

Catherine's Discomfort

Like the giddy laughter that can often follow a hard cry, it felt from the animated and energized conversations that filled the dining room at lunch as if there had been catharsis in all of the SAR groups. Perhaps, for a few, the happiness represented relief that the explicit section on homosexuality had not been as disturbing as they had anticipated. For most of the gay people present though, I suspect, there was joy in not only having the pain of their lives documented and understood, but also addressed compassionately by their heterosexual peers.

Kevin's nose wrinkled up with glee, and Betty's eyes watered with delight as Carla recounted for them and Dan an embellished tale of comforting a befuddled Latino hotel maid who had walked in on her as she got dressed for an evening out in Des Moines. Thomas and Lloyd, at another table, shared with George, Martha, and Beverly, comic impersonations of the dysfunctional Texas family characters who appear in *Sordid Lives*, the zany, gay and transgender-positive film planned for that evening. Nearby, Maggie, Wendy, Margaret, and Leona sat protectively with Charlie, and chatted about the power of the SAR process. Carol and I had lunch with our departing visitors, who were grateful for being included in the day's program, but who instinctively knew, even though they were gay or related to someone who was, that they were outsiders at that moment looking in on a community in transition.

"There's room for you here at our table, Sister," Chuck said as Annette surveyed the dining room, holding her plate of salad and glass of cranberry juice.

"Thank you, Chuck. I'd love to have lunch with you, but I'm looking for someone. You haven't seen Catherine, have you?"

"She's outside at one of the picnic tables in front of Higley," Tonya replied. "I just saw her head down there."

"Thank you, Tonya. I'll catch up with you all later," Annette said as she made a bee line for the exit, and walked down the hill.

"Do you mind if I join you?" she asked as she sat across from Catherine, who had a mouthful of tuna salad sandwich.

Catherine shrugged politely.

"Oh, that looks good. I should have tried some of that myself. That's pita bread isn't it?"

Catherine smiled as she swallowed, touched the napkin to her lips, and replied, "It's very good. And how are you doing, Sister?"

"Catherine, please call me 'Annette,' or I'll be forced to call you 'Reverend'."

"Certainly."

"Forgive me if I'm intruding where I'm unwanted but I've got the feeling that these sessions on gay issues are causing some conflict for you, and I wondered if you needed a sounding board."

"Discomfort, not conflict. It's very kind of you to think of me, but I think I know what I need to do."

"Can't I help?" Annette asked.

"No. It really doesn't involve you. I just know that I don't need to be where my values aren't affirmed."

"Oh dear, I hope that doesn't mean that you're thinking about *leaving*, Catherine. That would be awful, and I'd be *very* disappointed."

"I'd be sorry to disappoint you, Annette, but I don't feel this is a healthy environment for me."

"Oh, it wouldn't be *you* that disappointed me, Catherine, it would be *me* that was the source of my disappointment, and the failure of the program to provide safe space for *all* of us."

"Why would you fault yourself? You're not on staff."

"No, but I'm a participant who is fully invested in the workshop being a success for me personally *and* for the community that we've formed together. If you left because you felt unsafe or unwanted, I would see myself as partly responsible for failing to sense and address your needs."

"You're a unique breed, Annette."

"Oh, I don't think so, Catherine. I feel that there are many good people here who would be terribly upset if you decided to leave us. I can't think of a single person who would not take it personally. But, please tell me why leaving is so appealing. Your's is an important voice. It provides me the opportunity to challenge my own thinking. I welcome difference of opinion, and I'm eager to learn more about why you feel the way you do on any number of subjects. You leaving us would deprive me of that opportunity, and it would be a sad reinforcement of our world's propensity for polarization. 'Community' is an important concept to me, as I'm sure it is to you."

"And yet, you left your own," Catherine replied.

"Touché. But can you allow for the circumstances being a *little* different? I did indeed leave my community for another, not to find like-mindedness, but rather to be free to pursue a vocation of working with people with AIDS. My first community didn't allow for that option. But it wasn't about differences of opinion on moral issues. If that were the case, I, like many others, would have left the Roman Catholic Church many, many years ago."

"If you have doctrinal differences with the Church, perhaps that's the proper thing to do."

"Oh, not in my book. My commitment to my Church goes well beyond political or cultural differences. I can disagree with the hierarchy with my whole heart and soul on moral issues such as birth control, women's ordination, celibacy, gay marriage, etcetera, and still feel *very* connected to my faith, and to the community of believers who struggle in their daily lives to incorporate their understanding of Jesus. I'm really a child of Vatican II, Catherine, and a 'Theology C' believer, according to Bill's diagram. The quality of *relationships* is the determining factor in my life."

"And if you found yourself at a week-long workshop where the official staff position was that birth control was immoral, celibacy was required, and only heterosexual marriages were valid, and you were the *only* one there who felt otherwise, would you suffer through it, or go back home where you belong?"

"Is that how you feel? Alone? I'm so sorry that you feel that way. I know that feeling myself, and I know that it makes me want to run too. But is running away from such feelings the answer, Catherine? Isn't it possible to maintain your beliefs in the midst of opposition, to state them clearly, to listen compassionately to the voices of others, and to stay present to the feelings of isolation and loneliness?"

"Easier said than done," Catherine sighed as she looked away from Annette, and discretely dabbed away a tear that was forming.

"My dear Catherine, it pains me so to see you in such discomfort. Have you considered that this is *exactly* where you're supposed to be at this time? That perhaps something that happens this week will have a *positive* impact on the work that you're planning to do with the youth of your church?"

"Annette, I know that you're trying to be helpful, and I don't wish to offend you, but I'm no less convinced that leaving here is exactly what is supposed to happen."

"Tell me, if you would, what you feel is accomplished by leaving?"

"Brian spoke of the 'Swallowing' stage, and how gay children allegedly swallow poison about themselves. Well, there is, in my opinion, a lot of 'poison,' or unhealthy thinking, being served here this week, and I don't think it's good for me personally or professionally to swallow it. Like the young black man described in the film, I feel called to 'run as fast as I can' away from that which threatens me."

"I see. Well, I can understand how you've made the connection. Again, I'm very sorry for the isolation that you're feeling. I haven't felt the same mean-spirited attacks on conservative religious beliefs here this week that I know gay people endure for being who they are, but perhaps I've missed something. I actually feel the staff has been *very* respectful of differences of opinion, and of the people who hold them. But again, I'm not in your position."

"No, you're not."

"Would it matter at all to you in making up your mind if I offered to sit with you through the sessions, and you and I agreed to 'debrief' after each one? You wouldn't feel so alone and I would have the benefit of your differing views."

"That's very kind of you to offer, but ..."

"And Catherine, there's only one more session on gay issues. After this afternoon, it's over. Tomorrow, we're talking about something else."

"Yes, 'Monogamy and Its Alternatives.' Annette, it's not just the 'gay' thing. It's the whole philosophy here. You're not in the same situation as I am."

"I don't know. I think I *am* in such a situation in the Catholic Church, though admittedly I'm not alone. It could be very tempting to run away and join the Episcopal Church, particularly given its far more enlightened attitude on women's and gay issues, but I'm a Roman Catholic, and I'm stubborn. I have hope that with my efforts and those of countless others, my own Church might move away from its insane preoccupation with rules and 'tradition,' and toward the compassion for people that I see in the life of Jesus."

"That insane preoccupation with rules and tradition is what's guided the Church through centuries of social upheaval, and kept the institution focused on its mission of salvation."

"Henry the Eighth might disagree with you there," Annette said with a wink. "Stay and fight for what you believe in, Catherine. Share your perspective, and trust that it's having an effect on others. In my opinion, there's too much polarization, too much walking away from that which is uncomfortable. How many people left the Episcopal Church over the ordination of women? And how many more have left over the consecration of Bishop Gene Robinson because he's gay?"

"More than you can imagine. But that's another matter. I don't know how we got onto all of this. I very much appreciate your concern, Annette, and I'm glad that my presence has meant something to you. I think I'm going to take a little walk before the next session starts, if you'll excuse me."

"Certainly, Catherine. I fear I've worn you down. Please remember that I'm here for you, and that I will miss you terribly if you decide to leave us."

Catherine smiled politely as she swung out of her seat at the picnic table, stood with her plate and glass, and walked briskly back to Huntington.

Annette poked at her salad for a few minutes more, and then followed suit. Once back in the dining room, she politely handed her plate to the dishwasher, and then found Alison and Bill sitting alone, finishing their meals.

"I'm sorry for interrupting," she said as she sat down at their table. "I've just been speaking with Catherine, and I strongly suspect that she's going to be leaving us."

"Really?" Alison said with alarm. "Is she ill? Is there a problem at home?"

"She's not comfortable with our 'pro-gay' position," Bill explained. "I met with her this morning. She's apparently been struggling with this all week."

"Did she tell you that she's leaving?" Alison asked Bill.

"Not in so many words," Bill said. "I got her to agree to come to this morning's session. She was very quiet in group, but she has been all week. I had planned on meeting with her at dinner."

"I don't know that she'll be around that long," Annette said.

"I'll speak to her immediately. Do you know where she went?" Alison asked as she stood with her dishes.

"She said she was going for a walk."

"Thank you. I'll catch up with you both later. Please tell Brian and Carol that I may be late."

"Have you had many people leave early?" Annette asked Bill as Alison hurriedly headed toward the driveway.

"One in thirty years," I think. "She'd be the second."

Chapter Forty-Four

The Stages of Coming Out

"Hey, Kevin! Over here," Dan called out with a nodding of his head.

Kevin stood at the entrance to the downstairs meeting room, surveyed his options, thought for a moment about his decision, and was finally persuaded by Dan's sexy smile and plaintive, "Come on!" He sat cautiously next to Dan, but could feel himself melt as Dan put his arm around him and whisper, "Where have you been, buddy? I've missed you."

Peter entered the room, quickly looked around it, sat in a chair with a free one next to it, and placed his participant packet on the empty chair.

"Asshole," Dan whispered to Kevin, who sympathetically watched Peter politely wave away Annette who had tried to sit next to him.

"It's Catherine's," he explained.

"Of course," Annette replied kindly.

"I think I'll just sit back here with the two of you," Leona announced as she slid into the empty seat next to Kevin, placing her hand on his knee. "Unless, of course, I'd be intruding," she added with a smile at Kevin, and a stern glare at Dan.

"Make yourself at home," Dan smiled back as he massaged Kevin's shoulder.

"This afternoon, we're going to explore the stages that many gay people go through from self-denial to self-affirmation," Carol said from her spot in front of six easels at the front of the room. "We're going to guide you through the 'Homosexual Identity Formation' model created by Australian psychotherapist Vivienne Cass."

"Carol and I will talk about our own lives to help illustrate the stages, and we invite all of you to do the same," I said. "Cass has created a wonderful model, based upon her observations with hundreds of clients, but it's *your* stories and insights that will give it life today. As Carol begins to take us through this, remember that it's just a model and it may not accurately reflect your experiences. Some of us will see how we went through it sequentially. Others will see themselves jumping into the process halfway through it. Some of you will have skipped stages. Others will remember going back and forth between stages. The value for all of us in knowing the model is in better understanding ourselves as gay, lesbian, and bisexual people, and better understanding those in our lives who are gay. We think this is also a great model for the stages that transgender people go through from self-denial to affirmation, as well as family members and friends of gay, lesbian, bisexual, and transgender people. And, on a final note, at the end of the program this afternoon, we're going to be showing you Carol's and my favorite film of the week, which features senior gay men and women who have successfully come through these stages."

"The six stages outlined by Cass," Carol said, moving from one easel to another, "are 'Identity Confusion,' which is when you're aware that the topic of 'homosexuality' is creating an emotional response in you, 'Identity Comparison,' when you accept the possibility that you *might* be homosexual, 'Identity Tolerance,' when you start to recognize that you probably *are* homosexual and that you have social and emotional needs, 'Identity Acceptance,' where you accept rather than tolerate being gay, and start building a world that supports you, 'Identity Pride,' which is when you immerse yourself fully in the gay community and start seeing the world as 'us versus them,' and finally, 'Identity Synthesis,' when the walls that separate you from heterosexuals come down, and you fully integrate your sexuality into all of your life."

"Going back to 'Identity Confusion,' this is when you're swimming in a public pool, or you're watching television or a movie, and you realize that you're completely preoccupied with someone of the same sex," I explained. "You can have a funny sort of woozy feeling as you admire their looks, or their physique."

"Or their personality," Carol interjected.

"You feel a special connection," I continued, "that you don't quite understand. For me, it was physical attraction to a long series of men, from life guards at the pool, boy friends of my older sister and brother, camp counselors, pictures of Greek statues, coaches, and television and movie stars. The one television star that stands out the strongest for me was Robert Conrad."

Thomas and George started applauding, and Charlie carefully nodded his head in affirmation.

"Who?" Maggie asked.

"Robert Conrad was the very handsome and hunky star of the television shows *Hawaiian Eye*, *Wild, Wild West*, and *Ba Ba Black Sheep*," I replied. "He almost always took his shirt off in each episode, and I found myself waiting nervously for him to do it. When *Hawaiian Eye* was on the air, I was young and if you had asked me, 'Are you a homosexual?' I would have freaked out and probably been terribly offended. I wasn't a *homosexual*. I just loved watching Robert Conrad take his shirt off. And it's just a coincidence that every person I've ever had these feelings for were men."

"You watched all of these men undress, and you didn't know that you were a homosexual?" Leona said incredulously.

"I know that it makes no sense, Leona," I answered, "but look again at the whiteboard and all of the horrible words on it. And remember the guided imagery. There were no gay songs on the radio or gay billboards, or openly gay teachers, or gay dances. Everything was heterosexual. How do you find a context or a meaning for your attractions in that void of information?"

"I can see that," she nodded.

"Can I add Hugh Jackman to the list?" Lloyd asked. "And Tom Welling from *Smallville*."

"And how about Denzel Washington?" Thomas added.

"Now, *that* makes sense," Leona replied.

"As Brian said, when you find yourself feeling these attractions, you do everything in your power to deny that these feelings have anything to do with *being* a homosexual," Carol continued. "Cass outlined a variety of strategies that gay and bisexual people take. You pray for help. You seek a 'cure' on your own. You become an anti-gay moral crusader. You become asexual or heterosexually hyperactive. If you happen to have homosexual sex, you excuse it by saying that you were drunk or asleep, or that you did it on a bet, or that you were just 'experimenting,' or that you were taken advantage of. Homosexual and bisexual people who are in this stage are generally very threatened by, and often angry at, gay and bisexual people who accept their sexual orientations."

"Carol, was there someone you turned on to when you were young?" Dom asked.

"No, I didn't start focusing on women until later in my life, but how about the other lesbians in the room?"

"Jo on *Facts of Life*," answered Wendy.

"Xena," replied Gina.

"Jennifer Garner from *Alias*," said Lisa.

"Sheena, Queen of the Jungle," laughed Betty.

"Who?" asked Lisa.

"You're much too young," Betty winked.

"Okay, moving right along," I said, "some homosexuals never leave Stage One. They get married, stay celibate, or perhaps even enter a relationship with a same-sex person, but they don't validate their feelings of attraction, and, in some instances, they spend all of their time and energy fighting against homosexuality as a legitimate 'lifestyle.' Some of the most outspoken homophobic people in our culture are, or have been, closeted homosexuals."

"Like J. Edgar Hoover and Roy Cohen," George said.

"And most of the guys carrying signs saying, 'God Hates Fags'," Dan yelled out.

"But if the person accepts the probability that they are homosexual, they then move into Stage Two, 'Identity Comparison,' and they begin to explore the *consequences* of such a decision," Carol explained. "They start asking, *if* I am a homosexual, what will it do to my relationships with my family and friends, to my career, to my chances of getting married and having children, to my relationship with my Church?' What impacts them enormously at this stage is the amount of hostility about homosexuality they experience from heterosexuals they value. If, for instance, they come from a progressive Church or have a favorite gay relative, it makes it much easier for them to imagine living their lives as gay. They will then move on to the next stage. If, however, they see no opportunity for support, they will stay stuck in Stage Two. To cope with their situation, they may get married and have outside affairs, or they may enter a relationship with a same sex person but insist that they aren't really 'gay,' they're just in a 'special relationship.' Or, they might geographically move away from all of the significant people in their lives, and have gay relationships that are never acknowledged by anyone."

"There are a lot of people who live those kinds of lives," Thomas said.

"In the black community, it's called 'Down Low'," Lloyd said. "I know of lots of black men who have sex with other black men but insist that they're not 'gay.' For them, *gay* means sissy white boys. They see themselves as masculine, and they want to have sex with masculine men, often unsafe sex. They then go home, and have unsafe sex with their girlfriends or wives."

"Race, culture, and religion can have profound impacts on the ability of a person to leave Stage Two. But staying in Stage Two doesn't make them any less homosexual in 'orientation.' It merely affects their *identity*," Carol said.

"I remember," I added, "in my very early days of recognition, promising myself that I would never even imagine having sex with a man that I knew personally because that would be bad, but I could have fantasy or real sex with a stranger because love wouldn't be involved. I thought you could only romantically love someone of the other sex."

"That's why some men who have sex with other men won't kiss them or allow themselves to be kissed," Dan said. "For them, what's happening is just sex, nothing more. It would be *queer* for them to kiss another man. It would make them a *faggot*."

"That's right," Carol said. "And some women do the same thing, but in the opposite direction. They'll become emotionally connected with another woman, maybe even kiss, and snuggle, but keep it from becoming sexual. And they don't see themselves as lesbians."

"People who enter Stage Three, 'Identity Tolerance,' have accepted that they are gay, lesbian, or bisexual and that they need to find others like themselves for the sake of emotional and social support," I continued. "It's here that gay people begin to secretly join gay organizations at work or in church, go to a gay bar, look for gay movies or television programs, and discreetly read gay-theme books. The operative word," I explained, "is *tolerance,* and whether gay people move to the next stage or not is heavily influenced by the sophistication and maturity of the gay people they encounter. If their peer group is closeted with family and colleagues, and sees homosexuality as an unfortunate burden or sinful, then they will stay stuck in Stage Three. If, however, their friends are 'out,' and see being gay as natural and good, it is far more likely that they will progress into Stage Four, which is 'Identity Acceptance'. "

"I have to say that I had the *most* wonderful introduction into being gay that anyone could have," Carol said. "When I came to Thornfield for the first time, I came into contact with Brian as an open and self-affirming gay man, Susan Vasbinder, as an open and self-affirming lesbian, and this incredible staff of heterosexuals like Bill, Alison, Pam, Dick, Linda Roessler, and Mary Lee Tatum, who valued gay and lesbian people and their relationships the same as they did heterosexuals and their relationships. When I came to the conclusion that I was a lesbian, I had all of these great role models surrounding me who helped lessen all of my fears."

"Role modeling and mentoring are critically important, particularly at this stage," I said. "As we recall, gay, lesbian, and bisexual people generally don't come from gay families with long traditions of celebrating the goodness of homosexual feelings. When I was growing up, gay people on television were interviewed as silhouettes, and everyone who was closeted seemed ashamed. The first time I went into a gay bar, it was early in the evening, and the few people I saw there initially scared me. I thought they looked very sad. I was afraid to have anyone know that I was a member of this community.

"I then went to a conference, the first of its kind, on 'Homosexuality and the Catholic Church,' and I met all of these amazing priests, nuns, and lay people who were either gay or gay-supportive. They all seemed so happy and so proud, and it had a profound influence on me. I subsequently came home and wrote my next newspaper column for *The Michigan Catholic,* where I worked as a reporter, on the goodness of being gay. I was ready to come out.

"Then later, when I came out and lost my job at the paper, I was invited to speak to a gay audience at the University of Michigan. I was really eager and needy for acceptance by my local community, having lost the support of some family members and friends, and I was so upset when I was laughed at by the gay men sitting in the front row, who were dressed as a bride and bridesmaids, because I was in a coat and tie. 'What have I done?' I thought. 'Is *this* my new family?' I wanted to go running back into the closet.

"Yet, the more gay people I met, the more I found who I really liked, admired, and identified with. That made it a lot easier to be glad that I was gay, and no longer suffering in the closet. I get a lot of e-mail from gay men, particularly, who are afraid of acknowledging that they're gay because they don't see where they fit into the gay community. I encourage them to join gay men's discussion groups, bowling or softball leagues, political or religious caucuses, or any outlet other than just the bars, where they have the opportunity to meet positive role models who will help mentor them through the stages."

"As I say, I was really lucky to start my journey here," Carol repeated. "Now, if you *do* find self-affirming resources, and thankfully today there are a lot more of them available for gay people, such as Gay-Straight Alliances in the high schools, television programs such as *Will and Grace* that feature positive role models, movies and books and CDs, and places such as Provincetown, Massachusetts where you can go and be affirmed, then it's more likely that you'll move on into Stage Five, which is 'Identity Pride.' That's a really important word. *Pride*. Notice that the person has gone from *tolerating* his or her feelings of attraction for people of the same sex to having *pride* in those feelings."

"Identity Pride is the stage in which the gay, lesbian, or bisexual person sees being gay as being *fully legitimate*, and they immerse themselves in the gay culture," I explained. "They often move to gay-friendly towns or into gay neighborhoods. They find gay dentists, attorneys, therapists, plumbers, and doctors. They subscribe to gay periodicals, listen to gay music, go on gay cruises, put gay symbols, such as the rainbow flag, on their cars, and march in Gay Pride parades. They don't tolerate anti-gay bias from family, friends, or strangers. It's also at this stage that they get in touch with their anger at having endured a lifetime of anti-gay bias from the police, the Church, politicians, schoolmates, and family members. And, in the last couple of decades, AIDS has exacerbated that anger as gay men have watched in horror as their friends die of a disease that took 40,000 lives before the government began to respond.

"In many ways, that anger is very healthy and necessary. If gay people are going to move on in their lives, they need to deal with the feelings that have accumulated through the 'Swallowing' stage that we discussed this morning. How do you live in a world that describes you with these awful words," I asked, pointing at the whiteboard, "without feeling a lot of anger? The downside of the anger is that it often divides the world into an 'us versus them' paradigm, and it makes it nearly impossible for gay people to fully mature and to integrate their sexual orientation into all aspects of their lives. If all heterosexuals are the enemy, the gay person's life is *reactive* rather than *proactive*. We then live in our *victimhood*."

331

"And for the record," Carol added, "let me say that angry Stage Five gay people can scare the hell out of Stage One, Two, Three, and Four gay people, and they don't provide particularly positive role models in the long term."

"And they can scare the hell out of heterosexual allies too," Marjorie said.

"Why shouldn't queer people express their anger?" Dan defiantly hollered from the back of the room.

"Say more, Dan," I invited.

"You can have fashion queens dressing up straight guys and their apartments on television, but straight guys are still beating the shit out of high school sissies," Dan replied with agitation. "They're still raping dykes. The Catholic Church is still fucking with people's lives. People are so afraid of two queers getting married because somehow it's going to make their breeder marriages 'less stable.' You can kill for this country but only if you pretend that you're a straight killer. Queer kids are still dying of AIDS but no one gives a flying fuck because they're black or Spanish. So, because the Supreme Court says we can now fuck just like everyone else, and because we've got a few more gay stereotypes on television, we're supposed to put on a happy face? I don't think so."

"But what about straight people who want to be *supportive?*" Maggie asked nervously. "You're just going to scare them away."

"I don't *care* that my anger scares heterosexuals. I *want* it to. I want them to be damn scared about fucking with me," he replied, glaring at her intensely. "If they want to be supportive, then be supportive. Do it because it's the right thing to do. It shouldn't require that I smile to cover up my pain, and make them laugh by being a queeny little *Queer Eye* faggot." Here he stopped, took a deep breath, looked away, welled up, and slowly shrank into quiet exasperation.

A loud silence enveloped the room. Kevin reached over and pulled Dan's body close to him. Leona stood, came around Dan, and began to massage his tight shoulders. Everyone who had turned to look at Dan was now facing Carol and me. I stood still and silent for a complete minute.

"I share your anger and your frustration, Dan," I said slowly and softly. "I just don't show it like you do. I think every gay person in this room who grew up feeling like a piece of shit shares your anger. In some ways, I'm selfishly glad that you're as visibly angry as you are because it means that I don't have to show mine. There's a part of me that's happy you scare people because there's a part of me that wants vengeance. But I'm not happy for *you*, because I know from my own life that my unchecked anger is debilitating. It stunts my growth because it stops me from getting past my own ego. Festering anger makes me a victim, and I don't want to spend the rest of my life as a victim. I also know that my pain is my own, and while I have a right to it, I feel I don't have the right to impose it on others, especially innocent bystanders.

"Sometimes, Dan, I get so angry and so frustrated as a gay man living in a straight world that I just want to cry, to sit on the side of the bed and bawl, without even knowing the exact reason. And then I remind myself that there are lots of people out there who are just as angry and in just as much pain as I am, and some of them are angry at *me* for being male, or white, or financially stable, or for being able-bodied, or Catholic-raised, or for being a happy gay man. That thought doesn't make me less angry at the atrocities you listed, but it humbles me to think I'm not the center of the universe, that mine are not the only problems in the world, and that most people would be terribly hurt if they knew what kind of pain you and I are feeling, just as it hurts me to imagine that I have caused them pain. Ignorance is the enemy, not people. Ignorant people beat up sissies. They have to be stopped, but they also have to be educated. Watching them change their behavior when they get educated is what gives me hope and makes me less angry. I'm sorry for your pain, Dan, but I'm glad you felt that you could express it here so clearly and so strongly. Carol, if you would, why don't you take us to the next stage."

"Thank you," Carol said smiling and stepping gingerly over to the final easel. "Stage Six, 'Identity Synthesis,' happens when gay people feel their homosexuality integrated into *all* aspects of their lives. The 'us versus them' wall that Brian described comes down. That doesn't mean that the gay, lesbian, and bisexual people no longer feel anger, or pain, or pride. And they still may distrust heterosexuals, but they've come to understand that there's as much diversity in the heterosexual world as there is in the gay world, and they're less inclined to make quick judgments based upon a person's sexual orientation."

"Here, again, the quality of contacts we have makes all of the difference in the world," I explained, after taking a deep breath. "Encountering heterosexual people who challenge our stereotypes is critical in our ability to move from Stage Five into Stage Six. I think that I'll always have one foot in Stage Five and one foot in Stage Six. But the greater the number of heterosexual allies I meet, the less likely it is that I could ever retreat completely back into Stage Five.

"I was in Stage Five, 'Identity Pride' one time on an airplane where I was sitting next to a nun. I was particularly angry at the Catholic Church at the time because of some really offensive statement about gay people that they had recently made, so I decided to make a point of being gay by pulling out of my briefcase a copy of my book *On Being Gay,* which I left sitting on my tray table for the entire flight. I didn't make eye contact with the nun nor speak with her. At the end of the flight, as I was heading toward the door, she tapped me on the shoulder and handed me a note that read, 'God bless you. I support what you're doing.' I felt really stupid and very small, and I realized that I had missed a great opportunity to speak to an ally. It was my *heterophobia* that got in the way!

"A similar thing happened with a burly police officer. The car that was sent to take me from the airport to the university where I was speaking broke down in the middle of a snowstorm. I ended up in the back of a police car, waiting for a tow truck, as the student driver walked to the nearby service station and called for a ride. The student had informed the officer that I was speaking at the university. While we waited in silence, he turned and said to me, 'So, what are you talking about tonight?' 'Homophobia,' I answered a bit apprehensively. 'That's the fear of homosexuals isn't it?' the cop asked. 'Yes,' I replied. 'Oh, I got rid of that years ago. Our next door neighbor was gay and he used to babysit me. He was like an uncle. I loved him. My folks loved him. He was great!'

"Both of those experiences helped me begin to believe that people I suspect will be anti-gay might well be allies. A few years ago, that idea really got put to the test. I had just finished conducting two days of training for AT&T in New Jersey, and was flying home to Atlanta, where I lived at the time. The man sitting next to me on the plane introduced himself as a fundamentalist Christian businessman who would soon be addressing twenty-five hundred fundamentalists about 'morality in the workplace.' His wife, he told me, was an active member of Concerned Women for America, which is an ultra-conservative, anti-gay organization. 'Enough about me,' he said. 'How about you? Are you married and what do you do for a living?' With anxious determination, I told him that my partner Ray and I had been together for twenty years, and that I spoke in corporations and colleges on how to create a safe and productive work environment for gay people.

"He was astounded but genuinely curious about my work, and he asked for details on my program. I told him that the most effective tool I have in helping people understand the impact of inappropriate behaviors toward gay people was the telling of my story. 'Why not tell me your story?' he asked. 'I don't know any gay people.'

"Trusting that his interest was sincere, I did so. Over the next two hours, I calmly and patiently told him my story and answered his questions about my being raised as the middle child of seven Irish Catholics, about my sixteen years of parochial education, about knowing since I was young that I was gay and that I wanted to be a 'saint,' about my terrible loneliness and fear of my sexual feelings as a young adult, about being a super achiever who was highly-praised but nevertheless miserable in my isolation, about receiving an award for Christian leadership in high school and of then having my name taken off the plaque when I came out as gay, about drinking a bottle of paint thinner in a desperate attempt to ease my fear of the future, about finally coming out and subsequently being fired, and of my wonderful life of love with Ray, my soul mate. When I finished, he looked at me for a moment in silence and said with a warm smile, 'Brian, as surely as I'm sitting here, I believe that God had you sit next to me. My wife and I write lots of checks to groups that oppose civil rights for homosexuals, but the truth is, we don't *know* any homosexuals. You've put a face on this issue, and I won't ever forget that. I can't tell you how this is going to impact what I say to those businessmen I'm addressing next week, but I know that it will. I also know that this is going to be harder for my wife. She wasn't here with us, but I'll surely tell her about it'."

After a moment of silence, in which a few participants wiped away smiling tears, Carol said, "Let's take a break. When we come back, we'll process your feelings, and watch the film, *Silent Pioneers.* "

Chapter Forty-Five

Writing on the Board

When the workshop participants returned from their brief break, the words "fudge packer," "muff diver," "homo," "dyke," "faggot," and the others on the whiteboard glared at them from the right-hand side of the video screen. On the left-hand side, we had placed the easel with Cass's stage six, "Identity Synthesis."

"Before we move on," I said, as I eyed Alison slip into the room and sit next to Peter, "Carol and I want to go back and address these words. This collection of words and phrases, which were used to intimidate us as gay people, were swallowed whole and digested in our formative years. Many of us not only believed them to be true about others who were gay, but also true about us. We valued the opinions of heterosexuals about homosexuality more than we dared value our own feelings or those of our community members. But that 'mind set' changes for us during this process of Identity Formation. At some point, each of us is called to stand in front of the mirror, literally or figuratively, and assert with growing confidence, '*Faggot* doesn't define me! *Dyke* doesn't name me! Nor do *cock sucker, muff diver, sin,* or *abomination*'," I explained as I erased half of the words from the board and handed Carol the eraser to complete the job. "I am *gay*," I continued as I took a black marker, and smiled as a handful of participants applauded the wiping away of the derogatory words. "And *my* name is 'Brian'," I wrote in a bold script on the board.

"And I'm a *lesbian*," Carol said with a big, proud grin as she took a blue marker from a nearby table. "And *my* name is 'Carol'," she said as she wrote her name near mine.

We each then turned, faced the group of participants, and silently held out the dry-erase markers in our hands.

Betty stood immediately and walked briskly to the front of the room. "My name is 'Betty,' and I'm a lesbian," she declared as she wrote. Kevin was the next one up.

"My name is Kevin, and I'm a gay man," he said and wrote after her, and then handed his marker to Dan, who had followed him up the aisle. "My name is Dan and I'm *queer*," he emphasized as he wrote both words together, and then handed his marker to Wendy, who headed the line behind him. "My name is Wendy," she said, "and I'm a lesbian." Then, "My name is Gina, and I'm a lesbian. "My name is Thomas, and I'm gay." "My name is George, and I'm gay." "My name is Lisa, and I'm bisexual." And finally, "My name is Lloyd, and I'm gay."

When Lloyd sat down, the room was quiet in anticipation. Dick Cross then stood and strode with deliberation to the board and printed his name among the others. He said nothing and sat down. Bill Stayton followed suit, stating only "My name is 'Bill'." Alison, Pam, and Gail beamed with pride.

Again, we stood in awed silence. A full minute passed. Charlie then rose and several of us welled up as he solemnly walked to the board, wrote his name with Carol's marker, and said in a shaking but determined voice, "I'm Charlie, and I'm bisexual." He then handed the marker back to Carol, turned, smiled through his tears, and hugged me for several seconds.

Leona was the first to stand. She did so applauding, with her head nodding affirmation. "That's right!" she said. Beatrice, Margaret, Maggie, Dom, Paula, and Chuck quickly did the same. Seconds later, they were joined by nearly every heterosexual present. Alison, though, stayed seated with Peter, her hand on his shoulder, as she smiled approval.

"Thank you," Carol said. "You know, there is a lot of room on this board for the names of our heterosexual allies who don't care that someone might think that they too are gay."

To that invitation, Pam sprung to her feet, followed by Gail, Alison, Beatrice, Margaret, and Annette. Ben then wheeled his chair to the front of the room. Within a few moments, all but one had come forward and signed her or his name to the board.

"We're going to leave these names on this board throughout the week," I promised. "We'd now like to close this session by sharing with you a film that we feel nicely completes the snapshot of the journey we've worked to describe to you today. Gail, if you would, the lights, please?"

The 84-year-old Tucson rancher named Paul was in a monastery until he was 60. He came out as gay at 72, and now rides horses daily, greets each sunrise with yoga exercises, and wears an understated earring stud to church. "I'm very thankful that I am what I am, and that I'm who I am," he explained in the film *Silent Pioneers,* a profile of gay and lesbian seniors. "You can't define it, why anyone is gay. No one can. All I can say is that if you go that way and not fight it, you'll be happy. If you fight it, you'll be fighting it all of your life."

The grey-haired, heavyset black woman, who sat in the park with her adoring, guitar-strumming teenage granddaughter and infant great granddaughter, laughed giddily when she described her experience of kissing a woman for the first time. "When I finally named myself as a lesbian, I felt whole," Grandma said. "In my relationships with men, I always knew something was missing. I knew it would be nice to be with a woman, but I didn't expect the thunder, lightning, and comets that happened." In reflecting on her life, she said, "I think the legacy I'd like to leave as a black lesbian mother is to have my children have loving relationships, to learn to respect one another, and to learn to respect women as human beings. We have a double struggle as gay men and lesbians of color, to change what society thinks we should or shouldn't be."

Slow dancing at an event sponsored by SAGE, (Senior Action in a Gay Environment), the two lovesick men told us that they had been together for 54 years. "After 54 years, we're still in love," Gene said. "Lots of people stay under the same roof for that length of time, but they're not necessarily in love, and that sets us apart." Later, seated in their living room, Gene and his partner Bruce explained how they got involved in the gay civil rights movement. "After the kids had the courage to take to the barricades," at the Stonewall Riots in New York in 1969, Bruce decided it was time to step forward. "Their stand was something that could give John Wayne lessons in what 'true grit' really means," Gene added.

Myrtle had "lived straight" all her life, despite knowing at five-years-old that she was gay. A particularly endearing grey-haired woman, who had bussed tables as a waitress for 40 years, she one day decided "I was going back to my own." She started by going through the telephone directory looking for "gay" listings and could only come up with the bars. So she called them, she reminisced on camera with laughter, and she asked the bartenders "if there were any old lesbians in there who were looking to meet another old lesbian." Later she called a number that advertised "counseling for lesbians," and thought that she had hit the jackpot. Unfortunately, she got a recording each time she called. Finally she made a connection with a woman with whom she has been ever since. "I know that it's changing," Myrtle observed about public attitudes toward homosexuality. "I'm not asking anything from straight people, only just to accept me for what I am. I want to be free to live my life as they are free to live theirs." Then, surrounded by adoring birthday guests, she sang, "Oh tell me sweet Jesus, I really want to know, will there be gay people in heaven? And if there's not, who in the hell wants to go?"

When Gail raised the lights as the credits rolled, the room erupted into applause. Big grins filled the faces of all of the gay participants and nearly all of the straight ones too.

"That was great!" Gina said. "That was the best!"

"You have to always show that film," insisted Lloyd. "I *love* that film!"

"Does that group SAGE still exist?" asked Tonya.

"Yes. It's located in New York, and there are similar efforts being made to reach out to senior gays and lesbians in other cities," Wendy answered.

"There's a gated gay retirement community in Florida," Thomas said.

"And a big new one in New Mexico," Betty added.

"Do you see why the film is Carol's and my favorite?" I asked, and then, looking at my watch said, "We're running out of time. Any last comments?"

"Brian," Alison said, "I have something to say."

"Please," I invited as she stood.

"I hate the impact this will have on the wonderful mood in this room, but I report with great regret," she said solemnly after everyone had quieted down, "that one of our participants has found it necessary to leave us."

"Who?" Maggie interrupted as several people scanned the room with looks of concern and moans of regret.

"Catherine Mitchell," Alison replied. "I helped her secure transportation to the airport during the first part of this session."

"Is she sick?" Marjorie asked. "Is there a problem at home?"

"No, she's fine. She just feels that this workshop is not a good fit for her," Alison answered. "She asked me to say 'good bye' to all of you."

"What do you mean 'a good fit'?" Dom asked.

"She felt that though she was learning new things and enjoyed meeting new people that she would be more comfortable at home. Let me say," Alison quickly continued, "that I and the entire staff are deeply saddened by Catherine's decision to leave us. I attempted to dissuade her but her mind was made up. It's very unusual to have someone leave this workshop. Excluding those who have had to leave because of emergencies at home or for medical reasons, Catherine is only our second in thirty years to depart before the end of the week."

"We're due back in our small groups at this time," I explained, "but let's just take a few minutes to process our feelings. Does anyone have anything that they'd like to ask or to say?"

"I'm glad that Catherine took care of herself," Marjorie said after a moment of awkward silence. "If she didn't feel comfortable, then she should have left."

"A lot of us feel uncomfortable," Chuck replied. "I thought that was the purpose of the week. To push our buttons so that we could see where we needed to grow. I think it's a cop out to leave."

"Did we do something wrong?" Tonya asked.

"Did anyone on the staff speak to her about her feelings, other than you, Alison?" asked Joanne.

"I spoke with her this morning," Bill explained. "She said that she was feeling isolated in her views, that she didn't agree with what she saw as the 'liberal bias' of the presentations, and that she was considering leaving. I encouraged her to speak up about her views, and to challenge things she disagreed with. When we finished talking, I had the impression that she was going to give it more time."

"I fear that I pushed her over the edge," Annette said sadly. "I sensed that she was isolating and I talked with her over lunch about it. I told her that I wanted her to stay because she helped me clarify my thinking. I said that I would consider her departure a failure on my part to create a community in which everyone felt safe. Maybe if I had left well enough alone, she'd still be with us."

"You didn't do anything wrong," Margaret asserted strongly, "and you certainly didn't make Catherine leave. She left because she wanted to. It was her decision. I suspect that one day she will regret going home, that she'll see it as 'giving up'."

"Why should she see it as 'giving up'?" Peter asked. "What if she sees it as 'shaking the dust from her sandals'?"

"Jesus was talking about 'inhospitality'," George countered angrily. "This is anything but an inhospitable place. I think the staff has bent over backwards to accommodate other perspectives. Not once has a staff member put down people who think differently. We were all encouraged to examine our values so that we were aware of why we responded to situations the way we did."

"This doesn't have anything to do with *values*," Dan said. "Catherine left for personal reasons. This session got too close to home for her."

"Oh, please," Peter replied with exasperation.

"Are you willing to tell us that she *didn't* leave because she was feeling threatened?" Dan asked.

"It's unfair and unnecessary to speculate," Alison said. "I think it's time we moved on. Margaret is correct when she says that no one made Catherine leave. She made the decision based upon reasons that are known only to her. I know that we all wish her well. Like Annette, I wish she had stayed because I valued her perspective. But let's get back to focusing on our own journeys, shall we? I know that you've had a terrific presentation by Brian and Carol this afternoon. It's been very powerful. Let's now head to our small groups where we can continue processing what we've learned and felt today."

"Catherine was a pain in the ass since the day she arrived," Lloyd whispered to Thomas as they picked up their folders from the floor. "She isolated herself since day one. I think Dan's right. The 'gay' stuff got too close to home."

"I wish her well," Thomas softly replied with a slight smile. "I feel badly that she didn't want to stay. Can I catch up with you later, Lloyd? I want to check in with someone."

"Sure."

As Peter headed for the exit, Thomas cut around Martha, Beverly, and Judith and caught him at the door. "You doing all right?" he asked as he gently placed his hand on Peter's shoulder.

"Yes, fine, thank you," Peter replied politely.

"If you don't have any plans, I'd love to sit with you at dinner."

"Um, sure. That would be fine," Peter answered with a nervous smile.

"Good. I'll see you then."

As Peter approached the top of the stairs, he saw Annette standing against the wall, letting others pass, as she smiled warmly at him.

"Thank you for speaking to Catherine," Peter said as she moved alongside of him. "I know that she appreciated you reaching out."

"Did she say anything to you about it?" Annette asked.

"No, I hadn't spoken to her since the session before lunch. I just know that she would have appreciated your concern."

"I feel so terrible about her leaving."

"Me too."

"You're not thinking of going anywhere are you?" Annette asked with a look of concern.

"No, I'm here for the long haul. It's not always comfortable, but I'm here to stay," he said.

"Good. I really want you to stay. I *need* you to stay."

"Why's that?"

"Well, besides liking you very much, and wanting to better understand you, I've just got to believe, Peter, that we here can do a better job working things through than I'm seeing in the world outside. If you want to talk with anyone, please, please remember that I'm here."

Annette looked startled and then very pleased as Peter leaned down and kissed her on her cheek.

"Catch you later, Sister," he said as he headed off to Alison and Pam's small group session.

Chapter Forty-Six

Wendy's Map

"I told you I wouldn't be late again," Wendy said grinning as she entered Higley with a Diet Pepsi, and took a seat in the empty circle of chairs.

"Where is everyone?" I asked, my back to the door.

"We're here. We're here," Leona answered as she pulled open the door for the line of group members who all had cold drinks in their hands. "Be patient with us, Mr. Brian. We're running on fumes."

"Everyone pretty tired?" I asked as they all plopped into chairs.

"I'd be less tired after running a marathon," Dom said with a laugh.

"Oh, not me," Wendy countered. "I'm psyched. This day has been great!"

"It has been good, but I'd like to talk about Catherine if we can," Beatrice interjected softly.

"Sure," I encouraged with a nod.

"I'm really sad that she left. I didn't know her very well, but I'm sorry she felt so lonely here that she had to leave."

"I suspect that it wasn't about 'loneliness,' Beatrice," Margaret offered. "And if it was, I think maybe Catherine brought those feelings with her. I share your sadness that this week wasn't the positive experience for her that it is for me, but I trust that she learned what she needed to learn."

"I don't know about that," Wendy said. "But, I pity the gay kids in her church youth group. They don't have a chance."

"You never know," replied Margaret. "We all have the capacity for growth."

"Can we change the subject?" Leona said. "I don't want to talk about Catherine. I want to talk about Charlie. I lost it when you got up and signed that board," she said as she rubbed his back with her hand. "I was *so* proud of you. I nearly burst. Mind you, I still don't fully understand the whole thing, but I'm learning, and I know that was a really big thing for you to do."

"Thanks, Leona," he replied with a face-wide grin. "I was so scared when I saw the others get up, and I thought, 'Brian, how can you do this to me?' But then I thought, 'Hey, if I can't stand up and say I'm bisexual with *this* group, I can't do it with anyone.' When I actually wrote my name on the board, I felt this enormous weight come off my heart. And I thought, 'I've really got something now to put on my sexual journey map'."

"I was really happy for you, Charlie," I said.

"Me too," said Kevin, Dom, Beatrice, Wendy, and Margaret at once. Maggie smiled.

"Thanks," he said, and smiled knowingly at Maggie.

"Beatrice, was there anything more you wanted to say about Catherine's decision to leave?" I asked.

"Only that I wish she hadn't done it," she said.

"Me too," I said. "Are there any comments or questions about this afternoon's presentation? Anyone?"

"I liked the black grandmother in the movie," Leona said. "She was definitely cool."

"I liked her, and the saucy waitress," Dom said. "She had spunk."

"How about the guys, Dom?" Wendy asked with a smirk. "Did you like any of them?"

"Yes," he said with feigned exasperation. "I liked the guys too. I think the former monk was really amazing. I also thought a lot about what he said, and I think he's probably right. If you fight your gay feelings, you're going to fight them your whole life. If you accept them, then you have a chance to be happy."

"All right, Dom!" Wendy said enthusiastically as she reached out and gave him a high five.

Kevin clapped and Margaret laughed as they watched the two wink and smile at one another.

"Maggie, do you have anything that you'd like to share? Any impressions?" I asked.

"I knew you were going to call on me," she said shaking her head with resignation. "Well, of course, I imagined Barry getting up out of his seat and writing *his* name on the board. I'm sorry to keep doing this, but I can't help it. He's sitting right next to me every minute of this thing."

"Don't apologize. That's why you came here," I said.

"Yea, I know, but sometimes I'd like to have a reaction that had nothing to do with him. But I did see him get up and walk to the front of the room, and there was this part of me that wanted to yell, 'Sit down! You don't know what you're doing!' And then there was this other part of me that wanted to yell 'Go for it, Barry! I love you, and I want you to be happy!' So, I'm schizophrenic! By the way, Brian, he did get up and sign the board last year, didn't he?"

"Yes, he did, Maggie. He cried like Charlie, and a lot of people cried with him."

"I'm glad he had that experience. I am. It makes me sad for me, but it makes me happy for him."

"You're a wonderful woman, Maggie," Dom said.

"Thanks," she sighed.

"Have you gotten a better understanding of Barry's sexual orientation, Maggie?" Margaret asked.

"I have. If Barry is gay, as I think he is, I know that he didn't 'choose' his feelings of attraction, that they probably scared him to death growing up, that when he married me he hoped that his love for me would be enough, and that he's torn apart because he doesn't want to lose me or the kids."

"So, you don't think we 'turned' him gay?" I asked with a grin.

"No, I don't think that you 'turned' him gay," Maggie answered. "To tell you the truth, Brian, I'm *glad* that he came here. I really am. If Barry hadn't come to Thornfield, he probably wouldn't have come out, at least not for some time. I'd rather know what's going on than spend my life in a relationship with a man who wasn't happy. And I'm glad that he had you, Carol, and Kevin as role models."

"Thanks. And he's *really* lucky to have you in his life, Maggie," I replied. "Anything else? Anyone? Yes, Leona?"

"I was wondering why Dick and Bill got up and signed the board. Are they 'bisexual,' or is that something we're not supposed to talk about? "

"No, it's a good question, Leona," I replied. "I can't speak for either of them, but I've heard Dick explain that his experiences here at Thornfield have prompted him to question whether or not he has ever had, or could have, any same-sex feelings. This is one of the reasons that I love and admire the man so much. He *never* stops questioning, and he *never* stops growing. He came to the conclusion that being with a man would not be out of the question for him, so despite the fact that he's lived his entire eighty-some years as a heterosexual, he wants to acknowledge his bisexual potential. And Bill I've heard explain that while he also identifies and celebrates his heterosexual life and feelings, he too is aware of his capacity to be attracted to men. I think they're both primarily wanting to signify their solidarity with the gay and bisexual people in the room. Does that help answer your question?"

"Yes, thank you," Leona replied.

"Anyone else? Okay, then how about if we invite Wendy to share her map with us now?"

"I'm ready if you all are," Wendy enthusiastically replied.

"Go for it," Dom said.

Pulling her chair forward and unfolding her newsprint on the coffee table, Wendy began with an apology. "I'm afraid you'll find it pretty boring after all that you've seen and heard today, but it's my life, and I don't think there are any 'lies' here," she said, winking at Charlie.

"Good Lord, girl, look at those drawings!" Leona exclaimed. "We've got an artist in the group. I am definitely not showing my map after this."

"I'm glad I went before you," Beatrice said. "You're good."

"Oh, thanks. I like to draw," Wendy said. "Okay. So here you have five things that happened in my life so far that I think had a big impact on my sexuality."

Neatly, colorfully, and creatively displayed on her paper were five scenes, each outlined with a jagged-edged, but perfectly-aligned frame, like an old Polaroid photograph. In the first, there were four young, teenage girls in a circle with a bottle spinning on its side between them.

"Okay, so you know that I'm a lesbian, and that I work as a HIV-prevention educator in Cleveland, Ohio. What's not on this paper are pictures of my Mom and Dad, and of my three brothers, one younger and two older, and of my younger sister. I love them, and I know they've all had an impact on my sense of self, but when I had to choose five *big* moments of revelation in my life, they didn't make the cut," she explained.

"Dad's an accountant. Mom volunteers at the school library. My brothers and sister are all into sports, except my younger brother, who I think might be gay but he doesn't want to talk about it. I'm sure I scare him.

"Anyway, that's Mary Ellen Cassidy, Laurie Witherow, Tracy Pickens, and me, and we're playing 'Spin the Bottle.' We were all best friends, went everywhere together, did everything together. We're thirteen here at a sleep over, and Laurie said we needed to practice kissing, so we did. Everybody giggled, me included, but I knew I was having a better time than the rest of them, except maybe Laurie, who I suspect cooked the whole thing up so that she could kiss Tracy, who didn't seem all that interested. But *I* was sure interested, and when Laurie, who I had a big crush on, and I kissed, it was the first time I'd ever kissed a woman, and I want you to know that the black grandmother in that film was right. There was thunder and lightning and comets. I had to make myself cut it short so that nobody noticed how much I was enjoying it. I think Laurie noticed, but she never said anything. She just smiled knowingly. But we were both too afraid to do it again, or at least *I* was, and the other girls thought they got all of the practice kissing they needed that one day. But I was hooked.

"In this 'photo,' we find me and Jodie Henderson in a motel room in Gambier, Ohio, with me making love to another woman for the very first time. I was 19, she was 20, we were on Oberlin's soccer team. We were at Dennison for a weekend tournament. Jodie and I had flirted back and forth for a year, so when she asked me if I wanted to bunk up with her, I nearly died. I wanted it to happen but I was really afraid. She was more experienced than me, and she was wonderful! Patient, tender, considerate, loving. She went really slow. I know that some people, gay and straight, have a horrible experience the first time around, but mine was the best. So, 'thank you,' Jodie, for being my first.

"Okay, so moving right along, here I am, with Jodie and a whole group of other friends from Oberlin at the amazing 1993 March on Washington. Wow! I mean it. That thing changed my life. There were hundreds of thousands of lesbians and gay men from everywhere all together in D.C. for this massive march and rally. The signs said 'We Are Everywhere,' and we *were* everywhere, on the streets, in the subway, on the Mall, on TV, in the papers, on the planes coming and going, in the restaurants and hotels. Everywhere you looked, you saw smiling gay people. I felt so excited and so energized. I'm not kidding. It was so *empowering.* I finally saw in those couple of days what life *could* be like. It was awesome, and I knew that was the way I wanted my life to be from then on. I wanted to be surrounded by happy lesbians, gay men, bisexuals, and transsexuals. I wanted no more secrets, no more hiding, and no more being afraid. Maybe you had to be there, but it was something else.

"Okay, enough about the March. So, here I am with the first love of my life, Connie Butkus. As you can see in the picture, I'm crying, so this was not a really 'happy' moment for me. It started out really happy, but it ended up pretty sad. Connie left me for another woman, and it devastated me. I mean, *devastated*. We met right after I got out of college. She was this very cool, very sophisticated, very beautiful, fun person who swept me off my feet at 21. She was 25. We had a cute, little apartment near where she worked in Columbus. I was so in love, and I was sure that she was too. When she told me after four years together that she was leaving me for an older woman she had just met at a professional development conference, you could have blown me over with a feather. I cried and cried for weeks, maybe months. My friends were really worried about me. I lost all kinds of weight. I thought about suicide. I nearly lost my job. I just kept asking 'why?' and I kept thinking that I would never love again. I worried that I did something wrong, or that I wasn't pretty enough, or that I wasn't good in bed. I didn't know what to believe. She didn't want to talk about it. Turns out that it wasn't about me at all. But I never would have known that without the help of a therapist. I got this great, lesbian therapist who helped me grieve the loss and move on. She also helped me do some important work in self-esteem. I thought I had it all worked out as a lesbian. I thought that I was very 'with it.' Then I discovered how much internalized homophobia I was still carrying around. Anyway, I put old Connie down here because she represents an important point of growth for me.

"After Connie, I moved back to Cleveland where I met Linda, and we were together for four years too. I don't know what it is with these four-year romances. Anyway, Linda was a love but a pot head. I tried and tried to get her to stop smoking, but she said I was making a big deal out of nothing. If it wasn't a problem for her, why was it a problem for me? I found Alanon and learned that the best thing I could do for her was to take care of myself, so, I told her that if she didn't stop smoking grass, I'd have to leave. She wouldn't, so I moved out. That was a year ago.

"So, now I'm footloose and fancy-free, and I *love* my work, which is why I've put my co-workers in this last photo. Aren't they cute? That's Mark, Larry, Jack, and David. Being around them helps me capture the feelings that I had back at the March on Washington, and makes me look forward to going to work each day. When I moved back to Cleveland, I started working at a nursery. I love the outdoors and being around living things, but I was really lonely there, and I felt very isolated. Then I saw an ad on the Internet for an opening at the Lesbian and Gay Community Center. They needed HIV-prevention educators, and since I had worked as a volunteer with the Gay Speaker's Bureau for a couple of years, I thought, 'So, why not?' They hired me and I immediately made all kinds of great friends. They're amazing gay men and I love them all like brothers, but I have to admit, I'm really ready for some female companionship. They all say they're keeping their eyes open for me, but nothing so far.

"So, anyway, that's it! My life in a nutshell. Any questions?"

"Connie was a fool," Dom announced.

"She sure was," Margaret echoed.

"Thanks. I think she needed someone more mature, and more financially established," Wendy replied. "She's happy with her new life, and so am I, so all's well that ends well."

"Wendy, for the most part, your life growing up as a lesbian was pretty smooth sailing, wasn't it?" Beatrice observed.

"Yea, it sure was. I kind of feel guilty when I hear other gay people talk about all of the pain they experienced. I was initially confused about what I felt, and very cautious about telling people about my feelings of attraction, but I didn't feel the shame that so many others describe. I think it's because my folks are pretty liberal and not very religious. They're Presbyterians, but we never went to church much. I had some sex education in high school, and the guidance counselor used the word 'gay' respectfully. And then I went to Oberlin, which is about the most gay-friendly school you could go to. I also think there were a lot more positive role models available for me than say Brian might have had. So, you're right. It wasn't so bad."

"It's nice to hear that not every lesbian or gay man's life has been a nightmare," Margaret said. "I'm sure that lots of gay youths are still terrified of their feelings, but I'm glad to know that there are people like you, Wendy, who are out there who are a little less scarred."

"Wendy, how was it for you to do the map, and how did it feel to present it?" I asked.

"Doing it was fun, but not necessarily easy because there's so much that I wanted to put down. I mean, I thought Margaret did an awesome job by telling us what books influenced her. There were lots of books, movies, and women artists and athletes that influenced my sense of self too. Melissa Etheridge is a real hero, as is Martina Navratilova. And I know it's old, but *Rubyfruit Jungle* by Rita Mae Brown was an important book to me, as were the movies *Fried Green Tomatoes,* and *Thelma and Louise.* I also thought about putting down the Michigan Women's Music Festival, because it was a really big deal for me to go to that. I didn't like it. There was too much man-hating there for my taste, but actually getting up the nerve to go to it was a big thing for me. Then I thought, 'Do I tell them that I worked at a Dairy Queen in the summers or that I was a psych. major in college?' I'm not sure what that has to do with anything 'sexual,' but it's part of my story. So, to answer your question, I loved doing it but I hated cutting things out, and I had a good time sharing it with this group, because I'm so comfortable with all of you. You're wonderful. And, if I can say just one more thing, we're doing Maggie's toenails at the movie tonight."

"You're what?" Maggie asked with pleasant shock.

"We're doing your toenails. You said you've never had your toenails done. We promised you that we were going to do them. Leona's got the polish."

"You didn't bring any with you?" Dom asked with a smirk.

"Shut up, Dom," Wendy laughed.

"And Maggie, maybe then we'll get you an ice-cream sundae," Leona said seductively, "and who knows what other nice thing you might then do for yourself."

"I know where this is going," Maggie laughed. "I'll agree to the painted toenails. Thank you guys for being so sweet."

"Be prepared to be pampered," Wendy advised.

"Nice job, Wendy," I said as I observed people begin to gather their things. "You all know that you're now free until tomorrow morning. The film tonight is optional. And Leona, when we come back together as a group tomorrow, we'd love to have you share with us *your* map."

"I know. I know," she sighed. "But you sure know how to ruin a good mood."

Chapter Forty-Seven

Thomas and Peter Talk

Ben maneuvered his chair into the breezeway between Peabody and Huntington, and waited for Beatrice to walk up the hill from Higley. When he saw her, he waved enthusiastically and greeted her with a big grin.

"Got plans for the rest of the day?" he asked.

"Nothing other than painting Maggie's toenails," she said. "What do you have in mind?"

"I don't know. I just wanted to hang out with you. I'm getting a little anxious about how fast the week is going. We're free until tomorrow morning, except for the toenail thing. I thought we could get into our suits, stretch out on a blanket and get a little sun, and then maybe borrow a car and go into town for a nice dinner. Then we could come back and camp out under the stars. It's going to be a warm night. What do you think?"

"I think I'd like that," Beatrice replied with a shy smile. "Let me check with Leona and Wendy to see if I'm really needed tonight for Maggie's pedicure."

"Wendy's coming up right behind you. Hey Wendy," Ben hollered, "okay if Bea misses the pedicure tonight? We've made some plans."

"Absolutely. Leona and I can handle it. I think Margaret's going to join in anyway. Go for it, and have fun."

351

"Thanks," Beatrice said. "You'll tell Maggie that something came up for me?"

"You're covered."

As Ben and Beatrice headed for the dorm to change into their bathing suits, they passed Peter who was in his trunks, and then Dan, who was in his. Upon exiting Peabody, Peter walked toward the water, and Dan meandered across the lawn, found a spot, shook out his beach towel near where Betty and Carla were seated, and laid down in the heat of the late afternoon sun.

Outside of Peabody, Marjorie and Curtis sat together with their cigarettes and watched the comings and goings.

"My, this has been an interesting week," Marjorie sighed as she stretched out her sandaled feet and wiggled her toes.

"It's not over yet," Curtis replied with a raised eyebrow, "unless *you're* planning on going somewhere."

"Oh heavens, no. I'm having too good a time, and I'm learning *so* much. I thought I had it pretty much together but I've got to say I'm growing."

"Don't you think it's a little heavy on the 'gay' stuff?" he asked in a lowered voice.

"Not at all, at least not for me. Is it for you?"

"Yea, I could use a break."

"Well, I think you've got it now. There isn't anything else on the schedule that I can see. I just feel though that if we can't deal with the gay issue, we might as well not bother with the others. It's where the rubber meets the road," Marjorie replied as she pulled herself up straight on the bench and looked more intently at Curtis. "I don't think it's always going to need this much time and attention, but it sure does today. Do you know that the Religious Right spends more time and money battling gay issues than it does any other issue, including abortion? 'Gay marriage' makes them absolutely crazy."

"I believe it, but how much do *we* really need to know about it?" Curtis asked. "I mean, for instance, did we need to go through all of those stages?"

"Oh, see, that's what I was referring to when I said I was learning new things. That *really* helped me understand the differences between Peter and Dan, and between Wendy and Lisa. People are just at different stages of development. It makes perfect sense when you think about it, but who takes the time to think about it? Aren't you learning new things about homosexuality?"

"Yea, I am, but I'm not sure I need to know as much as I do."

"Maybe not, but I'm sure that you've got a good number of gay men and lesbians with disabilities who are your clients. I'll bet you'll ultimately find these sessions more useful to you in working with them than you'll find the one tomorrow on 'Monogamy and It's Alternatives'," she laughed derisively.

"Probably," he grinned, "but personally, I'm looking forward to that."

"Hello, you two," Annette said as she exited the dorm. "You haven't seen Peter or Dan have you?" she asked.

"You won't find them *together*," Curtis replied, rolling his eyes.

"Peter went down to the water, Sister, and Dan is over there on the lawn," Marjorie said.

"Oh, thank you," Annette answered as she walked in Dan's direction.

"Look out, Dan," Curtis sighed in a low whisper.

"He can handle himself," Marjorie replied. "And she's a good egg."

Down at the water's edge, Peter sat alone on the grass, his body dripping from his swim, his long arms wrapped around his knees, and his eyes fixed upon the rolling farmland across the lake. He stayed there for twenty minutes, breathing slowly but deeply, and listening to the sound of the rippling water break over the flat brown rocks that bordered the shoreline.

When he heard Beverly, Martha, Joanne, and Judith move from the picnic table and carry their animated, laughing conversation up the hill, he took in one last long breath, exhaled, stood, and followed them at a distance up for dinner.

Ben borrowed Carol's minivan, and he and Beatrice drove the short distance to Cazenovia for dinner at the small town's fabled inn. The rest of us chose between pasta with meat sauce and vegetable lasagna.

I met at a picnic table outside of Higley with Lloyd, Grace, Gina, and Carla to discuss their presentations at our 'skill building' workshop.

"We're meeting the day after tomorrow, and I haven't heard from any of you yet on who your intended audience is," I cautioned.

"I have mine right here," Carla said with a proud smile, passing me a neatly written page, and delicately patting herself on the back.

"Good for you, Carla," I replied appreciatively.

"Would you *all* like to know what I'm doing?" she continued coyly with the others.

"I would," Lloyd said.

"Gina's my partner, and she's been a great help with this," Carla said, sitting up straight, gently pushing her dirty dishes away from her, and folding her hands on the table. "Grace has also been an *enormous* resource. When it's my turn to present, I will be speaking to a group of engineers at a firm that bars discrimination based on gender identity and expression. Their department's diversity committee wants help in understanding transgender, or *bigender*, using your word, employees. They've scheduled this session as part of their yearly requirement to do diversity training. I've just got thirty minutes, so I'm going to speak to them for five to ten minutes as Carl, and the remainder of the time as Carla. What do you think?"

"I think that's a *terrific* idea. I'm very impressed," I said with a beaming look at Carla, then at Gina, and then Grace, who winked in response. "You've done your homework. You've used all of the right terminology. You've created a completely plausible setting, and your idea for a presentation format is intriguing. Nice going, Carla."

"Thank you, but don't act so surprised," she replied. "I'm not just another pretty face."

As we continued to discuss our day on Friday, Peter and Thomas walked slowly around the driveway.

"My heart really goes out to you this week," Thomas said as he searched Peter's face for a reaction.

"Thank you, but why?" Peter replied guardedly with a quizzical look.

"Because you seem very much alone, and when I put myself in your position, I feel sad."

"Hum. I guess 'sad' is a word I could use to describe my feelings this week. Sad and frustrated, and angry and confused."

"Will you talk with me about those feelings?"

"I will, but why?"

"Two reasons I guess," Thomas said, pensively stroking his chin. "I'd selfishly like to better understand you, and, to be quite honest, I think I imagine myself freeing you from those feelings."

"By convincing me that I'm not 'ex-gay'?"

"Yea, maybe."

"I appreciate your candor," Peter said smiling over at him.

"Tell me why you came here, Peter. The first day, when you announced that you were 'ex-gay' I thought maybe you came to proselytize, but you haven't done that. You haven't challenged anything that's been said. We're in different SAR groups, so I don't know what's been going on there, but I expected you to be trying to convince people that it's possible to be 'ex-gay'."

"I'm not sure why I came, to tell you the truth. When I read the description of the workshop on the Internet, I was intrigued. When I brought up the idea of my attending to my spiritual counselor, he was dead set against it. In fact, he was so strongly against it that it made me wonder why I should be afraid to come. I'm like that. Tell me *not* to do something, and it's all I can think about doing. I also thought it might be a great opportunity to safely test myself. If I was truly ex-gay, I should be able to go to a pro-gay workshop and survive. You could go to a workshop sponsored by the Religious Right, and still be gay, right?"

"This is all new to me, Peter. I've always thought of 'ex-gay' people as frightened, self-hating homosexuals or, more likely bisexuals, who have had bad experiences in the gay culture, and who latch onto Christian fundamentalism as the means of gaining social acceptance and religious 'salvation.' That's one of the reasons I wanted to talk. You don't seem to fit that mold."

"I fit some of it, Thomas. I haven't had any positive experiences in the gay culture. The two concepts seem contradictory to me. What's positive or life-giving about being obsessed with youth, beauty, and sex? If it's such a 'happy' lifestyle, why does it need to be fueled by so much alcohol and recreational drugs? Mention the name 'Jesus' in a group of homosexuals and they act as if you just farted. If you want their approval, talk about your trip to the baths or to St. Barth or to Barney's."

"I've never been to the baths, to St. Barth, or to Barney's, Peter, and I talk about Jesus with the ease and confidence of discussing a best friend, which, incidentally, for me He is. And for the sake of my health, I don't drink or take recreational drugs. Just as you don't fit my image of 'ex-gays,' I don't fit yours."

"You're an exception. Do you disagree with my description of the culture?"

"In some segments of it, you're right on the money. But ask yourself, Peter. What are you describing, a way of life, or the effect of oppression? Would you say that you didn't want to be black because after a visit to a slum you saw garbage on the streets, boarded up buildings, and street gangs? I mean, come on. Could Lloyd say as a result of being born into that environment and rejecting it that 'I'm ex-black'?"

"It's not the same, and you know it."

"It *is* the same! Or, at least, from my experience it's the same. Maybe not from your's. But let's not get hung up. I really didn't ask to talk with you because I wanted to argue. I apologize. You said that you could identify with some of my stereotypes of an 'ex-gay' person, in that you had bad experiences in the culture. Was there anything else?"

"I don't see myself as 'self-hating,' Thomas. I see myself as self-loving. I think that's what allows me to be here. I suppose you could say that I'm 'frightened' because I don't want to throw my life away. I don't want to waste it, and I think it would be wasted chasing my dreams in the gay culture. I suppose that like everyone else, I'd like acceptance but I don't think it drives me. I didn't expect to get much acceptance here and I came anyway. But you mentioned 'salvation' and I think that *really*, at least for me, is the operative word. You either believe the Bible or you don't believe the Bible. You either accept it on face value or you don't. If you don't, then don't worry about it. Go do your own thing. But I do believe it. I accept it as the word of God, and I really seek to follow it. The Bible says clearly that it is an *abomination* for a man to lay with a man as he would lay with a woman. It doesn't get any clearer than that, does it? So, I say, in response, 'I once was lost but now I'm found, was blind but now I see.' I was gay. I lived a gay life. I had gay sex, *lots* of gay sex. But, something inside of me kept telling me that I wasn't happy, that this was not the way life was supposed to be, that I was *wasting* my life. Then I went to a meeting I saw advertized in the paper. I got reintroduced to the Bible, and I decided that I no longer wanted to live the life I had lived. I no longer wanted to live 'gay,' so I took on the label 'ex-gay.' It says to me and to others, 'It's possible to do. It's possible to find happiness.' And to answer your initial question, I think that's why I decided it was unnecessary to speak up in the workshop sessions here. My being happy as an ex-gay man is testimony enough."

"Well said, Peter. I understand how you got to where you are today. But *are* you happy? You said earlier that you were sad, frustrated, angry, and confused. What do those words mean? And if I can, I wonder, do you think you'd be in the same spot you are today if you had come out and had wonderful experiences as a gay man? Let's say that you fell in love right out of college and that you and your partner have remained very much in love for many, many years. The sex that you have together is truly 'love making.' What if you two were active in your local church, you had a wide circle of gay and straight friends who shared your values, you were out at work, and had the complete support of your boss and colleagues? And what if you had a different view than you do now of what the Bible says, or *doesn't say*, about homosexuality? Or that you saw the Bible as only the first edition of God's revealing message to humankind, that He is still talking to us in ways that are intended to make sense to us at our level of understanding and evolution? What if you saw the message of Jesus as one of insisting that the law was made for man and not man for the law, and that the law had to be challenged and changed to address the needs of man, such as feeding people even if it violated the rules of the Sabbath? What if, Peter, your life as a gay man was emotionally, physically, and spiritually fulfilling and happy? Would you still feel the need to be 'ex-gay'?"

"But it isn't."

"But mine is."

"Then you shouldn't be ex-gay."

"Should you?"

"If it works for me."

"Does it work for you? What about feeling sad, frustrated, angry, and confused?"

"I said it works," Peter replied with a grin, "I didn't say it was easy."

"Is it about Dan?"

"What?"

"Are your feelings prompted by your dealings with Dan?"

"Oh, God, no. He's a pain in the butt, but I don't let him get to me. He wants to, but he's going to leave here frustrated."

"So, what's confusing, and what's frustrating for you? What's making you sad and angry?"

"To be quite honest, Thomas, I ask myself all of the same questions you just asked me about 'what if?' What if I had a love relationship like some of the people in the films? What if I'm stuck in Stage Three? What if Bill is right about Theology C? What if I find myself really attracted to another man? Have I actually only changed my 'behavior,' and 'identity'? That's confusing, and frustrating, and it makes me sad and angry. But that doesn't mean that I'm going to go back to being gay."

"Attracted to anyone I know?" Thomas asked.

"You had to pick up on that part didn't you?"

"Sorry. I think you're a really honest guy. It's Kevin isn't it?"

"What?"

"He's a wonderful man, and great looking."

"Are you planning on going to the film tonight? *Sordid Lives.* It's about time to start."

"I will if you'll come with me."

"All right. I'll give it a go."

"But what about Kevin? Are you attracted to him?"

"Let's go see the movie."

Chapter Forty-Eight

THURSDAY

"Lifestyles"

Initially, Betty and Carla were alarmed when they saw the overturned wheelchair lying next to the large mound of pillows and blankets in the center of the pine tree grove, but then they saw a little movement, smiled at one another knowingly, and continued on their brisk, early morning walk down the driveway toward the road.

Wendy passed them a short while later on her daily morning run.

"Keep your eyes open for deer," she said.

"We've already seen two dears," Carla replied to Betty's appreciative groan.

The breakfast room was filled with a buzz when Carol and I entered. Leona was insisting that everyone come and see Maggie's ruby red toenails. Maggie's freckled face was blushing but her smile betrayed the delight that she felt with the attention.

Thomas and Lloyd sat with Peter. Kevin joined them at Thomas's insistence.

"Good morning," Kevin said shyly, as he sat across the table from Peter.

"Did you like the movie last night?" Thomas asked him as he spread low-fat cream cheese on half of a toasted sesame bagel.

"It was *great*. I particularly loved watching Bill. Did you see him? He was crying, he was laughing so hard," Kevin replied as he peeled an orange.

"And did you hear Alison laugh?" Lloyd asked.

"She's got a great laugh, doesn't she," Peter affirmed, hoping that Kevin would look back at him.

A moment later, when Ben and Beatrice entered the dining room looking a wee bit self-conscious, spontaneous applause erupted from the different tables.

"What's that about?" Alison asked.

"I'll tell you later," Pam whispered, as she stood and gathered her things.

"Pam, if you've got some time, I'd love to talk with you," Joanne said as she met her at the dishwasher's station.

"I'd be happy to, Joanne," she replied. "How about if we meet at dinner?"

Gail's ringing of the school bell prompted the last of the stragglers to clear their plates, and head across the lawn to Ridings. As Judith and Tonya entered, they joined the circle that had formed to sing "I Love Myself."

Peter, who was flanked by Thomas and Annette, looked slowly around the group of faces, and felt a dull pang of sadness that Catherine's face was not among them. He nevertheless smiled as he joined the swaying back and forth which the bodies had begun to do to the rhythm of the music.

"I love myself, the way I am, and still I want to grow. The change outside can only come when deep inside I know. I'm beautiful and capable of being the best me I can. I love myself, just the way I am."

"Good morning! Before I lead us in a wake-up exercise," Alison said cheerily as we each took our seats in the semicircle, "we have some announcements to make, and I'll begin. First, if you haven't spent any time with the Quilt panels this week, please do so today. Virginia Montgomery is coming back tonight to take it down. I've loved having it with us, haven't you? Secondly, those of you who need a ride to the airport on Saturday, please let Gail know sometime today the departure time of your plane."

"Oh, please don't talk about leaving here yet," pleaded Maggie.

"I know," Alison replied. "I hate acknowledging that our time is nearly up."

"But we have two full days ahead of us," George reminded us.

"That's right! We do," Alison enthusiastically agreed. "But please do talk with Gail today if you have transportation needs on Saturday. Okay. Tonight, you'll have some film options. I'm going to be showing a wonderful film by Betty Dodson on the workshop that she conducts for women on self-pleasuring. I've attended the weekend program and can't say enough good things about it. For those of you who would like to see how she works with a group of women in helping them get to *know* their bodies and to *love* their bodies, and to know the difference between 'sensuality' and 'sexuality,' you can join me upstairs here in Ridings in the adjacent room there at 7:00 p.m. We'll have a discussion afterwards."

"Should we bring mirrors?" Marjorie asked with a smirk.

"If you'd like," Alison grinned back at her.

"Dick and I attended the weekend that she hosted for men. It was *great!*" chimed in Bill.

"Yes, you did," affirmed Alison. "And Bill, what will you be showing downstairs for those who want other options?"

"I'll be showing more episodes of *Sex in the City*," he replied.

"Thank you. Are there any more announcements? Yes, Bill?"

"I'll be meeting at lunch today with those of you who are getting credit for the week from Widener University," he said.

"Thank you. Anyone else? Yes, Carol."

"Three things. First, don't forget that in your participant packet are questions that need to be answered to get continuing education units from AASECT. You'll need to hand those in before you leave on Saturday. Second, there's also an evaluation form in the packet. Please fill it out. We always read them all, and we find them very helpful in reworking the week's format. The evaluation will be your ticket into the celebration tomorrow night. And third, speaking of the celebration, I need some volunteers who will take responsibility for decorating this room, and others who will organize refreshments."

"I'll help with decorating," Thomas said immediately.

"So will I," said Wendy.

"Great! Thank you. One of the things you'll be doing is decorating and hanging a large bed sheet that we'll provide so that everyone here can leave a message about your experience this week. We'll also be hanging sheets around the room from the last several years. You'll have a great time reading what past participants had to say. So, if anyone else would like to volunteer, please see Thomas and Wendy at some point today. And how about refreshments?" Carol asked.

"I'll help with that," Joanne offered.

"Me too," Dom said.

"Great! Thanks. You guys can collect some money from each of us. If anyone else wants to help, please see Joanne and Dom, and if anyone has a song they'd like to sing, a poem they'd like to read, a skit or a joke, please let me know. Okay. That's it for me," Carol grinned as she curtsied and took her seat.

"Very good. If there are no further announcements, let's everyone stand as you're able, form a tight circle, and prepare to wake up those sleepy muscles," Alison said.

Ten minutes later we were all wide awake, seated again, and having our attention drawn by Bill to the fifteen sheets of newsprint that he and Pam had earlier taped around the room. Each contained a description of a "lifestyle." The words were "Traditional Monogamy," "Child Free Marriage," "Single Parenthood," "Singlehood," "Cohabitation/Trial Marriage," "Group Marriage," "Serial Monogamy/Second Chance," "Swinging/Group Sex," "Communal Living," "Voluntary Extended Family/ Family Network Systems," "Synergamous Marriage," "Polyamorous / Open Ended/ Flexible," "Secret Affair," "Chaste Monogamy," and "Lifelong Chastity/Celibacy."

"This morning, we're going to talk about *lifestyles*, of which monogamy is but one option," he said with a big grin and raised eyebrows. "*Lifestyles*, as you recall, are the patterns around which persons organize for daily living. These fifteen lifestyles are the ones that we in the field have been able to observe as *choices* made by others. We're going to discuss these lifestyle choices today not with the goal of determining which one is 'right,' and which ones are 'wrong,' or which are 'moral,' and which are 'immoral.' As we stated clearly at the beginning of the week, these sessions are not about changing our values, but rather about *reassessing* them. We choose for ourselves what works best for us, but we know that what works best for us doesn't necessarily work best for others. Being familiar with why we make our choices, and why others make theirs, can only help us both personally, and in our work as professionals. So, let's take a quick look at the various lifestyle options, define them, and then explore our attitudes about each one."

Bill then read through the list and began to elaborate. "Monogamy literally means 'one spouse.' Traditional monogamy means being married to, and genitally exclusive with, one person throughout your life. Many people think that traditional monogamy is the norm, and that the rest of these are the 'alternatives,' but the fact is, as many of you know, that traditional monogamy is no longer the norm. Most people, at least in this country, either aren't virgins when they marry or don't live faithfully with the same person for the remainder of their lives. Half of all marriages in the United States today will end in divorce. Many younger people choose to live together prior to marriage. In addition, puberty starts at a younger age than it once did, and people today are marrying much later in life than their ancestors did. And, our life expectancy is 70-plus years whereas our grandparents and great grandparents often had much shorter lives. Though it is popularly romanticized as the 'ideal,' today most people, for a variety of reasons, do not spend their entire lives married to, and genitally exclusive with, the same person. What then are the other options people choose?"

"Bill? Before you continue," Marjorie interrupted, "I know that you don't want to talk about morality, but just for the record, doesn't the Bible prescribe monogamy?"

"No, it actually assumes polygamy," he said with a look that affirmed her astonishment.

"*Really?*" she said incredulously.

"Really," he replied. "The Bible neither prescribes nor proscribes monogamy. It actually assumes multiple wives but not husbands. The Talmud limits the number of wives to four. We'll be talking more about this in my skill-building group on Friday. But let's move on if that's okay."

Bill then continued with the list. Most of the other categories seemed self-explanatory, and many of them were not mutually exclusive. A "Single Parent," for instance, could also be a "Swinger" and/or engage in "Communal Living." Some terms, such as "Lifelong Chastity/Celibacy" described choices made about sexual activity. Other terms, such as "Voluntary Extended Family," described choices made about living arrangements or shared responsibilities.

"Serial Monogamy" described the situation of many Americans in which a partner committed him or herself to genital exclusivity with one spouse or partner, but had more than one spouse or partner in one's lifetime. "Cohabitation/Trial Marriage" was recognized as also a popular option.

"Every one of my children has tried that," Marjorie said.

"Mine too," Margaret added.

"Group Marriage" was defined as "threesomes or more." Generally, but not always, the consenting adults live together. "Communal Living," likewise suggested shared living arrangements, whereas "Extended

Family," might involve regularly-scheduled inter-family events, such as shared meals or vacations, but generally not shared homes.

"Secret Affair" was self-evident to most participants. It was different from the "Polyamorous/Flexible/Open Ended" lifestyle in that the latter choice assumed agreement between both partners that sexual activities with people outside of the primary relationship were permitted.

The two terms that seemed to need the most explanation were "Synergamous Marriage," and "Chaste Monogamy." The first describes a lifestyle in which one partner in a marriage simultaneously has a known and agreed upon long-term relationship with a third party. It is different from "Secret Affair" because it is not a secret, different from "Group Marriage" because only one of the partners is involved, and different from the "Polyamorous" lifestyle because the second relationship is *committed*, as opposed to being a "one-night stand."

The term "Chaste Monogamy" describes a lifestyle in which committed partners refrain from sex with others, and with one another. It differs from "Lifelong Chastity" in that the latter describes a choice made by a single individual.

"What I'd like to do now," Bill said after fielding questions of clarification, "is to have you each go stand beneath the sign that describes a lifestyle that you'd like to discuss further with others. We'll take about ten minutes to talk, and then you'll get the chance to explore one other option. Keep in mind that going to an option is *not* an indication that it's what you want for yourself, only that you'd like to explore it further with others. Got it? Okay, please move now to one of the lifestyles."

"Traditional Monogamy," by far, drew the largest group of participants the first time around. Maggie, Peter, Beatrice, Ben, Joe, Kevin, Carol, Tonya, Martha, Paula, and Grace stood together in a circle and began talking in groups of two or three.

"Okay, so why are we all gathered here?" Ben asked loudly enough for each of those in "Traditional Monogamy" groups to hear. "Is it because it's what we have, we want, or we're afraid to lose?"

"I know he said it's not the norm," Maggie replied, "but it's what *I* want."

"Even if it doesn't work out, it's worth working for," Kevin said.

"Yea, you have to have an *ideal*," Peter added with a warm smile to Kevin, who blushed.

"Extended Family" drew the next largest crowd. George, Annette, Dom, Gina, Gail, Margaret, Beverly, and Pam formed their circle and talked animatedly of the benefits of inter-generational networks of support.

"If this means what I think it does," Annette said, "I love the idea of being a part of others' lives in a really intimate way, and to have them be a part of mine. It's actually what the early Christian communities were all about."

Leona, Thomas, Wendy, and Judith went to "Serial Monogamy."

"Let's be honest," Wendy said. "It's the way things are."

"But is it what you want?" Thomas asked.

"I like the idea of 'second chances'," Leona answered.

"Open Ended" relationships attracted the attention of Dan, Lloyd, Charlie, Chuck, and me.

"Anyone notice that it's all men in this group?" Chuck asked.

"How many of you have tried 'Traditional Monogamy,' or are in that kind of a relationship now?" Dan asked.

The "Commune" listing brought together Dick, Betty, Marjorie, Joanne, Alison, Lisa, and Carla. When Marjorie saw Curtis standing alone under "Swinging," she excused herself and joined him there for the discussion.

"Thanks for coming over," he said with a sheepish grin.

"Hey, how do you even have a *conversation* about 'Group Sex' without a group?"

"Have you tried it?" he asked.

"No, but I've always wondered about it. In some ways it sounds like a lot of fun. How about you?"

No one stood at "Child Free Marriage," "Single Parenthood," "Synergamous," "Secret Affair," "Celibate Monogamy," or "Life Long Chastity/Celibacy."

After 10 minutes, Bill called "time," and asked the participants to move to a different heading. This time, "Commune," "Open Ended," "Swinging," and "Synergamous," attracted far more interest. "Celibate Monogamy," and "Lifelong Chastity/Celibacy," remained unattended.

When we came back together as a group, we processed the "advantages" and "disadvantages" of each. The most commonly cited advantages of relationships that were not traditionally monogamous were "increased opportunities to grow," "sexual variety and excitement," "more access to sources of support," and "freedom to explore wants and needs." The most commonly cited disadvantages were "jealousy," "lack of clear boundaries," and "increased risk of contracting a sexually transmitted disease."

"What was that like to do?" Bill asked when we had finished summarizing our small group discussions.

"It was fun," Wendy said, "because it was *safe*. We could say anything, or ask anything, without worrying about what someone was going to think about us. That was nice."

"It *was* nice," Margaret added. "It's my guess that most of my friends would love the chance to just talk about these options. It doesn't mean that you're going to act on any of it. It's just nice to be able to say, 'Hey, I've thought about that too'."

"It sure challenges 'ignorance' and 'secrecy,' doesn't it?" Pam affirmed.

"I was a little worried in the beginning that you were going to make us feel silly about choosing 'Traditional Monogamy,' as if it was outdated or oppressive or something," Maggie said to Bill. "But I felt free to go where I wanted, and say what I wanted, and I was really pleased that there were so many other people where I stood."

"I wouldn't want you to feel silly about *any* choice you made," Bill assured her. "Again, this is about getting in touch with *your* values. We need to ask ourselves, 'Why am I drawn to the choices that I'm making? And are my choices consistent with my values?' Do you remember how we talked earlier in the week about theologies A, B, and C? Those theologies determine for you which of these choices you find not only attractive, but *acceptable* for yourself. The significant second question is whether our theologies allow us to find acceptable the choices made by others."

Chapter Forty-Nine

Leona's Map

"Let's check in with each other before we process the last session, and move onto Leona's map, shall we?" I said as the members of our SAR group all settled into their usual spots around the circle.

"I'm in no hurry to do my map," Leona assured us with a chuckle, "so take as long as you like to talk."

"I found the last session interesting," Charlie said. "It felt good to be able to put names on the different lifestyles, and to see them as *choices*. I knew about most of them, except for maybe that syngemorphous ... "

"Synergamous," I corrected.

"Right. That thing," Charlie laughed.

"I actually have a couple of good friends who are in a synergamous relationship," I said. "One of the men has a gay partner on one side of the country, and a wife and grown children on the other."

"Don't be going and giving Charlie any ideas, Brian," Maggie scolded. "I think I can speak for your wife, Charlie, in saying 'Don't even think about it'!"

Charlie led the laughter, which eventually caught Maggie in its wave, and prompted a big grin and sigh of exhaustion from her. Charlie rose, walked around the room to Maggie, gave her a big kiss on the cheek, and sat back down.

"I don't want to leave this group," Dom said.

"Me neither," Wendy replied, shaking her head slowly.

"We've got this and one more full session together. Let's keep the magic going," I said. "Does anyone else have anything they'd like to say about the last session, or about anything else that we've covered so far this week?"

"No, but I'd like to point out that Beatrice looks mighty sleepy today," Leona said with an innocent look. "Didn't you get much sleep last night?"

"As a matter of fact, I didn't," Beatrice lightheartedly replied as she blushed crimson and shook her head in disbelief. "Ben and I laid under the stars and talked most of the night. It was wonderful. He's an amazing man."

"And how's he as a lover?" Leona asked with raised eyebrows of anticipation.

"Leona!" Dom and Wendy said in unison.

"What? I just asked a simple question. And if she answers that one, I have some others for her."

"Okay, moving right along," I interjected.

"I love you, Leona," Beatrice said.

"Me too," Kevin piped in.

"Me three," said Dom as Maggie, Margaret, and Wendy nodded their heads in affirmation.

"You all are going to make me blush," she replied, looking for a second as if she was working to control her emotions.

"Do you feel up to showing us your map?" I asked.

"Sure, I can do that," she said as she reached down to the floor and pulled her folded newsprint out of her participant packet. "But before I go and show you this thing, I have a few things I want to say."

"Why doesn't that surprise me?" Charlie said.

"Shut up, Charlie," Leona shot back with a menacing smile.

"It's all yours, Leona" I said.

"Okay. Well, as some of you know, I did *not* want to come here to this workshop," she said slowly as she looked around the room at each of us. "My director *sent* me, and it felt to me as if I was being 'punished' or something. As if I had done something wrong. I think if she was here, she'd say I have an *attitude* problem, and I can't say that I'd disagree. I think I'm a damn good educator. I seem to be real effective with the kids.

But I don't bother with political correctness, if you know what I mean. If I don't like something, I say so. It's just the way I am.

"Anyway, as I was saying, I didn't want to come here because I thought it was going to be all of these white folks sitting around taking notes and talking about how successful their teen pregnancy-prevention programs back home were. I never expected to meet anybody like Charlie, or Kevin, or Maggie here, or any of you, for that matter. And I didn't expect that I was going to have to make my own bed, clear my own dishes, or room with a transsexual lesbian either! I spent the first night here on a lumpy old couch thinking I was going to get attacked or something in the middle of the night. I moved out of Betty's room the next day, and to tell you the truth, I regret it more than anything else I've done in a long time, except maybe cause you pain, Charlie, by shooting off my mouth about 'homo heaven.' I'm sorry, you all, but I was just not prepared to be surrounded by so many gays and lesbians, and transsexuals.

"But I'm glad I did come. I'm glad I stayed. I'm glad that I'm in this group, and I'm glad that we all didn't sit around talking about nonsense all week. This has been one of the *best* weeks of my life, and I want to thank you all for that."

"And I want to thank *you*, Leona," Charlie said.

"Now, don't go interrupting me, Charlie, or I'll never get through this. I'm on a roll," she replied with an appreciative smile, and then fixed her gaze on the coffee table and the folded piece of newsprint. After a moment of silently staring at it, she drew her breath, unfolded the map, slowly and gently pressed out its creases with her hands, and said, "Now, I'm no drawer like Wendy, so don't expect much."

Before us sat a series of several stick-figure drawings, all in black, with one figure outlined in a big, shimmering, yellow, starlike frame.

"So here we go. I grew up in Washington, D.C. My daddy worked for the city and had a second job at night as a security guard. My momma worked in the cafeteria at the high school. There are five of us kids. Charlene, she's the oldest, that's her in that star there, Roy, me, and the twins, Florence and Milton.

"The two most important people to me growing up were my grandma, who lived in Roanoke, Virginia, and my sister Charlene. She's six years older than I am.

"As I understand it, we're supposed to put down the things that influenced us the most in our sexuality. Well, here I am at my grandma's, that I just *loved* to visit, and that's her banister in her house, and there's

Charlene and her friend Dorothy. Dorothy, who was a couple years younger than Charlene, and her brother Clarence, who was the same age as Charlene, were real close to us, like cousins, and they used to come with us to Roanoke when we visited my grandma. Which was just fine with my grandma. She was *the* most welcoming person you ever met. And she was the *happiest*. Nothing flustered her. Not even me and my sassy mouth. I loved being around my grandma. She always made me feel real special, like I was her favorite. But I knew that I wasn't. She treated everyone like that, like they were the reason she got up in the morning.

"When Grandma and I were alone in the kitchen together, she'd say 'Leona, tell me a story.' I used to be real good at making up fun stories. Grandma *loved* my stories.

"Okay, so I already told you about this time I slid down the banister, and Charlene and Dorothy knew I was feeling something special. I told you that, right? Well, when I was thinking about it, I thought that one of the reasons it felt so good to me, and why it was such a *good* experience was that it was happening in my grandma's house, where I felt safe and loved, and it happened with my sister Charlene, who was like my momma. Charlene's just about the nicest person you'll ever meet, unless she gets angry, and then, get out of the way. You do *not* want to make Charlene angry."

"Leona, I'm sorry for interrupting, but how old were you in this picture here?" Margaret asked softly.

"Six. I was six," she said. "Charlene was twelve. Roy was 10, and the twins were like three."

"Thank you."

"Okay, so here you see me when I was 10 and you see that I have a real sad look on my face. That's Clarence. He's sixteen, and as I said, he was like family, like a big brother. And that's his erect penis, which he got me to touch and then told me to lick it." Here she stopped, took a deep breath, and said slowly and softly, "And then he tried to put it in my mouth."

We sat silently together for a moment. Leona then continued at a faster rate.

"We were at my grandma's, and we were outside, just the two of us. I was playing on the swing, and he called me over to the shed and said he wanted to show me something. When he tried to push his penis in my mouth, I started coughing, and then I started crying, and he shook me and said 'Shut up. Shut up. I was only playing. Don't be a cry baby.' And he said if I told anyone, he'd say I was just making it up, just like I always do.

"I got real screwed up after that for a long time. I started not wanting to go to my grandma's house because I knew Clarence would be there. My grandma got real concerned. She said to Charlene, 'Something's wrong with that girl. Something's not right.' Charlene said she thought so too, and then one day she made me tell her. She said 'Something happened to you, and you're going to tell me!' I told her that she would think I made it up, and she promised me that she wouldn't. So, I told her what Clarence did, and she hugged me, and went right to my momma that night.

"Momma said, 'Leona, are you *sure*? You know how you like to tell stories. I can't believe that Clarence would do anything like that. Maybe you were just dreaming.'

"I was sorry I ever said anything. My momma started looking at me funny. Charlene got really angry but she didn't say anything at first. But the next time we all went to Grandma's, Charlene waited until everyone was in the same room, and she got right into Clarence's face, and told him that if he *ever* came near me again she was going to make him wish he hadn't. Clarence, of course, cried, and said I was making the whole thing up. My momma was very embarrassed, and said she was sure there was a 'misunderstanding,' and that it was best just forgotten. Charlene started yelling at Momma and stormed out of the house, but then Grandma spoke up and in a voice as calm and clear as if she was talking about how good the pie was, she explained that Clarence wouldn't be coming back to the house anymore.

"So, here you see Charlene in a big, gold star. She was my hero, and she stuck up for me all the time. But even though she and Grandma did believe me, my momma not believing me had a big impact. She kept looking at me funny and I started not liking my body very much. I sat alone and watched TV a lot, and I gained some weight. In high school, I didn't date much. I had a bad body image. I guess I had two boyfriends by the time I was a senior. Then I met William. That's William and me. We had both volunteered to decorate the gym for a school dance, and he asked me if I'd go with him. So I went, and we had a good time. He was a dancing fool. And we started going together. William said he thought I was the most beautiful woman he had ever seen. He said he had his eyes on me for two years, but was too shy to ask me out.

"William wasn't the first person I had sex with, but he was the first person who made me feel 'sexy.' He'd just sit there and look at me laying naked on the bed and he'd say 'You are so beautiful. You are my *queen*.' He was something else, and he helped me think that maybe I was too. So, William and I got married at the end of our senior year.

"William started in at the post office right after high school. I went to D.C. Teacher's College to get my teacher's certificate. At first we lived with his parents, and then we got a little apartment in the city. When I graduated, I started working at Anacostia High School in southeast Washington. I taught social studies, and guess I did pretty good at it. I got a 'Teacher of the Year' award from the district in '92.

"William and I didn't have any kids. William couldn't. But we were very happy. Very happy for nearly thirty years. That man made me feel like a million bucks. Charlene and her husband, Dwayne, loved him. We used to get together with them, and our friends Tyrone and Celia, for Thanksgiving, Christmas, birthdays, Easter, you name it. Then William had a heart attack, right on the job. He was delivering mail on a beautiful summer day six years ago. He said 'good bye' that morning. He told me that he loved me, as he always did, and he dropped dead at 46. He was the love of my life, and there will never be another like him. Never!

"It was real hard for me the first couple of years. Tyrone was great about checking in on me. He and Celia had me over a lot. So did Charlene and Dwayne.

"At first, teaching was a good distraction, but then school got to be too rough for me. Maybe I just got too old for it. I don't know, but I just wasn't up for it anymore. Metal detectors, cops in the hallway, drug testing, gangs, fights, no discipline, no respect. And then Dwayne got sick, and I just had enough. I quit three years ago. I took a couple of years off to be with Charlene, and I started with Planned Parenthood a year ago."

"What happened to Dwayne?" Maggie asked when Leona stopped for a sip of her ice tea.

"He died of AIDS," she replied. "We had no idea he had it either. We had no idea how he could have gotten it. But four years ago, he started getting really sick. Charlene begged him to go to the doctor to find out what was wrong. He finally broke down and told her what was wrong. He had AIDS, and he had been infected for a long time. He was sneaking his medications, hoping that he'd be fine. He was afraid that if Charlene, and the people at the church where he was a deacon, found out that his life would be over. But it caught up to him. Charlene took care of him until he died."

"Does she know how he got AIDS?" Dom asked.

"It was like Lloyd talked about earlier," Leona said. "He had a double life. He was a 'DL,' a down low, a bisexual or a homosexual, whatever, who had a marriage with Charlene, and who fooled around with other men. Who would have known it? Not one of us suspected. No one *would* suspect it. And not only did he infect himself," she said, her shaking voice rising in anger, "but he infected Charlene too."

Here she breathed two or three times and continued more calmly, "but Charlene is fine. Her health is good. She takes her medication and she hasn't had a sick day yet, knock on wood."

"I'm sorry," Wendy said. "I know that it's very scary, Leona, but HIV is a treatable disease today that most people can live with for a long, long time."

"I know. I know," she said with an appreciative smile but sadly. "It's just that she's so wonderful, it makes me sick to think of her having to deal with this."

"Leona, there's one more drawing on your map," Beatrice said gently. "What does the heart with the man inside, and the question marks mean?"

"Oh, that's Tyrone," she laughed. "Celia died of cancer about a year after Dwayne passed away. Tyrone's always been a wonderful friend, but I think he'd like it to be more than that with us. I've been keeping things real simple with him, just friends, because I don't think I'd ever be happy with anyone other than William. He spoiled me rotten. But just the same, all of these movies this week, and all of that lovemaking, not to mention seeing Ben in his hot red bathing trunks with that gorgeous body of his, has made me thinking maybe Leona has been missing out on something good for too long a time. So, maybe Tyrone will get a phone call when I get home on Saturday."

Everyone laughed and clapped together as Leona beamed a mischievous look of anticipation.

For the next few moments, Leona responded to questions about her story, and about how it was to do her map, and present it to us. Kevin then asked, "You said in the beginning that you really regret moving out of the room you shared with Betty. Have you told her that?"

"No, and I need to," she said. "If I could undo what I did, I would in an instant. I want to tell her that. I really do. I just haven't been able to figure out the time and the place."

Chapter Fifty

Alison and Dick on Aging

In *A Rose by Any Other Name,* the short film that began the session on "Sexuality and Aging," an elderly woman named Rose was threatened with expulsion from her assisted care facility if she didn't quit leaving her room at night and crawling into bed with her senior male romantic interest. Her behavior was considered scandalous, and she was reprimanded severely by the director of the clinic, and by her own daughter, for such "inappropriate" and "unladylike" conduct. Rose initially relented, but she and her male partner felt emotionally tortured by the regulation that forbid such inter-resident intimacy. Rose finally rebelled, and ultimately paid the price for her defiance of the rules.

Dick and Alison came to the front of the room when the lights were turned back on, took seats together facing one another, and began reflecting in casual conversation on the implications to them, and to all of us, of the message that older people should *not* be sexual.

"There are many issues that are brought up in this film," Dick started out in his authoritative manner, "but the one piece of it that most upsets me, Alison, is the attempt that was made to make Rose feel *ashamed* of her sexual feelings."

"Children don't like to think of their parents as 'sexual,' do they, Dick?" Alison concurred. "Not even *adult* children."

"We come up against this over and over again, this cultural bias about the lack of sexual feelings among seniors," Dick said with exasperation.

"We thought we'd take a few minutes to brainstorm with you on why we have this cultural bias," Alison said, turning her body and her attention to the participants.

"Yes, before we begin talking between ourselves about our own lives, we'd like to hear what you think about this matter," Dick said, now also facing the group. "If Rose had been *your* mother, how might you have felt about her liaison with the gentleman in her nursing home, and why?"

"I'd say, 'Go for it!' If others don't like it, that's their problem," Marjorie responded strongly.

"But, I'd want to make sure she wasn't being used," Joanne said. "We're assuming that Rose had all of her faculties."

"Yes, of course," Dick said, "but the question is, do we think of Rose as having sexual needs, and do we believe that she has the *right* to have them satisfied?"

"Yes, she is sexual, and yes, she has the right to have her needs met," Leona replied from her seat next to Kevin.

"How about hearing from some of the men?" Alison said. "What if Rose was *your* mother? And would you feel differently if we were talking about the sexual needs of her male companion? Do you think he has sexual feelings at his age and, if so, does *he* have the right to have them fulfilled?"

"I *hope* he has sexual feelings at that age," Dom said. "I'd like to think that I'll *never* lose mine, and I sure wouldn't want someone treating me like a child and telling me that I couldn't have my needs met. I'm an adult. Who's to tell me what's right for me? And, I'd guess that it would be the same for women."

"That's big of you," Wendy said smiling as she jabbed him in the ribs with her elbow.

"But I have to admit that if it was *my* mother," he continued, rubbing his side with his hand, "I'd have a hard time thinking of *her* climbing in bed with some old geezer in a nursing home."

"Careful, you're getting very close to home," Dick admonished gently.

"Sorry, Dick. If it was you, I'd have no problem," Dom replied with a red-faced grin.

"I think it's about body image," Ben said. "Going back to your original question about why there's a cultural bias against seniors being sexual, I think it's because we think of sex as being between two, young, trim, able-bodied people."

"White, and of opposite sexes," Lloyd added.

"I'm sure you're right. I don't know as much about that, Lloyd, as I do about the 'able-bodied' part. Most people don't think of people with disabilities as being sexual, or of having any sexual needs," Ben said.

"We know differently," Leona chimed in.

"Good," Ben laughed. "Then we've learned at least *one* important new thing this week. But older people, like people with disabilities, aren't seen as having the right bodies for sex."

"I also think it has to do with many people thinking of sex as 'dirty.' Some people use the expression, 'Doing the nasty'," Marjorie offered. "Nice people, 'nice' women especially, aren't supposed to have sexual thoughts. And orgasm is viewed as a loss of control. Our grandparents are not supposed to be 'nasty' or to lose control. We want them doing 'nice' things like baking cookies and fixing broken bikes."

"But we deny them their humanness," Margaret added.

"Yes, we do," Alison affirmed solemnly.

"You all are bringing up some very important points," Dick said. "We seem to have a very narrow idea of who can and should be sexual, and we also seem to have a double standard about the sexuality of women and of men. That reminds me of the old Sophie Tucker and Maurice Chevalier joke. It seems that Sophie and Maurice were having an argument about their choice of lovers. Each was 80 and was dating someone a quarter of their age. Maurice said to Sophie, 'Isn't it too bad that the world looks at you and thinks "Poor Sophie Tucker. She's so desperate that she has to go out with a 20-year-old." But they look at me and they say, "Good for Chevalier! He still has it, and can attract the attention of a woman who is so young".' To which Sophie Tucker replied, 'Oh, Maurice, you're just jealous.' 'Why would I be jealous?' he asked. 'Because everyone knows that 20 can go into 80 many more times than 80 can go into 20'."

George and Maggie clapped with delight from their seats in the front row, and were joined in laughter by the others.

"That's a wonderful story, Dick. And I, for one, love Sophie's attitude. But, let's get back, shall we, to the concerns we have about most seniors, women and men, being denied their sexuality. I particularly want to talk about the need for older people to be *touched*. Most older people are *not* touched, and yet we crave touch just as much as any person at any age. Rose and her male partner hungered for the intimacy that came with touch."

"We saw that in Jessie Potter's film earlier in the week," Dick added, "how many older people will pay to have their hair shampooed and cut just to be touched."

"Another way that people guarantee that they'll be touched is by getting a massage," Alison added. "That's something very high on my list of sexually-pleasurable experiences. It allows me to get back in touch with my body and all of its wonderful sensations."

"Me too. It's nonsense to think that you aren't sexual until the day you die."

"Well, we're here to set the record straight, aren't we, Dick? Get the message out. Older people have sexual feelings and sexual needs, and many of us are making sure those needs are met," she said strongly and then beamed to the appreciative applause.

"I'm 86-years-old. I've been married to the same woman for more than 60 years, and have raised five incredible children. I've been sexual throughout my life, and I have *no* intention of stopping," Dick said, turning again to face Alison.

"Me neither," said Alison, shifting her body to face Dick. "And I'm 76. I was widowed at 55, after raising three sons and a daughter, and I fully intend to stay sexual for the remainder of my life. But Dick, why don't we talk a little bit about what we mean when we say that we're 'sexual'?"

"Well, it's certainly not just sticking an erect penis into a vagina," he explained in his aristocratic manner.

"It's *attitude*, isn't it?" she offered.

"For me, it's about being open to experiencing my body and my feelings of attraction," he said. "And, if I so choose, consistent with my values, to express myself in any number of satisfying ways."

"That's right! When I see a handsome man, I might have a response in my body," added Alison enthusiastically. "When I see a bunch of guys on the football field in a huddle, for instance, I might think to myself, 'Wow, aren't those cute butts!' Being sexual means being open to your senses, to sight, sound, smell, taste, and touch, and to celebrate those feelings as good and wholesome. Many women experience their sexuality, for instance, through reading, thus the great popularity of romance novels. Being sexual means having an attitude that says 'I have feelings and needs, and I'm open to exploring those feelings and needs'."

"One of the great advantages I see in aging," Dick said, "is that you can let go of a lot of fears of what people might be thinking about you. Where before, when we were young, we were so conscious of a million things that stopped us from experiencing our sexuality fully. Poor body image, for instance, has prevented vast numbers of people from being in touch with their sexuality. At my age, I feel I have a very positive body image. Oh, that doesn't mean that everything works as I wish it would. I love to garden, and it's harder and harder for me to kneel down to do the planting and the weeding. But, for the most part, I'm very happy with the way I look. For example, I've become quite proud of my boobs."

Here he stood and gently cupped each of his large breasts in his massive hands. Several of the participants laughed and clapped with delight.

"There was a time that this might have bothered me, but not today. I enjoy the way they look, and I'm proud of them."

"I'm jealous," Carla said from her seat in the second row.

"You actually enjoy being naked, don't you Dick?" Alison continued with a big smile of approval.

"Oh, yes, very much," he said as he sat back down. "I enjoy the feeling of fresh air on my body. When I mention my interest in nudity, the typical response is, 'But after all, Dick, wouldn't you agree that 95 percent of human bodies look better off with clothes *on*?' And I ask if 95 percent of dogs and horses would look better clothed. What is so disgusting about human bodies? We'd all be better off if we could shed such inhibitions, and learn to appreciate the beauty of bodies of all types."

"I remember several years ago when I was in my sixties attending a weekend seminar in California. One evening, several of the participants had climbed into the hot tub, so I decided to join them. I didn't have a negative body image, but I don't think it was quite as positive as it is today. And I recall being quite surprised when a woman commented to me, 'Alison, you have beautiful breasts,' and I thought to myself, 'Why, yes I do, don't I?' I merely said 'thank you' though."

"Being able to appreciate our bodies is a very important component of sexual health," Dick said.

"Dick, do you remember the time a few years ago here at Thornfield when we all went down to the lake one evening for an AIDS memorial service? It was a very solemn event. When we finished our ritual of casting flowers on the lake in memory of people we loved who had died of AIDS, we stood around in silence not really knowing how to end the ceremony. I remember you whispering to me, 'Alison, you up for a swim?' and before you knew it, we each had our clothes off, and were out in the water, moving gently among the floating flowers. Do you remember that?"

"Now that you mention it," he said, "I do. Again, one of the advantages of getting older is one's increased willingness to try new things, to be inventive, to take risks, and not to worry so much about what others think. You, yourself, Alison, decided at age 69 to enter the Peace Corps. You were gone from this program for a couple of years as I recall."

"I was, Dick. I missed you all terribly, but I was fulfilling a dream by entering the Peace Corps. I spent my 70th birthday there. That decision was tied into my sexuality too, wasn't it. It was about experiencing myself as a woman, fully capable of taking on new challenges. It was a very gratifying and empowering experience. But Dick, you truly are *my* model of growth. I've watched in awe as you would try new things. Like learning to juggle, or rolling down the hill in your late 70s, or walking up to the board and signing your name as a bisexual. Talk a little about that if you would."

"I feel as if I've always had an interest in growing beyond comfortable boundaries," he replied. "Juggling looked like fun. I wasn't very good at it, but I had fun trying. Rolling down the hill was something that I used to enjoy as a boy, and I felt that there was no good reason why I shouldn't continue to do so. When I saw the others doing it for fun, I thought, 'Why not?' With regards to bisexuality, I've lived my whole life as a heterosexual. I've never really entertained homosexual thoughts or feelings. But, being here at Thornfield for the past decade and listening each year to Brian and Carol and the others talk about their lives, I've tried to imagine myself on a desert island with another man, and I've asked myself whether I could be sexually intimate in such a situation, and I concluded that I think I probably could. It wouldn't be my first choice, but I could certainly respond to affection. That prompted me to conclude that I was probably bisexual and, I suspect, the majority of the population is too. Cultural norms stop us from considering it, but I think I agree with Jung that everyone has bisexual potential."

"Dick, why don't we talk a little bit more about some of the challenges that face seniors sexually?" Alison said. "We've talked about the cultural attitudes that older people are not sexual, and that they don't need or want to be touched. I'd also like to add, as a single woman, that older women in my situation are *invisible*. We have no status without a husband. And sometimes, we're even seen as a 'threat.' I remember when Ernie died, very few couples were willing to include me in their social events. I knew my true friends were the ones who would invite me over. Getting out and putting yourself in situations where you might meet a new partner can be very challenging."

"But you've done so admirably," Dick said. "You seem to know no fear about taking on new challenges."

"Oh, I have fear, all right, Dick. I just try to not let it get in the way of living my life. But, let's you and I talk now a bit about the *physical* challenges that seniors will face in their lives, shall we? You mentioned in the beginning that sexuality was not just about inserting an erect penis into a vagina. I'd like to add into an anus. And I'm not just referring to gay men here, though gay men and lesbians get older too, and we're talking about their sexuality also, aren't we. But the truth is, for many men as they get older, getting or maintaining an erect penis can be a real challenge. Our bodies change as we get older. It's just a fact of life. Not only does our skin begin to wrinkle and sag, but our hormones become depleted and this has an effect upon women's ability to lubricate, and men's ability to penetrate. There are, today, means of addressing those issues, such as hormone replacement and Viagra, but they are nevertheless commonly experienced challenges."

"And for some people, such problems indicate for them the loss of their youth and of their sexuality. But that's nonsense and completely unnecessary," Dick said. "There are multiple ways of being sexual with one's partner."

"And of experiencing orgasms," Alison added.

"As you say, Alison, there are means of addressing the challenges that come up. You mentioned that women lubricate less easily. A little KY jelly takes care of that, but I actually prefer spit. I do so for three reasons. First, it's always available. Second, it's naturally warm and you never run out. And third, and this appeals to my Scottish heritage, it's free."

"Regarding the challenges some men have in getting or maintaining an erection, as we say, there is Viagra, as well as a couple of other products on the market," Alison said, "but there's also the possibility of being sexual *without* penetration. You don't need to penetrate to be a 'real' man, and you don't have to have an erection to have an orgasm."

"That's right!" he concurred excitedly. "We need to free ourselves up and use our imaginations. There are any number of wonderful ways of pleasing yourself and your partner. Massage, masturbation, oral stimulation, and digital stimulation of the clitoris and of the anus are all possibilities."

"The important thing is to talk openly and honestly with your partner, if you have one, about what is pleasing to you, and to him or to her,"

Alison said, "and if you don't have a partner, to be open to the options at hand, so to speak."

A few groans at the pun made her giggle.

"Mechanical or otherwise," she added with a grin, and then said more seriously, "Obviously, this is all within the framework of what you find acceptable for yourself, given your particular values. My values encourage me to live fully and with joy until the day I die. To wear purple more often and to carry an umbrella less, as the famous poem on aging goes."

"Will you be my mother?" Thomas pleaded from his seat in the front row.

"Mine too," Maggie said.

"It would be my pleasure," Alison smiled warmly back at each of them, "but if your own mothers are still alive, believe that the same passion for life burns within them. Our ability to manifest it is impacted by the circumstances of our journeys."

"Now don't go selling yourself short," Dick admonished. "Given the exact same opportunities, not everyone will choose to continue to grow as you have."

"Why, thank you, Dick. And as have you."

Chapter Fifty-One

The Universe as a "Turn On"

During the lunch break, George and Maggie started a wave of people rolling down the grassy hill toward the lake. Dick stood by and yelled enthusiastic encouragement as Thomas, Lloyd, Grace, Wendy, Gina, Lisa, and Margaret lay down and followed suit. Squeals of laughter filled the air around the dining room.

At a nearby picnic table, Bill met with those participants interested in getting academic credit for the week from Widener University. Grace hurried up the hill, grass stains on her khaki shorts, and breathlessly joined the group that included Betty, Beatrice, Tonya, Judith, and Ben.

Kevin took his plate of macaroni and cheese and tossed salad to the middle of the lawn, away from the "rollers," and sat alone, his legs folded, and his eyes keenly focused on the lake below. Beside him sat his Canon digital "Rebel" camera, which he hadn't taken out of his room since the first day.

Spotting Kevin seated alone, Peter gathered the courage to join him, and began heading out of Huntington when he spotted Dan cutting over from Peabody in Kevin's direction. Turning around, Peter saw Annette sitting at a table with Martha and Beverly, and decided to join their conversation about religious practice in Trinidad.

"Take my picture," Dan said grinning sexily as he plopped himself down next to Kevin.

The hot July sun comforted the weary bodies of the different groups who had stretched out on the lawn, and had closed their sleep-deprived eyes.

"I'm so tired," moaned Paula.

"You need to go to bed earlier," admonished Joanne.

"Look who's talking!" Paula replied with astonishment.

The meetings, picture taking, and sun bathing were soon brought to a close with Gail's ringing of the school bell. When we all had found our places in the upstairs of Ridings, Bill beamed with a smile of excitement as he prepared to pull the week of presentations together for us, and to offer us his theory on "The Universe as a Turn On."

"Here we are at the end of our five-day SAR," he began, "and we're going to take just a moment to reflect together on the process. Then, I'm going to offer you a *new* paradigm in thinking about this fascinating subject of our 'sexuality.'

"When we came together for our first full day last Sunday, we talked about this program of 'Sexual Attitude Reassessment' as being an opportunity to explore our *feelings* and assess our *values* about our own sexuality, and that of others. As you recall, we described the various components of 'Sexual Beingness,' as 'Sensuality,' 'Intimacy,' 'Sexual Identity' 'Sexual Health and Behavior,' and 'Sexualization.' Do you remember? We also defined 'sexual health,' using the words of the World Health Organization, as 'the integration of the physical, emotional, intellectual, and social aspects of sexual being, in ways that are positively enriching, and that enhance personality, communication, and love.' They also said that it was 'freedom from fear, shame, guilt, false beliefs, and other psychological facts that inhibit sexual response and impair sexual relationships'," he quoted by rote, once again.

"Then we suggested that there were three major obstacles to our sexual health. Can anyone tell me what those are?"

"Ignorance, secrecy, and trauma," Dom said confidently.

"That's right! Good, Dom. Ignorance, secrecy, and trauma," Bill repeated excitedly. "And we spent a lot of time together in both the large group, and in our smaller discussion groups exploring how ignorance, secrecy, and trauma *have* impacted our individual abilities to feel 'sexually healthy,' or 'sexually fulfilled.' In the large group, Ben, Kevin, Carol, and Brian all told us their stories, and of how they've had to face obstacles to experiencing their sexuality fully. Alison and Dick just did the same for us. Ignorance and secrecy are particularly challenging issues for people who grew up in their generation. Back in your small groups, we each also told our stories as we shared the maps of our sexual histories.

"In the midst of it all, we talked about our *theologies*, and how our theologies guide us and confront us as we navigate through *our* sexual feelings and behaviors, and through the sexual feelings and behaviors of *others*.

"We did all of this in a format that bombarded us with stimuli, through explicit films, stories, and guided imageries that forced us to leave our comfort zones on a variety of topics. The theory behind this format is that if we succeed in raising our anxieties high enough about these often uncomfortable subjects, we will have a breakthrough. The anxiety will drop, and we will become 'educable.' My guess is that those of you who came to get lesson plans, for instance, on how to talk to teenagers about homosexuality, are much better prepared today to implement those programs than you would have been had you showed up on Sunday and were handed by Carol and Pam a copy of that lesson plan."

"You've got that right," Dom said, nodding his head enthusiastically.

"No question," added Leona.

"I hoped you'd say that," Bill replied with a grateful grin. "The SAR has three components: Evaluation of our Sexual Attitudes, Knowledge Building, and Skill Building. We hope that we've succeeded with the first two goals. Tomorrow, we focus on 'Skill Building' during our daylong workshops. Any questions?"

"It's a great model, Bill," Margaret replied. "I can't tell you how much I've learned this week. I don't want it to end."

"Well, it's not over yet," he said with a conspiratorial smile. "Are you ready for just a bit more anxiety?"

"No more anxiety, *please*," pleaded Maggie with a playful grimace.

"It may not create any anxiety for you," Bill assured her. "Around the room, you'll see newsprint with the numbers '0' through '6.' This represents the Kinsey Scale on sexual orientation. Using this scale to indicate only *thoughts* and *feelings*, not 'behavior' or 'identity,' I'd like you to go place yourself on the scale, as you are comfortable doing. You have the right to pass. You can do so by staying seated, or by walking to a number with which you feel the greatest comfort. Do you all remember what the numbers represent?"

"Why don't you remind everyone?" Pam coaxed.

"The number '0' represents exclusive heterosexual feelings," he explained. "And '1' is for predominantly heterosexual, but with *incidental* homosexual feelings. 'Two' is mostly heterosexual with *significant* homosexual feelings. 'Three' represents equal feelings of sexual attraction for men and for women. 'Four' is mostly homosexual feelings, but *significant* feelings of attraction for the other gender. 'Five' is predominantly homosexual with *incidental* heterosexual attractions. And '6' represents exclusive homosexual feelings of attraction. All clear? Okay, let's move now to the place on the continuum that best represents our feelings."

"This is easy," Maggie said loudly as she stood to head to the '0,' and then felt awful embarrassment as she spotted Peter staying seated while those around him moved in different directions. "Sorry," she whispered as she passed him.

Peter watched the participants place themselves around the small semicircle of numbers. Dom, Chuck, Curtis, Ben, and Joe stood, or sat, confidently at '0,' along with Grace, Gail, Annette, Tonya, Maggie, and Leona. Most of the other women joined Dick at '1.' Carla stood at '2,' along with Judith. Lisa stood at '3' with Charlie, but Charlie eventually inched his way closer to '4' as the others found their places, and conversations ensued. The '6' end of the scale drew Gina, Wendy, Thomas, Lloyd, Dan, and George. I was just slightly over the '6' line toward '5,' but not as far as Kevin, Betty, and Carol.

Bill looked sympathetically at Peter, who sat alone in the center of the room. Peter looked up from the floor, saw Bill's wink, sighed deeply, and rose from his chair. For a moment, as he stood tall and still and locked his eyes with Bill's, the room grew very quiet. Peter then nodded his head slightly, smiled serenely, and walked slowly to Kevin's side.

For a few seconds, no one said a word, and then, led gently by Alison and Pam on the other side of the room, quiet conversations began again among the participants.

"Well, well, well," Dan said. "It's about time."

"Shut up, Dan!" Kevin demanded as he turned back to face him, his nostrils flaring.

"What?" Dan asked incredulously.

"He said 'Shut up'!" Thomas and Lloyd said simultaneously

"Well, fuck me," Dan said shaking his head with astonishment.

"Looks like your options are getting more limited," George whispered audibly, "unless you're into us full-figured gals."

Kevin reached over, squeezed Peter's hand, and smiled at him with admiration, and a nod of understanding.

"So how was that?" Bill asked, interrupting the conversations in the various groups.

"Very easy," Chuck said. "A lot easier than it would have been ten years ago," Wendy replied. "Still pretty hard," Carla added. "Scary," Charlie said. "Really scary, but liberating."

"Anyone else?" Bill asked.

Though many people hoped that Peter would speak, he did not. He simply stood, maintained eye contact with Bill, and allowed Kevin to continue to gently squeeze his hand.

"Okay, good," Bill said. "Now, can anyone tell us why I had you identify your feelings by placing yourselves on the Kinsey Scale?"

"To torture us," Carla replied to some appreciative laughter and applause.

"No, though there may be some here who might get 'turned on' to that," he said grinning.

"To help us take responsibility for our feelings? To know them, and to not be afraid to acknowledge them?" Thomas asked.

"Yes!" Bill replied. "If ignorance, secrecy, and trauma are the obstacles to sexual health, and we believe that the qualities of sexual healthy people, as we've said, include 'affirming one's own sexual orientation and respecting the sexual orientation of others,' what better place than here at Thornfield to practice what we've learned. Right?"

"Right!" Marjorie affirmed.

"Good. Then let's now take our seats, and talk some more together about what *really* turns us on.

"We've focused all of our attention this week in our films and in our stories, as well as in the exercise we just did, on our 'sexual orientation,' which is our attraction to *others*. We've explored the question of whether we're 'turned on' sexually by men, by women, or by both. But is that really all that turns us on, that makes our juices flow, that allows us to focus entirely on the pleasure of the moment? Many of you have been experiencing 'turn ons' all week, haven't you? For all of us, there have been a variety of 'turn ons' available to us if we opened ourselves up to the experience. Right? I want you to give me some examples. Besides perhaps being attracted to another person here, or to a person you saw in the films, what comes to mind when you think of being 'turned on'?"

"Sleeping under star-filled skies," Beatrice said after a moment of reflection.

"Yes!" Bill exclaimed as he wrote the words at the top of the newsprint pad.

"Sleeping?" George asked Beatrice incredulously.

"Immersing your body in a freshwater lake," Ben said, ignoring him.

"Good!" Bill said grinning as he wrote.

"Walking barefoot through dewy grass." "Rainbow-colored hot air balloons." "Pornography." "The smell of turkey cooking in the oven." "Skinny dipping." "Massage." "Breasts." "Cocks." "Fly casting." "The touch and smell of leather." "A warm bubble bath." "Getting a pedicure!" "A sexy novel." "Science fiction." "A mother deer and fawns drinking from a pond." "Slow dancing." "Hot apple pie a la mode." "Cross dressing." "Cooking." "Painting." "Snow in the woods." "Bonfires." "Shooting stars." "Walking in the surf." "Opera." "Late night talks with new friends." "Chocolate-covered strawberries." "Thong underwear." "No underwear." "Incense."

"Good!" Bill said. "And there are *thousands* more. Some of them we celebrate. Others we worry are 'pathologies.' How do we know? I've had clients who were directed to therapy by frightened spouses because they were 'turned on' by the smell of underwear taken from the dirty laundry basket. One man and his wife were 'turned on' by rubber sheets. They couldn't have orgasms without them. I once met a man, sent to me by his urologist, who masturbated to pictures of crocodiles. Nothing else turned him on, not even alligators. Carol is handing out to you now a list of the various recognized *paraphilias*. There you'll find categories and descriptions for people who *compulsively* rely upon unusual or 'unacceptable' stimuli to achieve orgasm. These include people who can only be aroused by partners who have, or appear to have, amputated limbs. That's called 'acrotomophilia.' There are people who are only 'turned on' when bondage and discipline are involved, or 'sadomasochism.' Some people are 'turned on' by being defecated upon, which is called 'coprophilia,' or by being urinated upon. Some people are 'turned on' by the thought of sex with animals, others with the thought of sex with children, which is 'pedophilia' or 'ephebophila,' depending upon the age of the child. There are some people who can only reach orgasm while they're cross-dressed. Still others require reading or listening to erotic narrative, which is called 'narratophilia.' The question for us becomes, 'What's the paradigm for these 'turn ons'?' How do we understand them and evaluate them in the full context of our sexuality *and* of our spirituality?

"I have a theory, and let me just say that some people get 'turned on' by their *theories*," he said with his mischievous grin and a little sashay of his butt, "that I believe helps us do just that, to understand and to evaluate our experience of the *universe* as a 'turn-on.' Bob Francoeur has titled it 'Stayton's Paneroticism.' It's based upon my belief that we are born *both* spiritual and sexual. And as Dick and Alison reminded us earlier, we're sexual until our passing from this world. Females, for instance, while still in utero, vaginally lubricate, and males in the womb have erections. These sexual response phenomena continue while we're sleeping, every 40 to 80 minutes, until we die. If human beings respond sexually from before birth until death, then this has important implications for our understanding of our *creation* as sexual beings, with the potential for sexual pleasure as a natural part of our life, doesn't it? It seems to me that one of the major tasks of our lives is integrating into wholeness these two aspects of our being, our sexuality and our spirituality."

Bill then turned, and with a black, dry-erase marker, drew his "Universe as a Turn On" model on the whiteboard. He drew a large circle, the center of which was a smaller circle, which he labeled "I." He then divided the circle into four parts by drawing two parallel lines from north to south, and two parallel lines from east to west. It looked like the intersection of two streets running in different directions, with the small circle in the center of the intersection. On the outside of the circles, he drew Kinsey-type continua of "0" to "6" at north, south, east and west. The continuum on the right-hand side represented our relationship with "Others." It was the traditional Kinsey scale with "Heterosexuality" at the "0" end, and "Homosexuality" at the "6" end.

At the bottom of the circle, the continuum was marked, "Me," and represented our relationship with ourselves, our *self-loving*. At the "0" end of the scale were the words "Self-serving," and at the "6" end were the words "Self-denying."

On the west, or left-hand side of the circle, was a continuum representing our relationships with "It," with "Animate Objects" at "0" and "Inanimate Objects" at "6."

Finally, outside the top of the circle he drew a continuum scale to represent our relationship with the "Thou." Here, "0" represented "Logic, Math, Science, etc.," and "6" represented the "Totally Transcendent Deity."

Bill then explained how the various "turn-ons" he and we had listed fit into the model. Obviously "shooting stars" didn't fit into the "heterosexual to homosexual" continuum, and yet it was a "turn on" for some. It was placed under "Inanimate Objects." So too were rubber sheets, dirty underwear, and skinny dipping. Animals, such as one's pet, a farm animal, and a crocodile were placed at the "Animate" end of the "It" scale.

"Some people are shocked to see the word 'Deity' on this scale, as if it was blasphemous to suggest that a person could get literally 'turned on' in their relationship to God, but Christian writings, and personal testimony, are *filled* with such references. The mystic writings of two medieval saints, Theresa of Avila, and John of the Cross, contain many examples of transcendental erotic expression. From my own youth, I recall fondly the Sunday night 'Singspiration' during which we'd sing the very sensual 'I come to the garden alone, while the dew is still on the roses. And He walks with me, and He talks with me, and He tells me I am His own'," Bill said as he swooned and fanned himself with his two hands.

"On more than one occasion, I've had a nun or a priest come up to me after I have presented this material and say privately, 'Oh, thank you so much. I once had a sexual reaction, an orgasm, while in the midst of deep meditation, and I thought that there was something terribly wrong with me. I thought I was rotten to the core.' I assured them that they were not, that such reactions are not uncommon. But what have we done as a culture to instill such senseless shame?

"It is my thesis that love, spirituality, and sexuality are inextricably bound together. Nature or God's intention seems to be to create persons who are sexual in the fullest sense of the word, with a sexual system that responds to sexual pleasuring. 'And God saw that creation was good.' To restrict sexual pleasuring to the procreational function, and to validate sexual pleasure only when it occurs in heterosexual relationships diminishes the creative capacities God gave humans for expressing love. So, how do we take all of the information we have explored together and work it into a theology of sexual pleasure that is relevant for daily living?

"If 'nature's intention' is to create persons who are fully sexual in every dimension of their relationships, then how do we present this aspect of our creation in a framework that *guides* peoples understanding and appreciation of their sexuality, and their decision-making about it? What pleasures are 'appropriate,' and what are 'not appropriate'? This is the challenge for all of us.

"And how do we make those decisions?" he asked.

"Through our individual value systems," Margaret replied.

"Precisely! If you believe that the sole purpose of sexuality is *procreation*, then you have to oppose every other sexual 'turn on.' That means that we see as 'wrong' being sexually aroused by our experience with God, with science, with all things animate and inanimate," he said crossing out the words with his marker. "There is no being 'turned on' by feelings for ourselves or for others, unless those others are of the opposite sex, and all relations with them are restricted to one person, for life, within the confines of Church-sanctioned marriage, involving only penile-vaginal penetration with the intention of conceiving a child always present.

"If, on the other hand, your values are guided by the belief that *relationship* is the criteria for judging sexual thoughts, feelings, and behaviors, then it opens you up to responding as sexual beings to far more in your life."

"But even then," Dom said, "you have to make a distinction between being 'turned on' by the smell of leather, and being 'turned on' by the body of an 11-year-old girl or boy."

"Yes, of course," Bill replied, "and *that's* where organized religion has, for the most part, failed us. The guidelines for 'life behaviors' of sexually healthy individuals that we offered to you earlier in the week come to us from the Sex Information and Education Council of the United States. And what did SIECUS say about 'sexually healthy,' or a theologian might say sexually *moral*, people?"

"That they discriminate between life-enhancing sexual-behaviors, and those that are harmful to self and to others," Dick replied strongly.

"That they engage in sexual relationships that are characterized by honesty, equity, and responsibility," said Pam.

"That they express their sexuality while respecting the rights of others," Alison offered.

"That they enjoy sexual feelings without necessarily acting upon them," Carol said.

"That they'll prevent sexual abuse," Marjorie added.

"Yes!" Bill affirmed. "Those and other values help us as individuals, and as a culture, to distinguish between which behaviors are appropriate, and which are not. Getting 'turned on' by the smell of leather is appropriate. Sex between an adult and a child is not.

"We have mentioned several times the three obstacles to sexual health, and to a theology that embraces the human experience. They are ignorance, secrecy, and trauma. There is a fourth. It is the Church's inability to *value* sexual pleasure, and its subsequent refusal to include sexual pleasure as a value in Christian education.

"The quest for wholeness and spiritual oneness with God, and with each other, is experienced in every period of history and among all peoples. When the integration of love, sexuality, and spirituality are experienced, God's intention is born anew in the world. Sexual pleasuring does *not* hinder either spiritual growth or service to humanity. On the contrary, it can *enhance* them. The current focus on sexual meaning in our time is a reaction of humans striving to understand the nature of their sexuality. Many are fearful of the implications. Maybe one of those implications will be the rediscovery that the entire universe is our potential sexual orientation, and that we can find sexual pleasure in all dimensions of our lives. That is what I believe. That is what *we* believe here at Thornfield. We encourage you to make your own decisions."

With that, Bill smiled, raised his eyebrows, sighed, and said, "It's time for your final small group sessions."

Chapter Fifty-Two

The Final SAR Group

"Why the glum looks?" I asked as I perused the circle of faces in Higley's living room.

"I don't want this group to end," Maggie moaned. "I want to take you all back to Racine with me."

"Too cold in Racine," Leona replied.

"Wendy and I are talking about getting together in Ohio," Dom said.

"Have you told your wife?" Leona asked.

"That *won't* be an issue," Dom assured her with a cocky grin.

"That depends," Wendy replied. "How cute is your wife?"

"Okay everyone," I gently admonished as Kevin and Margaret laughed, "let's get back to business. This is our last session together. I want to make sure that we've addressed any unanswered questions, and completed any unfinished business. I also want to make sure that we take some time to do 'closure.' There may be things that you want to say to each other before Carol comes around and takes our group picture."

"Do we get copies of the picture?" Maggie asked.

"Absolutely," I replied.

"All right!" she exclaimed excitedly.

"Leona, we left off with you. Do you have anything more that you'd like to say about doing your map?"

"I have something more that I'd like to say, but it isn't about that," she said. "I want to see your and Kevin's maps. Did you think you were going to get away without doing them?"

"You've already heard my story," Kevin protested.

"And mine," I added.

"Maybe, but for one thing, I'd just like to make sure that you *did* them like the rest of us, and second, I think we'd all like the opportunity to ask questions," she replied.

"I know that I have a couple of questions that I'd like to ask," Margaret said.

"Me too," Dom added.

"Okay, I said there might be some 'unfinished business.' Kevin, do you have your map with you?"

"Yes, but I didn't think I was going to have to *show* it. I didn't spend a lot of time making it look good."

"That's all right. Why don't you just unfold it on the coffee table, and then we'll see if there are any questions?"

"Okay," he said with resignation as he unfolded the newsprint on the table and revealed his series of quickly-drawn, stick figure characters. "Well, here's me at the movies, and that's supposed to be James Bond on the screen. And here's me watching that television program on transgender issues. And here's me with Bill Stayton and the group that meets at his office. You see Betty standing next to me. And here's me in the hospital bed having my reassignment surgery, and then here's me at my younger brother Tim's wedding where I was the best man. That last little squiggle is supposed to be the water down at the lake here. Thornfield has really impacted my life. As you can see, I didn't plan on showing this. I thought I was covered when I told my story in the big group. I could have made it prettier."

"The story is what's beautiful," Margaret assured him. "Your pictures don't need to be pretty."

"Thanks," he said.

"Kevin, can I ask you a question?"

"Sure, Wendy," he replied.

"Your story has had a really big impact on me. I thought I was cool on LGBT issues, but I've never spent any time with a female-to-male transsexual. I'm blown away by you. I really am. So, thank you."

"You're welcome," he smiled back.

"My question has to do with the lack of 'romance' in your story. Hasn't there been *anyone* who you've fallen in love with that you wanted to include on your map?"

"Sure, there are people who I've been 'attracted' to, but I haven't had any successful love relationships. Either I fall for the wrong guy or the wrong guy takes an interest in me. I wish I did have someone special to tell you about. To tell you the truth, it makes me very depressed that I don't."

"Now don't try to tell us that gay men aren't interested in you?" Leona said with a raised eyebrow. "You've got them crawling all over you this week, even the ones who aren't supposed to be gay anymore."

"But it never seems to work out," Kevin said with a sad sigh. "I don't know. I guess for some people I'm a 'curiosity,' maybe even a 'challenge.' And some are afraid of my body."

"But you're so *handsome*," Maggie said. "And *sexy*."

"I think I know what Kevin's talking about," Beatrice interjected. "I think Ben has had to go through the same thing. He's good looking, and has a great body, but he never knows if someone has taken an interest in him because of his disability, and he never knows if someone he's interested in will be turned off by their fear of what sex with him might be like."

"Exactly!" Kevin said.

"But you can't live your life worrying about such things," Beatrice said. "One of the things that most attracts me to Ben is his *confidence* in himself as a fully sexual man. He's nice looking but his real appeal comes from his self-confidence. If others are attracted to him out of some sense of 'charity,' they'll be very disappointed. He's not a victim that needs rescuing. And if they pass up the opportunity to be with him because of fear of what sex will be like, it's their loss, not his."

"Are you listening?" I asked Kevin.

"Yes, I'm listening," he smirked.

"Kevin, if I could give you anything, it would be the confidence that you're a very sexy man," Wendy said.

"Even with a 'zut'?" he asked.

"Hey, it's not what you've got … "

"It's what you do with it," Kevin finished her sentence. "I know, I know, but try telling that to a size queen."

"To hell with them," Wendy replied without hesitation. "I say we start promoting 'Zut Power.' It will become the 'in' thing. And if the size queens don't like it, let them screw themselves."

For several minutes, members of the group laughed with Kevin about the proposed new motto. Dom even suggested having T-shirts made up, and felt confident that Dick would wear one proudly. Leona then brought the attention to me.

"Okay, Brian, it's your turn."

Dutifully, I pulled out my map, unfolded it on the table, and displayed drawings that had been shared with many groups before them. Through the past twenty-some years, though, there had been several additions and subtractions. It was in the safe and encouraging climate of Thornfield, for instance, that I first, but not initially, addressed the sexual abuse I experienced as a child, and it was here, more than a decade ago, that I added a wine bottle with the 'not allowed' red circle and slash logo over it to indicate how my new sobriety had profoundly impacted my sexual journey. The poison sign on the bottle of turpentine, and the yellow halo above my head as a child, remained the same, as did the big heart which enveloped Ray and me, and the "Thornfield" road sign.

"You've spoken about most of this in the large group," Margaret said, "but you haven't really said much about Ray. Will you talk about him?"

"If I had my choice, I'd spend the entire week talking about my relationship with Ray," I replied with a broad smile, "but unfortunately, we still need to talk a lot about the *oppression* gay people face, which doesn't leave a lot of time to talk about the *joy*."

"The joy is evident in your life," Margaret countered. "We really *do* need to hear about the loneliness of growing up gay, or at least I do. Your guided imagery really drove the point home for me. Understanding now how gay youths grow up feeling so isolated and afraid will make a big difference in how I approach my youth work back home. But I still want to hear about Ray."

"He's my dearest friend, my soul mate, my lover, my spouse, and the best thing that ever happened to me," I answered. "We met back in 1976, and have been inseparable ever since. We're both one of seven children, both Irish Catholic Midwesterners, both spent time in the seminary or monastery, are both in recovery, and are both serious about growing spiritually. We had a civil union ceremony in Vermont with an amazing 80-year-old justice of the peace on our 25th anniversary, and two years later got married in Ottawa. I can't imagine my life without him."

The group then asked a variety of questions about Ray's and my relationship, our spirituality, and our families' levels of support. Finally, Margaret commented on how very grateful she was that Ray and I had found such great happiness in our lives. She wished the same for all gay people.

I thanked her, and then, feeling that they were out of questions, I folded up my map and brought our attention back to the need to say "good bye" to one another and to the group.

"Quite honestly, I'm feeling a little afraid to leave this group," Charlie said.

"Me too," Maggie jumped in. "I don't want to go home. I like it here. I feel as if you understand me, and support me, even in my wackiness."

"You're not wacky," Charlie protested. "You're perfect, just the way you are."

"You see, that's what I mean," she said. "Here, I'm perfect."

"You're perfect at home too, Maggie," Margaret said. "It's just that you don't feel that way because you can't compete with Barry's attraction to men. If Barry was here, I'm sure he'd say you were perfect too. You're a perfect friend and a perfect mother. You're just not a man."

"Margaret, I'm going to miss having you around," Dom said. "You say things that I'm thinking, but in a way that I just can't. And you have the best insights. Why don't you come back to Ohio with Wendy and me?"

"That's a wonderful offer, Dom, but I've got my hands full back in Indianapolis. If it's okay though, I'd like to go back to Charlie and his opening statement that he's afraid to leave this group. Charlie, will you say more about that?"

"Thank you," I mouthed to Margaret.

"I feel that while I've been in this group, I've been honest for the first time in my life," he said sadly. "I can't talk like this with my family and my friends back in Oklahoma City, and I sure can't talk as openly with the members of my congregation. Talking with you about my bisexual feelings is like deep breaths of fresh air. I don't want to go back to holding my breath."

"But you *can* find some people with whom you can be honest," Beatrice reminded him. "You said that you were going to find a therapist. That's a start, right?"

"It is, but I still feel scared."

"I can understand your feelings, Charlie. They're normal, and to be expected," I assured him. "But I'm only a phone call or an e-mail message away."

"Me too," said Margaret, Maggie, and Beatrice in unison.

"Thanks," he said. "Whoever thought I'd ever stand up as a Kinsey 3?" he asked, shaking his head with disbelief.

"A Kinsey 4," Leona corrected.

"What?" Charlie asked.

"A Kinsey 4," Maggie answered. "You started at '3,' but you ended up at '4'."

"Boy, you guys don't miss a thing, do you?" he laughed.

"Charlie, it's been so helpful to me to have you in this group," Maggie said. "I know that you and Barry are maybe different in your degree of attraction to men, but you're both wonderful men, and watching you struggle with your feelings has really helped me have more understanding and sympathy for Barry. I'm not saying that it's now easy for me, but it's easier."

"Thanks for saying that, Maggie. That means a lot to me to hear," he replied.

"This has been a great group," Beatrice said enthusiastically. "I have learned so much about sexuality, and about my own values. I can't tell you how powerful this week has been for me."

"Yea, I want to thank everyone," Wendy said. "Dom, Beatrice, Margaret, Charlie, Maggie, Leona, Kevin, and Brian, this has been awesome. I know that we're not supposed to compare groups, but there's no way the other groups were as good as this."

"It *has* been an awesome week, Wendy, and my guess is that in every group, someone is saying to the others what you just said to us, and that's good. We want all of the groups to be as successful as ours was. But I want to thank each and every one of you for putting yourselves out there, and for trusting the process as you did. We said at the beginning of the week that you get out of this what you put into it. That's always been true for me. I also want to thank you for taking responsibility for the smooth running of the group. You've all been terrific about asking each other questions, and keeping the conversation flowing. And we've done a pretty good job of staying focused on our feelings, as opposed to getting carried away with our heads."

"What do you mean *pretty good*?" Leona challenged. "I'd say we did a *very good* job of staying focused on our feelings, and you were a great help, Mr. Group Leader. I just want to say that I am very, very glad that I didn't go home after the first day. You all are the best. I can't say that I've got it all worked out in my head, but I do know that every time I hear the word *transgender* I'm going to think of my friend Kevin here, and every time I hear the words *gay* or *lesbian,* I'm going to think of Brian and Wendy, and every time I hear of the word *bisexual,* I'm going to remember old Charlie, who I love. I won't forget you, I promise. And let me just say that every time I hear the word *handicapped,* I'm going to think of that hunk of a man, Ben, in his hot red bathing suit."

"This group just wouldn't have been the same without you, Leona," Dom said. "You brought a life and an honesty to this group that we would have sorely missed. And I'd just like to say that I'm glad that *I* didn't go home either."

"Were you thinking about it, Dom?" Maggie asked with surprise.

"Not too seriously, but I have to admit that I was pretty worked up about having to watch the gay male sex films. And I surprised myself. I found them to be 'enlightening,' and even at times, I don't know, *natural.*"

"Well, I'll be," Leona replied, shaking her head in disbelief. "Well, let me also say that when I hear the words *Italian football coach,* I'm going to think of Dom here, and how he is just something else."

"Thanks," he said beaming. "And Wendy here has said that she'll help me think about how I can be a better ally to the gay kids."

"Good for you, Dom" I said.

"Can I add just one more thought?" Margaret said as she saw me look at my watch, and heard the sound of laughter from the other groups' participants as they assembled on the lawn for their pictures.

"Please," I invited.

"When I hear the word *sexuality* from now on, I'm going to think of all of the wonderful stories I've heard from you all this week as you did your maps, and all of the wonderful stories I heard from the other participants in the large group, and down at the lake, or over a meal, or while laying in the sun. It's a rich word, isn't it? A *spiritual* word, really."

"Once again, well said," Dom replied.

"Hey, how about a group hug before we get our picture taken?" Wendy asked enthusiastically as she stood with her arms outstretched.

"Sounds good to me," Kevin nodded and smiled.

Chapter Fifty-Three

The Last Staff Meeting

Each group had its own idea of how it wanted its picture taken. One laid down on the grass with all of the participants' heads together in a circle. Another had Carol lie on the ground and shoot up at the circle of smiling faces that looked down upon her. My group wanted Higley in the background, so we sat on the top and the seat of a picnic table in front of our meeting place. Charlie stood beaming on the right of the table with his arm around Leona, who sat at his side. Dom flanked the table on the left with his arm around a grinning Wendy. When the shot was finished, Kevin hurried to his dorm room for his camera, and was followed by several others who wanted their own keepsakes of the workshop.

Carol was, with good reason, the last to join the final staff meeting of the week. The remains of the cheddar cheese, Triskets, seedless green grapes, and cashews she had brought with her in the car from Virginia sat on the table along with Bill's and Alison's scotch and waters, Dick's and Pam's Chardonnay, and my water.

"Get yourself a drink and join us," Alison invited. "I know that Dick didn't facilitate a small group of his own, but I've asked him to sit in on this session."

"Of course!" said Pam. "We couldn't do this without you, Dick."

He smiled appreciatively.

"No, we certainly couldn't," Alison affirmed. "I'd like us all to check in, and report on the work we did with our SAR groups. Then I'd like to talk about the future of the workshop. Where do we go from here? And, finally, I'd like to know if we're going to do anything as a group for the celebration."

"The answer to the last one is easy," I replied. "I don't think we have the time to come up with anything new, but I'm open to suggestions. I would, though, like to know how everyone's group went."

"Great. Just great!" Bill said excitedly. "Of course, we had Catherine leave, but other than that, we had a very good week."

"Good going," I said. "Everyone did good work?"

"Oh, yes," he said. "I think so. Chuck, the guy from Mississippi, really stretched this week. He's an eager learner."

"That's great. I didn't get to spend much time with him, but he seems like a nice guy," I replied.

"And funny," Bill said. "He had us in stitches."

"How about the rest of you? How did your groups do?" I asked.

"Our group was a little slow getting started but it did some wonderful processing together," Pam said. "Peter, in particular, did some very important work this week, I think."

"Me too," Alison confirmed. "They all did good work, but Peter really searched his soul. Having George and Lloyd in the group helped a lot, didn't it. They kept prodding him on, and keeping him honest. And Peter and Annette really bonded midweek. I think he trusted that he could let his guard down in the group. Respecting confidentiality, he knows that he has a lot yet to sort out. But I think he's really glad that he came."

"That's great! Good for him! And how about Beverly and Martha?" I asked. "How did they do?"

"Who?" Bill asked with a befuddled look.

"Beverly and Martha, the women from Trinidad," Carol explained. "Beverly is in *your* group, Bill."

"Oh, *that* Beverly," he laughed. "She was terrific! She's a little shy but when she had something to say, people really listened. She's talking about sending others in her agency here next year."

"And what about Martha?" Pam asked.

"She was in *my* group," Carol said. "What a beautiful woman she is. She had us spellbound with her story."

"I'm glad," Pam said. "And Leona? How did Leona do?"

"Leona was one of our biggest successes, I think. The change in her this week is truly amazing," I replied.

"It is. It's *amazing*," Carol confirmed. "If you told me on the first day that someone was going to leave this week, I would have put my money on Leona. She seemed unhappy with *everything*. Now, she tells me that she'd like to be on the staff if ever there are any openings."

"Wouldn't that be a kick?" I laughed.

"Yea, you and Leona could co-facilitate a group," Carol replied with a smirk.

"I could do that," I assured her. "She's solid. She's still got some work to do on the gay issue, but she's well on her way."

"She just needed some time to find her place," Pam said.

"I agree, but she also had some negative attitudes to examine, and some style issues to confront," I replied, "but she did that."

"I want to know about Dan," Alison said. "He has worried me the most this week. He seems so angry and so alone."

"He *is* angry," Carol replied. "He's *very* angry, and he tends to isolate. But he's going to be all right. He lives 100 per cent of his life in gay politics. It's all he thinks about. All of his friends are gay and transgender activists. He's not used to being around so many heterosexuals, especially people who aren't completely supportive, for such a long period of time."

"Can you tell us *anything* about his story without violating his confidence?" Pam asked. "It would sure help me to know how to be more empathetic with people like Dan."

"He's had some really bad experiences as a gay man," Carol said. "I know he wouldn't mind my telling you that several years ago, he and his best friend were brutally gay bashed by a group of teenagers in West Hollywood, of all places. His friend was in critical condition for a long time, and was left permanently scarred. And when Dan was just coming out as a teenager, he was lovingly mentored by a group of gay men who later died very sad and horrible deaths from AIDS. Some of them had been abandoned or disowned by their families. He's got a lot of anger about the way gay people are treated in this culture."

"Thank you, Carol," Pam said with obvious appreciation. "I knew there *had* to be something going on there, but I just didn't know what. Everyone has a story, don't they? We just need to figure out a way to hear it."

"Is he glad that he came here?" Alison asked.

"I think so, but I also think he's too proud and stubborn to say so," Carol replied. "It was good for him to be in the group with Thomas, Carla, Gina, and Lisa. They gave him a lot of support and challenged him. But I'll tell you, it was Dick here who I think had the *biggest* impact on him."

Dick smiled and shrugged his shoulders in response to the compliment.

"Good for you, Dick," Alison said. "What did you do?"

"I don't have the slightest idea," he replied honestly.

"Oh, come on, Dick," Carol said. "You cried when he told us his story about being bashed. You told him that you understood his anger, and that it was justifiable. You also talked honestly about how you got past your own prejudices about homosexuality. He trusts you, and he admires you."

"I don't know about that, but thank you for saying so," he replied softly.

"So, your group went well, Carol?" I asked.

"It was great," she said.

"And what about Carla?" Bill asked. "She and Betty have certainly bonded."

"Oh my God, Carla may *never* go home," Carol exclaimed. "She may hide out here and wait until we come back next year. She says she's never felt so free to be herself, and so accepted by others."

"Isn't that wonderful?" Alison said with delight. "And, Brian, how about your group?"

"One of my best, I think," I said. "We had a lot of personal breakthroughs. Maggie leaves here pretty much healed of the awful wounds she brought to Thornfield. She's got a much better understanding of her husband's homosexuality, and even an appreciation of what happened to him when he was with us last year. And Charlie will *never* be the same. He was a gift to Maggie, as she was to him. They're both a little nervous about going home, but they'll both be fine. Dom, of course, is a gem, and I think he'll be a *terrific* role model for the kids back home. Wendy has had a big impact on him. They're leaving here buddies. Margaret could have been my co-facilitator. I love her. She reminds me a lot of Mary Lee. And Leona, as we've already said, has learned so much. It was a great week. It really was."

"And how did Kevin do?" Bill asked.

"Oh, I think this was a powerful week for Kevin too. He was pretty quiet in group, which is normal for him, but I think he's more confident and happier than I've ever seen him," I replied. "He certainly got his share of attention from the boys this week."

"And the women," Pam said. "I know of three women who would like to take him home with them."

"Does that count me?" Alison laughed.

When we had completed our reflections on the week, Alison proceeded with the next item on her agenda. "It's time now to talk about the future of the workshop. In that regard," she said sadly, "I'm afraid that I have some very troubling news for you. The future of Thornfield as a retreat facility has come into serious question. I've just learned today that they probably will *not* be accepting reservations for next year. It's simply not a moneymaking operation for the diocese. In fact, it's a drain. As you know, the facility needs constant maintenance, and the revenues they bring in from workshops such as ours, and from weddings, don't come close to meeting their expenses. I understand their dilemma. It's happening all over the country with church-related sites, but it creates a bit of a problem for us, doesn't it. As I've been told, their plan is to spend a year assessing its future use. So, we will most likely be without a home next year, and perhaps thereafter."

We all sat in stunned silence for a moment. While we ourselves had questioned how long our program might continue to run, given the impact of the economy on agencies' budgets, the federal government's negative attitude toward comprehensive sex education programs, our frustration with how hard it had become to fill seats in the workshop, and our own increasing age and dwindling staff numbers, we nevertheless preferred to not have the decision about the workshop's future made for us.

"When will we know?" I asked.

"We could always go somewhere else," Carol suggested.

"It just wouldn't be the same," Pam replied.

"This is our home," Dick said.

"Is there anything we can do?" Bill asked.

"I don't know when we'll know for sure," Alison replied. "And though we certainly could go elsewhere, I agree with Pam and Dick, this is our *home*. One thing that I'd like you all to do is to write the bishop and tell him what this place means to you, and why it's so important to us to stay put. Perhaps that will make a difference."

We talked for twenty minutes more, mostly about our attachments to the place, our memories of the good, fun, and sometimes sad times we shared, and of what we would miss most – Mary Lee's and Susan's trees, the walks around the driveways, cutting wildflowers, the lake, and the spaces in all of the buildings that had been made "sacred" by the tears, laughter, joy, and anger that had accompanied the stories told to one another over the past three decades. We all pledged to write letters to the bishop upon our return home.

"Okay. Let's move on," Alison suggested. "So, what are we doing at the celebration?"

"I've run off the songs that we've sung for the past couple of years," Carol said, "but I think we should practice. How about if we get together after dinner tomorrow, and we'll go through them?"

"Sounds good," Dick said, making a note on his daily schedule.

"Do you have me down for anything?" Bill asked.

"Did you *tell* me that you wanted to do anything?" Carol replied.

"I don't know. Did I?" Bill laughed.

"No. I've got Dick down for a couple of jokes. Brian is going to do 'Ernestine.' Alison has a reading, and Pam's got a poem. What would you like to do?"

"Let me think about it and I'll get back to you," he said.

"I brought a wig, a make-up bag, and a dress," I said. "We could dress Bill up."

"What?" Carol and Pam asked together.

"I brought a wig, a make-up bag, and a dress," I repeated.

"Where did *you* get a wig and a dress?" Carol asked incredulously. "I thought you'd *never* do drag."

"I hadn't until last summer," I replied grinning. "I was at a gay naturist event … "

"Where?" Alison asked.

"Gay nude camp," Carol answered.

"And a guy in my cabin was a make-up artist, and 'dresser' for a big television show. He set up 'Fifi's Emporium' for the week, which was sort of a drag queen's 'Stop 'n Shop.' He also did a 'Drag 101' workshop, and I attended. When he found out that I had never done drag before, he offered to use me as his canvas. Inspired by the role modeling of growth I get around here, I said 'yes.' So, Fifi put a big lavender wig on me, false eyelashes, and make-up. And I was beautiful."

"Did he give you the dress?" Pam asked.

"No. I just had my towel. I wrapped it around me as if I had just come out of the pool. When he finished with me, I walked back to my cabin to show my other cabin mates how I looked. They said, 'Who are you?'

and I said, 'I'm Brian,' and they said, 'Brian who?' and I said, 'Brian McNaught,' and they said, 'You're *kidding*!' It was very exciting. My first drag. So, one of my cabin mates said 'Darling, that towel just won't do. Here, try this on,' and he gave me a pink, black, and white disco shift."

"And you brought it?" Alison asked.

"Yes," I said.

"Go get it," Bill said, clapping his hands. "I want to try it on."

"You do?" I asked.

"Yes! I've never done drag either," he said excitedly.

"Me neither," Dick said, his eyes brightening. "I want to try it on too."

Amidst the laughter of disbelief, I took Bill by the hand and led him to my bedroom where I pulled the wig and make-up bag from a dresser drawer, and the disco shift from the closet. "Here, see if this fits," I said, handing him the dress. When he had disrobed, and put it on, I carefully placed on his head the lavender wig and the pair of long black eyelashes. "You're beautiful," I promised him. "Go show the others."

Bill giggled as he walked into the Higley living room, and was greeted by gales of laughter and applause.

"Oh, God, Bill, you look like a piece of Good 'n Plenty. Wait. Wait," Carol said. "I've got a tiara and a wand. Don't move."

"And get your camera!" Pam shouted after her as she headed to her bedroom.

"You're adorable, Bill" Alison said as Bill paraded around the room, and admired himself in the full-length mirror on the back of his bedroom door.

"If Kathy could see me now!" he exclaimed with laughter.

"If the folks at Widener University could see you now," Alison countered.

"Bill, you *are* beautiful, but it's Dick's turn," I said. "Come on, Dick. You're next."

In my bedroom, Dick dutifully dropped his trousers and donned the shift, which came to just below his boxers, and well above his knobby knees. Next, he received the wig, and waited as Bill reluctantly removed the eyelashes and put them on Dick's deeply-wrinkled, patrician face. "Here's the tiara and wand," I said as he stood patiently like an old St. Bernard that had been dressed up by it's six-year-old mistress. "A real 'show stopper,' Dick. Go show the others."

The screams that greeted him were hysterical. Alison laughed so hard that she cried. Bill did so too, wiping away the tears from his eyes as Pam kept saying in disbelief, "Oh my God, Dick. Oh my God."

"You're *beautiful*, Dick," Carol assured him. "But your eyelash is upside down. Here, let me fix it. Okay, now turn this way if you would, and lift your wand up as if you were Glinda, Good Witch of the North, waving good-bye to the Munchkins. Good. Now throw your head back and laugh." Dick followed instructions as if he was a well-paid model, striking pose after pose at Carol's request.

"Okay, Brian, it's your turn," Pam said. "Let's see you in drag."

"I will," I replied, "but it's not Brian that you'll be seeing. It's Tippy. Tippy Day."

"Tippy who?" Pam asked.

"Tippy Day. It's my drag name. Your drag name is your first pet's name and your mother's maiden name. Everyone has a drag name."

"Not me. I never had a pet," Pam said. "I was too allergic."

"No pets?" I asked with amazement. "Not even a goldfish or a turtle?"

"Well, my Aunt Marian had a dog that was like my own. It's name was Mimi."

"Oh, that's good! You look like a 'Mimi'," I replied.

"And *you* look like a 'Tippy'," Carol said. "Now go get dressed, Tippy."

I did so, and was by far the 'prettiest' of the three. Then it was Pam's turn, then Alison's, and finally Carol's. Each posed for pictures in wig, dress, lashes, tiara, and wand. Hands down, the most enthusiastic model of all was Bill, who nevertheless decided it was not a costume he would wear to the celebration.

"Let's go visit Mary Lee's and Susan's trees," Bill suggested enthusiastically. "We haven't done it as a group this year, and we may not get the chance again, *ever*."

"Okay. Okay, but wait 'til I change," pleaded Carol who was still in the lavender wig and disco shift. "I'll only be a minute."

"No, don't change," I pleaded. "Mary Lee and Susan would *love* it. Please. Please. Come as you are!"

"Oh, what the hell," she said as she grabbed her bottle of non-alcoholic beer, and headed for the door. Bill and Alison picked up their drinks too, and we processed as a group up the hill toward Peabody and the driveway.

Playful catcalls, applause, and laughter greeted us as Carol struck poses along the path, and 'blessed' each group with her wand.

"You're beautiful!" Carla yelled from her spot on the hill next to Betty and Dan.

"And I want that wig!" Dan yelled.

"You'll have to fight me for it," I answered.

"That can be arranged," he replied.

Chapter Fifty-Four

FRIDAY

A Stranger in Our Midst

After a heavy but delicious chicken Parmesan dinner, and a long walk with Paula around the driveway to talk about her gay son, I slipped away to my room, propped myself up against rolled blankets and pillows on the bed, and picked up where I had left off in reading *The Ladies of Llangollen*. Eleanor Butler and Sarah Ponsonby, the most celebrated "virgins" on the 18th Century, who lived and loved together for more than 50 years in Wales, were mourning the death of their faithful servant and friend, Mary Carryll. The next thing I knew, someone was gently lifting my head onto a single pillow, taking the book from my hands, covering me with a blanket, and turning off the light.

"I fell asleep," I announced groggily.

"Yes, you did," Carol confirmed in a whisper. "Stay asleep. I'll see you in the morning."

"No, come talk to me," I said as I moved my body to the side of the bed closest to the wall, and patted the place beside me. "What time is it?"

"It's a little after midnight," she said as she stretched out on the bed above the covers, and let me hold her spoon style. "You missed all of the excitement."

"What excitement?"

"Peter and Kevin were down at the beach snuggling in front of the fire, and Dan came down. It was quite a scene. First they started fighting, and then they ended up in a *threesome*."

"No!" I said, sitting up, now fully awake.

"No, but it was a good story, wasn't it?" she laughed.

"I hate you," I said, lying back down.

"No, you don't. You love me," she replied confidently.

"So what *did* happen tonight?" I asked.

"Nothing. Alison had a big group at her Betty Dodson film. A smaller group went down to the beach after *Sex in the City*, and played 'I Never' for awhile. The late night drinking crowd is still at it over in Peabody, but most everyone else went to bed pretty early. Pam and I've been working on our program for tomorrow."

"Hey, what are you two doing?" Pam whispered as she poked her head in the door.

"Just talking. Come on and join us," I invited as Carol and I moved closer to the wall.

"You sure conked out early," Pam said as she lay sideways with her back to Carol. "Where'd you go after dinner?"

"Paula and I went for a walk around the driveway. We had a good talk."

"I was out there walking with Joanne. I didn't see you," Pam said. "Carol, can you move over a bit? I'm falling out of bed."

"Suck it in. It's a twin bed, for cripes sake," she laughed.

"I didn't see you either, but it's a big circular driveway. What's up with Joanne?" I asked.

"Oh, she just wanted to talk about stuff that's happening at SIECUS. She knew I was once on the Board."

"I haven't connected much with her this week," I confessed. "It's this way every year. No matter how hard I try, I still leave here not knowing much about half of the group."

"It's the same for all of us, sweetie," Carol replied. "Joanne was in my group though, and I really liked her. Not as much at first, but when I got to know her I did. She's part of the late night crowd at Peabody."

"What are you three doing? Having a pajama party?" Alison asked as she stepped into the room.

"Yes, come join us," I said. "How did your session go?"

"It was *very* successful, I think. We had a big crowd, and a good discussion. Where am I supposed to lie?" she giggled.

"Get on top of Carol. She can handle it."

Alison entered the bed from the end, and climbed on top of Carol who grunted, "I can't breathe."

"Shush. You're fine," I assured her as Pam laughed and pushed against the side of the desk to stay on board.

We laid like that for several minutes as Alison recapped the conversation that followed the film on female self-pleasuring. "So many of the women had never looked lovingly at their vulvas. It was an eye-opener for some of them. But I think that Joe really got the most out of the evening. As he explained, he's eager to learn so that he can be a better lover to his wife. He asked at least a dozen questions, and all of the women were more than glad to answer them for him."

"I think he's very cool," I affirmed.

"You guys, I have got to go to bed," Pam finally said as she carefully pulled herself from the pile and blew kisses to us. "I have to get up early in the morning. Carol, are we still planning on meeting before breakfast upstairs in Huntington?"

"Yes," she grunted.

Alison then rolled off Carol and said that she too had a big day coming up and needed to get some sleep. "Good night, darlings," she said. "Sweet dreams."

"I'm coming. I'm coming," Carol said as she kissed me, and swung her legs to the floor. "See you in the morning, Tippy."

"I love you, Carol," I said.

"I know you do," she replied.

The crows seemed to be in particularly good voice at dawn as they talked back and forth from the limbs of the many pine trees that towered over the dorms. I laid there for a long time listening to them, and then suddenly jumped from bed fearing that I was late. Dom and Wendy were waiting for me, and graciously accepted my apology for holding them up on our Friday morning run. Marjorie absolved me with a blessing and toasted us with her coffee mug as we headed down the driveway for the road. It was a beautiful, sunny day, and I reflected out loud on how grateful I was for the fun times we were having together.

Later, though, when I arrived in Huntington for breakfast, I had a strong sense that something was wrong. There was a constraint in the atmosphere in the dining room, and I found the lack of joyful banter a bit unsettling. It was almost as if the participants had already pulled back from the edge of intimacy, perhaps to protect themselves for the trip home. But that was unusual at this point in the day. Normally the emotional armor didn't start going on until the end of the celebration that night.

When we gathered in Ridings and formed our circle to sing "I Love Myself," the reason for the change in the environment became apparent. There was a stranger in our midst. Standing next to Betty, where Carla would normally be, was a man. He looked like Carla, but he didn't "glow" like Carla. His face was washed clean of make-up. His hair was pulled into a neat ponytail at the base of his neck. His beige linen shirt fell straight against his flat chest. He wore khaki shorts and brown sandals, and he smiled a bit painfully at the participants as he looked around the circle and sang, "I love myself, the way I am, there's nothing I need to change."

When we took our seats, Alison offered a cheery "good morning," and began making her announcements. Today, she reminded us, we would be breaking into our "skill building" groups, with Carol and Pam meeting upstairs in the large room in Huntington, and Bill in the adjacent library. I would be with my group downstairs in Ridings, and Alison would be meeting in the carpeted area upstairs.

If we hadn't already done so, we needed to let Gail know of our travel plans for Saturday. Also, would we please make sure that our personal e-mail and postal address information were correct on the master copy of the mailing list that was located on the registration desk. We were also instructed to strip our beds in the morning, to put all bed linen and towels in a pillow case, and leave it outside the door to our rooms.

"Are there any more announcements?" she asked.

"It's not an announcement," said Annette. "It's just an observation, but I miss seeing the Quilt hanging at the front the room."

"I do too," affirmed Alison.

"And I miss Carla!" Dan shouted out from his seat.

"Yea, where is Carla?" Dom asked.

"I think someone ought to go and see if they can find Carla," Margaret suggested.

"It seems we *all* miss Carla," Alison confirmed.

"I do too," replied Carl appreciatively, "But she'll be back soon. She just needs to do a presentation in Brian's workshop, and then she'll return in all of her glory. I promise."

Several people started clapping, and soon everyone joined in. Betty put her big arm around Carl's shoulder as his eyes welled up, and he waved his hand to say "please stop."

After requests were made for more help with decorating and securing refreshments for the celebration, Alison turned the floor over to Carol.

"We have two things to do before we go to our workshops," she said, "and they're both two of my *favorite* things that we do here. The first is our 'wake-up' exercise, which is a 'car wash,' which I'll explain in a minute, and the second is our group photo. After the car wash, we'll gather on the lawn in front of Ridings and have our picture taken."

"Then I'm changing *now*," Carl said as he stood and headed toward the door. "Start the car wash without me. Carla's going to be in that picture."

Carl was out the door before he had time to hear all of the cheers of affirmation that filled the room. When it died down, Carol grinned with delight and proceeded to explain the "completely voluntary" wake-up exercise.

Following her directions, we went outside and formed two parallel lines on each side of the sidewalk that led back to Peabody.

"Okay," she said, calling our attention back to her, "it's a beautiful day and we're going to have the bodies of our cars 'washed.' Now, when you drive into a car wash, what's the first thing that happens?"

"They break off your antenna," Chuck answered.

"No, that comes later," she laughed. "What do they do first?"

"They vacuum the car," said Thomas.

"Right! They vacuum the car, so you first few people in line need to be the 'vacuums.' Then what? They 'spray water' on the car, right? And then they 'scrub' the car," she said rubbing herself all over vigorously. "Get it? And then what do they do?"

"They drip hot wax on you," George said smirking.

"Ooh, baby," replied Bill with a look of excitement.

"Okay, 'hot wax,' and then what? They 'blow dry' you, and then they 'rub you down' with cloths. Right? Got it? Okay, I'll go first. It helps if you close your eyes and walk slowly. Then someone from the head of the line follows, and we keep going until everyone gets a chance. You with me?"

"Turn off the radio, lower your antenna, and put it into neutral," Dan directed as Carol headed down the sidewalk, her eyes squeezed shut, her arms pulled close to her sides, and a big smirk on her face. Ben then maneuvered his wheelchair in behind her but kept his eyes open. "You're all safer that way," he advised. "But feel free to scrub the undercarriage."

Squeals of laughter, double entendres, whooshing sounds of "spraying water," moans of pleasure, and vigorous massage rubs carried the "cars" down the line. A few participants walked through quickly with nervous looks on their faces, but most of them smiled with delight and walked slowly through the mostly-appropriate, tactile attention they were getting. Only a handful opened their eyes. Peter was one. He kept them closed until he came to the spot where he surmised Dan would be standing. There, he opened his eyes, smiled with raised eyebrows at Dan, and said, "Don't even *think* about it." Dan responded with a feigned look of wounded shock, but abided by Peter's wishes. Hands off.

Carla came running from the dorm just as the exercise was ending. "Wait, please! Just one more. I promise I'll be quick." Without hesitation, the car washing apparatus came back up to full speed and gave the giggling, beautifully made-up and accessorized, self-described "fire-engine red, BMW convertible" the wash of its life.

When we had finished rubbing Carla down, Carol led the applause for the event, and then asked me to organize the participant pose for the large group photo while she ran to the office to ask Kit, a conference center staff person, to come take our picture. But before I could give my first instruction, there was a mass migration to Peabody where participants grabbed their own cameras. When they returned, they made a large pile of their Cannons, Nikons, and Kodak disposables, and then joined the group of sitting, kneeling, and standing comrades.

Ignoring my request that the tallest people stand in the back and that the shortest people go to the front, most of the participants gravitated to the side of the people with whom they had most bonded during the week. Maggie and George knelt together in the second row. Behind them stood Charlie and Leona. Betty, Carla, and Dan also stood nearby. Annette wanted to be near Peter, who wanted to be near Kevin, so they sat together in the first row. Martha and Beverly weren't going to be separated either, nor were Chuck, Dom, Wendy, Gina, or Lisa. Thomas had his arm around Lloyd, and Beatrice knelt next to Ben, in the wheelchair he had positioned on level ground at the end of the second row. Marjorie and Curtis shared a quick smoke as we were getting organized, and found adjacent places in line near Ben. Margaret and Joe stood serenely independent, and the remaining participants gravitated toward staff members whom they liked.

In the background, directly behind us, arose the swooping roof of Ridings, with its cross at the peak. To our right, at the bottom of the hill, was the still water of the lake that would soon reflect in its choppy waves the early weekend boating activity. I hoped that both of these significant landmarks, the building and the lake, would make it into what I feared would be our last group photo at Thornfield.

It was a full ten minutes before Kit had finished learning how to focus and shoot the fifteen or twenty cameras that sat at her feet. With the last one, she said, "I'd say 'smile,' but this group doesn't need any help in that department. What a bunch of happy campers!"

"Three cheers for Kit," Alison said. "Hip, hip hurray. Hip, hip hurray. Hip, hip hurray."

"Thank you, Kit. Okay, everyone, grab your cameras and head to your workshops," Carol announced. "The next time we're together as a group is the celebration!"

"So, what happened to lunch?" George asked.

Chapter Fifty-Five

Leona and Betty Talk

Carol and Pam had, by far, the largest group. Fifteen participants followed them as they headed up the outside stairs of Huntington. Bill's group was close behind with nine.

Chuck, Dom, and Margaret were perhaps the most eager to get help in planning their programs for youth. The others all had some experience in the field of sexuality education.

The morning would be spent with Pam and Carol helping their group focus on the "foundations" of sexuality education – the goals, philosophy, underlying values, and best practices. Pam took the lead on reviewing one of the "best practices," which was called the "experiential learning cycle." This emphasizes the role of the educator as a "facilitator," rather than as a "lecture-style" teacher.

"The key is to conduct fun, participatory learning activities, but then to ask open-ended questions that lead students to explore what happened during the activity, what they learned from it, and how they plan to *use* what they learned," Pam explained.

"We've brought lots and lots of handouts for you with ideas for activities," Carol later told the group. "We're also going to model some activities for you, and then, this afternoon, have some of you share your activities with us."

"I need lots of help getting ready to answer students' questions about sex," Dom said at his first opportunity.

"You mean, like, 'How do two men have sex?' and 'What does sex feel like?' and 'When you have a wet dream, what do you do when your mother comes in and sees your bed?'," Carol replied.

"Yea, and 'What does 69 mean?' and 'What's a douche?'," Chuck added grimly.

"Thank you. Those are *great* questions," Pam replied. "How about if we start by modeling how *we* would answer them, and then we'll have *you* practice answering some of them. And, we'll give each other feedback. That way, when you go back to your programs, you'll be more comfortable and more prepared to answer these kinds of questions."

"That would be great!" Dom said. "Would you start with the one about two men having sex, please?"

"You want to take this first one, or would you like me to?" Carol asked Pam.

"Why don't you go ahead," Pam replied.

"Okay," Carol said. "The first thing you do is *affirm* the student for asking the question. You want them to know that you're *glad* they asked the question. I'd say, 'Great question! The only difference between two men having sex, and a man and a woman having sex, is that there isn't a penis *and* a vagina involved. Remember that having sex can be so much more than the act of a penis in a vagina. Whether it's two men, two women, or a man and a woman, they can have sex by touching, massaging, kissing, etcetera. Oral sex, which is a mouth on a penis or on a vulva, might be involved for some couples'."

Next door, in the library, Bill and his group were sharing the content of the daily journals they each kept during the week. The assignment was to reflect on how they reacted to the lessons of the day in light of their spirituality. Peter confessed that the week for him was loaded with "land mines," and that there was often an explosion when his personal reactions to events in the workshop hit up against his religious beliefs. Of particular concern to him, he said, was the reaction he had to the hand exercise with Kevin, and his belief that the pleasurable feelings that came up for him were completely contrary to God's will for him.

"My head is a jumbled mess," he said with an exasperated look and plaintive smile at Kevin, who sat across the circle from him at the table.

"Sorry about that," Kevin replied. "My head is kind of a mess too."

As was always true in Bill's workshop, passages from the Bible came up as either sources of *conflict* for individuals, or sources of *support*. As such, once each of the participants had the opportunity to share from his or her journal, Bill offered his thinking about the Holy Book as it relates to sexuality.

"There are four basic, but not mutually-exclusive, approaches to the Bible," he explained. "The first, and these are listed randomly, is that the Bible is the most evil book ever written. Some people feel that it has destroyed more lives, generated more violence, and excused more atrocities against humankind than any other book in history. A second approach to the Bible is that it has value because of its literary beauty, and as a historic record of the journey of a people, and of their relationship to their God. A third perspective is that of the 'literalist' who believes that the Bible is the one and *only* word of God, written without error in stone for all generations. Finally, there is the contextual view that says that the Bible can offer guidance to our everyday lives when the experience of the author reflects a universal truth, but otherwise should be understood as limited by the cultural context in which it was written. The one position that, in my opinion, is impossible to defend and to incorporate with meaning into one's sexual/spiritual life, is the third view."

Bill then spent a significant amount of time citing passages from the books of Leviticus and Deuteronomy, as well as sections from the New Testament, that made the Bible, for him, an unreliable guide for moral decision-making. "Who today would stone their son to death because he spoke harshly to his father, or who could avoid sitting in a chair that a menstruating woman at one time had sat in? Who could avoid wearing clothes that mix fabrics? And who dares quote St. Paul's admonition that women should *never* offer guidance or counsel to a man? What would you do with all of our women clergy, therapists, doctors, teachers, counselors, police officers, nuns, tax consultants, CEOs, or nurses?"

Across campus, Alison was explaining to her group her philosophy that one's sexuality needed to be truly integrated into one's life. "To do so, you have to have self-esteem and you have to ask for what you want. Self-esteem is multifaceted, but one very important component is our body image. We *are* what we like, and what we don't like, about ourselves. And what we don't like about ourselves significantly influences our ability to integrate our sexuality fully. Also, we need to learn to ask for what we want. It's been my experience as a marriage and family therapist that women who reached their goal of enjoying their sexuality were women who were able to negotiate with their children, their spouses, or their partners that they had one hour a day, every day, to themselves to do with as they pleased."

A short while later, Maggie was standing in the center of the circle in Alison's group, talking about what she liked and disliked about her body. "When we *hide* it, we can't *own* it," Alison explained. "If we practice, in this safe setting, what we do and don't like about ourselves, our negative feelings become less mitigating factors in our lives. It's *all* 'me.' It's who I am."

"I *hate* my freckles," Maggie said as she rubbed her arms to show her area of concern. "I think they're ugly."

"I, on the other hand, *love* your freckles," quickly replied Dick, who, with Ben, were the only men in the group. "I think they're *beautiful*."

Downstairs, Lloyd was getting feedback from me, Carla, Grace, and Gina on his half-hour telling of his story.

"You did an *amazing* job, Lloyd," I began. "Given that your audience was high risk teens, and that your message was about lowering one's risk of contracting HIV, your personal story was extraordinarily powerful. I'm aware that in a few days you'll know for sure your HIV status, but using your own experience of 'screwing up,' and telling of the enormous anxiety that you're feeling now was *spellbinding*. And you did it all in the thirty minutes you were allowed. You get an '11' out of a possible 10 points."

"Thanks," he sighed with relief and appreciation. "I thought a lot about what you said, that 'the messenger *is* the message.' I figured if I was going to connect with these teenagers, they had to trust that I knew what they were going through. But how would you change it, once I get home and get my test results?"

"Well, *you're* going to know the answer to that when the times comes," I replied. "Let your message pour out of your heart. If you find, as we all hope, that you're 'negative,' you still have a gem of a story to tell them. Stay in touch with the feelings that you have today. That's your gift to them. If you end up testing 'positive,' search your soul for how, if at all, your message to these kids changes."

"Lloyd, can I just say what an incredible gift it was to hear you this morning," Grace said. "When I signed up for this workshop, I really never expected to be so deeply touched, or to learn so much. I'd love to figure out a way to get you in front of a corporate audience. I just don't know what the business 'tie-in' would be. I need to give it some thought."

"That took a lot of courage," Carla said, rubbing Lloyd's back vigorously with her right hand. "I was *proud* of you."

"Yea, you were awesome," Gina said. "I'm not sure what I'm supposed to do now for an encore."

"You're a different 'messenger,' Gina," I said. "You've got a different message. You've got Gina's message. Stay focused on that, and don't compare yourself to Lloyd. You can't be a black gay male who is possibly HIV-positive. And Lloyd can't be you, or touch people in the same way that you'll touch your audience. Besides, you've got plenty of time to think about it. Grace is up next, and then, after lunch, Carla will present. You'll be last, but not least."

"Who do have in mind for *least*?" Carla asked coyly.

"Why do we have to have a 'least'?" I replied. "What if everyone gets an '11'?"

After offering Lloyd our positive feedback, we spent some time giving suggestions on what he might do to improve his effectiveness. It was then Grace's turn. Forty-five minutes later, we were headed for lunch.

Carol and Pam's group ended their morning session before Bill's, but Leona stayed upstairs as the others headed down to lunch, and sat near the door to the library. When the door finally opened, she smiled and waved enthusiastically at Kevin and Charlie when they walked out, and then jumped to her feet when she spotted Betty.

"Girlfriend, can we talk?" Leona asked with a warm smile as she looped her arm through Betty's. "I swear I'm gonna burst if I don't get to say to you what I've been wanting to say for days."

"Sure, Leona," Betty replied gratefully. "Do you want to get a sandwich and a drink, and go sit by Mary Lee's and Susan's trees? It's where you saw Carla and me talking the other day."

"That sounds good to me," Leona said. "Give me 10 minutes to get rid of my things and to grab some food, and I'll meet you at the door leading to the driveway."

Fifteen minutes later, the two of them were sitting crossed legged on the ground, each slowly eating the chicken salad in pita bread sandwiches they had brought with iced teas to the grove of blue spruce across the stone bridge.

"I know we've got to get back to our groups, so I'll get straight to the point," Leona said. "Have you ever had a meal that was so good and that you ate so fast, that when you were done you wished you could start all over again, so that you could *really* enjoy it?"

"Sure," Betty replied. "That's why I'm as *big* as I am. I do it all of the time."

"Oh, Betty, please. You're beautiful. *Big* and beautiful. I don't mean *fat*, because you aren't fat. But you *are* a big girl. Oh, Lord, how did I get on that? Betty, help me please, you know what I'm saying, right?"

"Yes, Leona, you're saying that I'm a big-boned beauty," she smirked.

"That's right! But of course, that's not what I came out here to tell you. I wanted to say that this week has been like that really good meal, and I know that I missed a lot of it because I was so busy being scared, and defensive, and ornery. I came here with a bad attitude, and the first thing I ended up doing was asking to be moved out of your room because you were a transsexual lesbian. I can't tell you how many times this week I've kicked myself for doing that, not just because I'm sure I hurt your feelings, which makes me very ashamed, but because I *know* I missed an opportunity to learn from you, and to maybe even become friends. I'm so sorry, Betty. If I could do it all over again, I would. I'd like to do the whole *week* over again, and maybe next year, I'll come back and do just that. I know that I can't go back and 'undo' what I already did. I wish I could. I just want you to know I'm sorry, really sorry. I wish you were still my roommate."

"Oh, Leona, you have made my day," Betty said as she moved over and pulled her into a long, warm hug. "Thank you so much for telling me that. I know that meeting me was not what you expected on your first day, but I'm so glad that you loved this week, and that you wish we had become friends. Right after you moved out, I came here and talked to Susan. That's her tree there. She told me that everything would turn out, that I should 'trust the process.' She was right, wasn't she, Leona? She was right."

"I guess she was, Betty. I guess she really was."

"Thank you for seeking me out. I know that it couldn't have been easy," Betty said.

"It was a lot easier than going home and *not* having talked," Leona replied.

As Betty winked at her, hugged her again, and began to get up off of the ground, Leona said quickly, "Betty, can I ask you to do one thing for me?"

"Sure," she said sitting back down. "You name it."

"Do you mind if we hold hands for just a minute?"

"No, not at all, if you'd like to."

"Thanks," Leona said as she took Betty's left hand into her right, closed her eyes, and began slowly and gently rubbing Betty's fingers with her thumb.

"Well, I'll be damned," Leona said, opening her eyes. "It really *was* you! At the touch exercise, when we rubbed hands for a while, but then had to stop and move to someone else. Do you remember? I know that I came over and checked out your ring after the exercise, but I didn't *really* believe you had been the one I was getting so 'turned on' to. We had our moment, though, didn't we?"

"We did indeed, Leona. And it's just between us girls."

When we came back together as a group in the basement of Ridings, Carl had set up four chairs, cleared away the others, secured an easel to display his transgender continuum, placed a glass of water on a piano bench near where he would stand, and, with the help of Gina and Lloyd, had brought down the whiteboard from upstairs. He handed me the introductory remarks he wanted me to make, and sat nearby in his beige linen shirt, khaki shorts, and brown sandals waiting for his cue.

My introduction of him, at his request, reminded the audience that there were "a growing list of states, including Minnesota, California, New Mexico, and Rhode Island, and several major corporations such as Lucent, IBM, Lehman Brothers, J.P. Morgan, American Airlines, and Apple Computer, that prohibit discrimination based upon gender identity and/or expression. The motivating factor for such measures, particularly among the corporations, was the desire to attract and retain the best and brightest employees. They needed, therefore, to create a safe, equitable, and productive work environment for everyone."

The four of us who would be listening to Carl, I reminded them, were engineers in a company that banned such discrimination. Our department's diversity committee had set up this program as part of our yearly training. "Carl Gunther, our speaker, is a church organist who is married and has two grown children."

Carl stepped forward into the silence that followed my words, and shook each of our hands firmly as he said, "Good afternoon. As Brian said, my name is Carl. I'm a husband, a father, and a musician. Thank you for inviting me to speak with you. Your company currently prohibits discrimination based upon gender identity or expression. It does so because it wants to make sure that people such as me who fall on the transgender continuum trust that at the end of the day, they will be evaluated based upon their skills and performance, and not because of how they see themselves, or on how they 'present' their gender to their colleagues. I know that while some people may agree that this makes good business sense, for many people the subject of 'cross dressing' is nevertheless unsettling. In the brief time that we have together today, I'd like to help break through some of that discomfort by putting a face, my face, on the issue for you."

Carl then picked up the guitar that he had placed beside his chair and began strumming softly a familiar tune. "How many of you remember Jerry Herman's popular song from *La Cage Aux Folles* entitled 'I Am What I Am'? Gloria Gaynor did a disco version many years ago that some of us are old enough to have danced to, but I prefer a slower version." Here he stopped talking and began to sing slowly in a beautiful voice, with rich accompaniment from his guitar, the words to the often-sung gay and transgender "anthem."

"My favorite line from that song," he said when he had finished singing, "is 'So what if I love each feather and each spangle. Why not try to see things from a different angle?' In the time that we have left, that's what I'd like to offer, 'a different angle.' I'm going to tell you my story of growing up with an awareness that I was 'different,' and of how that knowledge paralyzed me with fear. As I tell you my story, I'm going to periodically walk behind this whiteboard and alter slightly my appearance. I'm going to keep talking, but at any time, I'd like you to raise your hand to indicate that I have just stepped over the threshold of your 'comfort zone.' Will you do that for me?"

For the next twenty minutes, Carl told his story, careful to make eye contact with each of us. As promised, he periodically stepped behind the whiteboard as he spoke, and a moment later emerged with his appearance slightly altered. First his hair was pulled up from his neck into a pony tail at the top of his head and a few bangs were combed down onto his forehead. His beige shirt was also accented with a thin gold necklace, and his brown belt was replaced with a colorful one. Strumming softly again, he talked about his fear of being 'gay' when he realized he needed to express his feminine side, and of the awful misgivings he had about telling his wife of his desire to cross dress. His two beloved children and their need for emotional safety were always at the top of his mind, so he never did anything that might confuse or alienate them. But he was *miserable*.

Placing the guitar back down, Carl went back behind his "curtain" and reemerged with a small bottle of perfume and a set of tiny earrings. "These were the first things that I allowed myself," he explained as he sprayed a little perfume at his neck and wrists and inserted the earrings. "And I found that when I did these little things, in the privacy of my bathroom, late at night, when everyone else was asleep, I smiled genuinely for the first time in a long, long time as I felt the tension leave my shoulders, neck, and lower back. Though I washed the perfume off, and tucked the earrings away, my wife and children commented for the next several days that for some reason I seemed to be in a very good mood. Which I was, and seem to always be, when I'm free to tap that side of me that needs to be expressed."

The experimenting became more frequent, Carl explained, and he soon sought out the advice of a counselor, who luckily sent him to a therapist who had some experience with transgender issues. He then began reading literature, and eventually was brought into a small discussion group of others who shared his need to cross dress. He came to trust that he wasn't "gay," but rather "bi-gendered," meaning that he had the ability, and the *need*, to express both his masculine and feminine natures. As he explained this to us, he went one more time behind the whiteboard, and added a touch of lipstick and make-up to his face, and reemerged with a slightly more feminine gait.

"No hands up yet?" she asked in a bit more of a velvety tone as she scanned the room. "My, aren't you a sophisticated group? How about if we now discuss which *bathroom* at work I'm going to use when I'm cross dressed?" she laughed playfully. Dutifully enacting our roles as members of her engineering audience, we each raised our hands slowly to indicate that we thought we had each just found our threshold of comfort. "Ah, the bathroom," she smirked. "Personally, I wish they were all unisex, but I know that your company is working on an agreeable policy for all of us."

Here she stopped, looked briefly at her watch, and walked with hard outstretched to each of us. "My name is Carla," she said warmly, "and it's been a pleasure being with you. My time is up, which is a shame, because there's so much more that we could talk about. Thank you for your time and attention." And then, picking up her guitar and strumming out the thematic tune, she sang with a wink and with great flair, "I am what I am. I am my own special creation. So, give me the hook, or the ovation." To which we enthusiastically responded with the latter.

An hour and a half later, as the five of us meandered slowly across the grassy hillside, giving "high fives" on the scores of "11" that each of them deserved, we spotted Wendy and Thomas running excitedly toward Kevin who was sitting at a picnic table with Peter.

"We apologize for interrupting," they said breathlessly, but we need you and your camera, Kevin."

Chapter Fifty-Six

Saying "Goodbye" to Thornfield

Just after 7:00 p.m., the staff walked together across the lawn from Higley to Ridings where the celebration was about to take place. Alison, Pam, and Carol were all beautiful in the one long dress each had brought for the occasion.

Like most everyone else, we had eaten our dinner quickly, and had hurried off to prepare for the evening. While we were practicing songs in our dorm, Dom and Joanne and the refreshment crew were spreading out onto long tables a feast of M&Ms, honey-roasted peanuts, wedges of assorted cheese, strawberries, and a huge chocolate sheet cake. Likewise, Thomas and Wendy and their volunteers were decorating by hanging the autographed bed sheets from previous years around the walls of the first floor room, moving the whiteboard that displayed nearly all of our names up from the basement, stringing colorful crepe paper and balloons from the ceiling, and unveiling their very special surprise of the evening.

"Oh, my goodness," Alison gasped as she raised her hands to her mouth with a look of delighted shock. "Have you *ever* seen anything so wonderful?"

"That is *so* cool," Carol exclaimed as we all walked to the wall that had previously displayed the Quilt, and now admired with awe the decorated bed sheet that was flanked by Wendy and Thomas, the beaming proud creators. "It's just amazing," Pam said. "You guys blow me away. You really do."

"Sex Camp" it proclaimed at the top of the sheet in bold black letters and quotation marks. *"The world's best kept secret,"* was written just below. And underneath that, smiling out at us with faces of pure glee, was an extraordinary drawing of the entire workshop group, thirty-seven in all, just as we had appeared in the photo taken earlier in the day. The likeness of each character was astounding. And to my delight, there, behind the group, was the sweeping roof of Ridings with its cross at the top, and to the left, the pine trees and the shimmering blue water of the lake.

"How did you *do* this?" I asked incredulously.

"It was Wendy," Thomas said. "She's very talented, as you can see. We got Kevin to retrieve the photo that Kit took on his digital camera. Wendy worked all through her break and dinner on this. It's amazing, isn't it?"

"It was Thomas's idea to add 'The world's best kept secret'," Wendy said. "And he's right. It really is."

For the next several minutes, person after person came forward in shock and delight, and then laughed with joy when they spotted themselves in the drawing. "You even got my freckles," Maggie exclaimed. "Hey, I'm thinner than that," George insisted with laughter. "Look at you, Ben," Beatrice said. "He looks hunky even in that drawing," Leona added. "How about a big round of applause for Wendy and Thomas?" Dom suggested.

Then, at Alison's nod, Gail started the boom box, and the familiar introduction to our song began to fill the room. Taking the cue, we moved into a circle and all began to sing from memory the words to "I Love Myself." Everyone seemed to be aware that it was the last time we would be singing it together as a group. As was my custom, I tried to make eye contact and smile "good-bye" at each person in the circle. I noticed that many of the others were trying to do the same. By the final verse, we were rocking back and forth in rhythm, our arms around the shoulders or waist of the person on either side. When we were finished, the participants followed the staff's lead and took seats in the circle of chairs behind us.

"Let's move these chairs into a nice tight circle, shall we?" Alison invited.

"Now is the time to begin our 'good-byes,' and to prepare to re-enter the worlds from which we came," she said after we had moved closer together. "I'd like you to begin the process by slowly looking around the room at the faces of the people who only a few days ago were strangers. How do you feel about these faces today? What would you like to say to them? I, for one, will have a very hard time saying 'good-bye' to you. You truly are the most wonderful group of people that I've had the privilege of working with for a long, long time.

"There was great energy surrounding us this week, wasn't there? Energy and intimacy. You all seemed to work so hard at examining what was stopping you from crossing the bridge to your own sexual health and happiness, looking at what was at the end of your rope. We laughed together, and we cried together, and we grew together as we made our individual journeys by telling stories about ourselves. 'Well done' to all of you. You now see why we refer to this as 'holy' space.

"We're going to spend a little time tonight saying our farewells," she continued. "I want each of you to feel free to share whatever you like, if anything at all, with your new friends. But before we do, I'm going to ask the staff to offer you their thoughts about leaving here and going back into your homes, your families, and your work environments. They've all learned from past experience about some of the hurdles that we'll face, and some of the things we can do to minimize the shock, and to keep those internal fires burning. Carol, why don't you begin?"

"Thank you, Alison," Carol said, sitting up straight in her chair. "I just want to say really quickly that I agree *completely* with Alison. You're an amazing group. I'd like to take you all home with me. My guess is that many of you are feeling the same way, and I want to remind you that you're all just a phone call or an e-mail message away from one another. Don't feel you have to lose touch. We've got lots of participants from years past whom we still hear from. Secondly, when you go back to what some people refer to as the 'real' world, remember that what happened here was real too. We really did break through our fears this week, and we created honest, intimate friendships. It's possible to do with our family and friends, if we haven't already done so."

"But remember," Pam added, "that they *weren't* here for this experience, and they *aren't* going to understand it right away. Don't overwhelm them with your enthusiasm as soon as you walk in the door. You're excited about the week, but they probably aren't. You may even find them a little resentful that while you were here having great breakthroughs in *your* lives, they were at home doing double duty with the kids or with household tasks. And the people at work may have been handling your workload too. I suggest that the first thing you do when you get back is to ask them how *their* week went. Let them first tell you about all of the things that happened at home, or at the office. And then, when you do tell them about your experiences here, do it in small doses."

"Yea," I said, "I wouldn't go home and say, 'Oh honey, you should have been there. We had two transsexuals and one cross dresser, and a nun, and two football coaches, and an 'ex–gay' guy, and lots of homosexuals, and we watched films of men and women masturbating and making love, and men and men, and women and women making love, and then this guy in a wheelchair went for his first swim, and this woman priest left, and this bisexual minister came out, but his wife and his congregation don't know about it yet, and we heard about this guy who could only get turned on by a crocodile, and we watched women look at their vulvas with mirrors, and I talked about how you were non-orgasmic, and it was really *cool*!' A little bit at a time would be more effective."

"It helps to have had a spouse and colleagues who have been through this experience," Bill said, laughing with the others. "My wife Kathy knows why I'm so energized when I come back from Thornfield, and she *really* looks forward to our first night in bed. But I *do* want to support what Carol said about this experience being *real*. There will be times, perhaps even as early as when you get to the airport tomorrow, when you'll find yourself questioning whether you should trust what happened this week. You'll probably experience some discouragement or depression because you can't seem to keep alive the wonderful feeling of intimacy that you've had here. When the people in our lives back home get upset about mundane things, like the weather, we'll be thinking 'Why are they spinning their wheels? What does that have to do with their sexual and spiritual health and happiness?' And then we'll find *ourselves* complaining about politics, and work, and the weather, and we'll wonder if this week at Thornfield really happened, and if it did, what was the point? When that occurs, I want you to remind yourself that everyone in your life, deep down inside, wants to feel what you felt this week. It's just that they don't get the opportunity to practice. But we can help them practice, if we remember and trust our experience here at Thornfield."

"I'd like to say something about that," Dick said, as he cleared his throat. "There seems to be much discussion about what is *real*. Is what happens here at Thornfield 'real,' or is what happens in our everyday lives outside of Thornfield 'real'? It reminds me of a dialogue in a much-beloved children's story by Marjorie Williams in which the same question is asked. A Velveteen Rabbit, a new toy in the nursery who wanted very much to be loved by his young owner, seeks counsel from another toy, the Skin Horse, on how to determine what is *real*."

"'The Skin Horse had lived longer in the nursery than any of the others'," Dick began from memory in a kind, grand-fatherly manner. "'He was so old that his brown coat was bald in patches and showed seams underneath, and most of the hairs in his tail had been pulled out to string bead necklaces. He was wise, for he had seen a long succession of mechanical toys arrive to boast and swagger, and by-and-by break their mainsprings and pass away, and he knew that they were only toys, and would never turn into anything else. For nursery magic is very strange and wonderful, and only those playthings that are old and wise and experienced like the Skin Horse understand about it.

"What is REAL?" asked the Rabbit one day when they were lying side by side near the nursery fender, before Nana came to tidy the room. "Does it mean having things that buzz inside you and a stick-out handle?"

"Real isn't how you are made," said the Skin Horse. "It's a thing that happens to you. When a child loves you for a long, long time, not just to play with, but REALLY loves you, then you become Real."

"Does it hurt?" asked the Rabbit.

"Sometimes," said the Skin Horse, for he was always truthful. "When you are Real, you don't mind being hurt."

"Does it happen all at once, like being wound up," he asked, "or bit by bit?"

"It doesn't happen all at once," said the Skin Horse. "You become. It takes a long time. That's why it doesn't often happen to people who break easily, or have sharp edges, or who have to be carefully kept. Generally, by the time you are Real, most of your hair has been loved off, and your eyes drop out, and you get loose in the joints and very shabby. But these things don't matter at all, because once you are Real you can't be ugly, except to people who don't understand."

Sighs, moans of delight, and gentle applause filled the room when Dick finished, which he acknowledged by smiling and nodding his head gratefully.

"Thank you, Dick. You are *our* Skin Horse," I said in the quiet that followed.

"Yes, thank you, Dick," Alison nodded. "And now, it's *your* turn," she said, gesturing with her hand to the circle of participants. "If there's anything that *you'd* like to share, now would be a good time to do it."

We sat as a group in reflective and awkward silence for a minute or two. Lisa was the first to speak.

"I know that I've been very quiet this week," she said. "I tend to stay on the sidelines and observe. Maybe it's my shyness that's at the end of my rope. I just wanted to say, though, that when we came here the first day and sang 'I Love Myself,' I had to stop myself from laughing out loud because I thought it was the *dumbest* song I had ever heard in my life, and I thought there was *no way* I was going to stand here all week and sing it. But a funny thing happened. I can't believe that I'm actually going to say this, but I grew to *love* the song, and I think I'm going to miss singing it with you all more than anything else this week. And it's not the words so much that I love as it is just watching individual people sing the words. To see the looks on their faces while they were singing told me that they really *meant* the words, and that the words meant a lot to them. Like watching Carla, and Betty, and Kevin, singing 'I love myself the way I am,' and Ben singing 'there's nothing to rearrange,' and watching Leona look at Betty, and Dan look at Peter this last time around while they're singing 'I love you just the way you are,' I feel like you all *really* mean it, and that makes me feel *really* good inside. And as someone who's struggling with her own identity as a bisexual, it's meant a whole lot to watch Charlie, and all of the gay and lesbian people here singing arm in arm with the heterosexuals about loving themselves. I don't know. It's just had a really big impact on me, and I wanted you all to know it, and to know I'm going to miss singing that dumb song with you."

"Why, thank you, Lisa," Alison smiled gratefully. "That's wonderful to hear."

"And I'm going to miss Bill wiggling his cute butt, and Alison, your cheery 'good mornings,' and Dick's great T-shirts, and Carol and Brian's bantering, and Pam's gentle counsel," said Joanne.

"And Gail ringing that damn bell," Curtis added.

"I'm going to miss my SAR group, which was the *best* SAR group here," Dom said.

"Oh, no it wasn't!" Chuck countered.

"I'd like to say 'thank you' to the *whole* staff," Margaret said. "You were all terrific. The material you presented was clear, well-organized, and very helpful. But the feelings of mutual respect and affection that you have for one another is what I'm taking home with me. It was a real pleasure to witness, and it made me feel very safe."

"Here, here!" George echoed as he led the applause.

"Thank you," Alison said. "We do indeed love and respect each other. I feel very lucky to be working with such a great group of professionals who are also dear members of my extended family."

The room grew quiet again as we waited to see if there were any further reflections.

Carla was now the first to break the silence. "First, I'd like to say how nice Alison, Carol, and Pam look in their long dresses," she said smiling and nodding at each, "but they're not the *only* ones who brought something special for the occasion," she chirped as she stood, held out the sides of her lovely, chintz dress, tossed her head back in delight, and twirled in a circle in front of her chair to the anticipated applause of the group. "I have had *so* much fun with all of you this week, and you've been the most *wonderful* group of loving supporters that a girl could ask for. I know it hasn't been easy for all of you. This cross dressing thing can take getting used to. But I don't think I've ever been as happy, primarily because I've never felt as free to express my feminine side for so long a period of time. It's been heaven, and you're all angels. And the biggest angel of all, and I'm not talking about her size, is, of course, my new best friend, Betty. She is clearly the wind beneath my wings. She's been my big sister all week, and I trust that we're going to be in each other's lives forever. But, you've *all* been great, and I want you to know that I'll never forget this time we've had together. Never!"

"Carla," Chuck said in his strong drawl, once the applause had subsided, "you're right when you say that it wasn't easy. At least, speaking for myself, I'd have to say that when we sat next to each other that first day, and you introduced yourself as a 'cross dresser,' I thought that everyone would see my face turn bright red. I'm glad that no one noticed it. I thought to myself, 'People back home don't say what you just said and live to tell about it.' Now, maybe I'm overstating it a bit, but you get the point. But, I'll tell you Carla, you're the *best* thing that happened to me this week. You and those gay male sex films were my biggest hurdles, but hey, look at me. Not only did I make it through in one piece, but I've come to like and respect you, and Betty, and Kevin, and all of the gay folk here. Although, Dan, I'd have to say that your anger was a little hard to swallow at first, but I've seen you mellow this week, and I sure feel that I have too. So, thank you Carla, and thank you everyone, for being who you are, and for helping me to understand and support you."

To that, Carla jumped up, ran over to Chuck in the midst of our strong applause, and gave him a big, long hug and kiss on the cheek. Following her lead, Dan jumped up, ran over to Chuck with a big grin on his face, and did the same. Chuck's face was now crimson, his head and shoulders shook with laughter, and he wiped away a tear.

"Well, as long as we're handing out hugs and kisses," Leona said standing and walking to the center of the room, "I'd like to give Betty, there, a hug and a kiss for being the best roommate I never had, and," finishing her hug of Betty, and turning to her right, "I'd like to give my friend Charlie a hug and a kiss for being one of the bravest and nicest white man I've *ever* met." Returning to her seat, she continued, "This week has been a real eye opener for me, as many of you know. I'd surely like to come back here next year and do the whole thing all over again. There's so much more that I'd like to learn. And maybe next time, I'll keep my mouth shut more so that I have a better chance of hearing what you all are saying. But, if I do come back, I'm going to need all of you to come back too."

"Thank you, Leona," Alison said when the applause for her had subsided. "Wasn't that a wonderful way to bring this segment to a close?"

"Alison?"

"Yes, Peter?" she replied.

"Before you do, I have something that I'd like to say," he said softly.

"Of course," she replied. "What is it, dear?"

Peter smiled back at her and sat motionless in silence for several seconds. I held my breath in anticipation, and was aware that others were unconsciously doing the same. Each head turned to face him, all with looks of concern. Kevin, who sat at his left, slowly reached over and gently squeezed his knee. Peter's face registered his gratitude.

"When I came here," he started slowly.

"Can you speak up, please?" Alison coaxed.

"I remember you doing that the first day, when I introduced myself," he replied with a grin and in a stronger voice. "When I came here, I did so with great curiosity about how you all were going to deal with me and my 'ex-gay' identity. I didn't expect to fit in, but I thought it was a good place for me to test myself, and to perhaps help others see a way out of their homosexuality. I know that my being here was upsetting to some of you, and confusing to others. Trust me, I didn't come to cause turmoil. I should have realized, of course, that I would, particularly to the gay people present, and I apologize for any bad feelings that my being here caused. You all, though, were great. Except for one major clash with an unnamed participant," he said, smiling at Dan, "my week has felt very safe, and I have felt very welcome. You all have been extremely kind. Annette, you and Thomas in particular, went way out of your way to make me feel wanted, which was especially helpful after Catherine left.

"I know that I spent a lot of time alone this week, which was no one's fault but my own. I haven't wanted to isolate. I've just needed to think. As you may know, a lot has gone on for me in the last seven days, and I still haven't sorted it all out. I'm not sure when, if ever, I will, but I'm grateful for you, and I'm grateful for the confusion. Faith is an *action* verb, right? If I say I'm a believer and I feel some turmoil around my beliefs, it means that my faith is alive, and I need to take a closer look at what's not working for me. I just want to thank you all for accepting me for who I am, or who I wish I was, or even who I might become. Whatever. You've all been great, and despite my comment about 'shaking the dust from your sandals' when Catherine left, I think this place, and all of you, have been extraordinarily hospitable. And, I think I want to thank you, Dan, especially, for pushing me so hard. Your anger scares me. It really does, but I'm also *attracted* to your self-assurance and to your pride. So, 'thank you.'

"I don't want to take up any more of our time, but I do want to say that as hard as you all have tried to make me feel at home, and as hard as I've tried in the last couple of days to find my place in this community, I still feel as if I'm on the outside, and I've felt this way since midweek. I'd like to remedy that, right now, if I may."

"How is that?" Alison asked for all of us.

"I'd like to sign the board," he said. "Mine is the only name not up there."

Annette's eyes immediately brimmed with tears, which started a small chain reaction as Peter stood and slowly walked in silence to the whiteboard, picked up a dry erase marker, scanned the names for a moment, and then wrote his name next to Kevin's. He turned, nodded his appreciation to the group, and said, "I don't know what it means to each of you to see my name up there. I only know that I needed to do it. Thank you." He then walked back to his seat.

Dan was the first on his feet clapping. There was a collective sigh, and a drawing in of deep breaths in the room, as boxes of Kleenex were passed around the circle.

"Thank you, Peter," Alison said with calm dignity. "Having your name on that board with all of the others makes me and everyone else here very, very happy."

433

Again, we all applauded, Peter included, what had just transpired.

"Before we leave this circle, take a break, and move into our celebration," Alison said, "I need to share some sad news with you. We have kept this from you because we didn't want it to impact your time here in any way, but we have learned to our great regret, that we are most likely going to lose our home at Thornfield. The Episcopal Diocese, I am told, has decided to refrain from accepting any reservations for the facility next year as they look seriously at the financial viability of maintaining the property as a retreat center."

For the next several minutes, Alison and the staff affirmed the participants' statements of sadness, shock, and disappointment, and answered their questions about the future of the workshop.

"Thank you for not telling us," Margaret said. "It *would* have made a difference in the week for me. I'm glad that I didn't know."

"Me too," affirmed Joe. "I'm sorry that you had to keep it to yourselves, but I'm glad that you did. I had a wonderful week of growth, and had I known that this might be the last year here, I think I would have spent a lot of my time trying to take care of the staff."

"We really only had it confirmed yesterday," Alison said.

"Well, nevertheless, thank you for not telling us before," Marjorie said. "Is there anything we can do?"

"Yes," Alison replied. "There is. We could all write to the bishop and tell him what being here this week has meant to us. I'll give you the address if you'd like. But more important, what you can do is enjoy yourselves completely for the remainder of our time here in this holy place."

Chapter Fifty-Seven

The Celebration

"I hate to write on this beautiful work of art," Margaret said as she began to inscribe her message with a blue felt-tipped pen at the bottom of the "Sex Camp" sheet.

"But your thoughts will only *add* to its beauty," Thomas assured her as he stood on the other side of the hanging, pensively staring at the ceiling, and stroking his chin.

"When you two have finished, I'd love to show you something," I said from behind them.

Gail had filled the room with the disco beat of "Jump" by the Pointer Sisters as we took our bathroom break and prepared for the celebration. George and Maggie immediately started dancing in the center of the room, as did Wendy and Gina. Several people began swaying to the rhythm as they milled around the room, looking for inspiration at the messages that previous participants had left on their sheets. Others stood waiting their turn to write on our own keepsake.

"I came to Thornfield to learn new skills, and I fell back in love with life," Grace wrote.

"Tell me where you're going, and I'll follow," Charlie said.

"As hard as it was to say 'hello,' it's a lot harder saying 'good-bye'," wrote Dom.

"Click your heels three times and say, 'There's no place like Thornfield'," Thomas said.

"I take a piece of each of you with me," Annette wrote. "You will always have special places in my heart."

"It wasn't what I expected, but it was more than I hoped for, growled Dan, your queer friend."

"Come to Trinidad and help us fight ignorance, secrecy, and trauma," wrote Martha.

"We create our own suffering. Let the bliss we found here guide our steps forward," said Margaret.

When they had finished, Thomas and Margaret sought me out. "What was it you wanted to show us?" Thomas asked.

"Come this way," I said, taking each of them by the hand. "You've heard us all talk about our friend and former staff member, Mary Lee Tatum. She was a truly remarkable woman, and someone very dear to all of us. I feel certain that if she was alive today, she'd gravitate toward the two of you. Like her, you're both 'old souls.' I want to point out where she signed the sheet the year before she died, just to help you make a personal connection with her."

When we found the spot, Margaret chuckled. Mary Lee had written "Follow your bliss."

"Pretty close to what you wrote," Thomas said.

"Okay, everyone, find your places. The show is about to begin," Carol announced like a ring master. "We have a full evening of songs, poems, jokes, games, and skits. And who would have thought that just yesterday I had only *one* act lined up? First on our program, is Carla, the one act I knew I could count on. She's going to play the guitar, and lead us in a song. Can we have a big hand for Carla?"

"This one's for Betty," Carla said as she began strumming. "You all know the words. I'd love to have you join me if you would. It's called 'Wind Beneath My Wings'."

Carla's beautiful voice was solo for the first two verses as we all sat in stunned silence and watched either the intense passion on her face or the grateful blush on Betty's. We each then joined in with the familiar lines, "Did you ever know that you're my hero, and everything I would like to be? I can fly higher than an eagle, for you are the wind beneath my wings."

"That was beautiful," Carol said as Carla finished, and Betty jumped up to give her a big hug and kiss. "Nice job," she said over the applause.

Dick came up next with three jokes, which he had told with great expression and expert timing at each celebration for the last several years. The first involved an Irishman who was the proud owner of a 12-inch pianist which he had secured from a hard-of-hearing leprechaun whose life he had saved, and who promised to grant him one wish. Undaunted by the groans which usually greet such humor, Dick proceeded to tell us of two Greek statues, male and female, which stared at each other longingly for many years. When, through the intercession of a sympathetic god, they were brought to life for a limited amount of time, they dumbfounded the god by choosing to forgo sex and instead seeking equitable retribution on the pigeons who had "crapped" on them throughout time. And the third of Dick's jokes, which he dedicated to Bill, relayed the story of an elephant and a mouse who each counted on the other's help at different times to escape quicksand and certain death. The mouse employed his red Corvette convertible to pull the elephant from near death. The elephant, on the other hand, straddled the pond and had the mouse grab hold of his prodigious penis. The moral, of course, was that if you have a big enough penis, you don't need a red Corvette. "For many years," Dick explained, "Bill has driven such a car."

Next up were Thomas, Lloyd, Gina, Wendy, Dan, George, and Betty. Thomas, having borrowed my lavender wig, played the role of Alison. After giving us an enthusiastic and cheery "good evening," in a voice reminiscent of Queen Elizabeth's, he reminded us of the "touch" exercise where we had closed our eyes and used our hands to express our feelings of joy, sorrow, and affection.

"Tonight," he said, "we're going to explore the *other* senses, which as you recall Bill saying, are the 'aphrodisiacs' of sex." Those of us who were seated were asked to watch and make sure that his volunteers didn't "wander off or get hurt." Those standing in the center of the room were instructed to turn around three times, "and then find a partner. Now, I want you to use your wonderful sense of *smell* and sniff them 'hello.' That's right! Good. Now, please get to know their smells and let them get to know yours." To this, Lloyd, Gina, Wendy, Dan, George, and Betty began sniffing under each other's arms, around each other's heads, and at each other's butts. The laughter these antics prompted was hysterical.

The sniffing went on for several minutes as they were asked to "express your joy over hearing good news," and "express your anger at one another. Okay, now sniff and make up."

"Well done," clapped Thomas regally as he flipped lavender strands of hair from his face. "Now, say 'good bye' and find another partner, whom I'd like you to lick 'hello' to." Groans of disgust from the outside circle greeted this new instruction. "*Taste* is a very important sense," he said, attempting to control his laughter. "We must *taste* our sexuality. Are you ready? You have just heard some very sad news. Very sad news indeed. I want you to comfort your new friend and communicate how very badly you each feel for him or her. Go ahead, please lick away."

Lloyd, Gina, Wendy, Dan, George, and Betty were now laughing too hard to continue. They were relieved to hear Carol start the applause, to which they responded by joining hands with Thomas and taking several long bows. Kevin clicked photos furiously.

Carol next motioned to Ben, who then wheeled himself to the front of the room. "I have a poem that I've written for the occasion," he said, "but before I read it, I want to say 'thank you' one last time for this whole week – for my incredible swim, which I'll never forget, and for the sensitivity you all showed in your language, like saying, 'Stand as you're able,' and 'Move to the front of the room,' as opposed to *walk*. That meant a lot to me. I also want to thank you for asking me to tell you my story, but also for not *focusing* on my disability all week. It's all been great. From the moment I rolled in the door of Huntington that first day and saw Gail's bright, smiling face at registration, and how she juggled things to make sure I could stay with the other participants in Peabody, I knew this was going to feel like 'home.' You all are the best! And I won't forget you."

"And I won't forget *you* in your hot red bathing trunks either," Leona said.

"Me neither," Dan assured him.

Ben's poem, which he read after grinning appreciatively at both Leona and Dan, was an enchanting free verse affirmation of life's "turn ons," much like the list that we had composed with Bill, though Ben's personal compilation included the frequent, enthusiastic repetition of the line "and sleeping under the stars with a honey Bea." The women, particularly, moaned their appreciation of the sentiment, and smiled at Beatrice playfully.

Pam followed Ben with a poem that she explained often made her cry. The author described a scene in which a group of people, who each had one stick of firewood, sat around a dying fire on a frigid night and ultimately opted to freeze to death rather than share their wood with the others who were rich, black, unemployed, white, or otherwise unlikable.

Marjorie and Joanne were up next with sheets of newsprint that displayed the words to a beautiful song called, "Hasn't Anyone Ever Told You" that they were excited about us singing together. Alison then read a favorite passage from a book by Virginia Satyr. Next, Bill told a joke about a priest, a rabbi, and a minister who argued over who should get the one parachute on their nose-diving airplane. The staff then came up and sang an old song about Thornfield, written by Carol, to the tune of "You Are My Sunshine." Beverly and Martha next taught us to do a fun dance from Trinidad. And Tonya had a group exercise that involved passing a balloon from person to person under your chin.

Kevin continued to take pictures throughout the production, as did everyone else who had remembered to bring their cameras.

"Okay, I'm now pleased to announce that it's time for the appearance of a *very* special guest," Carol said excitedly. "Ernestine Tomlin is back to visit us at Thornfield. Ernestine?" she said, gesturing to me as I made my way to the chair at the front of the room.

Ernestine Tomlin, I explained to the multi-generational audience, is a character developed by lesbian comedienne Lily Tomlin. She is a telephone operator who has been with the phone company for many, many years. "She attended this year's workshop on sexuality," I said, "and is now back home at her switchboard station.

"One ringy dingy. Two ringy dingies," I snorted through my scrunched-up nose and puckered mouth. "A crisp, businesslike 'hello.' Have I reached the party to whom I am speaking? Ms. Mills? Ms. Leona Mills?"

Leona screamed from her seat next to Charlie, as the others in the room applauded and laughed.

"Ms. Mills, this is Ernestine Tomlin from your SAR group at 'Sex Camp.' Yes, hello. I'm calling to see if you wouldn't like to make a sizeable contribution to the Ernestine Tomlin Vacation Fund. 'Fat chance,' you say? Well, Ms. Mills, I wonder if you'd be willing to listen to a little tape recording of mine? Yes, dear, that *is* your voice. Wait a second. Wait a second. I want to hear this part again. Oh my goodness, Ms. Mills, the things people can do with banisters. What's that? Confidentiality? Isn't that cute! No, Ms. Mills. I never signed such a document, and all I can say is 'Who's SARry now?' I beg your pardon? You say you don't care if I send this tape to your employer? I see. Well, Ms. Mills, are you near a computer? Then, please take a look at this picture that I'm just a 'click' away from sending to *The Washington Post*. Yes, that *is* you, laying a big, fat, wet kiss on a known lesbian transsexual. What's that? Oh, well now, that's the spirit, Ms. Mills. And how much did you say you'd send? Oh, that's *very* generous. And, yes, a check will do nicely. Thank you. And, Leona, before you hang up, please don't take this personally. You're just the first on my list."

In the next couple of minutes, Ernestine called Charlie Tatewell and Dom Paluzzi. When she thought she had enough cash, she made one last call.

"One ringy dingy. Two ringy dingies. Peter, is that you? I got the moolah, babe. And if you'll 'ex'-cuse me, Good Looking, it's off to Bimini we go!"

Peter came over as I took my bows and gave me a big hug, to which I responded by "swooning," and fanning my face with both hands.

Carol then called Carla up, who brought us together in a tight circle as she talked and strummed on her guitar. "I've had a super time this week with you as we've all let our hair down – well, actually, I pulled mine up, didn't I? We came together to explore our sexuality, and in particular, our sexual health, as guided by our individual theologies. Tomorrow, my hair goes down, and yours goes up, as we head home to our loved ones and to our work. As you may recall, my work is as a church musician, and I thought maybe I could put on that hat just briefly tonight to lead us in a song that everyone knows and most everyone, regardless of their theology, enjoys singing. And it's not the words that seem to touch us, or really *matter* that much, is it? It's more about the impact the 'music' has on our spirits. At least, that's what I think. Join me now, if you would, in singing "Amazing Grace."

We all spontaneously joined hands as we sang full voiced the old, familiar tune. "I once was lost but now am found, was blind but now I see," Thomas and Peter belted out with big grins and repeated squeezes of each other's hands.

"How sweet the sound, indeed," Carla said when we had finished, and as she accepted our applause, and took her seat.

"That was wonderful, Carla. Thank you," Carol said. "And now, the staff has a final song."

Taking our positions in line, according to the number of years we'd spent at Thornfield, we held our hands together in front of us like the von Trapp children, and sang about the sad sort of clanging from the clock in the hall, and the absurd little cuckoo in the nursery, that compelled us "to say 'good-bye' to you." One by one we stepped forward and sang to the tune of "So Long, Farewell," our individual messages of closure. As each of us finished, the nursery clock mechanism of gentle shoves, kicks to the butt, and bops on the head propelled us forward, one at a time.

I was the second to last to sing. "Gay, straight, trans, bi, please celebrate your lives. It's all we've got, so please buy my book."

When Alison was finished, we came back together as a group, and repeated the opening verse. As we finished, we waved "good-bye" to all of the participants and walked off into the hall to the sound of their claps and whistles.

"Thank you, everyone!" Carol said upon our return to the room. "Please dig into the food, and let's start the music!"

As soon as Gail had inserted a tape into the boom box, Dan made a bee line for Kevin.

"Hey, handsome, how about a dance?" he asked.

"Sure," Kevin replied.

The music was fast and they were soon joined by Ben and Beatrice, Carla and Betty, Thomas and Lloyd, Wendy and Gina, Dom and Margaret, George and Maggie, Gail and Carol, Pam and Bill, and Charlie and Leona.

"It's hot in here," Dan said into Kevin's ear. "You want to get out of here and go for a swim?"

"Oh, not now. Maybe later," Kevin said. "I want to do some dancing and say my 'good-byes'."

"Why don't you come down later and say 'good-bye' to me on the beach?" Dan said grinning, and raising his eyebrows in anticipation.

"Yea, maybe," Kevin replied.

"That sounds like a 'no'," Dan said as he playfully tousled Kevin's hair.

The next song was fast too, and Betty excitedly announced and started a 'Conga' line. Eventually, nearly everyone jumped in, holding the waist of the person in front of them as the line snaked its way around the big room in Ridings, out into the hall, past the bathrooms, and back to the source of the music.

"Look at that," I said to Carol who stood next to me on the side. "Look at Chuck holding Carla's waist, and Peter holding Dan's waist, and Leona holding Wendy's waist. I mean, if you told these people last Saturday when they arrived that they were going to be doing the Conga with one another they would have said, 'Are you nuts?' If you think I'm dancing with a cross dresser, or if you think I'm dancing with an 'ex-gay,' you're out of your mind."

"It's magic, isn't it?" Carol sighed.

"Yea, it is. And it's fun to help make it happen, isn't it?"

When the music stopped and the dance ended, Dan pulled his hands down to his waist and around those of Peter. "Well, hello there," he flirted, turning his head. "Nice to have you on board."

"I'm not sure what 'board' I'm on," Peter replied, "but thanks, Dan."

"Well, why don't you come down for a swim later, and we'll see what 'board' you're on?" Dan grinned sexily, still holding his hands.

"You are *incorrigible!*" Peter laughed as he carefully disengaged.

"I'll take that as a 'maybe'," Dan replied with a wink.

Eventually the music turned slow and the dance floor thinned out. Beatrice sat on Ben's lap as he gently rolled back and forth to the rhythm. Wendy and Gina, who had built a nice friendship during the week, talked animatedly as they danced. So too did Thomas and Lloyd.

Kevin and Peter sat with Annette on the sidelines for several minutes before Peter found his voice. "Would you like to dance?" he asked Kevin.

"Yea, that would be great," he said, unable to conceal his blush.

"Did you ever think you'd be sitting here watching this?" Chuck whispered to Dom as they eyed the same-sex couples in each other's arms.

"Nope."

"How you doing with it?" he asked.

"Better than I ever would have guessed," Dom smiled back.

"Me too," replied Chuck.

"Sweetie, I thought you were going to bed. You said 'good-bye' to me ten minutes ago," Pam said as I stood and watched the dancing. "Don't you have a real early flight?"

"I do, 6:30," I replied. "I haven't said 'good-bye' to Dick yet, and I've been waiting for a slow song. There's something I want to do."

"What's that?"

"Ask Charlie to dance. I don't think he's ever slow-danced with another man. What do you think?"

"I think it's sweet. Go for it," she said.

Charlie initially looked nervous when I asked him, peering over his shoulder to see who might be watching.

"What am I doing?" he laughed as he caught himself. "I'd *love* to dance. But I get to lead, right?"

"No way," I said.

When the dance was over, I leaned over and gave Charlie a quick peck on the lips. He smiled and said, "That's the first time I've ever kissed a man in public."

"How did it feel?" I asked.

"It wasn't long enough, but it felt great!"

"I'm glad. Good night, Charlie."

I then sought out Dick, who was sitting by himself, enjoying the sight of the dancers.

"Good night, Skin Horse," I said.

"Up for a swim?" he asked.

"I can't do it, Dick. I've got an early flight. I need to say 'good-bye'."

"Well, good-bye then," he replied.

"I love you, Dick," I said, reaching down and giving him a big hug.

"I love you, too," he replied awkwardly.

Before I went to my room, I made a detour to Mary Lee's tree.

"Looks like this is it, Mary Lee," I said as I stroked a branch. "They're kicking us out of here. It's been an amazing experience, hasn't it? I hate to leave, and I'll miss this crazy, crooked tree. But, I'll be back to see you, I promise."

After I finished packing and making sure my plane ticket was easily accessible, I read a little more of my book, then set my alarm, turned off the light, and listened to the laughter and banter of the people who had carried the celebration down to the beach. They were wonderful, sweet sounds of joy. The giggling made me smile as I drifted off to sleep.

Suddenly, my room was filled with light. I had no idea if it had been two hours or six hours since I had lain down. All I knew was that it was still dark out, and there was no more noise coming from the beach.

"Psst, Brian," Kevin whispered loudly as he stood at my opened door. "Are you awake?"

Postscript

Our beloved staff member and friend, Dick Cross, died before the completion of this book. Up until his final day, he was enthusiastically involved in sexuality education. His legacy in the field is monumental, and his presence in our lives is greatly missed.

With the completion of every couple of chapters of *"Sex Camp,"* I would send my manuscript to each staff person for his or her review. Dick wrote back, "First and foremost, I love it! I think you have done a remarkable job of capturing on paper the atmosphere of Thornfield ... you have provided a precise, accurate description of what goes on at Thornfield and I am grateful for it." He then took me to task for not having more bisexual characters among the participants.

A tree in memory of our Skin Horse was planted next to those for Mary Lee and Susan. On our last visit to the site, the remaining staff copied the passage from *The Velveteen Rabbit* that Dick often recited from memory, and buried it among the roots of his tree.

The Episcopal bishop of the diocese, in response to my letter, wrote, "I hear clearly your reference to Thornfield as 'holy ground,' and understand your desire to continue meeting there. I too have had significant spiritual experiences at Thornfield, as have my children, and so I do not take the action of closing Thornfield lightly ... I wish you, the staff and attendees of the Workshop on Sexuality well as you continue your work. I hope you are able to find a new location for your gatherings that will, eventually, be as meaningful to you as Thornfield has been."

We've to date taken no action to find a new site, but a promise has been made among the staff that as each of us dies, a tree will be planted among the others in the place we came to think of as our home.

About The Author

Brian McNaught is a sexuality trainer and author whose primary focus are the issues facing gay, lesbian, bisexual and transgender people, and those who live or work with them. Named "the godfather of gay sensitivity training" by the *New York Times,* he has worked primarily with heterosexual audiences in major corporate and university settings since 1974. He is the author of the classic "coming out" book, *On Being Gay - Thoughts on Family, Faith and Love*, as well as *Gay Issues in the Workplace* and *Now That I'm Out, What Do I Do?* Brian also produced and/or is featured in five highly-praised videos, three of which have been aired regularly on PBS affiliates. He lives with his spouse, Ray Struble, in Provincetown, MA, and in Ft. Lauderdale, FL.

For more information on Brian or his educational materials, go to www.brian-mcnaught.com.

For additional copies of this book, please go to www.sexcamp.us.

CPSIA information can be obtained
at www.ICGtesting.com
Printed in the USA
LVHW090304240221
679786LV00010B/62